QUEST OF THE HIGHLANDER

Crowns & Kilts, Book 5

QUEST OF THE HIGHLANDER

Published by Boxwood Manor Books
ISBN: 978-1-948053-36-5

The cover image: Period Images
Cover artist: Teresa Spreckelmeyer
Interior formatter: Author E.M.S.

Published in the United States of America.

For all the wonderful members of my Rakes & Readers Group on Facebook! I appreciate all of you and am very grateful for your friendship, support, and cheerful posts.

Quest of the Highlander

Chapter One

Spirit Tower
The Isle of Skye, Scotland
March 1541

"Oh, Lennox. How splendid!"

At the sound of Violette's soft, French-accented voice, Lennox MacLeod straightened, his blue-tipped paintbrush stilled in mid-air. He glanced back at his sister-in-law then followed her gaze to the mural he was painting in the tower house entry. After a moment's reflection, he gave a tentative nod.

"It's nearly finished," he said. "Do ye approve?"

"Approve? It is utterly magical." Lifting her skirts, Violette descended the tier of shallow stone steps until she was beside him. Together they studied the mural of a birlinn sailing on the wave-tossed Minch, bound for Duntulm Castle, the clifftop stronghold that had once been their family home. "It reminds me of the day two years ago, when Ciaran and I sailed back to the Isle of Skye after our unexpected marriage in Edinburgh." She turned her delicate face up to him, smiling wistfully. "You were waiting for us outside Duntulm Castle's sea gate, looking just like an ancient Viking warrior."

"It seems much longer, so much has happened." He raked a hand through his tawny-gold hair and sighed. "I know Ciaran requested this mural, but I can't help wondering if it will serve as a painful reminder of the night the MacDonalds attacked and stole the castle away from us."

"I think he has come to understand that pain is part of life, especially for you Highlanders." She paused to rest a hand on the curve of her belly, as if reminding herself of the babe who would join their family in the summer. "Loss can give way to new beginnings, if we allow it."

Lennox sent her a sidelong glance. "It is difficult to imagine my brother indulging in such tender emotions."

"Perhaps, but Ciaran has learned to soften his heart, at least with me." Violette gently touched his arm. "And what of you, Lennox? Your grandfather is chief of Clan MacLeod, yet you do not seem very concerned about fitting into the mold of a Highland warrior."

"Because I enjoy artistic pursuits more than dreams of battle?" He shrugged. "'Tis who I am. When Grandfather begins to lecture me, I simply nod and go on about my life. It helps to wander, away from the Isle of Skye."

"But do you think you'll ever find true happiness here, among your clan?"

"I cannot say." Lennox had learned, long ago, to deflect such penetrating questions with a light-hearted smile. "I sometimes suspect the faeries must have left me at Dunvegan's sea gate, in a basket, when I was newly born."

Just then, the heavy door to the tower house swung open, and Ciaran MacLeod appeared, bringing with him a damp gust of wind. The two brothers had always been opposites, not only in physical appearance but also in their natures. Since they were young, Ciaran had been dark and cynical, while Lennox had been born with the coloring and heart of a lion.

"Put your paints and brushes away, brother," Ciaran said. "Have ye forgotten that we must go to help our sister today?"

"Oh, aye. I did forget Fiona will journey to Stirling on the morrow."

"But first, you both must pause for a bowl of mutton stew," Violette said. "It is nearly ready. Can you not smell it?"

"And who prepared this stew?" Ciaran sniffed the air suspiciously. "You—or Old David?"

It was, Lennox knew, a familiar jest in their family. Old David had long been employed as a MacLeod cook, but when Violette first came to Skye, they realized his food paled in comparison to the French-flavored dishes she prepared.

Violette laughed and went into her husband's arms. "What if I tell you that I dispensed advice as he cooked?"

Leaving them to their banter, Lennox packed up his supplies and went outside to clean his brushes. It would be good to get away for a few hours, he told himself. To sail with Ciaran to the island's Waternish peninsula and spend some time with their sister and her tiny bairn, Lucien. Tomorrow, mother and child would leave Skye, traveling several days to reach Stirling Castle. There they would join Fiona's husband, Christophe, a master mason who was now overseeing the great building project undertaken by King James V.

Lennox paused outside on the grassy slope overlooking Loch Dunvegan. Through a veil of misty clouds, he could see the imposing shape of the clan MacLeod stronghold, Dunvegan Castle. It was the home of Alasdair Crotach, his grandfather and the clan chief, and most of his relatives.

In his heart, Lennox asked the questions he had just evaded with Violette. Why was it that, even as a lad, he had never quite felt part of this powerful clan? And now, as the mural was nearly finished, Lennox felt the familiar urge to roam.

An urge to go far away from the Isle of Skye…in search of a part of himself that always felt just out of reach.

Lennox and Ciaran walked side by side over the brow of a hill overlooking the Cottage of Dreams, the home Christophe de St. Briac had built for their sister, Fiona. They paused for a moment, the wind catching the edges of their belted plaids as they surveyed the scene below. Smoke curled from the chimney, baby lambs frolicked near their mothers, and just then, little Lucien came through the doorway, closely followed by Fiona.

Lennox had been haunted for hours by a strange sense of unease. It tugged inside his chest, like an itch he could not scratch, but the sight of Fiona and Lucien brought a smile to his face. He took a slow, deep breath.

"Our sister grows more bonny by the day," he remarked. "Even with her husband far away at Stirling Castle."

"Aye, Fi is a strong lass." As Ciaran spoke, she began to wave, beaming, and Lucien gave a squeal of excitement. "No doubt she has a long list of chores for us."

Soon enough, they were inside the light-filled cottage, and Fiona was giving them directions. As Lennox worked, he looked around at the cozy environment Fi and Christophe had created for their home. Other cottages on the Isle of Skye were dim and dreary, with tiny windows, walls of turf blocks, and a hole cut in the thatched roof to let out cooking smoke. Most people lived like that, except for the fortunate few who resided in a castle or tower house.

But Christophe, an architect, had created a different vision. Under a vaulted ceiling, the whitewashed walls of this cottage were lined with jewel-like paintings and sturdy shelves filled with books. Fiona loved books better than anything except her family, and thanks to her aristocratic French husband, she now had more than she could count. Lennox knew she had already begun reading aloud to baby Lucien, who was not yet two years of age.

As Ciaran dragged a big carved chest across the stone floor, he pretended to complain, "Fi, do ye mean to take every single possession in this cottage?"

She stood, hands on hips, her glossy black hair coiled softly at the base of her neck. "It could be a year before this project is finished at Stirling, Christophe says. Maybe longer! Something keeps happening to cause a delay."

"No doubt your husband will remedy that," said Lennox. "I'm surprised he wasn't called in long ago to take over as master mason at Stirling Castle."

"The king has been asking for him through intermediaries, I

think, but we were both reluctant to make such a commitment. In the end, it was our old friend Bayard who begged Christophe to join him at Stirling. We were both unable to resist his coaxing."

"I will always have a special place in my heart for Bayard," Ciaran said with an ironic smile. "He has been a true friend to me."

"So true. We all love Bayard. He's like a great bear." Fi turned then, pointing to a shelf on the wall near the bed. "Lennox, I nearly forgot that book, the one bound in garnet leather. It's one of my very favorites. Can you reach it?"

Lennox nodded. He stepped around Lucien, who sat on the floor with Raoul, the big family hound. Just as Lennox reached up for the leather-bound volume, Raoul unexpectedly let out a bark, and Lennox's hand bumped a silvery casket, knocking it from the shelf. One glance told him that the ornamental box was on course to strike Lucien. Without another thought, Lennox flung himself forward and managed to deflect the silver missile in mid-air, saving his nephew from harm. As he fell hard against the stone floor, he heard a metallic crash.

Little Lucien stared, wide-eyed, a bite of bannock in his pudgy hand. Raoul clambered up onto his long legs and began to howl. Fiona rushed over to where Lennox lay sprawled, the decorative case cracked open beside him.

"Are you all right?" she exclaimed.

"Oh, aye." He laughed ruefully and rolled onto one shoulder, looking for the broken casket. As he focused on the case and noticed the lid's distinctive enamel inlay, a chill crept over Lennox.

"I can see you remember," Fiona said softly, looking first at Lennox, then at Ciaran.

"Aye," said Ciaran. "Ma called for this on her deathbed. Inside was that ancient Viking brooch she wanted ye to have."

Lennox looked from the shattered silver box to his sister's face. "It's ruined. Can ye ever forgive me?"

"'Twas only a mishap," Fiona assured him. "There is nothing to forgive, for you saved Lucien from harm."

Bits of the enamel from the lid were strewn on the floor. As Lennox bent to pick them up, he noticed that the bottom of the casket had broken apart, revealing what appeared to be a hidden compartment, its contents sealed away inside until this moment.

Gradually, he focused on a miniature of a man, framed in gold. It was painted on porcelain, the likeness standing out against a background of cerulean blue. Next to the miniature, Lennox realized, was a lock of hair secured with a bit of black riband.

No one spoke. Time seemed to stop as a strange, airless fog descended on them. Lennox couldn't explain what he was feeling, but the back of his neck prickled and he realized he had stopped breathing. He looked at Ciaran. The utterly stricken expression on his older brother's face caused his heart to clench.

Suddenly, Fiona spoke. "I'll just clean this up before Lucien swallows something he shouldn't."

"Right," Ciaran put in. "I'll help."

Lennox was all too aware of the tension in the air. "Wait." He reached for the miniature, brushing Ciaran's hand aside as he snatched it up.

"'Tis nothing," cautioned his brother.

"If it is indeed *nothing*, ye won't mind me having a look."

With that, he rose lightly to his feet and went to a window, where the light was better. He felt his family watching him, but he ignored them. Slowly, Lennox opened his sun-darkened hand and stared at the miniature.

"Jesu." The word came out in a gust of breath. He blinked. "It's me!"

Although Lennox felt he was looking at his own reflection, the man staring back at him was no Highlander. He was clad in a fine black doublet sewn with rubies. The stranger's fair hair was neatly tamed, unlike his own wild locks, and crowned by a plumed cap of soft velvet.

After scanning these details, Lennox drew a deep breath and looked more closely. He noticed that the man's hair waved beside his right ear, in just the way Lennox's did. The man was turned slightly, yet his striking, sea-green eyes gazed out from the miniature in a way that felt calm and faintly amused, even affectionate. There was something about him that felt hauntingly familiar.

Lennox raised a hand to his chest, as if to banish the raw emotions that tangled inside him. "I don't understand," he said at length, his voice choked. Walking toward Fiona and Ciaran, he thrust the miniature toward them. "We three plainly know this is not me, but who the devil *is* it?"

"I couldn't say," protested Fi. "I've never seen it before! It appears to have been hidden inside a secret compartment."

"Hidden, perhaps, but not by a Viking, unless doublets came into fashion much sooner than I thought." Lennox recoiled from the direction his thoughts were taking, but couldn't stop himself from saying, "This silver casket belonged to Ma."

Fiona picked up the lock of hair and held it next to his. The strands varied in hue from tawny to pale gold. "I'd swear this was cut from your head. I've never met another MacLeod with hair quite like this."

Turning to Ciaran, Lennox saw his brother's face go pale. "Ye know who this is! I can see it in your face."

"I do not!"

"By God, do not deceive me. Since we were bairns, I could always see it when a secret passed over your face."

Fiona stepped between them. "Ciaran, is this true? Do you know who this man is?"

"Nay." In a low tone of dread, he added, "But… I can guess."

"Ye must tell me, then." Lennox's heart was pounding as he grasped the front of his brother's shirt and stared hard into his eyes. "I deserve to know!"

"Aye." Ciaran swallowed. "Ye should know the truth. But

there is so much pain that comes with it." He paused, sighed deeply, and continued, "Ma quarreled with Da when I was a bairn, and she took me away for a season or more. Later, when I was older, Ma revealed that ye were conceived during that time. Da has always loved ye as a son, but—"

Lennox's heartbeat filled his chest and echoed in his ears. Sweat broke out on his brow as he struggled to translate what seemed to be a foreign language. "Are ye saying that I am no MacLeod after all?"

Pointing to the miniature, Ciaran said raggedly, "I suspect this man is your true father."

Fiona had come up behind Lennox, wrapping her arms around his chest. "This changes nothing," she said, and began to weep.

"How can ye say that?" Outrage boiled up in him. Turning, he held her at arm's length. "It changes *everything*! I am not truly one of you. I don't belong here. No wonder I have always felt it, deep inside. Perhaps I have always known the truth but couldn't face it."

"You are still our brother!" cried Fiona. "And the bonds between us run deep. We have shared our lives, Lennox MacLeod! Nothing can change that."

"I cannot speak of that now. Ye must see how my life has been turned on end by this news." Lennox pointed again at the face that so closely resembled his. "*Who is this*?"

"Truly, I know not," insisted Ciaran. "And Da swears he does not know."

"Why did ye not tell me?" The notion that the two of them had been sharing this secret, holding it from him, discussing it behind his back, filled Lennox with an indescribable rage and frustration. "Would ye have let me go to my grave believing this lie about my own life?"

Ciaran began to pace, and Fi led Lucien away to the table, where she gave him a small dish of porridge. Lennox knew he should not have carried on in front of his little nephew, but a storm was raging inside him.

"I could not bring ye such pain," Ciaran replied at last. "I agonized over it with Violette. I feared one day the truth would come out, but I dreaded that time."

"So even Violette knew." Lennox clenched his jaw and demanded, "Who else?"

"Ma, obviously." Ciaran winced slightly. "And Grandfather."

"Ach." Lennox felt sick. "That explains it."

No one asked what he meant, for they must have known full well the subtle ways Grandfather had held Lennox at arm's length. He'd told himself he didn't care about winning the favor of the powerful clan chief, since he had no interest in becoming a true Highland warrior. If Grandfather had ordered him to take a position of power within the clan, Lennox would have refused, so he told himself it was all just as well that he was overlooked. Excluded. Not that Grandfather or Da were cold to him, but they'd always seemed rather relieved each time he announced he was going away.

At least I now understand why I never felt comfortable in this world, Lennox thought. And yet his eyes stung, and his heart ached.

When Ciaran pressed a cup of whisky into his hands, he drank, welcoming the sudden burn, the spreading glow, the easing of his torment. After a long minute of silence, Lennox said, "Ye have kept the truth from me since we were lads. How can I now believe that ye do not know who my father is?"

Together, they stared at the miniature. "I want to swear on our bond as brothers, but no doubt that would cause ye to scoff," Ciaran replied ruefully. "I can only tell ye what I know."

Fiona spoke up quietly from her seat at the table with Lucien. "I want to hear this as well. If there has been a secret, all our lives, I knew nothing of it!"

Ciaran pressed a hand to his eyes. "When Ma took me away with her, I was so young, I can scarcely remember it—except that I was frightened. I remember being inside a great castle with Isbeil, our nurse, but little else." He threw up his hands. "Ye may believe me or not, but I speak the truth."

Lennox turned to look at Fiona. "Isbeil never spoke to you

of this while she was alive? Ye were closer to her than any of us."

"Nay!" she exclaimed, meeting his gaze. "And you well know Isbeil would have died before betraying any secret our mother kept."

"Then I must go to Dunvegan and demand the truth from Da. He doubtless knows more than he has revealed."

Ciaran seemed to swallow a protest. "All right, then. I will come as well."

"And so will we." Fi stood up, holding little Lucien, and put out her chin defiantly. "Do not refuse me. I am still your sister!"

Although Lennox wished he could use his pain to build a protective wall around himself, he was glad for Ciaran and Fiona's support. They were, after all, the only family he had ever known.

Chapter Two

The morning's wet, gray clouds had gusted away, and now a sunny breeze pushed Lennox's small galley over the waters of Loch Dunvegan. In the distance, he spied the great rocky pedestal that held Dunvegan Castle aloft like an ancient crown. Adjusting the sail, Lennox glanced back at his family members. How many times over the years had the three siblings sailed together in this very boat, laughing, talking, utterly at ease as they approached their clan MacLeod stronghold? Now, however, he clearly saw how different he was from them. It was impossible to remain blind to the truth: Lennox stood out like a hound among a flock of sheep.

"Mind the rocks," warned Ciaran as he took the tiller. "Your thoughts are clearly elsewhere."

High on the stony plateau, guards were posted outside the castle's sea-gate, but they waved at the sight of the three MacLeods. When Ciaran had brought the galley onto the shore and helped his sister and nephew to disembark, Fiona turned to Lennox.

"Will you please carry Lucien?" Her blue gaze was penetrating.

It pained him to look at the wee lad, for it felt as if the newly-revealed secret had carved out a gulf between them. "Aye." Lennox opened his arms to the smiling bairn, forcing himself to smile in response. Lucien thought of him as his easy-going, kindhearted uncle, who was always ready to laugh and hoist him high into the air. Nay, Lennox could not punish the child for the sins of adults.

Lucien leaned trustingly against his uncle's broad shoulder and reached for the clan MacLeod badge affixed to his cap. Since he was a babe, Lucien had been drawn to the badge, and it had become a ritual between them. Often, Lennox detached it from the woolen bonnet and gave it to him to hold, but not today.

Today, the very thought of the *Hold Fast* insignia was like a dagger in Lennox's heart.

When they had ascended the carved stone steps, passed through the sea-gate, and entered the shelter of the castle's outer courtyard, Fiona came closer.

"Wait." She caught his sleeve. "I beg you, do not harden your heart against your family."

"Do ye imagine I can behave as if nothing has happened?"

"Lennox MacLeod, you are still my brother, even if it's only Ma and a lifetime of shared memories that bind us together. I have not forgotten the words our mother spoke to you on her deathbed."

"I cannot bear to feel this now," he said in a ragged whisper.

Fi leaned closer, forcing him to look at her. "She called you her 'beautiful lion' and begged that you guard your tender heart."

"Can ye not see, everything I thought was real was a secret. A *lie*. I would be a fool to smile as before and open my heart to those who hid the truth." He sent a fiery glance toward Ciaran, who was watching them from a short distance away. "Tell me ye know this, Fi."

She drew a shaky breath. "Aye. But Lennox—"

"I'm going now to speak to Da and Grandfather."

"I have never heard so cold a voice from you," Fiona protested. "When all the other men have buried their feelings, I could always count on you to show kindness. Caring. Tenderness."

Lennox shook his head. "I cannot feel anything now except pain—and anger."

With that, he set Lucien down to play with two of his little cousins and strode on ahead of the others, into the castle. He soon found his father in the cavernous hall, immersed in a game of chess with his half-brother, Tormod.

Magnus lifted a weathered hand in greeting but did not look up from the ancient chessboard. Just two years ago, after the loss of their family castle to clan MacDonald, he had been a shell of his former self. His gradual return to health had been a source of deep satisfaction to Lennox, but all those warm feelings now seemed spoiled.

"I would have a word with ye and Grandfather," Lennox said without preamble. Even as he spoke, he realized with a shock that Alasdair Crotach was not his grandfather any more than Magnus was his da.

"In a bit," Magnus replied absently, fingering the berserker, one of the ancient ivory chess pieces carved from a walrus tusk. "I am on the verge of conquering Tormod for the second time today."

Ciaran approached the table and cleared his throat. "Da. Stop what ye are doing. This matter is more important."

This deliberate show of support from Ciaran only increased Lennox's feelings of harsh confusion. Without a backward glance, he started toward the spiral staircase that led up to Alasdair Crotach's chamber. He could anticipate every worn place in the broad stone steps, every arrow-slit window that let in the damp breeze from Loch Dunvegan, for he'd climbed these stairs since he was no bigger than Lucien.

Arriving in the clan chief's bedchamber, Lennox saw that the old man was sitting up in a chair, a warm plaid wrapped around his bony shoulders. He had lived more than nine decades and was the oldest person Lennox had ever known. It seemed to the proud members of clan MacLeod that Alasdair Crotach might never die.

"I was near asleep," the old man said in a raspy voice.

Ciaran came to stand on Lennox's right side, and Fiona appeared on his left.

"Grandfather," Ciaran said loudly, "Lennox wishes a word with ye."

Magnus came into the room then, still holding the berserker chess piece. "What the devil is this all about? I don't trust Tormod to leave the board undisturbed!"

Lennox raised a warning hand at Ciaran. "I do not need ye to speak for me." He looked at Fiona. "Both of ye, leave us."

Fi again looked stricken, but she tugged at Ciaran's sleeve and said, "We must do as our brother bids."

When they went out, Lennox closed the heavy door behind them and gestured for Da to take a seat on the bench near Alasdair Crotach's chair. Both men were now regarding him warily. The emotions that surged inside Lennox, like fire in his heart, were so unfamiliar he felt a moment of terror.

"I know now that I am not a MacLeod by blood, and ye two have kept this secret all my life." he said harshly. "Today, I demand the *truth*."

Magnus's hazel eyes widened with shock. "How did ye learn this?"

Reaching into the leather pouch he kept belted to his plaid, Lennox withdrew the miniature and thrust it in front of them. "Ma had hidden this in the base of that silver casket she gave Fi before her death. We discovered it today."

All three of them stared at the exquisitely-painted miniature of the man in the jewel-trimmed doublet, who looked exactly like Lennox. The rasp of Alasdair Crotach's breathing filled the tower room, while the blood drained from Magnus's face.

"So, that must be your true da," Grandfather said at last. "A nobleman, from the look of him."

The words cut straight to Lennox's heart. His *true da*. With a glance, he saw that Magnus's eyes were wet. "'Twould seem so," he agreed, wishing he could feel as hard as his voice sounded. "Who is it?"

Grandfather glanced away. "If ye came here expecting me to have these answers, ye have wasted a journey."

It stung that Alasdair Crotach could dismiss this event that had shaken the very foundations of Lennox's existence, yet it was not surprising. The old man had not maintained his rule of their clan for seven decades by dispensing kindness and sympathy.

Lennox deliberately turned away from his grandfather, toward Magnus. "What have ye to say, Da? I know ye have held this secret every day of my life. If ye care for me at all, prove it by telling me the truth."

"I… I am as stunned as ye are to see that man's face. It brings back a deep pain I'd thought was in the past," Magnus said, his voice raw. "Lad, I have always loved ye as a son, for I thought ye were mine until after your fourth birthday."

Lennox pulled up a wooden stool, sat down, and stared at him. "Tell me everything."

"Ach! Ye would think no other bastard had e'er been born in all of Scotland!" scoffed Alasdair Crotach with a wave of one gnarled hand. A sudden warning glance from Magnus caused him to draw a wheezing breath and fall silent.

Magnus addressed Lennox in beseeching tones. "I know how much ye loved your ma. I feared it would break your heart to know she had been untrue to me…and that I was not your true da."

"That is a poor excuse for living a lie and keeping me in ignorance." Lennox leaned forward, filled with a steely resolve. "*Tell* me."

"Aye, I will, but I only know part of the story." Magnus coughed. "I accept my share of blame for your ma taking Ciaran and leaving Skye. She was very angry with me." His face went red with shame. "I dallied with a kitchen maid, and Ellie walked in on us. I was a fool."

"Where did she go?" he pressed.

Magnus shook his big head. "She would not tell me—or speak to me at all. Her nurse, Isbeil, brought a brother to travel with them in one of our galleys. The day they sailed away, with little Ciaran sitting between them on the bench, I thought my heart would break."

Lennox mulled this over, imagining the scene and Magnus's despair as he stood on the cliff outside Duntulm Castle and watched his family depart. Yet there must be more to the story. His mother, Eleanor, had been a strong, kind woman, and it surprised him that she would walk away without giving Da a second chance. "How long were they away?"

"The full summer. When Ellie returned, she said she came back to me because she'd discovered she was with child and knew we must restore our family bond. I was overjoyed and did not question the notion that ye had been conceived before we parted. Later, when ye were born, everyone agreed ye resembled the long-dead, distant Viking ancestors of clan MacLeod."

Grandfather hacked up some phlegm, as if offering his opinion of that theory.

"And then what happened?" pressed Lennox.

"We were happy, all of us. Years passed." Magnus sighed deeply. "One day, I discovered a letter hidden in your ma's things. It was filled with words of love." He pointed an accusing finger at the miniature. "From *him*."

Lennox's heart pounded with a mixture of dread and anticipation. "And what name was signed to this letter?"

"No name. Only an initial. *R*, I think. And no matter how I raged, she would not reveal to me his identity."

Lennox's mind spun at the thought of all the men in Scotland with a surname or Christian name starting with *R*. It was a useless clue! "How can I believe you truly do not know more than this?" He wanted to grab Da and shake the answers out of him. "Swear to me!"

"Lad, I swear on the robe of St. Columba, on the memory of your beautiful mother, that I do not know who that man is." Magnus swiped a hand across his eyes and pointed at the miniature again. "If I could tell ye, I would. But there is one thing I can say…"

Lennox felt a spark of hope that Da would actually divulge a secret. "Go on."

"Ye may have that man's blood, but I raised ye, Lennox

MacLeod. I was the one who made a home for ye and taught ye to sail, to hawk, the way to wrap your first clan tartan."

"That's well enough, but all of it pales next to the *truth*," Lennox whispered. "I have felt for years that I was different from the rest of the clan, but I couldn't understand why. Now I do." Lennox paused to stare at Alasdair Crotach, who looked back under hooded lids. "This is the reason I have not been given a proper clan brooch, is it not?" He pointed to the circular brooch that fastened Grandfather's plaid to his linen shirt. It featured the MacLeod bull's head in the center and was inscribed with the clan motto: *Hold Fast.*

Before Alasdair Crotach could speak, Magnus interjected, "Perhaps ye have forgotten that I too was misbegotten? I have spent my manhood standing in line behind the legitimate offspring of my own da, taking the leftover scraps tossed to me by William, Tormod, and the others."

"But it's all different!" raged Lennox. "Ye are the natural son of the chief of clan MacLeod!" He pointed to the brooch that gleamed at Magnus's shoulder. "Ye have every right to wear this, as does Ciaran. Your place in this family is rightful, but I am not even a true Highlander. Ma was born near Edinburgh." Lennox brandished the miniature. "And this fancy fellow looks more like a member of the royal court than any Highlander we know!"

Grandfather reached over to pluck at Lennox's sleeve. "Has it ne'er occurred to ye that 'twas your openly expressed discomfort with the clan that stopped me from fixing a brooch to your sash?"

Lennox stared. Perhaps that *had* crossed his mind, but now it seemed everything he'd once casually considered had been twisted with new meaning. Even Dunvegan Castle, the fortress at the center of his life, felt unstable today.

"'Twould seem I do not belong here on Skye," he murmured. "Perhaps I never did."

A loud knock sounded at the bedchamber door, and Lennox crossed to open it. There stood Ciaran.

"I could not bear to wait another moment," his brother said. "What have ye learned?"

In spite of everything, Lennox was heartened to see the emotion in Ciaran's dark face. "Very little, as ye predicted, but I may have one clue. Do ye remember that old Isbeil had a brother? Da says it was he who took them away in a galley, when ye were but a babe."

"Her brother?" Ciaran looked past Lennox to lock eyes with his da. "Were ye speaking of Duncan?"

"Oh, aye," Magnus nodded. "I remember now. Duncan."

"He labors for me in our shipyard," said Ciaran. "His cottage is nearby."

Lennox's heart leaped. "We must find him. If Duncan was with them, he may have the answers I seek."

Twilight was gathering as Violette came into the hall of Spirit Tower, followed by Old David who carried a tray of glasses and an open jug of wine.

"This is my favorite time of day on Skye," Violette said in her charming French accent. "The light is sublime, don't you agree? Pink and gold."

"Aye," agreed Ciaran, sending a conspiratorial smile to Lucien. "'Tis the faeries' doing."

As Lennox watched them, his thoughts drifted. As soon as he could tear Ciaran away from his little family, they would go together to visit Isbeil's brother, Duncan. What would the old man tell them? Lennox couldn't help imagining the stories he might hear, of his mother arriving at a grand castle, of the scene when she had met his father. The notion that Duncan might point at the man in the miniature and say his name aloud made Lennox feel oddly dizzy.

Across the room, Fiona began to show Lucien how to roll a ball for the new family puppy, a brown-and-white ball of fur called Gaston. Once she could see that her little son was feeling confident, she returned to the group at the table. Old David had just entered the hall with a platter of venison pie, roast carrots, and spring peas.

"I thought we were going to see Duncan," Lennox said as he watched Ciaran help himself to a wedge of pie. He knew he sounded edgy, but what did they expect? His whole life seemed to hang in the balance this evening.

"Aye, and we will," Ciaran replied evenly. "But first we must eat."

The thought of food made Lennox's stomach clench. "For years ye have kept the truth from me, and now that I have stumbled across it, ye still delay helping me to find more answers."

Ciaran sent him a stormy glance. "If I go without food, my temper will be as foul as yours." He pushed the pie across the table.

"And where the devil is Da, I would like to know?" Lennox complained as he grudgingly cut himself a wedge of venison pie. "He is more to blame than anyone, for he has known the longest, and yet he could not be bothered to come with us tonight."

Fiona patted Lennox's shoulder, looking worried. "I have never seen you like this before."

Before he could reply, there was a loud bang at the tower house door, and it swung open with a loud groan. Lennox looked up and was surprised to see Magnus entering the hall. Close behind him walked a wiry man with a grizzled beard, an old tartan bonnet pulled down over his ears.

"Da!" Ciaran rose and went forward to greet the two men. "Who's this with ye?"

"I've brought Duncan, Isbeil's brother," said Magnus, leading the older man forward. His eyes held a naked plea as he looked at Lennox.

The others rose to greet the visitors and call for additional refreshment, while Lennox struggled to quell the emotions that rose up inside him. It was so much easier to feel resentful and angry toward Da, to silently compile a list of grievances, but this simple demonstration of love from the only father he had ever known brought stinging tears to his eyes.

Magnus came to sit down on the bench beside Lennox. "Here then, Duncan, take a seat." He patted the place on his other side and turned back to Lennox, speaking to him in a low voice. "This is what ye wanted, isn't it?"

"Aye, Da."

" I know ye feel I've failed you, lad. All I can think of now is to try and make it right, going forward."

Fiona leaned over to make eye contact with Lennox. He knew she wanted him to embrace Da and tell him all was forgiven, but Lennox's heart, usually quick to warm and forgive, resisted. Instead he nodded at Magnus, mumbling thanks, and turned to Duncan.

"Our nurse, Isbeil, was your sister, was she not?"

"Aye. May the saints be with her." Duncan raised his glass and drank to his departed sister.

"Is it true that ye came to the aid of our mother, when she and Isbeil had to travel from the Isle of Skye? Our da remembers that ye were the one who took them over the water to…" He let his voice trail off, hoping that Duncan might quickly supply the answer he sought.

"Aye, I did help them. 'Twas many years ago." The old man glanced at Ciaran and smiled nostalgically. "This proud warrior was but a wee bairn. I recall that he took a liking to my old hound, Rufus. They'd curl up together in the bow of the galley, like kittens."

Feeling impatient, Lennox leaned forward. "Tell us more. Where exactly did ye take them?"

Duncan removed his bonnet and scratched his balding pate. "As I recall, we traveled to a tower house, where your ma was welcomed."

"Was it Hilltower?" Lennox supplied, holding his breath. That was the name of his mother's ancestral family home, north of Edinburgh.

"Could be. My memory's not what it once was."

Da poured some whisky into the man's cup. "I wonder where it might have been?" he asked. "Near Edinburgh?"

"Nay. By the western edge of Scotland, closer to Oban, I think." Duncan drank again and looked at Magnus. "Ah, now I recall. There was a big lass staying there who might have been kin to your lady. A sister?"

The MacLeods exchanged glances. "Aunt Tess," breathed Lennox. Of course! His ma had always turned to her older sister for guidance and love.

"What else can ye tell us?" Ciaran asked.

Duncan shrugged. "Nothing more. Your ma declared she would ne'er return to Skye, and so I left them there and sailed home alone."

Magnus had gone pale as a ghost, but Lennox could spare no sympathy for him tonight. In a voice hard as stone, he said, "I must find Aunt Tess."

It was Fiona who spoke first. "Just this week, I had a message from our aunt, in reply to the news that Lucien and I would soon travel to join Christophe. She wrote to say she has been named a lady-in-waiting to Queen Mary! The royal court always spends Easter at Stirling Castle, so we will be together there soon." She came over to rest a hand on his shoulder. "The way forward is quite clear. You must come with Lucien and me to Stirling."

Lennox thought of the miniature, tucked inside a pouch at his waist. In his mind's eye, he clearly saw the man who resembled him so closely. Was it possible that the truth could be revealed when he arrived at Stirling and spoke to his aunt?

"Aye," he said softly. "I'll go, Fi."

She threw her arms around him. "How wonderful it will be to travel together! Christophe has been worried for our safety."

Darkness gathered outside Spirit Tower as they made plans for the three of them to depart on the morrow, but Lennox felt strangely disconnected from this family he'd known since birth. Candles flickered in iron sconces set into the stone walls, illuminating the newly-painted mural of a birlinn on the waves near Duntulm Castle. Lennox stared at it. Originally he had imagined it to be a scene of homecoming, but now it seemed to hold a very different meaning.

Perhaps, without even realizing it, he'd painted a galley sailing *away* from Skye, bound for an unknown future.

Chapter Three

April 1541
Stirling Castle, Scotland

Nora paused at the tall leaded-glass window and emitted an appreciative sigh. Stirling Castle was set high on a soaring stone plateau, and Nora's perch in the tapestry work room offered a breathtaking view of the charming village and emerald-green countryside that encircled the fortress.

"Oh Father, I'm so glad we came here," she said, smiling.

William Brodie was hunched over a richly colorful tapestry spread over the surface of a worktable. "We had no choice," he rumbled, peering through tiny spectacles at one section of the beautifully woven tapestry. "The Scots king needs me, now more than ever, since the *Hunt of the Unicorn* tapestries have arrived from France." William frowned. "See here, another area that is imperfect."

As Nora looked at the place indicated by his long, knobby finger, she silently gave thanks that King James V had purchased the magnificent set of tapestries. The six works of art depicted a unicorn hunt, from the first sighting of the mythical beast and ending with the dead unicorn being brought to the castle in triumph. Woven in Flanders, the tapestries were a gift from King François I, intended to decorate and warm the walls of the new palace still under construction. In addition to the priceless tapestries, the king had also sent a huge loom that had recently been assembled in this newly-renovated workroom. It was the first loom of its kind in Scotland, and Nora's father had great plans for it.

"Ye must care for not only these newest treasures, but all tapestries in the royal collection. Cleaning, mending, storing, hanging..." William was describing the work Nora would be doing as a tapestry keeper, known as a tapisier, for the royal court of Scotland. She seemed to only hear half of what he said. He slanted a proud glance her way. "Perhaps, if ye prove yourself, ye may be allowed a bit of true restoration. With the proper supervision, of course."

Before Nora could reply, they were interrupted by a knock at the open door. "Mistress Brodie?"

Nora looked over to see Grant Carsewell, a tall youth with expressive gray eyes who had extended a hand in friendship since her arrival at Stirling Castle in early March. "Hello, Grant. How nice it is to see you."

Her father cocked his big head. "We are laboring, young lad."

Grant beamed, looking only at Nora. "I've come to say that ye two are invited to sup with the royal court tonight. The king and queen are in residence, and they wish to celebrate the arrival of the new tapestries!"

"How thrilling it would be to dine in the great hall of Stirling Castle," Nora said, feeling a rush of excitement as she imagined the scene.

Grant smiled as he crossed the floor to peer at the tapestry spread over the worktable. "Oh, 'tis splendid indeed! Did ye help to weave it?"

"Nay." William shook his head. "Grand tapestries like these are woven in the lowlands of Flanders." He paused. "By those who have devoted their lives to perfecting this art."

"But aren't ye a weaver yourself, sir?"

Nora could see that her father's patience was running low. "Although I am quite capable of performing all the weaver's tasks, my real gift is drawing the pattern for a tapestry. It is called the cartoon, and it can take many weeks to create."

"And what of Nora?" asked Grant. "Will she do the drawing or the weaving?"

"Neither. She is a lass." William adjusted his spectacles and returned his attention to the tapestry, effectively ending the conversation. "Great weavers and cartoon artists have always been men, and the best among them reside in Flanders or France. 'Tis virtually impossible for a lass in Scotland to achieve such standing."

"But I do intend to become a master weaver," Nora dared to say. "It is my dream."

"Ye are gifted and will doubtless achieve more than other lasses," William said gruffly. "But we live in a world of rules. We must accept what is possible."

Nora bristled but made no reply. Long ago, her Flemish mother, Ada, had advised, "Your father is a rigid man. He finds comfort in structure. Life will be much easier if you simply do and think as you please without challenging him." A year later, when William announced they were moving to England to look after Henry VIII's growing tapestry collection, Ada simply refused to go. Nora had felt torn between her two parents. Although barely ten years old, she already saw herself as a weaver, and in the end she felt compelled to accompany her father. Although she'd not seen her mother for more than a decade, she had never forgotten her advice.

"Father," she said now, "I am going outside for some air."

He frowned. "Ye know well enough that our work leaves nary a moment for leisure." William gestured toward the red velvet bed hanging that servants had delivered to them just an hour ago. In raised work of gold and silver, it was decorated with a hunter and a stag, and it was meant for the king's own bed. "Ye should feel honored to bring your needle to repair a hanging like this one. Do not tarry!"

Nora wasted no time. She caught Grant by the sleeve of his blue doublet and led him out of the cavernous workroom. When the door was closed behind them, she sighed. "I have a deep regard for my father, but he can certainly make me yearn to escape," she confided.

Grant was watching her as they walked down the broad

curving staircase. "Ye put me in mind of a bird I saved when I was but a lad. Eventually, I realized if I truly loved him, I wouldn't keep him in a cage."

"Exactly." Nora laughed softly and lifted her skirts. "Of course, I owe Father everything, and he has been a wonderful teacher. But as much as I respect him, I am determined to make my own way in the world. One day, I *will* be a weaver, creating magnificent tapestries for royal courts like this one."

They emerged into the bustling, walled inner close, and Nora sensed Grant's skepticism even before he spoke. "I suppose dreams are a good thing, and I admire your determination," he allowed. "But it seems that men have the power, and the truth is, a lass must be governed by their rules."

"You are very young," Nora replied, turning sober. "And you have not known me long. I am not like other women. I have lived in Europe, England, and now Scotland. I have seen the world, and I mean to have my way with it." She paused, her body growing taut as a bowstring. "I will not be constrained by my father or any other man. The only true obstacles between me and my dreams are my own talent and strength, and I know they can overcome anything."

For a moment, Nora thought she saw stars in his eyes. One day, the lasses would be flocking around Grant Carsewell, but for now he was suspended on the precipice between adolescence and manhood.

"I want to be like you," he said.

"It's easy enough! Repeat this, morning and night," Nora urged. "*I alone am master of my own future.*"

Just then they were interrupted by a female voice calling Grant's name. He turned his head and gave a cry of delight. "Look there, it's Fiona!"

Nora realized that these people, who had the look of newly-arrived travelers, must be the friends Grant had told her about. His stepfather Bayard de Nieuil, she knew, was one of the French masons working with Christophe de St. Briac on the construction of the new palace here at Stirling.

Grant now turned to Nora, beaming. "Will ye come to meet my friends?"

He drew her along with him until they reached the small band of travelers, but he released her arm in order to embrace a young brunette woman with a warm smile. The newcomer wore a traveling gown of slate-blue wool that seemed to enhance her beauty in spite of its simplicity.

"This is my friend, Fiona MacLeod," said Grant. "And the wee bairn is Lucien, her son. They are the family St. Briac has been waiting for."

Although Nora smiled and spoke words of greeting, she felt awkward. She was taller than Fiona, and her curling mass of reddish hair struggled to burst free from the long braid down her back, while Fiona's ebony tresses were coiled neatly at her neck.

"Hello, Grant." The deep male voice spoke from a distance.

The speaker was a tall, broad-shouldered Highlander who stood apart from the others. He wore a belted plaid that revealed lean-muscled legs, but Nora's gaze was drawn to the man's wild, golden-tawny hair.

"Lennox!" exclaimed Grant. His face lit up. "Are my eyes deceiving me? How did ye come to be in Stirling?"

The man called Lennox smiled broadly in response. "I brought my sister and nephew from the Isle of Skye," he said, glancing her way as he explained. "And, as it happens, I've some business of my own." As Grant chattered in reply, Lennox slowly turned to look at Nora. His eyes were a startling shade of sea-green, and he lifted sun-bleached brows in a question. "I do not believe we've met, my lady."

To Nora's consternation, she felt her face grow warm. "There's no need to address me as if I were nobility. I am simply Nora Brodie."

Grant drew her closer to Lennox and made a sweeping gesture with one hand. "Yet there is nothing *simple* about this fair lass," he proclaimed. "Nora is a gifted weaver of tapestries! She and her father have come from the Tudor court in

London, at the behest of King James himself, to look after the Crown's priceless collection of tapestries."

Lennox angled an ironic glance between Grant and Nora. "Since my young friend can speak of naught but you, Mistress Brodie, it seems I must make my own introductions. I am Lennox MacLeod, from the Isle of Skye, brother to Fiona."

Under his warm regard, Nora became aware of a stirring deep inside, a restive yet pleasurable tingling. This was a part of her she'd taken pains to keep buried, for female instincts only interfered with her dreams—nay, goals. And so she steeled herself and, with a backward step, gave Lennox MacLeod a polite smile. "I hope you will enjoy your time in Stirling, sir."

"Lennox is a painter," Grant announced. "He is artistic, as ye are."

"How nice," Nora replied. Yet, in spite of her resolve to hold him at arm's length, she wanted to know more.

"I am very interested in the art of weaving," said Lennox. "And I've always wanted to see the sorts of priceless tapestries I've heard about all my life. Ye have seen them with your own eyes?"

Nora couldn't help smiling. "I have. I was raised in Flanders, where the most magnificent tapestries of all are made." She was gratified to see a bright glint of interest in his eyes. "My father has given his life to creating cartoons and weaving tapestries. It has been my privilege to join him in that world."

"I'd be grateful if ye would show me some of the tapestries that are in your care here at Stirling Castle," he said.

"We do have some truly splendid new works that have recently arrived by ship from France," she said, as enthusiasm bubbled up inside. "The *Hunt of the Unicorn* tapestries."

"The unicorn has virtually become the symbol of Scotland, it seems."

"It is true!" She felt drawn to the Highlander by an invisible thread. "My father says the unicorn is a metaphor for Christ himself."

"Fascinating." Lennox gave her a smile that dazzled like the sun itself. "I hope ye will be good enough to enlighten me further, Mistress Brodie."

"Perhaps. But please call me Nora."

"Agreed." He looked into her eyes. "And I am Lennox."

Nora suddenly found it hard to breathe, and an inner alarm sounded within her. Ever since she'd grown old enough to experience even twinges of amorous desire, she had learned to tamp them down as quickly as possible. Once again, she reminded herself that if she meant to achieve her aspiration to become a female weaver, there could be no room for romance in her life, not even at a distance.

And so, with a polite nod to Lennox MacLeod, Nora turned away. "And now, I really must return to our workroom. Good day."

She smiled and made farewells to the others, but avoided the Highlander's questing gaze. So quickly did Nora turn and hurry off, she felt the low heal on her shoe come off, but the last thing she wanted to do was call attention to herself by stopping to retrieve it. Perhaps Grant, who followed in her wake, would pick it up.

"What's amiss?" the youth whispered as he drew alongside, taking her arm. "Are ye ill?"

"I merely realized the time. Father will be looking for me."

"But," teased Grant, "I thought ye resisted such confinements."

"I wish I could." Nora didn't understand why she had felt so warm, even breathless, in the company of Lennox MacLeod, but she knew she could not allow it. "Unfortunately, I live in Father's world, and I must find ways to achieve my goals without being singled out as a rebel."

Quickly, she traversed the inner close, weaving among the noisy clusters of stone masons and carpenters who were building the new palace. Just before she stepped inside to climb the tower steps, she felt that someone was watching her. Turning to scan the courtyard, she saw a tall, slender man with curly dark hair and a rakish beard. He was openly staring at her, grinning, and when their eyes met, he swept off his plumed cap and bowed low.

Nora hurried inside, feeling unusually precarious as she lifted her skirts and rushed up the turnpike stairway, back to the safety of the tapestry-filled workroom.

For his part, Ciaran wished he were back at Duntulm Castle on his beloved Isle of Skye. He had no use for a city like Edinburgh, with its crowds, noise, and dwellings that climbed upward and jutted out haphazardly above the streets. Perhaps worst of all was the stink. He glanced down a dark, twisting lane, called a close, that veered off from the High Street. A half-starved dog had cornered a rat, while two grubby little boys made mischief nearby. Even as Ciaran wondered how people could live in such wretched conditions, an upstairs window was flung open and a man dumped a chamber pot of waste onto the filthy cobbles below.

"We've just arrived, and already I long to turn around and go home," Ciaran said under his breath.

"Cheer up." Violette reached over and lightly cuffed his arm. "Soon you will be in the palace, feasting with the king and all the fine members of his court. No doubt that will improve your mood."

He sent her a dark glance. Violette was well aware that he cared little for rich food and crowds of people making merry. He would rather be standing on a mountaintop, with the grandeur of the Isle of Skye spread below him, or sailing a galley from his grandfather's fleet as the sea spray flew in his face. Or even doing battle with a brutal MacDonald foe. Anything but socializing with a lot of fancy courtiers who believed the Highlanders were their inferiors.

"I think ye know me better than that," he said. "This is the last place I would choose to be."

"Yet our lives cannot always be as we might wish," came Violette's wistful reply.

He looked over, suddenly aware that she might be speaking of herself, not him, and allowing him a glimpse into her secret feelings. Not for the first time, Ciaran wondered what Violette was hiding. "I suspect you refer to your own life and wishes."

"My own?" she gave a little laugh. "I wish only to be of service to the household of Magnus MacLeod." And as his gaze sharpened, she looked away.

Moments later, Ciaran was distracted by the sight of a mammoth gatehouse looming up at the foot of the Canongate. Beyond the gatehouse rose the towers of Holyrood Palace.

"Ach," his grandfather grunted. "At last."

Ciaran could only imagine how difficult such a journey must have been for a man of Alasdair Crotach's advanced age, yet the MacLeod chief summoned the will to sit a bit straighter in his saddle. He turned his weathered face into the mist and nodded, as if reminding himself of his title, his clan, his heritage.

At the gatehouse, Magnus went ahead to speak to one of the guards and they all passed through the arched portal to the spacious inner courtyard. No sooner had grooms appeared to take their horses than a cluster of well-dressed men emerged from the palace to greet the MacLeod party.

Two clansmen from Dunvegan helped Alasdair Crotach to dismount and come to the front of the group. One of the Lowland courtiers strode toward them. Clad in a leather jerkin, he was muscular, with a receding hairline and a thick, dark beard. The centerpiece of his flushed face was a twisted nose.

"On behalf of His Majesty the King of Scots, I bid ye welcome," the man said in a deep voice. He looked first at Alasdair Crotach before sweeping his gaze over the rest of the group. "I am Hector Shaw, Yeoman of the Chamber. We are honored that ye have traveled so far at the invitation of the king."

Another portly fellow introduced himself as George Balglavy, the Keeper of Holyrood Palace, and it quickly became apparent that he was in charge of the MacLeod clansmen, not the self-important Hector Shaw. Ciaran watched Shaw curiously as Balglavy took over, ignoring the yeoman in the leather jerkin.

"If ye will all follow me," Balglavy said, "I'll show you to your apartments." Turning to Alasdair Crotach, he added with a wink, "No doubt ye are weary from so long a journey, sir, and would welcome refreshment. Ye will find the king's whiskey to be very fine."

After the MacLeod chief and his clansmen had started off across the courtyard, Hector Shaw turned toward the servants who remained behind. "Come with me," he said. "Ye will have lodgings near the palace."

Ciaran lingered nearby. He found that he was reluctant to leave Violette with this stranger, especially since she was the only female. Of course, he told himself wryly, it wasn't as if she was irresistibly tempting to men. In fact, standing off to one side in her soiled dun-colored gown and crumpled headdress, she looked more like something the cat had dragged home. Still, Ciaran went around the others to speak to her.

"I could find other lodgings for you," he said softly.

To Ciaran's surprise, Violette looked up with flashing eyes. "Do you imagine that I cannot fend for myself?"

"Nay! I merely thought ye might…" *Might what?* Even he didn't know the answer to that. It was more a feeling in his gut. "I mean, we know nothing of that fellow." He inclined his head toward Shaw. "Have a care."

"Might he wish to ravish me?" She swept a hand in front of her soiled, ill-fitting dress.

Now she was making light of his concern. "I only meant to offer ye a choice, lass." Ciaran bent closer, until he caught an unexpected whiff of meadow grass from her damp skin. "Since ye do not require me, I'll be on my way."

He saw the burly yeoman, Shaw, watching him as he turned and followed the MacLeods into the palace. Just as he passed inside, Ciaran looked back over one shoulder and glimpsed the bedraggled figure of Violette Pasquiére. To his chagrin, she raised one hand just enough to proudly wave him on.

Sitting beside her father in the castle's magnificent great hall, Nora watched as servants entered with platters of roasted swans in full plumage, their beaks artfully gilded. A harpist played an ethereal tune near the high table, where the king was now being seated in a carved wooden throne, flanked by a dozen trusted courtiers.

"I thought it was your great desire to attend these festivities," said William Brodie, nearly shouting to be heard above the other voices, laughter, and music. "Are ye not impressed?"

Looking over at her father, Nora realized that she'd been chewing at her lower lip. It had always been a sign to those who knew her best that she was ill-at-ease. "I am impressed indeed." She gestured toward the splendid hammer-beam ceiling high above them. "I did not realize anything quite so grand existed in Scotland."

"Aye, that's part of the reason I wanted to bring ye here to Stirling. Ye know little of your true heritage, lass, and the rest of the world seems to think Scotland is a wild and backward place."

"I suppose I always had the idea you left here for that very reason," she said.

Her father shrugged and lifted a cup of wine to his lips, to hide a smile, she suspected. "When I was young, I knew I would have to travel to pursue my dreams. I heard rumors that great art was to be found in Europe. Once I got there and was apprenticed to a fine weaver, I knew I had found my place in the world."

"And then you met Mama," Nora interjected.

His eyes grew wintry. "Aye. With your birth, I thought we were making a true family, but your ma could not submit to the will of her husband. She—" Her father broke off with a shake of his head. "Pay no attention to me. This wine has loosened my tongue."

Farther down their long table, Nora saw Grant sitting with his stepfather and mother, Bayard and Judith de Nieuil. Judith was a beautiful, prickly woman, but Bayard was a warm bear of a man, whom Grant loved like a true father. It seemed Bayard was even able to light a flame inside Judith's chilly heart.

Nora had learned from Grant that Bayard had been a master mason laboring here at Stirling to build a new palace in the French style. However, when Christophe de St. Briac had arrived in recent weeks from the Isle of Skye, Bayard had gladly relinquished that position to his mentor.

Now, Bayard sat with the newly-reunited St. Briac family, conversing animatedly, while Christophe held his baby son on his lap and fed him bites of roasted lamb. Fiona was there too, looking blissfully happy. When Nora caught her eye, the two women exchanged smiles.

At that moment, Lennox MacLeod entered the hall. Nora saw him immediately. She couldn't help staring, for he resembled a mythical Norse god come to life. He wore a snow-white linen shirt and a belted plaid, with a sash bisecting his wide, hard chest. A thousand candleflames seemed to illuminate every strand of gold in Lennox's tousled hair, and the smile he turned her way made her feel lightheaded. Nora dared to smile back as he took a seat next to Grant, though she knew she shouldn't. Any contact with this man was dangerous, like reaching out to recklessly touch a flame.

"Ah, at last we meet," a voice murmured into her ear.

Startled, Nora came back to reality. She glanced up to see the dark, curly-haired man from the courtyard, bending down to make himself heard. Before she could think of a response, her father spoke.

"'Tis Sir Raymond Slater, am I right?" William boomed. "'Twas your ship that brought the magnificent unicorn tapestries and our grand new loom to Scotland. My name is

William Brodie. My daughter Nora and I are the tapisiers who are charged with caring for those treasures." He looked expectantly at Nora. "Lass, will ye not give thanks to this fine man?"

Before she could speak, Slater was sweeping off his peacock-feathered cap. "Mistress Brodie, it is I who must speak words of appreciation. Your exquisite beauty illuminates this entire hall."

Nora rose to stand before him, feeling more uncertain than shy. "You are too kind, sir." Yet she couldn't help basking in the realization that she looked pretty in this, the single fine gown she owned. Fashioned of pearl-gray velvet and white silk, it had been a gift from a female weaver in London. Nora suspected the lady, named Marianne, had felt sorry for Nora with only William to look after her. Her father had scoffed when Nora unwrapped the gown, saying she would never have good reason to wear such a creation, but tonight when she emerged from her chamber in the pearl-gray gown, he'd beamed.

"Ye will put the queen to shame, lass," William had said proudly.

And she did look pretty. The gown accentuated Nora's rich, coppery locks and striking blue eyes. Usually, her looks were the farthest thing from her mind, but tonight was different.

"Will ye share a cup of wine with us?" William asked the Englishman.

Sir Raymond Slater nodded and took a seat beside Nora. He was richly garbed in a jerkin of sapphire-blue velvet trimmed with gold braid, worn over a slashed, blue-and-bronze doublet, and Nora couldn't help noticing the contrast between Slater's appearance and the simpler clothing worn by Lennox MacLeod. As her father continued on about the tapestries, explaining why they were so rare, so valuable, Nora sensed that Sir Raymond was scarcely listening. She could feel his gaze on her face, and the sensual part of her that had been ignited today by the presence of Lennox MacLeod began to flicker again.

"Did ye know," William was continuing enthusiastically, "a

set of tapestries such as this one could cost as much as a great warship?"

"Indeed?" Slater replied coolly. "Then perhaps I should have kept them for myself and sailed on, past Scotland."

Nora sensed her father's deep shock at such a notion. He froze beside her then abruptly began to laugh and reached over to clap the Englishman's shoulder. "Ha, sir! I know ye are in jest, but I must advise that ye not repeat such remarks. I suspect others would not be amused."

A thin, liveried servant was approaching and came to a stop beside Nora's father's chair.

"My good sir," the young man greeted William, "the king requests that you join him at the high table so that he might impart a few words of appreciation."

Nora felt a wave of happiness for her father. "Only a few days have passed since the royal court arrived from Linlithgow," she whispered, "and already His Majesty has heard about you, Father."

"Aye." William colored slightly and rose to his feet. "But I cannot leave you here alone, lass."

"Never fear," Sir Raymond Slater said with a grand gesture. "I shall look after your daughter in your absence, sir. It would be my honor."

When William had left them, Nora fell silent, waiting for the next course to arrive.

"You are a very beautiful woman," Slater said suddenly. He leaned closer, and she could feel the heat of his scented body and smell the wine on his breath. "I suspect your father has sheltered you from the pleasures of the world, yes?"

Nora's stomach jumped. "Certainly our work does keep us apart from the world, but it is also my choice," she replied.

"And how old are you, Nora?"

His use of her Christian name made her feel even more nervous. "Two and twenty," she replied softly, well aware how many females were wed and mothers many times over by the time they reached her age.

"Such a shame, for so much beauty to go *untasted*." In the next instant, he moved away, and his tone lightened. "My apologies, Mistress Brodie, if I was overfamiliar. I fear I was momentarily overpowered by your charms. Allow me to make amends."

Nora softened. After all, he was a very handsome man, and she did not want to be stiff and prim. It was not the way she saw herself at all. "There's no need to apologize."

He reached inside his jerkin, and a moment later he withdrew a small emerald-encrusted box. "In this case I keep something very special: rare sweetmeats from the West Indies." Slater pushed at a tiny clasp and the case opened. "I only share this delicacy with a few close friends."

She wanted to say that the two of them were hardly close friends, but Nora's mouth watered at the sight of the sweetmeats. Sugar was her weakness, and when was the last time she had eaten such a delicacy? "You're very kind, sir."

The Englishman wore jeweled rings on his long, pale fingers. Nora watched, spellbound, as he reached out to pluck one of the sweetmeats from the case and put it in her hand. "I promise, you will find it *sublime*."

Chapter Four

Lennox ate the sumptuous meal and listened as Grant excitedly detailed King James V's plan to confine lions at Stirling Castle.

"There is a courtyard being constructed in the center of the new palace that the king has named the lion's den!" Grant shook his head as he spoke. "It's shocking, don't ye agree? Lions belong in the wild jungles of Africa, not in a stone enclosure. I intend to find a way to stop this mad scheme."

Lennox nodded, listening with half an ear as he cast a sidelong glance at Nora Brodie. She sat with her father at another table, clad in a gown of pearl-gray velvet with lightly slashed sleeves revealing puffs of ivory satin. Her thick curls were swept back in a style that was at once simple yet elegant, set off by a French hood trimmed in silver and pearls. Even from a distance, he could discern the sparkle in the lass's blue eyes, the graceful line of her neck and jaw, the animation in her gestures as she conversed with her father. What was she saying? What brought that radiant smile to her lips? She was, Lennox decided, the most beautiful woman in the entire great hall.

Nay, he corrected himself. Nora Brodie was the most beautiful woman he had ever seen. Anywhere. A strange desire came over him to go and sit beside her. Did he not have a perfect excuse to do so? Earlier that day, he had retrieved the broken heel of her shoe in the courtyard, and now it was concealed in the pouch at his belt, along with the miniature of his true father.

Aye, he could join her at the table, return the heel, and then they would find themselves engaged in easy conversation. Lennox felt a rush of euphoria as he imagined divulging the story of his quest with an openness he could not grant even to his family members. Deep inside, he sensed that Nora would listen and understand, and then she would share her own life story…

A hand cuffed his arm. "Have ye heard one word I've said?" cried Grant. The youth followed his gaze and gave a low snort. "Ach, I see ye are taken with Nora."

"I needn't be *taken* with a lass to admire her." Although Lennox's tone was casual, he felt his face warm. By the saints, was he *blushing*? Before Grant could call him out, he added, "Perhaps ye are the one who fancies her?"

The youth sat up straighter, brightening. "I won't deny it. I confess, if I were older, I would do battle to win Nora's hand."

Just then, Lennox was rescued when Fiona gestured from the other side of the table. "Come and sit with me," his sister invited softly. "I have news."

Remembering that Fi had pledged to discover if their Aunt Tess had come to Stirling with the king and queen, Lennox pushed to his feet.

"We will continue this fascinating discussion at a later time." With a smile, Lennox leaned down to pat Grant's thin shoulder, then started around the table. The great hall felt stifling to him, warmed by the bodies of countless perfumed courtiers and their ladies. How could these people live this way, day in and day out?

"Do sit with me," Fiona greeted him. Reaching up, she caught his hand and drew him down on the bench beside her. "The king has summoned Christophe to meet William Brodie, the master weaver, to discuss the plans for placement of the tapestries in the new palace. It seemed a perfect time for us to talk."

Lennox saw that Lucien, his little nephew, was occupied by Bayard, who sat nearby with his wife, Judith. The robust

French mason held the boy on his lap and showed him a little carved wooden lion. Beaming, Lucien brandished the toy and growled, showing his tiny teeth.

"It's nice that the wee lad is allowed to join you in this formal setting," Lennox remarked.

"Oh, I believe they are so happy to have Christophe here to oversee the last stages of the new palace, he can do as he pleases." She reached out, still smiling, to touch Lennox's face. "How handsome you are, brother. You put these other fancy courtiers to shame."

"Ye view me in a favored light, sister," he laughed. "The rest of the court stares as if I have escaped from that lion's den the king wants to build."

"You're mad." Fiona shook her head fondly and speared a bite of marchpane tart with her eating knife.

"Did ye summon me only to say that? I was expecting news of our aunt."

"As it happens, I do have news." She held another morsel of the tart up to him. "You must try this. I can promise, you've never tasted anything like it on the Isle of Skye." She waited, then pretended to frown. "Do open your mouth!"

Lennox obeyed with a sigh, allowing his sister to feed him. "I agree, it is delicious. But what about Aunt Tess?" Even as he spoke, his attention wandered briefly back to Nora Brodie, and he allowed himself a brief look in her direction. To his surprise, her father had disappeared from her side, replaced by a richly garbed courtier with black hair and a pointed beard who leaned forward, as if intending to block Lennox's view.

"Are you listening?" Fiona demanded, nudging him.

He gave himself a mental shake. If he kept glancing toward Nora, Fiona would quickly pinpoint his weakness and proclaim it aloud. "Of course I'm listening. But who is that man over there with the ridiculous peacock plume in his cap? Do ye know him?"

"Oh, that is Sir Raymond Slater. He is the captain of *Hercules*, the ship that brought the grand *Hunt of the Unicorn* tapestries from France. Ever since the king arrived, His Majesty has been fawning over the Englishman." She paused to give a disparaging sniff. "Christophe tells me, however, that Sir Raymond is a swaggering knave who basks in the praise that comes his way. He takes so much credit for the tapestries, one would think that he wove them himself!"

Lennox wanted to rise and make his way to Nora's table, to find a way to remove Slater and take the Englishman's place at her side. Should he find out if she needed his assistance?

"Forget about that man, will you please?" Fiona reached out to lightly tap his cheek. "Honestly, Lennox, sometimes I think you should be on a *different* sort of quest—one that has to do with your future rather than some secret from the past."

"What are ye going on about now?" Of course, he knew well enough. She'd given him this speech several times during their journey from the Isle of Skye to Stirling Castle.

"Why not search for a bride instead of your lost father? Sometimes I suspect you are doing this merely to avoid what is right in front of you... You need someone to share your life with, to give you bairns, to—"

Lennox held up a hand to silence her. "Leave it alone, Fi. Talk to me about Aunt Tess."

"I wouldn't badger you if I didn't love you so." Sighing, Fiona continued, "Aye, I do have word of our aunt."

"Word?" Lennox had assumed that, as a lady-in-waiting to Queen Mary, Tess would be present. "Is she not here tonight?" Even as he spoke, his attention firmly returned to the real reason he'd traveled to Stirling Castle. In his mind's eye, he saw the face of the man in the miniature. Had he not upended his entire existence to embark on this quest? He must be on guard against distractions like the bonny Nora Brodie.

Fiona was shaking her head. "No, Aunt Tess is not present in the hall. It seems that Her Majesty will soon be delivered of a child, and she has taken a small band of trusted household servants to be with her at Falkland Palace, preparing for the birth. She had a son, Prince John, just last May, and it is very happy news that soon he will have a new brother or sister." Pausing, Fi smiled to herself, and Lennox recalled that she had become a friend to Mary of Guise when the Frenchwoman was a new bride, in 1538. "As her lady-in-waiting, our aunt was among those who traveled to Falkland rather than coming to Stirling with His Majesty and the rest of the household. They will all be reunited after Easter."

"But why did ye not tell me this sooner?" Lennox demanded, his voice rising.

"Perhaps I only just learned this news myself! Have we not just arrived at Stirling?" She cuffed his arm. "Unlike you, I have been asking questions about Aunt Tess, and unlike you, I have found the answers."

He covered his face with both hands. "God save me. What next?"

"Falkland Palace isn't very far away. Perhaps you'll have to travel there to speak to her." Fiona stared hard at him. "That is, unless you have a better reason to stay right here at Stirling Castle?"

"Nay." Even as he denied it, Lennox stole another glance in Nora's direction. To his surprise, he saw that her place at the table was empty, and for an instant it seemed the candlelight dimmed in the great hall. "As ye say, I will go to Falkland Palace. I have no choice."

Nora found that she couldn't walk on her own. The stone floor seemed to spin under her feet and she had to lean against Sir Raymond Slater. What was wrong? If only her father hadn't gone to sup with the king, she wouldn't have to rely on the kindness of this imposing Englishman when she began to feel ill.

"Don't fret, my dear. I will take you to your rooms," he was saying, holding her up as they started across the inner close, toward the wing of the old palace where the Brodie rooms were located. "Look, do you see how bright the stars shine tonight?

The night sky is like velvet and the stars like diamonds."

When she tried to tip her head to look up, it seemed she would fall backward, but Sir Raymond caught her and held her for a long, reassuring moment. "I don't know what's wrong with me." Her tongue felt thick. "This has never happened before. Could it have been the sweetmeat?"

"Nay. I ate two myself! More likely, in the evening's excitement, you imbibed more wine than you are accustomed to," he soothed. "I'll have you in your own rooms soon enough."

Though her mind was clouded, Nora was certain her father would be outraged if he knew she was alone with this stranger. "We should call for someone else," she said. "Another lady."

"But which lady would you ask to leave the grand festivities?" he asked, even as he led her across the courtyard. "The music has just commenced. Besides, I have been wanting to see the loom I brought all the way from Flanders for the royal weavers to use. I heard your father has already made great progress in assembling it."

He continued on, telling her how difficult it had been to get the loom's two giant rollers into the hold of the ship, how he had taken care to remind his crew that this was a treasure that would one day produce great pieces of art. As he spoke, they entered the wing where the Brodies had rooms adjoining the workroom. Slater's tale began to seem tedious to Nora. Why had she imagined she had anything to fear from this man? After all, everyone at the court treated him with great reverence, as if he were a true hero, and he did not appear to be any threat to her innocence.

When Nora wobbled on the first step of the spiral staircase, the Englishman startled her by swinging her up into his arms and nimbly ascending to the tapestry workrooms. "I beg you, my lady, do not protest," he said with a debonair smile. "You are as light as air."

Nora started to laugh and caught a whiff of his heavy scent: a mixture of ambergris and musk. "I am taller than most, good sir." Glancing down, she saw that he could not manage to open the door. "Perhaps I could just sit here and wait for Father…"

"Did you know your own queen is as tall as most men?" Without waiting for her response, he continued to speak in conversational tones while persistently working at the door latch. "I met Mary of Guise once, when I visited France to receive a cargo from her uncle, King François. In those days, she was the Duchess of Longueville. Had you heard that, after she was widowed, King Henry VIII sought her hand in marriage? They said he simply couldn't bear to think of James V claiming her."

Nora sagged against his shoulder, feeling dizzy and grateful for his strong free arm around her waist. "Nay, I did not know that." She was surprised to hear that her words were slightly slurred.

He replied as if nothing at all were amiss. "When your queen refused Henry's offer, she said, 'I may be a big woman, but I have a very little neck.' 'Twould seem she had no wish to follow Anne Boleyn to the block." Sir Raymond gave a bark of laughter and arched a dark brow at this reminder of the English queen's gory death.

Nora was so distracted by this odd tale that she scarcely noticed that he had finally gotten the door open. Still, a part of her was alert enough to remember he should not be alone with her inside this private space. "I thank you for bringing me this far, and now…" With a careful effort, she finished, "I must bid you good evening, sir."

"Ah, but you promised to show me the loom!"

"Did I?" Nora blinked, trying to remember. "In truth, I do not feel well."

Slater firmly led her to sit in a low, mahogany chair before lighting a single candle with a taper from the fireplace. "I will bring you a cup of wine. It will do wonders to revive you."

No sooner had he started toward the shelf where her father kept their spirits than Nora closed her eyes. She felt as if she were sinking into a cool, deep pool of water. It was lovely…as long as she didn't let her head drop below the surface.

"Here you go."

He was lifting her head, and a cup was poised at her lips. With difficulty, Nora opened her eyes. "I—I am not really thirsty."

"Do you not wish to feel better? Of course you do."

His deep voice seemed to purr beside her. Had he just touched her ear with the tip of his tongue? "But..."

"I must *insist* that you drink. I cannot leave you alone until I know you are feeling better."

She tried to sip the wine and discovered that she was much thirstier than she had realized. As he tipped the cup higher and higher, Nora drank more. A dark heat spread through her limbs, rendering her unable to move even before her mind had formed the thought.

"Fear not. I will put you in your bed, and then you'll rest, pet."

In her bed? Nay, not there. She tried to protest, but could not make a sound. Slater was lifting her up, carrying her through the shadowed room. He peered first into her father's chamber, then turned to the other door and pushed it open. The gown she had worn earlier that day was spread over a stool, identifying the space as hers.

"Such a sheltered life you lead. Like a nun!" He clucked his tongue, dropped her down on the bed, and straightened to his full height. "But it needn't be a permanent condition. I have just the remedy. You want that, don't you?"

Nora stared up at him through a blur of moonbeams. She attempted to shake her head, but could not move even her toes. Suddenly, he was kneeling on the edge of her mattress, and she saw him fumbling with the padded protrusion of his striped codpiece. The scene felt like a nightmare. Aye, perhaps it truly was but a dream! Bile rose in her throat, and tears trickled down the sides of her face. *Please, go away*, she tried to shout. Perhaps she had spoken but simply couldn't hear, just as she was unable to move.

Slater tugged at her bodice, but thankfully her breasts were covered by layered undergarments that could only be removed one at a time. The room began to spin as he pushed her skirts up, pried her thighs open, and climbed on top of her.

"Sorry, pet, no time for pleasantries," he grunted.

Nora managed to turn her face away from him, only dimly sensing what he was doing. She tried not to inhale his musky scent. Her body was numb. After a few moments, she was aware of a searing pain, as if something had given way deep inside her, and then it was over.

When Raymond Slater clambered off the bed and readjusted his clothing, Nora could only stare at him, mute. Her head began to pound and her throat was dry as dust. Every part of her, including her vibrant spirit, was numb.

"That wasn't much, but you'll improve with practice. Are you not grateful to me for introducing you to the ways of womanhood?" His tone was smooth as he pulled her skirts down over her bare legs. "And you needn't worry, pet. This interlude will be our little secret."

Chapter Five

"Perhaps she has merely gone out for a moment of privacy," Fiona said.

Lennox, who was staring pensively across the great hall toward the table where Nora Brodie had been sitting a short while ago, drew a harsh breath. "A moment? It has been much longer than that."

"If she needed to relieve herself, it would take time," Fi whispered. "Lasses have layers of skirts and petticoats to deal with."

"I don't know..." Her absence nagged at him. "I feel that something is amiss."

"You *feel* it? My dear brother, you barely know the lass. All your life, you have rescued those in need...but is it your place to intervene with Nora Brodie?" Fiona lifted a delicate brow. "Even if it were up to you, she does not strike me as the type who wishes to be rescued."

She had a point, he knew, but uneasiness stirred in him all the same. As soon as Christophe returned to the table, Lennox found an excuse to slip away. It was easy enough to weave unnoticed through the crush of guests, for some of the boards were being removed, and dancing had begun.

He passed under the arched, torchlit doorway, into the cool open space of the inner close, a courtyard ringed by magnificent royal buildings. Alone except for guards who blended into the shadows, Lennox paused to scan the indigo sky for familiar starry landmarks. A smile touched his mouth at the sight of

Venus and the bright W pattern of Cassiopeia. Even though the stars were at their most dazzling above the Isle of Skye, he found it comforting to see the same ones wherever he traveled.

The sound of footsteps reached his ears, and Lennox saw the man in the vivid blue jerkin who had been sitting beside Nora, now coming toward him from the other side of the courtyard. It was, he recalled, Sir Raymond Slater. The Englishman glanced right and left as he continued to advance toward the flickering torchlight.

"Good evening, sir," Lennox greeted.

For a moment, it seemed Slater would continue past without speaking, but then he seemed to reconsider. Pausing, he forced a tight smile. "Good evening."

Before the man could continue on his way, Lennox said in a strong voice, "We have not met, but your reputation precedes you, sir. My name is Lennox MacLeod, of the Isle of Skye."

"Hmm. Well enough." Moonlight silvered Slater's sharp features as he gave a distracted nod. "I must go."

"Wait, sir. I am in search of Mistress Nora Brodie, the tapisier. Have ye seen her?"

The sea captain blinked before his manner abruptly turned friendly. "Ah, yes, the bonny Mistress Brodie, as you Scots would say! I did encounter her a short time ago. She mentioned feeling overcome by the crush in the hall and said she was going to her rooms to lie down, so I offered her safe escort to her door." Slater fingered the fur trimming on his jerkin. "If there is nothing more I can do for you, I must be on my way."

"Of course. Good night." Lennox tensed as he watched the Englishman stride off toward a far wing in the old palace, where he doubtless had been given rooms of honor near the royal apartments. Something about the fellow was unsettling, but before Lennox could ponder this further, he caught sight of the thin, slightly stooped figure of William Brodie emerging from the great hall.

"Have ye seen my daughter, Nora Brodie?" The master weaver exclaimed without preamble.

Lennox went to meet him and introduced himself. "I have not seen Mistress Brodie myself, but Sir Raymond Slater mentioned that she retired to your rooms."

"Ach! My Nora, retired to her bed?" His thick gray brows lowered in concern. "'Tis hard to believe she would depart before the dancing, yet mayhap she overindulged. Nora is not accustomed to so much rich food and wine. I'll go up now to see for myself." Brodie's expression lightened as he added, "Sir Raymond Slater is an impressive man, is he not? He brought the unicorn tapestries and our magnificent loom all the way from France! How kind he was to see my lass to her door while I supped with His Majesty."

Lennox tried to relax, to sigh with relief, yet the strange, unsettled feeling persisted. "Indeed," he agreed politely.

Nora's father started off across the uneven, cobbled surface of the torchlit courtyard, but after a few steps, he paused to look back. "Ye said you're a MacLeod? Brother-in-law to Christophe de St. Briac, the mason I met with tonight?"

"Aye."

"I knew your da, years ago, in Edinburgh."

Lennox's heart leaped like a stag in the forest. "My…da?" No sooner had the words escaped in a choked whisper, than Lennox realized Brodie was, of course, referring to Magnus MacLeod, the man who had raised him.

"Ye are interested in art? Come round to our workroom, and I'll show you the *Hunt of the Unicorn* tapestries. We have great plans for the new loom as well."

"I would be pleased to do so." Lennox drew a breath at the thought of being with Nora in their workroom and talking to her about the tapestries. "My thanks, sir."

Brodie stared at him for a long moment. "Our door is open as long as ye do not forget my foremost rule: my daughter is not available to be courted, no matter how pure your intentions may be. Long ago, Nora chose a different, more *serious* path in life. As an artist, ye must understand what that means."

Lennox wanted to continue their conversation. He had so

many questions about Nora, about their work, but this was not the time. So, instead, Lennox watched as the older man continued on his way, until he had passed through one of the entrances to the darkened palace.

As clouds passed overhead, Lennox realized he was standing all alone in the courtyard, bathed in a pool of silvery moonlight. Behind him, the great hall blazed with light, and the air fairly vibrated with the strains of music, laughter, and raised voices, but he stood, unmoving, until he saw a candleflame flicker in one of the upper rooms of the royal building where Nora and her father lodged.

Lennox drew a harsh sigh. He wished he could have accompanied William Brodie, just to see for himself that Nora was all right. Lowering his head, he paused to rub the side of his jaw, wondering again what caused this sense of disquiet.

You barely know the lass, Fiona had reminded him. *All your life, you have rescued those in need...but is it your place to intervene with Nora Brodie?*

Nay, Fi was right. Lennox inhaled an almost painfully deep breath of night air and realized he must return to his own rooms. If he planned to travel to Falkland Palace on the morrow, there were preparations to be made.

Nora lay wide awake in the darkness, feeling as if someone had wrapped her entire body in cotton batting and now was attempting to split her skull with a dagger. Her mouth was so dry. Her legs tingled as if tiny pins were pricking her flesh, and she gradually became aware of a raw pain at her very core.

Bile rose again in her throat as the memories returned in jagged pieces. Sir Raymond kneeling beside her on the mattress, untying the strings of his codpiece. Lying on top of her, groaning, his weight forcing the breath from her lungs, as he pushed and pushed himself into her body.

Had it truly happened? Sick with dread, Nora drew her

skirts up just far enough to touch between her legs. Her tender flesh burned, and a sticky fluid coated her fingers. She could have wept with despair.

Another memory returned, from the tapestry workroom in London's Whitehall Palace. Nora's young body was blossoming and one of the old weavers had noticed how some of the men were looking at her. The elderly woman pulled her aside one day, warning, "*Keep your skirts down and your legs closed, young miss! If a man plants his seed in you, you'll give birth to a bastard!*" And in the years since, her father had muttered similar warnings, although no one had offered any clear information.

My God, Nora thought, *what have I done?*

Suddenly she was overcome with a need to wash. Her father might return and come in to check on her. The substance between her legs had a distinctive scent. What if her father should enter, see her rumpled bed, and detect the odor? Shame and panic swept over her as she imagined such a scene.

It was unthinkable.

How much time had passed since Sir Raymond Slater left her chamber? Gathering her resolve, Nora managed to sit up and bring her legs over the side of the bed. The room swayed up and down for long moments then gradually righted itself. Reaching out, Nora held on to the back of a chair and came up to a standing position. Nearby the candle beckoned weakly to her, its flame sputtering in a pool of melted tallow. As Nora lifted the candlestick, wax dripped down the sides, and the flame came alive again. She set it on the deep sill of her mullioned window and rested against the stone surface, trying to get her bearings.

In the courtyard below, radiant light continued to pour from the tall windows of the great hall, and the strains of music rose through the night air. Thank God the festivities continued! Perhaps her father was still inside, talking to the king. Tears stung her eyes. She hoped he would stay there and, for once, forget about her.

Just then, a flash of gold caught her eye from the shadowed courtyard. Leaning forward, Nora made out the back of a tall man, lean yet powerful, his fair hair agleam in the starlight. Her gaze touched the man's snow-white shirt and the dark plaid belted at his waist. Her breath caught. Could it be Lennox MacLeod?

Nora leaned closer to the bright candle flame at the same instant the man turned and stared directly up at her window. Indeed, it was Lennox, and he seemed to gaze into her heart, piercing the distance and the darkness.

Hot shame flooded Nora's body. At that moment, she couldn't even face herself, let alone meet this splendid Highlander's kind green eyes. As she turned away, clutching the candlestick, Nora prayed he hadn't really seen her after all.

More desperate than ever to wash away Sir Raymond Slater's seed, she stumbled to the chest, where a jug of water, a cake of lavender-scented soap, a soft cloth, and a basin were arranged. Sobs rose in her throat. She hated feeling this way—soiled, as if she'd committed a terrible sin, and she told herself it was not her fault. But was that true? Perhaps her memory was fuzzy, and she hadn't meant to do anything wrong, but it had happened all the same! Her mind went round and round, trying to piece together the events of the evening, but every memory led her down a dark, confusing alley.

With shaking fingers, Nora removed her underskirt. When she saw the blood smeared over the linen of her petticoat, she thought she might be sick. *Oh dear God.* Just as she poured water in the basin and braced one foot on a stool to wash the most intimate parts of her body, a hesitant tapping came at the door.

"Lass? Are ye unwell?"

Father! Nora's heart leaped with panic as she yanked down her petticoat. "I am fine," she managed to reply in a low, even voice, praying he would not open the door and see her standing by the washstand. "I had just fallen asleep."

"Oh!" he sounded surprised. "I did not mean to wake ye, but I feared ye might be ill."

"Not a bit," Nora replied, forcing a light tone. "I merely wanted to be fresh for our morning's labors."

"Ah, ye make me proud, abed while all the other ladies of the court indulge in rich food, spirits, and dance."

"Good night then, Father."

"I wish ye peaceful sleep, lass. Ye are quite right: there is much to discuss on the morrow. I had a long conversation with His Majesty tonight, and when we rise, I will tell ye all that he said and all the golden opportunities that lie in store for us here at Stirling Castle."

When her father had gone, Nora gave in to the urge to weep, leaning against the cold wall. For years, she had been building private dreams and plans for a future that was out of reach to other women. A future that would require her to put her commitment to art above any other human need, including romance, love, or even a family of her own.

As Nora began to wash, she was swept by a wave of terrible foreboding, a realization that no amount of soap and water could undo the events of this night. The moments when Raymond Slater had lain atop her might well have reduced all her shining dreams to ashes.

Chapter Six

Lennox rose at first light, hoping to ride away from Stirling Castle before any distractions could appear. The night before, he had gathered his few possessions and rolled them into a blanket, and now he emerged into the courtyard, the bundle tucked under his arm. Perhaps, on his way to the stables, he might stop in the great castle kitchens and ask for some food to carry him to Falkland. Over years of traveling, Lennox had learned that female cooks were generally quite eager to feed him, especially if he paused to smile and jest with them.

It promised to be a fine day. Soft dawn sunlight streamed into the inner close, which was surprisingly busy. Servants hurried to and fro, busy with the tasks of the new day, while the masons and carvers were climbing the scaffolding that surrounded the stone façade of the new palace.

The kitchen and stables were in the outer close, and Lennox tried to blend in as he started off in that direction. He was eager to be on the other side of the high castle walls, to inhale the sweet spring air and discover what views lay in store when he wound his way down the mighty volcanic crag that served as a pedestal for Stirling Castle.

However, after only a few steps, he heard a familiar voice call his name.

"Lennox, *mon frère*!"

With a wry smile, he stopped to greet Christophe, who was now master mason at Stirling. "I am very impressed by the scale of your project," Lennox said after shaking his brother-in-law's hand.

"Ah, you know it's largely the king's doing, not mine. His Majesty has elaborate plans for his new palace." He gestured toward the work a group of masons were doing nearby. "At Falkland Palace, we carved a few roundels into the stone outer walls—likenesses of royal favorites. But here at Stirling, there are plans to cover one entire *ceiling* with at least forty-five medallions carved of oak, and each one must be painted in detail by a true artist." St. Briac arched an ironic brow. "Are you seeking employment, by chance?"

Lennox blinked, taken aback. "Have ye not heard from Fiona that I am embarking on a quest of sorts, to discover the identity of my true father?"

"*Oui*, I heard. Magnus may have his faults," the Frenchman replied quietly, "but he did raise you, and he loves you."

Lennox's heart contracted as he absorbed Christophe's plain words. "Da kept the truth from me all my life, even though he and Grandfather well knew that I did not fit in with the rest of clan MacLeod." With that, he reached into the pouch under his belt and found the miniature that resembled him so closely. Withdrawing it, he cupped it in his big palm and watched for Christophe's reaction. "Surely ye can see why I must find this man. It is as if I am missing a great piece of myself."

Christophe cocked his head slightly and sighed. "I do understand."

Just then, Bayard came lumbering toward them. His arms were spread wide to carry one of the large, carved medallions toward a doorway to the new palace. Grant followed a few steps behind, carrying a toolbox with two wooden mallets and an assortment of chisels.

Bayard smiled broadly as he paused to show them the circular oak carving of a noblewoman holding a tiny greyhound. "I've been laboring over this for a fortnight. *Eh bien*, what do you think?"

Lennox knew an urge to offer suggestions about the paint colors they might choose, but stopped himself. Instead, as the two Frenchmen conferred, Lennox turned to Grant. "I seem to recall that ye were learning to carve on Skye, when Bayard and Christophe built the tower house for my brother Ciaran. Are ye now an apprentice to your stepfather?"

Grant nodded proudly. "Bayard is giving me my own set of tools, one by one, as long as I take proper care of them. I enjoy carving. I think it will be a fine trade for me, but I must confess that when I encountered Sir Raymond Slater this morning, I nearly asked if I could come along and join his crew. Wouldn't that be a fine life, sailing off to explore the world?"

Lennox paused. "Is Slater leaving Stirling?"

"Aye, or he will be away soon enough. Perhaps an hour ago, I came upon the captain and his men eating breakfast. His groom said they were off to St. Andrews to board Sir Raymond Slater's grand ship, *Hercules*, for a voyage to Spain."

Lennox took a deep breath, relieved. No matter how many times he had told himself to put Nora Brodie out of his mind, he'd continued to think of her...and the candle in the window. The woman's form he'd glimpsed there, briefly, had been indistinct at best, but somehow Lennox *felt* it was Nora. Was something amiss? Perhaps not, but he was glad all the same that Slater was leaving Stirling Castle.

Smiling, he reached out to ruffle Grant's dark hair. "Don't let your mother hear ye speak of sailing off to Spain," he chided gently. "I'm quite certain she wouldn't approve."

Before the boy could reply, Bayard gave him a nudge. "Back to work now, lad."

"I must be on my way as well," Lennox said, nodding to the trio and offering a wave as he started off again toward the kitchens.

He had walked only a short distance when he spied a familiar figure hurrying out of the chapel, a cloak wrapped tightly around her slim body, her bright locks nearly obscured by a gable-hooded headdress. But what struck him most was the way the lass bowed her head, as if shielding herself from the world.

"Nora?" he called uncertainly.

When she glanced up for an instant, Lennox saw how pale she was. Her wide eyes reminded him of a doe surprised by a hunter.

"Oh, good day," she said in a strained voice. "I cannot tarry, sir. My father awaits my return."

With careful movements, he came closer. "I have something for ye." As she watched him, Lennox reached into the same pouch where he kept the miniature. "Actually, I am only returning it."

Nora blinked when he held out the low blue heel from her shoe. "How—?"

"It was lying on the courtyard cobblestones when ye took your leave yesterday. I remembered the blue toes of your slippers, peeking out from under your skirts, and I was certain it must belong to you." He tried to hold her gaze, smiling. "I hoped to return it last night, but when I had a moment to do so, ye had already gone."

When she reached out to accept the small offering, Lennox let his fingers gently graze her palm. "You are going away?" she asked, glancing at his bundle.

"Aye. I'm bound for Falkland Palace, to see my aunt."

"I wish you a safe journey."

As she started to turn away, Lennox put a hand on her arm. "I will return, Nora. I still hope to visit your workroom, to speak to you about your weaving and learn more about the unicorn tapestries." Then he dared to touch her pale cheek with his forefinger. Softly, he asked, "I sense that ye are troubled. Can I help?"

Nora lifted her chin and summoned a smile. "Worry not, sir. I am not myself this morning, but I shall recover. Do you never have days when your spirits flag?"

Slowly, Lennox nodded. "I do indeed have such days. More than anyone knows." He fought an urge to offer more comfort, even to gather her into his arms, but instead simply returned her smile. "I hope that whatever burden ye carry will soon lighten."

With that, Lennox stepped away from Nora Brodie and started down the cobbled pathway leading to the kitchen. When he glanced back and lifted a hand in farewell, he expected the lass to have gone on her way.

However, Nora stood rooted to the spot, looking wistful, even lost, as she watched him go.

When Lennox approached the stables, eating the last of the warm oatcake the cooks had given him, he saw a gathering of men. Holding the reins of their horses, they shuffled their feet impatiently.

"When is the captain coming?" complained one, craning his head to look toward a small group of storage buildings behind the kitchen.

"When he is good and ready!" replied another.

"Perhaps you mean good and *finished*," said a third, guffawing.

They were Slater's men, Lennox realized, as a chill crept over him. Something was not right. A rustling sound, followed by a muffled female protest, reached his ears. Lennox started off toward the voice.

"Don't go that way, sir," called Slater's young groom. Winking, he added, "Ye might disturb the captain before he's finished swiving."

Lennox dropped the food he had been eating and walked toward a narrow space between the buildings. Turning into the passageway, he saw onions spilling across the ground beside an overturned basket.

Just out of sight, an anguished voice implored, "I beg ye cease, sir! I am newly married. I love my husband!"

Fury rose up in Lennox as he rounded the corner. There, a plump, red-cheeked young woman was pinned against the wall of rubble stone, her white cap askew, her skirts and apron pushed up to her waist. In front of her, Sir Raymond Slater was grabbing between her legs, as if he had every right to invade the most intimate part of her body.

With his other hand, the Englishman pulled at her bodice, exposing one of her breasts. The kitchen maid began to weep as Slater warned, "Quiet! Someone will hear, and then all the castle will know you are a trollop, wandering about alone, inviting the attentions of lusty men like me."

Her eyes were squeezed tightly closed. "Please, sir."

"That's better," he approved, pretending to misunderstand her meaning. "*All* women want me. You should be thanking me."

The Englishman was fumbling to untie his codpiece when Lennox came up softly behind him and pushed the point of his sharpened dirk into his back. "Unhand the lass and turn around."

Clearly shocked, Slater obeyed, hands raised as he swiveled to face him. To Lennox's disgust, the man's red, semi-erect penis was exposed. Their eyes met, Slater's flashing with defiance while Lennox could only stare in contempt.

"My good fellow, perhaps you misunderstand this situation," the Englishman said with what was doubtless meant to be a roguish, man-to-man grin. "Surely you can see I wasn't *harming* the wench. Quite the opposite! You know how it is, they always pretend to protest, but in truth the chit wants it more than I do."

Lennox would not reply to Slater's repellant comments. To the cowering servant, he said kindly, "Mistress, straighten your skirts, pick up your basket, and go back to the kitchen. Ye may rest easy; no one will hear a word of this."

Her hands shook as she rearranged her clothing and hastened off through a door at the back of the building. Lennox looked around to see Slater's men clustered together at the end of the passageway. Wide-eyed, they watched their worldly captain's humiliation at the hands of a Highlander.

"Go on, then." Lennox nudged Sir Raymond Slater with the tip of his dirk. "Ride away from here. Get out of Scotland and do not return."

Shoving his flaccid member back into the striped, padded codpiece, Slater glared at Lennox. "Pray that our paths do not cross again, or I will have my revenge."

Lennox gave a cold laugh and sheathed his dirk. "Ye are the one who should be saying that prayer. If I catch ye mistreating another lass, I'll have your head on a pike." Arching both brows, he added, "Ye are a loathsome excuse for a man."

His heart pounded with anger and revulsion as he watched Sir Raymond Slater saunter off to join his men, laughing as if it had all been a bit of twisted mischief.

Lennox rode all day to reach Falkland, stopping only to rest and water Chaucer, his chestnut stallion.

Although the roads were more passable than the rough tracks of the Highlands, most people still trudged along by foot, for few owned a proper horse, and only the royal family dared attempt to travel the rutted lanes by coach. The green countryside was lush and liberally dotted with sheep, and though the villages Lennox passed through were charming, he felt none of it could compare to the windy, untamed beauty of Skye. In those moments, he ached for home. He had to remind himself that his mother was born and raised near Falkland, and his real father, dressed as he was in the small portrait, could not have been a Highlander. Perhaps, as the truth of his heritage revealed itself, he would come to see himself in a different light.

Dusk was deepening into night as Lennox came into the burgh of Falkland. Torches were lit outside the palace. He was bone tired as he drew in on Chaucer's reins and spoke to the guard who emerged from the gatehouse.

"My name is Lennox MacLeod, of the Isle of Skye," he said in a forceful tone. "I am the grandson of the chief of Clan

MacLeod, and I have come a great distance to see my aunt, Lady Tess Lindsay, who attends the Queen."

The man went off and conferred with someone else inside the guardroom before disappearing into the inner courtyard. Lennox rubbed his weary eyes and spoke quietly to Chaucer. "Soon," he whispered, "we will both rest."

A few minutes later, the guard returned and admitted him, and a groom took his horse. A serving maid led him into the old wing of the palace, where he was given a small chamber on the second floor.

"Lady Tess asks that you wait upon her tomorrow," the servant said before she left him. "Someone from the kitchen will bring food to you."

Lennox smiled his thanks, but when he was alone, he began to pace, his earlier fatigue replaced by impatience. After coming so far to speak to his aunt, how could he wait another day?

He paused at a small window overlooking the courtyard. Candles glowed at one end of an adjoining wing, and the sound of female laughter drifted out on the spring breeze. Lennox needed but an instant to decide on his course of action. He changed into a fresh shirt, rewrapped his belted plaid, combed his wild golden hair with long fingers, and started off to find his aunt.

The queen, he knew, would soon deliver a child, so doubtless her meals would be confined to a small group of her ladies. Lennox made his way down the torchlit turnpike staircase that connected the two ranges of the palace and emerged into the courtyard, following the light and the voices. When he reached the outer door to the room, which he guessed must be a hall designated for the queen's private use, a menacing guard appeared. Torchlight flickered over the man's meaty face as he looked Lennox up and down.

"The queen is dining with her ladies, and no one is allowed inside," the man announced gruffly, one hand on the hilt of his sheathed sword.

Lennox attempted a winning smile in the style of his brother-in-law, Christophe. "Quite understandable, but my aunt is a lady-in-waiting to Her Majesty, and she has invited me to join them." He paused, sensing that it hadn't been quite enough. "I've ridden since dawn from Stirling Castle. I have brought word from His Majesty, the King."

The guard continued to stare, clearly unconvinced. "Who exactly is your aunt?"

"Lady Tess Lindsay. Ye might tell her I am here. Lennox MacLeod, of the Isle of Skye."

When the guard opened the door and went inside, Lennox stood in the wedge of light that spilled into the courtyard and scanned the room. His eyes were drawn to the magnificent ceiling, painted with costly verdigris, indigo, and gold, before he searched the long table of women for his aunt. Two dogs, a brown terrier and a greyhound, roamed about the edges of the table, in search of scraps. The Queen of Scots sat at one end, chatting amiably with her ladies, a gown of claret velvet covering her great bulk. Servants wearing the crimson bonnet of the queen's livery carried platters of roasted capon and spring vegetables.

Lennox hadn't seen his mother's sister for several years, but he remembered that she was a big woman, taller than many men, and he quickly saw her near the queen. Tess's kind face was lined, her gray hair nearly hidden under a French hood. Her brow furrowed at the sight of him.

"Lennox MacLeod?" she queried, looking surprised. "I did not expect to see you tonight."

He cocked his head slightly and came a bit closer. "Did you not? I thought…"

The guard, who was conferring with an usher, straightened. "Ye were meant to wait outside!" he scolded Lennox.

Queen Mary looked among them with interest. "Who might this handsome visitor be?" Her eyes twinkled in the candlelight. "A Viking raider, perchance?"

As his aunt made introductions, Lennox came to bow before

the queen, smiling in a way he hoped would dispel any lingering doubts. "I apologize for the interruption, Your Majesty," he said. "I must have misunderstood the message from my aunt."

"We are pleased to have you among us, good sir," replied the queen. She gave him a look that was subtly laced with coquetry, and it came to Lennox that they must be nearly the same age. "Do join us. My people will make a place for you beside your aunt."

When he was seated and had drunk a goblet of Burgundy wine, Lennox looked at Tess. "I have something of great import to discuss with you, Aunt."

She blinked. "I am glad to see you, lad, but you should not have interrupted this meal. Her Majesty is meant to be in her chamber for these weeks before her lying-in, but she chafes against confinement. So, when she ventures out, as tonight, her ladies surround her. But *you* are a man." Her voice was gentle, but firm.

Chastened, Lennox turned his attention to the queen. She was speaking of her young son, Prince John, who was less than one year of age, but who lived in St. Andrews with a household staff of his own. "Soon, I am told, he will take his first steps. How I wish I could be with my boy," she said, sighing, and Lennox felt the grief underlying her words. "With both my little sons!"

Tess leaned over and explained softly, "The queen has one more child, born before her marriage to King James, who has remained behind in France, living with Her Majesty's family. Little François is but five years of age, and our queen has to content herself with letters that bring news of him across the sea." Pausing, Tess sipped her wine. "Thank God none of our family were born royal."

"I suspect ye have seen a great deal during so many years at court," Lennox ventured, hoping to steer the subject in another direction. He could feel the miniature concealed under his belt, pressing against his hipbone. Would his aunt think him selfish if he began to ask questions about his mother?

"More than you can imagine." Tess lifted her pearl-handled eating knife and gestured toward his untouched serving of capon. "But we will speak of other matters later."

His heart sank, yet he could not force this subject. "Later tonight?"

Just then, Queen Mary went pale and set down her goblet of wine. "I am unwell," she proclaimed. Beads of sweat shone on her brow, and her hand went to the great curve of her belly as she moaned, "This should not be happening. It is too soon!"

Aunt Tess rose, calm but concerned. "We must escort you to your chamber, ma'am." She joined the other ladies in assisting the queen, and just before they left the table, Tess glanced back at Lennox. "When the time is right, I shall send for you."

Within minutes, he found himself alone at the table, surrounded by plates of rich food and half-drunk goblets of strong wine. The dogs lay nearby, gnawing on bones.

I have waited a lifetime, Lennox thought, sighing. *I can wait a few hours more.*

Chapter Seven

Nora stood before the magnificent loom, welcoming the wave of anticipation that came over her. This was the one bright spot in her life.

Over the past fortnight, since the dark, confusing episode with Sir Raymond Slater, Nora had alternately felt either numb or consumed with trepidation. She was unable to summon her usual zest for life, except during these moments when she could see and touch the loom and imagine sitting before it, weaving art.

Since its arrival from France, magnificent loom had been completely rebuilt in a spacious room of its own. William Brodie had been laboring over the design for a new tapestry, and today five weavers would be chosen to begin the creation of a huge tapestry called *The Prodigal Son*.

Nora could scarcely wait. Surely this would be the moment when she could officially make the leap from a confined role as a female tapestry keeper to that of a true artist. A weaver.

It was thrilling to see that her father's pattern for the tapestry, called a cartoon, was now in place. Behind the cartoon, plain warp threads stretched vertically between the two large rollers, to make a grid formation. Shuttles wrapped with specially-dyed weft threads of silk, wool, and costly metals were already assembled to one side of the loom. The craftsmen would manipulate the shuttles by hand, weaving the colored weft threads between the warp threads.

The process was magical, Nora thought. Her heart beat faster as she envisioned the masterpiece slowly coming to life over a period of months. And one day *she* intended to oversee the entire process, as her father now did at Stirling Castle. Her imagination was bursting with secret ideas for her first grand tapestry project and all the ways she would make it stand out from those made in Europe. Whenever memories of Sir Raymond Slater threatened to engulf her, she clung to her dream, to this craft that was in her very blood.

And she prayed that her worst fear, lurking in the shadows, would prove unfounded.

"Ah, there is my girl."

"Father!" Nora turned to see him entering the room. She colored slightly, as if fearing he might be able to read her mind about Slater. Thank God he seemed to be too consumed by this project to notice how pale she had grown and how little she had been eating.

"It's time we spoke about your duties in the coming weeks," announced William Brodie, spreading a sheaf of parchment over the worktable.

Was he avoiding her eyes? Nora felt a chill. "Duties?"

"Aye." He cleared his throat. "As it happens, there is a tapisier who has been here for a good many years, a Frenchman called Jacques Habet. He has very firm ideas about the role of any lass who might be involved in our work."

Nora suddenly felt that there were threats all around her. "I see."

"It isn't easy for me to come in here and usurp all the authority from this fellow, as ye may guess. We must tread carefully. But he does have many consequential tasks in mind for you." Her father's tone became hearty as he pointed to the list. "First, ye will organize the castle tapisiers to clean and organize the existing collection of royal tapestries. I must admit, they are more impressive than I had expected. I am told His Majesty inherited many from his mother, Margaret Tudor, who must have brought them from England as part of her dowry. And there are some exquisite cloths that came from France with Marie de Guise."

Nora knew he was referring to Queen Mary, whose name had been anglicized when she became the Queen of Scots. She looked ahead, down the list of tasks. She was to supervise the repair and storage of all manner of hangings and embroideries, choose which pieces would move each season with the court, and oversee the servants who would hang the tapestries by rings in the other royal residences.

"These duties will be *quite* consequential," her father said at the very moment she looked up at him.

"I suppose it might seem so, to another sort of person." Nora heard the decided edge to her own voice, but she couldn't help it. "However, I suspect any castle housekeeper could do as much. When you were offered the position of master weaver to the royal court of James V, and we came here from London, I believed I would work with you."

"Lass, have I not told you, many times—"

Nora broke in. "I wish to be a weaver. Part of the creative process, at the loom."

"Ye are stubborn, Nora Brodie. Headstrong. Just because ye want something, it does not mean it is possible. I cannot simply push this Habet fellow aside and insist that one of the royal weavers must be a lass. They would think me mad." He paused, adding for good measure, "Habet has already said no lass has the strength to work the loom all day long."

Nora blinked back tears. How could this be happening? All her life, he had encouraged her aspirations. Hadn't she left her own mother behind, in Flanders, to be at his side so that she might grow up to become a master weaver?

"Father, you have promised me."

He stared in consternation. "I have ne'er promised that ye would be a true weaver! Ye must have dreamed it! With your gifts and determination, ye may have a grand life as a royal tapisier, which few women could even imagine. But a master weaver?" William shook his head. "Nay."

Her eyes stung. "You know I can do it."

"This is a world of men. I cannot change that! No master weaver has ever been a—"

She broke in, her tone impassioned. "I know what you are going to say, that women cannot assume such a position, but I mean to break that rule. I *will* be a master weaver before I die." She watched his eyes widen and hurried on. "It is a big dream, bigger than such a dream would be for a man, so I have no time to waste with this..." Nora poked a finger at the sheaf of parchment. "This *list*!"

Her father moaned and rubbed his brow as if she had caused his head to ache. "Even if ye were a lad, there would be years of apprenticeship ahead. I cannot simply wave a hand and allow my daughter to move past the *men* who follow the proper path."

Apprenticeship? What about all the years she had spent with him, learning to weave magnificent tapestries at her father's side?

"I am being punished because I am female," Nora declared angrily.

"I did not make this world!"

Suddenly, Nora's throat was thick. "I thought you were my ally."

"I am, lass. Your ally, but no wizard."

She turned away. "I must go outside, Father. Perhaps I only need a bit of air."

"Aye, go on, then. But do not tarry." He waited until Nora reached the door before adding, "If ye will be patient, perhaps we shall find a way. Ye must show them all that ye are willing to give your life to your art. That's what it will take if ye mean to do what no other woman can."

She felt a surge of hopeful determination at his words, but no sooner had she emerged into the busy inner close than the dark cloud of worry returned, wrapping itself around her like a heavy cloak.

"Nora!"

Looking up, she saw Grant. The youth emerged from a small group of masons and carvers, loping up the cobbled pathway from the bakehouse with an oval loaf of bread in one hand. He seemed to grow taller every time she saw him, and if she were not so preoccupied with her own problems, his attentions to her would seem sweet.

Nora put on a smile and waved. Almost before she could speak, he was at her side. "Where have ye been these past few days?"

"I have been very busy. We are about to begin the first tapestry on the new loom."

"But that is a good thing, and I can see in your face that something is wrong." He was staring at her, an unruly shock of dark hair falling over one eye. "Come with me."

Sighing, she let him pull her along, into the still-unfinished new palace. Because work was being done on the other side of the building, there was no one about as they made their way along a wide passageway. When they reached the doorway to the king's outer hall, Grant pointed inside.

"The heads are going to decorate the ceiling in here." He pointed to the plain, coffered ceiling high above them, and she realized he was referring to the large portrait medallions she'd seen them making. "I've been helping with the carving! Bayard has taught me so much."

On they went, until Grant opened a door leading into a large, three-story-high courtyard with stone walls and many windows. It opened to the blue sky overhead.

"How lovely!" exclaimed Nora. "But it would be much nicer if it were a garden."

"It's meant to be a place to exercise the king's lion," Grant replied casually. "I think it's outrageous, but there's no time to speak of that now." He led her to a low wooden bench against one wall. When they were seated side by side, Grant tore off a large chunk of rough trencher bread and handed it to her. "It's still warm."

Lately, the thought of food had made Nora sick. Everything

made her feel sick, in fact, which was part of the reason she felt anxious, night and day. This bread, however, felt comforting. She took a little bite and sighed. "It's delicious. Thank you."

Grant stuffed a piece of bread the size of her fist into his mouth and chewed. "Lennox told me how to charm the kitchen maids," he confided, grinning. "They give me lots of things."

"I don't doubt it." She smiled but felt an odd pang when she thought of Lennox.

"Aye, I'm growing up." Grant swallowed and leaned closer. "Will ye tell me what's amiss? Ye are like a different lass."

Of course, Nora could not tell him the real truth, so she said, "The castle tapisier wants to relegate me to caring for the embroidered cloths rather than weaving at the side of my father and the other men."

"I do not think ye would be daunted by such a challenge, Nora." He watched her. "What is truly bothering you?"

His plain-spoken question caught her off guard. "Some things…a lady cannot discuss."

"Why not? I am your true friend."

Nora began to weep and found she could not stop. "I… Oh, Grant, you are right. My problems are much bigger than anything to do with weaving." She couldn't look at him. "I fear my life is ruined!"

Awkwardly, he gathered her near and patted her back. "How can that be? Whatever it is will pass, will it not? Now, ye must tell me what has happened." After a brief pause, Grant added, "I give ye my word that I will keep your confidence."

Drawing a deep breath, she felt a surge of relief. There was no one else to talk to, and she couldn't keep her terrible problem inside any longer. "You will find this very shocking."

"Nay. Nothing ye could do would shock me."

"I—" She could scarcely say the words aloud. "I believe I am with child."

"How can that be?" Grant's eyes were round with disbelief. "Are ye saying that ye have lain with a man?" His expression told her that he believed this was impossible.

Determined to pull herself together, Nora straightened her shoulders and dried her eyes, but her chest ached as she told her terrible story. She had reached the part where Slater escorted her to her chamber and then helped her to her bed when Grant looked as if he were in the grip of a wild fury.

"Ye are about to say that he took you by force!" he cried, his cheeks red with emotion. "I will find him and murder him!"

Nora lay a hand on the boy's arm. "It wasn't truly like that. Part of the confusion for me is that I am not completely certain what happened. I grew ill. The floor kept moving. I couldn't gather my thoughts. Perhaps the wine affected me, and I said something to him that was misunderstood?"

"Nay! Damn his eyes, he is no gentleman or this could not have happened!"

"I want to think you are right." She drew a ragged sigh. "But perhaps he is used to lying with women who are carried off by his fine looks, his wealth, his position at court...and thought he was doing me a favor."

"I will not listen to one more excuse ye might make for that jackass!"

"Believe me, I do not wish to excuse him. In truth, I hope to never see him again. I wish I could put it all out of my mind now, but I deeply fear that my life will never be the same." She twisted her fingers together until they hurt.

"How can ye know it—know that he's made you with child?"

Nora thought of the semen Sir Raymond Slater had left between her legs, the tangy scent of it, the way it felt when she touched it and tried to wash it away. He had put his seed in her, and if her monthly flow did not commence soon, she would be forever ruined.

"It is the way of life," she said sadly. "Men do the dishonoring, and women are left behind to pay the price." Tears slipped from her eyes. "Perhaps I wanted too much. My dreams...may have been too big after all."

Grant jumped to his feet and began to pace back and forth

in front of the bench. "I will not let you suffer dishonor at the hands of that scoundrel!" he shouted. "I will marry you myself!"

His voice rose, echoing against the stone walls of the lion's den, and Nora reached for his hand and brought him back to her side. "Please, do not shout. People will hear you!"

"Marry me." Shaking with emotion, he framed her face with the big hands he'd yet to grow into.

"Grant, please stop. You are only making this worse. I am years older than you, and I would never steal your future away like that." Nora managed to smile at him tenderly. "Besides, you have dreams of your own to chase before you marry."

He looked deflated. "But ye must wed *someone*. It's the only way."

"Why must a *man* be the solution to every problem in life?" she demanded. "I will think of something, all by myself. And meanwhile, perhaps this terrible fear will prove unfounded."

Looking thoughtful, Grant tore off another chunk of bread. "When we lived in Edinburgh, Ma had a friend with a problem just like yours. Her name was Bess." He paused to chew slowly. "Bess was telling Ma about it one night and I overheard from my bed. The man she had lain with had disappeared, much like Sir Raymond Slater, but Bess found a solution."

Now that Nora had brought her dark secret out into the light, she found that she felt better. "What did Bess do?"

"As I understood it, she lay with another man, a craftsman who owned property. She then told him she was with child, and they were wed."

As he spoke, Grant offered her another piece of bread, but Nora could only stare at it, aghast. "That is deceitful!"

He shrugged. "I thought so, too, but Bess declared that it was no worse that the tricks men play on women every single day."

"I could never do such a thing."

"Of course not." Grant patted her hand. "I wouldn't even suggest it."

"I must go. Father is waiting for me." Rising from the bench, it came to Nora that perhaps her own father had tricked her with empty promises. Her heart hurt. Impulsively, she turned back to embrace Grant. "Thank you for your friendship."

His arms tightened around her for an instant. "It is my honor."

Nora left him then, lifting her skirts as she hurried out of the lion's den. She felt an urge to run faster, faster, as if her slippered feet might know a secret route that would carry her to freedom from her problems.

Chapter Eight

The weather was fine in the orchards behind Falkland Palace, where a small table and two stools had been placed among the trees. Plum blossoms swirled down like snowflakes, a few of them landing on the gold-and-silver royal chessboard.

Lennox bit back a yawn as he watched his opponent, King James V, stare at the board. After a moment, the monarch lifted first a rook then the queen. Another long pause followed as he frowned.

"I fear ye have trapped me," the young king lamented, stroking his reddish beard with white, bejeweled fingers. He was so fair that even his lashes were pale.

"Nay, sire." Lennox managed a casual smile. It was a dull business, playing chess with someone you were not permitted to best. "Ye are a much finer player than I."

"Hmm." The king returned his attention to the royal chess pieces, made for him of jasper and rock crystal.

It seemed impossible that a full fortnight could have passed since Lennox had arrived at Falkland Palace, intending to speak to his aunt immediately so that he might carry on with his quest. Instead, Queen Mary had begun laboring that very night, surrounded by all her ladies, all of whom were French except for Tess. His aunt had been needed to communicate with the Scots castle staff, and Lennox had been forgotten.

Soon enough, King James had arrived from Stirling, overcome with joy by the birth of his second son, Arthur. Two more weeks had followed. The queen had her "upsitting" when the baby was three days old, but she was not permitted to leave her chamber for the christening. Lennox had attended, hoping to see Aunt Tess there, but she merely lifted a hand to him at the end, on her way back to the queen's bedside.

To Lennox's surprise, it was the king himself who sought him out each day. His Majesty's favorite companion, Sir James Hamilton of Finnart had fallen out of favor and been executed only a few months ago, and now the monarch was missing someone to join him in a game of chess or tennis. Lennox had become his new comrade, and one did not refuse the king.

"Do ye Highlanders hunt on the Isle of Skye, young MacLeod? I don't recall seeing a forest there, let alone a proper deer park," James said, toying with the pomander that hung from a chain round his neck. "The queen and I like to hunt fallow deer in spring. I am also in the process of bringing boar from France. My gamekeeper is building a special fold for them."

Lennox tried to appear interested. "I am at your service, Your Majesty, if ye should desire to hunt with me."

Suddenly, the moody young monarch got to his feet and looked around for the lackey who waited nearby. "I am thirsty. I shall return to the castle now."

Lennox wore a bemused smile as he watched him go. *How convenient to be the king and be able to simply walk away from a game ye cannot win.* After a moment, he rose. He had brought a roll of paper and case of tinted chalks to the orchard, hoping he might have an opportunity to sketch, and now he took them up. On his way back to the castle, Lennox passed by a long open gallery that adjoined the royal apartments.

"Monsieur!" a female voice called softly.

He looked over, shocked to see the queen herself sitting on a bench under the sheltering half-roof. In her arms, she held a swaddled infant. Only one of her ladies was with her, a young French girl who gazed shyly at Lennox.

"Your Majesty," Lennox said, approaching the edge of the gallery. He bowed to her. "I am surprised to see you…and this very handsome young prince."

She gazed down at the tiny baby as if he were a treasure. "They like to keep my son from me, swaddled so tightly, in a darkened room," confided the queen. "But my cousin has brought him to me, and we are stealing these moments together." After a pause, she tilted her head to one side, observing him. "How do you find Falkland Palace, m'sieur? Your brother-in-law, Christophe, was instrumental in making it so beautiful."

Lennox smiled, relaxing. "I think the palace is splendid, Your Majesty, but I am more taken with the sight of ye holding your new son. I must be bold and ask, would it be possible for me to make a sketch of ye two together?"

She blinked in surprise. "You are bold indeed, m'sieur. Others would be shocked that you are speaking to me at a time when I am supposed to still be hidden from the world."

He noticed that she hadn't refused. "Shall I leave you?"

Queen Mary laughed softly. "*Au contraire*! Please, do make the sketch, but with all possible speed. If your *tante* should appear, we would both receive a scolding."

And so, Lennox stood at the edge of the gallery, using the stone ledge as his table. Filled with a familiar sense of pleasure, he opened his wooden case of charcoals. His fingers moved quickly. Perhaps, he thought, if she liked the sketch, she would invite him to paint them.

When he had finished, he handed the paper to the queen, who stared at it in wonder. "*Mon Dieu*, you have captured our likenesses perfectly in so short a time."

Lennox leaned against a pillar and smiled. He had centered the drawing of mother and child on the paper, but the baby's face was so sweet that he had also made a sketch of Prince Arthur's tiny face in one corner.

"I am very happy that ye are pleased," he told the queen.

"How can I thank you, m'sieur?"

Lennox took a breath. Of course he was not expected to actually request anything in return, yet had he not waited more than a fortnight for just such an opportunity? "Your Majesty, I traveled to Falkland Palace to have an important conversation with my aunt, Lady Tess Lindsay, wife of Sir Stephen MacFarlane. Circumstances have made that impossible…"

"Ah, I see! *Oui*, I shall gladly intervene." Marie de Guise beamed. "Someone will bring you word of a time and place where you can meet with my dear lady. But now you must go, before anyone else sees you. I am not supposed to be outdoors, especially with my tiny babe—let alone in the company of a man! But should not a queen be permitted to break a rule or two?" She gave him a tiny wink before returning her attention to the sketch. "*Au revoir*!"

Two mornings later, Lennox was on his way to meet with Aunt Tess.

At last! he thought. All the long days of waiting now were paying off. He strode quickly through the spacious gallery that fronted the south range of the palace, the loose folds of his belted plaid moving against his thighs. As he walked, Lennox found that his attention was drawn to the large tapestries displayed in a continuous line along the inner wall of the gallery.

Pausing, he studied the hunting scenes that covered the wall, noting the way each colorful stitch blended with others to become part of the grander scene. His thoughts soon turned to Nora Brodie, to the animation that showed on her lovely face as she spoke about weaving and the sadness he'd sensed in her that last morning, when she had avoided his gaze in the courtyard at Stirling Castle. When he returned, Lennox would ask to visit William Brodie's workroom. Perhaps Nora would even give him a weaving lesson.

He felt a sharp twinge of arousal as he remembered the dream that had awakened him in the middle of the night. Nora had been in his bed, her full breasts and long legs pale in the moonlight, her burnished hair spread across his pillow.

"Ah, nephew!" called a woman's voice in tones of amusement. "You must be thinking of a lass."

Startled, Lennox looked over to see his Aunt Tess standing in the doorway to the royal chapel. "I was merely admiring the tapestries," he protested, but felt his face grow warm.

"Indeed?" She teased, coming closer, and he noticed again how much bigger a woman she was than his mother. Clearly, she enjoyed good food, and her eyes gleamed in a way that put him at ease. "Let us go outside and take a turn around the gardens while you explain what has brought you to Falkland Palace, so persistent in your need to speak to me."

When they had emerged from the courtyard into the gardens, Tess slipped a hand through his arm. "How good it is to see you, Lennox MacLeod. Your ma was so proud of you." She looked him up and down as she spoke. "All three of Eleanor's children are bonny indeed, but you are truly splendid. As Her Majesty said, you appear to have sprung from one of the Norsemen who invaded the Isle of Skye."

Her tone was warm, even light, but Lennox stiffened. "Ye speak as if I do not share the same da as Fiona and Ciaran."

"Ah, well, perhaps the faeries intervened during your conception," Tess chuckled. "As I recall, the folk on Skye believe in that sort of thing."

They had come upon a narrow path leading into the bluebell wood. After they had walked a bit farther, Lennox spied a lichen-crusted bench under a great oak tree and gestured to invite his aunt to sit with him.

"I did not seek this interview with you so that we might jest about the faeries," he said plainly. "I have come on a quest of real importance. It involves the very essence of my life."

"By my troth," she exclaimed with a nervous laugh. "I am surprised to find you so serious. My sister always said that you were her golden, caring son, while your brother Ciaran was the dark one."

He rubbed a hand over the tense planes of his face. "Aunt, I must be very frank. There is no time to spare, for I fear that someone will call ye away, and I may not have another chance to ask ye these questions."

"All right." Tess folded her hands in her lap and straightened her spine. "I am listening."

"I have always felt…different from the rest of my family. Cared for, aye, but different." He felt the miniature through the folds of his plaid, and now his hand curved around it. "Do ye understand?"

"What exactly do you mean?" Her cheeks seemed to pinken, though perhaps that was simply the deepening afternoon light.

Lennox felt as if he stood on the edge of a great black chasm, his future calling to him from the other side. Suddenly, a part of him wished that he'd never felt discontented with clan MacLeod, never gone to Fi's house to help her pack, never accidentally bumped the little casket with the enameled lid. Why couldn't he have been happy with the life he had, the one he'd known since birth?

In this moment, sitting beside Aunt Tess, his chest hurt and his eyes stung. "I have learned at last that Magnus is not my real da. I'm no MacLeod at all," he said, hearing the catch in his own voice. "I've been told that Ma left Skye with little Ciaran and her nurse, Isbeil. They sailed south, to you. When she returned to Skye, months later, it seems I had been conceived." He paused, hearing his own heartbeat. "No one else can help me but you, Aunt Tess."

After drawing a deep sigh, she nodded. "Aye, I remember that summer well. I had gone to stay in the tower house of an old family friend, to help him through his last illness." Misty-eyed, Tess added, "'Twas Ian MacDougall. Such a fine man. But you would not remember him."

"Aunt, I implore you." Lennox had an irrational fear that, at any moment, someone would appear to summon Tess back to the queen, and he would have missed his one chance. Deftly, he reached in the folds of his plaid and brought out the pouch containing the miniature. "Look at this face."

Seeing the man's image again here in the sunlight was rather startling to him as well. Lennox hadn't taken a good look at it for more than a fortnight, and now he was struck by how much his true father resembled a high-born member of the royal court. It wasn't just the rich, gem-encrusted clothing he wore, but also something in his face. One brow was slightly arched, as if he had been amused, and there was a knowing, intelligent spark in his green eyes.

It came to Lennox that the man looked *civilized.*

"Why, nephew," Tess said in tones of wonder. "This could be you!"

"Perhaps, if I owned a doublet sewn with rubies, but such finery is hard to come by in the Highlands." He leaned forward, letting her feel the ironic edge of his emotions. "Aunt, I have traveled from Skye to Stirling, and now to Falkland, in search of the truth. I have waited here for a full fortnight to ask the question only ye can answer." Pointing to the miniature, Lennox demanded, "Who is this man?"

Tess shook her head. "By my troth,I do not know!"

Lennox had never been quick to anger, but now he felt a strong urge to grip his aunt by the shoulders and shake her. "I do not believe it!"

At this, she got to her feet and pointed a finger at him. "You forget yourself, Lennox MacLeod. Do you wish to hear what I have to say, or shall I leave you?"

"Nay, do not go." He felt as if his head would explode. "It's just that… I had such hopes. Accept my apology, please."

She perched on the edge of the bench, clearly poised to flee if he misbehaved again. "Your beautiful mother did not raise you to behave in such a manner."

As she was speaking, Lennox heard raised voices from the direction of the palace. Heart racing, he sensed that time was running out. "Aunt, I will be grateful for anything ye can tell me."

Tess looked into the distance, as if seeing back to a long-ago summer on the western coast of Scotland. "I remember well the day Eleanor arrived, with little Ciaran and her old nurse, Isbeil. The old woman's brother brought them over the sea from Skye. It isn't far, as you know." She smiled wistfully. "I had written Eleanor to tell her I would be with Ian until he passed from this world. He was a great friend of our parents and had been like an uncle to us."

Were the voices growing louder? Lennox wanted to hurry his aunt along, but feared the worst if he tried again to force the story from her.

"Eleanor told me of the trouble with Magnus…" She looked over at him and he nodded to let her know he was privy to this drama. "My heart ached for her. She had made up her mind that she would never go back, but where could she stay? Clearly, Ian's tower house was not the solution. He was dying, and Eleanor knew that she could not impose upon his small staff." Tess gave him a rueful smile. "You may imagine what your brother Ciaran was like as a wee lad, chasing Ian's wolfhound up and down the stone steps."

"What did Ma do?" Lennox asked, praying his aunt wouldn't hear the commotion that seemed to increase with each passing minute. Something was clearly wrong at the palace.

Seemingly oblivious, Tess continued, "One day, an invitation arrived for a hunting party at Duart Castle, on the Isle of Mull. Of course, Ian could not attend, but he suggested that Eleanor go in his stead. She was already acquainted with Hector Mór, the chief of clan MacLean, and so she packed up Ciaran and Isbeil. Ian's squire took them across the Firth of Lorn in his small galley, to Duart Castle."

"And then?" he urged, his voice hoarse.

Tess gave a philosophical shrug. "I never saw her again that summer. Ian passed on, I returned to my own home here in Fife, and when next I had word from Eleanor, she had gone back to Skye. She wrote that she had…reconsidered her marriage." Tess paused, inclining her head toward the palace, and he knew she now heard the voices. Almost as an afterthought, she added, "And then you were born, Lennox."

The sound of twigs cracking and gravel crunching reached their ears. Someone was running along the path, headed in their direction. "Please, Aunt, will you tell me one more thing?"

Tess struggled up from the bench, waiting and watching, and now she was the one who looked impatient. "Be quick."

Lennox rose to face her and held the miniature out so that she could have a second look. "Could this man be Hector Mór, the MacLean?"

She squinted at it. "I think not, but I only met him once. I suppose it is possible, but still, what Highland chief would wear such clothing?"

Lennox felt a memory stir and take shape. "Aye, that's true. I'd almost forgotten, I saw him once too. Ciaran and I sailed to Oban once, perhaps a decade ago. Ma bade us stop at Duart Castle and convey her greetings to the MacLean." His heart clenched like a fist as he remembered that long-ago day. How innocent and trusting he had been!

Just then, a page wearing the queen's black-and-crimson livery burst into the clearing. "Madame, at last I have found you!" he cried in a French accent. "Her Majesty has need of her ladies. Word has come that Prince James is gravely ill, and the king has ridden with all possible speed to reach his side."

"Oh, how terrible!" exclaimed Tess. She glanced back at Lennox. "I must go to her at once."

"I fear there is more," interjected the page. "Soon after His Majesty left for St. Andrews, Prince Arthur's wet nurse noticed that the new babe is very warm. Feverish. He has been sleeping so long, everyone is worried. The queen is beside herself."

"Both little princes are ill, in different castles?" Tess exclaimed in disbelief. "How can this be?"

"Allow me to escort you." Lennox took her arm as they started down the path. "Perhaps there is something I can do to help."

It was the young page who responded, his face chalk-white against his crimson bonnet. "*Oui, m'sieur*, there is something. You may pray for our two tiny princes."

Chapter Nine

Late afternoon was softening into evening when Lennox stabled Chaucer at Stirling Castle and walked through the arched entrance to the inner close. His eyes stung with fatigue, he was ravenous, and he needed to wash, but first he must find Fiona. As a caring friend to the queen, his sister would be anxious to speak to him about the princes.

Lennox's heart constricted with pain whenever he thought of the terrible tragedy that had befallen Queen Mary and King James. It was unthinkable, to lose two babes on the same day, but it seemed royal folk were not protected from grief and loss. Nay, sometimes it seemed they had more than their share.

In the courtyard, the masons, carvers, and glasswrights were putting away their tools. There was no sign of Christophe, but Lennox caught sight of Grant and waved to him.

"Ye are back," the lad exclaimed, rushing to his side.

"Aye." He put a hand on Grant's shoulder. "I fear I cannot linger, lad. I'm here to get the rest of my things and bid my family farewell, for at dawn I depart for Duart Castle on the Isle of Mull."

Grant's eyes were wide. "Duart Castle! Ach, I've heard it's a wondrous place."

"Will ye tell me where I might find my sister?" As he spoke, Lennox looked over the top of Grant's head, scanning the crowd for Fi's familiar face.

"She went to visit Nora in the tapestry workroom, to see the new loom now in use." He grinned.

This news made Lennox's breath catch for an instant. *Nora.* He'd been trying not to think of her and wishing he had the ability to banish her from his dreams as well. Soon he'd be far away from Stirling Castle, which was just as well. Nora Brodie's aspirations were much grander than simple romance, and it would be folly for Lennox to bring a lass into his life when he didn't even know who he really was.

Still, he was leaving on the morrow. What harm could come of seeing her one more time? A pleasurable frisson of anticipation crept over him and he sent himself a stern reminder: *Only look. Smile, perhaps, but nothing more!*

"Grant, will ye take this up to my chamber for me?" Lennox proffered the bundle of his possessions. "I will find Fi, then we'll all dine together later, one last time. I want to hear what's been happening in your life this past month." Raising his eyebrows, he added, "I swear, ye are taller than when I left."

Fiona leaned forward and placed the back of her cool hand against Nora's brow. "My dear, are you unwell? How pale you are."

They were standing together at the great loom, and Nora had been doing her best to talk about the *Prodigal Son* tapestry that her father had designed. It was impossible to concentrate, though, and Fiona's words made her stomach knot.

"Perhaps I am spending too much time indoors," Nora said, offering a wan smile. "There has been so much work to do."

Work, yes, but none of it at the loom, unless her father brought her there later in the day, when the men had gone. The problem was that weaving such a treasure required very good light, so by the time Nora sat down at the loom, it was impossible to see each fine detail.

Not that it mattered. Nearly a fortnight had passed without the onset of her monthly courses, and with each day that passed, she slept and ate less. The thought of food made her ill.

Her father thought her sad, touchy mood was due to her disappointment at being passed over as a weaver, when in fact Nora was terrified at the prospect of telling him that she was with child.

Lying awake in the middle of the night, the words would go round and round in her mind, but no matter how many ways she planned the speech, it was wrong. No explanation could be sufficient. She was ruined! Her father would stare at her, his own expression reflecting shock and disappointment and shame. He would declare that she had thrown away everything they had ever worked for. Had all her vows to pursue an artistic life, without a husband or children or any other encumbrance, been nothing but fabrications?

The soup Nora had eaten at midday seemed to curdle in her stomach. There was absolutely no way forward, yet how long could she hide her condition? Where could she go? Back to Flanders, to her mother?

Even if a plan were possible, she had no means to carry it out.

"Look at you, my dear," Fiona whispered. "You are clammy with perspiration. Is it a fever?"

Just then, Nora heard someone entering the outer rooms. She waited for her father to call out to her, but the footsteps came closer. When Nora turned away from the loom, she was surprised to behold Lennox MacLeod, so handsome, his wide shoulders filling the doorway. Was she imagining the golden light surrounding him?

"Dear brother!" exclaimed Fiona, beaming at the sight of him. "How good it is to see you. Did you rescue any maidens in distress while you were away?" Glancing toward Nora, she added lightly, "It is his specialty, you know."

"Fi," he warned in a low voice, even as he crossed the room to embrace her. Turning then, he spoke kind words of greeting to Nora.

She managed to smile without blushing. "May I offer you a cup of wine? We have our own, from Flanders."

"Thank you, but no. I will not stay," he replied. He looked toward his sister. "I am travel-stained and hungry, but before I go to my chamber I wanted to speak to you about Queen Mary."

"Only last evening we received word about the baby princes," Fiona replied in softly anguished tones. "Oh, Lennox, how could this have happened?"

He stood beside the big loom, and Nora saw the genuine sadness in his green eyes. "Only God knows, I fear. First, word came to Falkland Palace that Prince James was gravely ill in St. Andrews, and immediately the king rode to his little son's bedside. Barely an hour later, the newborn Prince Arthur became feverish. By the next nightfall, both babes were dead, though of course those of us in Falkland did not learn of Prince James's passing until later."

"Our poor queen," Nora murmured.

"My heart aches for her," agreed Fiona. "I cannot imagine her pain. How could such a thing happen to both princes, in different castles? Is it not chilling?"

"Aye," Lennox replied grimly. "It is hard not to suspect foul play, though there is no proof."

"Who would do such a terrible thing? It's beyond imagining!" Fiona exclaimed.

Lennox lifted a strong shoulder up in a half-shrug and sadly shook his head. "There are many noblemen who stand to gain power if the heirs to the throne are removed. Some within the royal court whisper of poison." He reached out to touch his sister's arm. "The queen is a strong woman. This tragedy will not break her. Frankly, it is King James who I worry about. He looks truly haunted."

Fiona nodded slowly. "His Majesty has always been prone to melancholy."

"I was fortunate to share a brief interlude with Queen Mary, shortly before her sons fell ill," Lennox said pensively, looking first at his sister then at Nora. His gaze held rare depths for a man, she thought. "Walking back to the palace one afternoon, I came upon the queen, sitting in the gallery with her newborn son. I had my chalks and paper, so I asked if I might sketch them. To my surprise, she agreed. I rather quickly made a likeness of them together, with a small sketch of Prince Arthur's face in one corner. The queen was very taken with the drawing and asked if she might keep it, as a memento of the afternoon when she broke the rules, holding her swaddled babe and sitting outside in the sunshine with him."

Nora's heart ached as she listened and imagined Queen Mary looking at the sketch now that Prince Arthur was dead. "It is doubtless her only lasting keepsake of her newborn son," she whispered.

"Aye. Thank God I happened upon them."

Fiona went closer to Lennox and rested her head on his broad chest. "You are a good man, even though your urge to save those in need can sometimes get you in trouble. I'm very proud to call you my brother." She paused to lean back and give him what seemed to be a particularly meaningful look. "How good it is to have you back with us at Stirling."

Nora felt this, too. The very presence of this man brought her a much-needed sense of calm and safety, as if he could somehow shield her from harm.

"That's another thing I came to tell you, Fi," Lennox said tentatively. "I cannot stay. I will be leaving Stirling at first light, bound for Duart Castle on the Isle of Mull. I'll explain it all when we dine tonight, but know that I must go, hoping to find there the answers I seek."

Nora watched them exchange glances, sighing to herself. How lovely it must be to have a real family—loved ones who would rally round in times of trouble and support one another. Then Lennox's words sank in. The Isle of Mull! She was surprised at her own deep reaction to the news that he would be leaving again so soon.

"But you will come back?" Nora asked impulsively.

Lennox gave her a rueful smile. "I had been looking forward to spending more time here in this workroom, learning more about your art. But unfortunately I cannot stay, and I do not know when or if I will return to Stirling."

Midnight was at hand when Lennox undressed in a beam of moonlight and got into bed. His small room was referred to as a closet, and the bed was too short for his long frame, with a straw-filled tick set upon loosely-strung ropes. It would have been tempting to spread his blanket on the rush-strewn floor and lie there if it were not too much trouble. He was simply too weary.

The evening had been filled with family conversation, as Lennox told Fiona, Christophe, and Grant about his time at Falkland Palace and his conversation with Aunt Tess. He'd hoped Fi might have an inkling what their mother had been doing at Duart Castle, but she was as surprised as he was.

Lying now in the darkness, Lennox let his thoughts drift back to Nora Brodie. He'd been visited by erotic dreams of her during his weeks at Falkland Palace, yet when he saw her today, the aura about her had been so unsettling that he felt discomfited by those memories. As he had dined with his family tonight, Lennox had casually mentioned Nora to Fiona, wondering if the lovely tapisier might be grieving a loss or dealing with a crisis of some sort. Fi assured him that she had asked Nora the same question, but the girl had denied any problem. At that point, Grant had glanced up, alert, but after Lennox changed the subject to his impending journey west, the lad returned to his trencher of roasted peacock with wine sauce.

Fi's words came back to him yet again: *My dear brother, you barely know the lass. All your life, you have rescued those in need...but is it your place to intervene with Nora Brodie?*

Nay, he had more than enough problems of his own, without shouldering Nora's as well, even if she wanted him to, which she clearly did not. Lennox sighed and closed his eyes.

Dawn would be here soon, and he needed sleep so that he might focus on his quest.

No sooner had he drifted off, than a tapping came at his door. Immediately wide awake, Lennox bolted upright and reached for his sword, propped at the side of the bed. Was he going to open the portal completely naked except for his weapon? It seemed he had no choice, for he could see, in his exhaustion, he had forgotten to bar the door.

However, as Lennox swung his legs over the side of the bed, a soft voice spoke.

"Lennox MacLeod? Is this your chamber?"

"Nora!" he said hoarsely, shocked. Moving back against the pillow, he drew the sheet over the lower half of his body. "Come in."

The door swung slowly open, and Nora's face came into view, pale and uncertain in the moonlight. She was wearing an emerald-green cloak, the hood pushed back to frame her mass of long curls.

"I cannot rise to offer greeting without revealing more than ye want to see," he explained with a note of irony. "Close the door and come over here. What the devil has brought ye to my chamber in such an unexpected manner?"

Nora did as he bade, seeming almost to float as she approached. Indeed, Lennox thought as he watched her emerge from the shadows, she could have been a spirit with her luminous skin and haunted blue eyes. However, as she sat down on the edge of his bed, he perceived that her mood was hardly ephemeral.

"I have come to ask for your help." There was a tremor in her voice. "You must help me!"

Taken aback, Lennox reached for her hands and found them cold and damp. "By the saints, what is it?"

"Promise. I beg of you!"

"Nora Brodie, I will assist if I can, but first ye must tell me what is wrong."

"I cannot confide all, not yet, but you must believe that my circumstances are *desperate*." She closed her eyes for a moment, and Lennox almost imagined he could hear her heartbeat in the silence between them. "Please, take me with you when you leave Stirling Castle."

Lennox could not believe his ears. "Are ye in jest? I cannot do such a thing. Ye would be ruined and your father would see me hanged. Or worse."

"What if I told you I have been thinking of you? That I have…feelings for you and cannot bear to think of you leaving forever?"

Now Nora came closer, sitting near so her soft hip touched his hard flank, and he inhaled her fresh scent, like linen and sunshine. Their eyes met. She reached up and touched the muscled planes of his chest.

"Lass, I think ye have gone mad," he managed to whisper.

In the next moment, Nora had slipped a hand to the back of Lennox's neck. "If you will not take me away, then grant me one kiss."

A groan seemed to rise up from the core of him as her sweet lips lightly brushed his. All the times she had visited him in dreams suddenly were real, and arousal coursed through him like a wildfire. *"Nora."* Had he spoken?

Her mouth opened under his, and he tasted her, so sweet, his tongue lightly touching hers. Gently, then with building intensity. Her cloak had come open, and Lennox realized that she wore only her shift beneath it. It was open halfway in front, affording him a glimpse of the inviting curve of one breast. His cock, already stiff with need, throbbed. For an instant, he imagined drawing her down with him on the bed and opening her shift. Finding her breasts. He already knew what her nipple would feel like in his warm mouth, for they'd been naked together in his dreams.

Yet another part of Lennox sensed something was wrong. His strong inner voice was telling him to stop. Tasting salt in her kiss, he drew back. Could it be that she was weeping?

"Nora!"

"Don't you want me?" she whispered.

"By God, I want ye far too much, but this is not *right.* I cannot lie with a woman like you in such a way, and I know damned well ye don't want that either. Not truly. Did you think, if ye gave your body to me, that would persuade me to take ye away?" He heard the ragged emotion in his own voice.

"Isn't that the way of it with men?" Nora covered her face and turned away from him, clearly ashamed. "It seemed my simple plea was not enough, and I have nothing else to offer."

Lennox leaned forward and firmly closed the front of her cloak. "Ye misjudge me, lass. I am not like those other men. Tell me plainly why ye must leave Stirling, so I may make a reasoned decision."

"Why can you not trust me when I say it is a matter of true urgency?"

Just as he tried to get a clearer view of her face, a cloud covered the moon, and the chamber grew even darker. "What does this mean? Are ye in danger?"

Nora stared at him. As their eyes met for a long moment, he seemed to see into her soul. "If I stay," came her soft reply, "I truly do not know what would become of me." She swallowed. "I am filled with fear. I have no choice but to leave, quickly."

"What of your da? Can he not protect you?"

"It is Father who may well threaten me," Nora whispered urgently. "Please believe me when I say that I simply cannot speak of this matter. Do not ask me to say more."

He drew a deep, scorching breath. "Aye, then. I will do it."

For some reason, he expected her to react as other women had when he he'd granted a heartfelt plea, exclaiming in joy and coming into his arms. But Nora Brodie's response was merely a solemn nod.

"I have prayed you would agree," she said. "Thank you."

"Just before dawn, I will come to your door. Listen for my one soft tap."

"I am truly grateful." Her chin trembled for only an instant before she rose and started toward the door.

This is mad, Lennox thought again, remembering William Brodie. "Nora, what about your da? Do ye intend to leave his care without a word? He will believe I've kidnapped his fair daughter and raise a hue and cry!"

"Nay. I have already written a letter. I will leave it behind, so he understands I have gone by choice." The faintest of smiles touched her mouth. "In it, I have reminded him that I am two-and-twenty years of age. A woman grown. And this is Scotland, where I am free to live my life as I choose."

Back in her own bed, Nora lay awake for the next few hours. Everything was in readiness. She had packed only a few essentials into a satchel, yet in a weak moment, Nora had slipped out to the workroom and taken a few finger-shaped wooden bobbins of her favorite yarns, dyed in bright hues by mixing herbs like weld, madder, and woad. She also rolled up and stowed two smaller tapestries. One choice was purely sentimental: the first little tapestry she'd woven as a child. It portrayed her pet rabbit, one ear up and one down, the weaving neater, tighter, cleaner on the top than the bottom. Nora had never forgotten the strange thrill she'd felt as she became increasingly capable of weaving at a small loom without her father's assistance. It was a passion that only grew stronger through the years as her skills sharpened.

Before dawn, Nora rose and washed one more time. She was grateful to feel numb again, for if she stopped to truly consider what she was doing, she might have wept. All her life, her father had been her guide and often her only friend, the one person who understood her. It would break his heart, she knew, to find that she had run away.

Yet there simply was no other choice. It was impossible to tell her father the truth of her situation, impossible to stay at Stirling Castle while carrying Sir Raymond's bastard. During the many nights she'd lain awake, it had occurred to Nora that she might say that Slater had forced himself on her, but the entire court seemed to be so dazzled by him, who would believe her?

And so Nora stood just inside the doorway to her chamber, wrapped in her green cloak, clutching her satchel, feeling sick. She prayed that she was right about Lennox MacLeod, that his word was good and he would come for her. Licking her dry lips, she glanced back at the letter to her father. It lay fairly glowing against the deep blue cover of her bed.

Where was Lennox? Had she misjudged him, and he had decided to go without her?

Just then, a candle flame flickered from the direction of the workroom. As it danced over the shadowed wall, coming closer, Nora thought her heart might cease beating.

"What's this all about?" cried William Brodie, looming up in the doorway to her chamber. "Where do ye think you're going, lass?"

Chapter Ten

Nora met her father's challenging stare, speechless, wishing she could make herself invisible. Her heart was pounding so hard she felt certain he must be able to hear it.

William Brodie's eyes were moving over her, touching on her satchel, her cloak, the letter on her bed. "I demand an *answer*," he rumbled. "What the devil is happening?"

Just then, a soft tap came at the outer door. Nora's heart leaped with a mixture of relief and trepidation, for it was her father who wheeled around to throw open the portal. There stood Lennox, looking quite undismayed by the sight of a red-faced William Brodie.

"So ye are to blame for this!" thundered the older man. "Ye doubtless intend to dishonor my daughter, MacLeod, but I will see you dead first!"

Nora watched, stunned, as Lennox gave a reassuring smile and put a hand on her father's arm. "Dishonor? Never. In truth, I mean to protect her."

"Do ye think to trick me? Get out!"

Instead of obeying, Lennox stepped into the room and looked at Nora, sending her a message with his eyes. She went forward, trusting him somehow to carry them safely through this stormy drama.

"Father," she said, "it is not what you are thinking."

Lennox reached for her hand and put it through the crook of his elbow. "Aye, sir. If ye will only attend me—"

Nora felt as if her heart might tear in two as Father grasped her other arm and tugged, glaring at her.

"Take your hands off my daughter!" Brodie was shouting now, heedless that he might wake others in the palace.

"Calm yourself and do Nora the honor of listening to what we have to say."

"*Nora?* Ye have no right to use her Christian name!"

"That will soon change," Lennox replied calmly.

It was Nora's turn to stare at him in surprise. What could he possibly mean? Before she could form a question, the Highlander smiled down at her and touched a tanned finger to her lips.

"Nay, love, do not protest. Your father deserves to know to the truth." Looking back at William Brodie, Lennox said, "I am in love with your daughter and mean to make her my wife."

The older man's face reddened in shock. "Bah!" he spat. "If that were true, why would ye spirit her away in the hour before dawn, without coming to me as a man of honor and asking for her hand? And why would my lass run off without so much as a farewell to her father?"

"Ye pose a reasonable question, sir." Lennox rubbed his jaw. After glancing again toward Nora, he said, "As it happened, there was simply no time. I was called away from Stirling on a family matter of great urgency…"

At last, Nora saw an opening in the conversation that she could fill. "And when Lennox broke the news to me that he must leave at dawn, I realized I could not bear for us to be parted again, especially so soon after his journey to Falkland Palace. I begged him to take me with him without fully considering any of the consequences."

"Oh, did ye indeed?" shouted her father. "I think ye have gone mad! What about your *calling*? The gift ye have nurtured since ye were a wee lass, always proclaiming that weaving meant far more than any trifling dreams of romance?" He paused, breathing hard. "If ye meant to run away with this wild Highlander, why did ye berate me about becoming a weaver at the new loom?"

"Wild?" Lennox echoed, raising one tawny brow. "A rash judgment, sir."

"Allow me to speak," Nora said, raising a hand. "Father, you may recall that when I spoke strongly to you about my aspiration to become a master weaver, you told me it could not be. You said the dream I had nurtured since I was a child was impossible, simply because I am a woman, not because I lack the skill."

At this, to her aggravation, her father gave Lennox a sidelong glance, as if to exchange a commonly-held belief about females. "This slip of a lass cannot seem to understand that a *true* weaver must possess a great deal of physical strength in order to operate that great loom."

"You see?" cried Nora. "All my life you encouraged my dreams, but when the time came for me to reach out and make them come true, you found many reasons why it could not be!"

She saw real, raw pain flash in his eyes. "Is that a reason to leave me and everything we have shared since the day you were born?"

For a moment, Nora wavered. Perhaps it was truly mad to run away with Lennox MacLeod, to abandon her father and the world of tapestry weaving to which she was so deeply devoted. But in the next breath, she remembered the babe Sir Raymond Slater had put in her. It would be far worse for William Brodie to discover that shocking and shameful secret than to think she had left because she'd fallen in love with Lennox. And even if she did tell the truth and Father could somehow understand, it would be impossible to hide her condition or explain the babe to the rest of the royal court.

"Father, you said it yourself. At the royal court, weaving tapestries is a man's domain. Perhaps, in my future with Lennox, I can find another place to apply my skills as a weaver."

Defeat, then grief flashed across William Brodie's face. Nora feared he might weep, but then his strong chin jutted out, and he stared defiantly at Lennox. "If ye think I will allow ye to lure my daughter away and defile her, ye are sorely mistaken!"

As Lennox regarded the older man, Nora waited, wondering what he could possibly say to that.

"I am no defiler of innocent lasses," he replied evenly. "I love your daughter and intend to marry her."

Nora pressed her lips together to suppress a stunned gasp. Good God, what was Lennox saying? And now that he had spoken so rashly, how could he undo such words later?

His jaw still out-thrust, William nodded angrily. "Aye! And well you should wed, before ye leave Stirling Castle."

Lennox took Nora's arm again. "I fear there is no time now. A family crisis demands that we depart now, but we shall have a proper wedding very soon."

"I know a remedy for this," her father persisted, reaching again for Nora's other arm. He tugged on her. "Ye will handfast. *Now*. With me as the witness!"

She looked at Lennox, expecting him to finally admit the truth: that he had no desire to take Nora with him, let alone wed her, and now he would be on his way, leaving father and daughter to sort out their problems alone.

Instead, Lennox continued to study William Brodie. "Handfast?" he echoed with a hint of challenge.

"I may have spent most of my life in Flanders and England, but I was born a Scotsman." Her father narrowed his eyes at Lennox. "Surely, as a mighty Highlander, ye know all about handfasting!"

"What does it mean?" Nora queried nervously.

"Your bridegroom is in a great hurry, so let us demonstrate rather than explain," her father said. He wore the expression of a cat who has cornered a particularly elusive mouse. "'Tis simple enough."

If Lennox was disturbed by this unexpected turn of events, he gave no sign of it. Instead, he took Nora's hand in his and put his other around her waist. It was comforting to feel the strength of his fingers.

"Your da is quite right," he murmured with a grim smile. "We should say our vows for him to hear."

"Go on then," William Brodie folded his arms over his chest, watching them with an air of suspicion.

"Nora Brodie, I take thee to my wife," Lennox said simply.

She blinked, waiting for more. What sort of ceremony was this, without a church, an altar, or a priest?

"Now ye must say it, lass," commanded her father. "It's what ye want, is it not?"

Tears stung her eyes. Lennox squeezed her hand encouragingly, and Nora wondered why he was being so kind, so good to her.

"Just repeat the vow back to me," he whispered. "Then we can go."

She drew a deep breath and said, "Lennox MacLeod, I take thee to my husband."

Her father paled. "Aye, then. It's done." He made a dismissing motion, and Nora saw his hand tremble. "Farewell, daughter."

It came to her then how severe this rupture in her life truly was. She ached to put her arms around her father and tell him she loved him, that he had been her rock, her mentor, her guide through life. But already he was turning away, head bowed, and she knew that anything further from her would only twist the knife in his heart.

"Let's be away," Lennox said in a low, firm voice. Picking up her satchel, he clasped her elbow through the green wool of her cloak and guided her to the door.

Just as they passed through the portal, Nora looked back and saw her father angled in profile, watching them go. He suddenly looked like an old man. Impulsively, Nora called out, "Father… I left a letter for you, on my bed."

Shaking his head, William Brodie averted his face again. "I no longer know ye. Be gone from me."

Nora heard the catch in his voice, but what could she do? Instead, drawing a deep breath, she stepped off into a future filled with secrets, half-truths, and uncertainty.

Chapter Eleven

As the first light of dawn crept over the castle walls, masons began to assemble in the courtyard. Lennox guided Nora along the shadowed, colonnaded gallery, heading toward the stables. He tried to stay out of sight, for the last thing he wanted was an encounter with any of his family. How could he possibly explain Nora's presence by his side?

Glancing over at Nora, Lennox saw that she had retreated inside herself. She had drawn the edges of her green hood closer to her face, and her expression was pensive, even troubled. Did she feel ignored by him at a time when she might need reassurance?

"I don't mean to be cold," he said in a low voice. "I just want to us to be away."

Nora looked over in surprise, almost as if she had forgotten he existed. "Oh, yes. Of course, I am feeling the same."

Soon enough, Lennox brought Chaucer out of the stable and into the Nether Bailey. He turned to Nora and gestured toward the padded pillion that he'd attached behind his saddle.

"We must ride together for now."

Lennox was surprised to see her cheeks go charmingly pink, and suddenly their situation was tinged with pleasure.

"I am grateful to you for taking me away, and I shan't complain of any discomfort." She bit her lip and her blush deepened. "Not that riding with you would be unpleasant."

"I'm relieved to hear it." He gave her a wry, tentative smile and put both hands around her waist, preparing to assist her up to Chaucer's back.

"MacLeod!" a male voice shouted from behind them. "Lennox MacLeod!"

He groaned. "I knew it would be impossible for us to depart unnoticed." Turning, Lennox saw his brother-in-law emerging through the ancient north gate that opened to the outer close. "Did we not make our farewells last night?"

Christophe de St. Briac came toward them. Clad in a worn doublet of dark leather, he lightly held a small chisel in one hand. "We did indeed, and so I was not surprised to see you pass through the courtyard this morning without another word to me," the Frenchman said before turning his crisp, blue eyes on Nora. "And *then* I saw Mistress Brodie. When you told Fiona and the rest of us that you meant to go to Duart Castle, you forgot to mention that you would have a traveling companion." He arched a brow for emphasis.

Lennox felt Nora watching him, waiting to see how he would respond. He stared back at Christophe and cursed himself for allowing his family to think they had the right to intrude into his private life.

"Nora is coming with me," Lennox began. "We are…wed. I cannot explain now, but ye may tell my sister that I'll send word soon."

"You two are *wed*?" Christophe replied, cocking his dark head in disbelief.

"Aye, we are! But I can say no more at this time. We must be away." Lennox was relieved when his brother-in-law took a step backward.

"*Eh bien.*" Christophe's gaze traveled to Nora. "I wonder how our friend Grant will take this news?"

Nora spoke up. "I do not think Grant will be shocked by this turn of events," she said in a firm voice. "Please encourage him to take some time and consider everything that has happened in recent weeks."

What the devil was that supposed to mean? Shaking his head,

Lennox extended a hand to Christophe. "Fear not. All will be well."

"I hope you are right," Christophe said. "*Bonne chance, mon frère.*"

As they mounted Chaucer's back and started through the North Gate, Lennox glanced back to see his brother-in-law still rooted to the same spot, watching them go. When would he be with Christophe and Fiona again? Perhaps his entire life would be different when that day came…

Nora was warm against Lennox's broad back, her woolen skirts and kirtle hiked up so she could sit astride. As Chaucer passed the guards and left Stirling Castle behind, Lennox thought he could feel her sigh against him. When they were safely away and slowly descending the steep, twisting lanes of Stirling, he paused before a turning, drew in on the reins, and looked back at her.

"Are ye all right?"

Nora met his gaze, and Lennox was struck by her gleaming, cornflower-blue eyes, rich with emotions he could only guess at. Softly she asked, "Why did you do it?"

He blinked. "Do what, lass?"

"Tell my father that you wanted to wed me, that you loved me." With each word she spoke, more rosy color washed her cheeks.

"Because it seemed the only way," Lennox said honestly. "We were caught."

"But…the vows. What do you call it?"

"Handfasting." He gave her a rueful smile.

"Can it truly be that we are lawfully wed?"

"Aye. That's the way of it in Scotland." He felt intensely curious to know what Nora was thinking. What desperate secret had driven her to beg for his protection? And now that they had exchanged vows, did the notion of being his wife repel her? It was ironic to consider that although many lasses had pursued him, he had never come close to settling down with any of them. "Fear not. Handfasting need not be binding. But knowing we exchanged vows set your da's mind at ease, and we can travel together as man and wife." Seeing her eyes widen, Lennox added, "It will help to keep you safe."

Dark clouds were gathering in the western sky, bringing with them a chill, gusty wind. Chaucer lifted his proud head, sniffing for rain, as Nora's hood slipped back to reveal a cloud of brandy-hued curls. How lovely she was, Lennox thought. An alluring blend of vulnerability, determination, and mystery. A sudden desire to kiss her mouth came over him like a warning.

"Get out the way!" shouted a scrawny boy as he passed them, driving a handful of goats down the rutted lane.

"The journey to Oban will be long," Lennox said, turning his body forward again. "We should be on our way—unless ye have changed your mind?"

"No," came Nora's reply. He felt her move more closely against him. "I must go. There is no other choice for me."

Cool, misty rains swirled around them throughout the day, as Chaucer carried Nora and Lennox away from Stirling and into a picturesque series of wooded hills and glens. They spoke little, for each time they stopped, Lennox complained that the weather was slowing them down and they must not tarry. He had planned well, she discovered, packing bannocks, cheese, and plums. He made certain there was always a stream nearby to furnish long drinks of cold water.

"How did you manage to do all of this, in the short time between our conversation in your rooms and the time we left this morning?" she asked once, as he handed her another piece of cheese and a bannock.

"All of this?" Lennox gave a sardonic snort. "I made no additional preparations, but went back to sleep after you left me last night. We are eating only the food I brought for myself, when I thought I was traveling alone."

"But..." Nora bit her lip, considering. "Will there be enough?"

"Enough for today, at least," he said ruefully. "Fear not. I will see to it that we don't starve, but it's also important that we make haste to reach Duart Castle."

Questions intruded in Nora's mind, but she pushed them away. If she began to doubt Lennox or even consider what lay ahead in her own future, she feared she'd drown in a wave of fear. It was far more pleasant to live in the moment, enjoying the fantasy of running away with her splendid, handfasted husband.

They rode for hours, pausing only to let Chaucer rest and drink from streams that rushed by. Nora kept waiting for Lennox to turn onto a better road so that they might find proper lodging for the night, but they continued on rutted, muddy tracks, the only sign of civilization being the occasional thatched roof of a croft house in the distance.

Finally, feeling the damp chill through her cloak, Nora spoke. "Do you never intend that we should travel on a real road?"

Chaucer had slowed to negotiate a rocky stretch in front of them, and Lennox took that opportunity to look back, his face inches away from Nora's. "What did ye have in mind?"

He sounded almost amused, which irked her. "I'm certain you must know what I mean! A *road!* A proper thoroughfare that passes through villages, where we might find an inn to offer us a warm meal and a clean bed." Nora paused and widened her eyes for emphasis.

Lennox laughed as a gust of wet wind nearly took off his cap of tartan wool. "Do ye imagine there is such a thing nearby? This is Scotland, lass. In the Highlands, there are neither *roads* nor *inns*." He spoke the two words as if they were vastly amusing to him.

She gave a soft gasp of disbelief. "A tavern, then, with a meager chamber for let."

"Nay. None of those either, at least not between Stirling and Oban."

"But where, then, shall we sleep?"

"Oh, I will think of something." Lennox smiled in a way that made her feel warm. His eyes rested on her mouth and she flushed.

"What is it?" Nora put a hand up to her lower lip. "A blemish?"

He merely gave a soft laugh and shook his head, urging Chaucer forward. "I know ye have enjoyed a life of comforts that doubtless did not include sleeping outdoors, but it may well happen tonight."

She held onto him, feeling his back muscles against her cheek. "But it is raining!"

"Perhaps ye prefer to return to Stirling Castle?"

Nora thought of the babe that must be growing inside her, so tiny that there was no sign of it yet. Reminding herself that Lennox was doing her a favor, she resolved to endure whatever trials lay in store for them.

At least, if they were going to sleep in a ditch during a storm, he would be unlikely to claim his rights as her new husband…

Thankfully, the rain had stopped by the time Lennox turned onto a path leading into the woods. Before long, they came upon a snug little clearing, and Chaucer halted of his own accord. Smiling, Lennox patted the horse's flank, dismounted, and reached up for Nora.

"We'll rest here," he said, hoping she wouldn't protest.

Nora wrinkled her nose doubtfully, but came down into his arms all the same. Holding her, Lennox realized that he didn't want to let go. Desire rose up from his core, mingling with something new and sweet. Affection, perhaps? Her hair was fragrant against his face, and he wanted to bring her closer, to fit her body to his.

Chaucer broke the moment by nudging them with his nose.

"There is a burn nearby," Lennox murmured. "Listen. Can ye hear it?"

He thought he could sense her heartbeat slowing as she nodded. "That's your Scots word for a stream, is it not? Chaucer must be thirsty."

"Aye. We'll camp here for the night." Reluctantly, he let her go and turned his attention to the chestnut stallion.

When they had all seen to their needs, Lennox filled a jug with water from the burn and brought it back to the little clearing. Darkness was gathering as silvery clouds scudded across the sky. Chaucer had found a patch of grass on which to graze, and Lennox suddenly realized that he was painfully hungry. He spread out his blanket and hunkered down, sitting back on his heels as he brought out the same food they had eaten at midday.

"Will ye not you join me, lass?" He glanced toward Nora, who was standing off to one side, watching.

She bit her lower lip before approaching and tentatively lowering herself to the blanket.

"I regret that I cannot provide a fire, since the wood is wet. Otherwise, I would gladly hunt some wild game to cook for our wedding supper." He kept his tone light, and Nora rewarded him with a faintly nervous smile.

"I will confess, it's not the sort of wedding day I could have ever imagined," she said.

The bannocks were now dry as stones, but Lennox broke one in two and handed half to her. "Nor would I."

"I apologize for drawing you into my…problems. And for my father, who made everything worse."

"I don't suppose ye want to tell me yet what this is really all about?"

Panic flared in her eyes. "Please do not ask me to say more about it."

Lennox uncorked a flagon of wine and drank, then offered it to Nora, who copied him. He heard the tender note in his own voice when next he spoke. "I have already vowed that I am not a man who would force ye in any way. I merely thought ye might be relieved to share the secret that troubles ye so deeply, lass."

The night air was growing chilly, and she moved closer to

him. "I am grateful for your kindness, sir, more grateful than words can express."

"Even though it means eating cold bannocks and sleeping on the ground?" he teased lightly.

Smiling, Nora accepted the wedge of cheese he held out. "I will no doubt look back on this night as a great adventure."

Lennox wanted to offer to make it a much greater adventure than she could imagine, but he held his tongue. Still, he allowed himself a brief fantasy of Nora, wrapped in his blanket with him, letting him undress her, opening her mouth to his kisses, moaning as he explored her body with his fingers...

"I almost forgot." Nora broke into his thoughts, sounding excited. "I picked some berries near the stream. Won't they be delicious?" She brought the plump brambleberries out of a pocket sewn into her cloak.

"Aye. Delicious." He couldn't keep the ragged edge of desire from his own voice.

Nora put one of the berries in her mouth and closed her eyes, sighing. "Oh, but it is sublime. Especially after a day of only bannocks and cheese. Let me give you some."

He watched as she took his hand, opening his long fingers to reveal the rough surface of his palm. "Your hands are so large," she observed, her own fingers slim and pale against his.

"Aye," murmured Lennox. He let her see the heat in his gaze before adding. "I am a man, after all."

Her cheeks went pink. "I am aware of that." Nora put several of the brambleberries into his hand, yet it seemed that her fingertips lingered over his. She licked her lips. "Is there more wine? I find I am still thirsty."

"Drink, lass. Ye need the warmth." He passed the flagon to her, waiting until she had finished to ask, "I know very little about your life before Stirling Castle. Tell me about the finest meal ye have ever eaten. Perhaps it will take our minds off the ways this one is lacking." For Lennox's own part, he hoped her tale would distract his cock, which was hard and aching even though they had scarcely touched.

Not yet, at least.

Nora leaned back against a tree trunk and brushed errant curls from her brow. "When I was about ten years old, and still living with my parents in Brussels, we three traveled to Paris. Papa had been the master weaver on a magnificent tapestry that was purchased for the Palais du Louvre. What a great adventure that was! The night before we returned to Flanders, we dined at the palace with King François I. For a girl my age, it was as if we had been transported into a fairyland. I had never been in such sumptuous surroundings, and they served more food, more courses, than I had ever imagined, each one announced with a trumpet fanfare!"

Lennox had a dozen questions about her childhood in Flanders, but they would have to wait. Instead, he prompted, "What was your favorite?"

"The liveried servants carried platters overhead with peacocks in full plumage, their beaks gilded. I thought perhaps it was merely paint, but Mama assured me they had actually melted gold." Nora paused to sigh, beaming at the memory. "It was also the first time I had ever seen a fork."

"Were the sweets delicious?" he asked, enjoying the sight of her smiling face.

"Oh, yes. The thing I remember most was the amazing array of confections that were made to look like something else. Animals, birds, even fish!" She laughed before smoothly moving the subject to him. "And what of your best memory of a feast? I know nothing about the Highlands apart from the rumors that all of you are a bit rough."

"Perhaps ye believe them now that ye see we lack such civilized comforts as roads and inns," Lennox parried lightly, a smile tugging at the corner of his mouth.

"You are teasing me, I know." Her gaze moved to the sharpened dirk, sheathed at his waist. "Yet your weapons look rather savage. And you don't wear a doublet…"

He felt torn between defending the splendid place where he had lived all his life and revealing that he was not truly a

Highlander at all. "Would ye think more highly of me if I wore a doublet instead of a belted plaid?"

"Of course not. I want to learn about this isle called Skye." Coming closer, Nora put her hand on his forearm. "It must be a magical place."

"Aye." His heart began to ache.

"No doubt you enjoyed many meals that linger in your memory."

Lennox closed his eyes and let himself go back in time. "The stronghold of Clan MacLeod is an ancient stone castle with views of a sea called The Minch." He heard Nora draw a breath and felt her sense of wonder. "Nearby, in plain sight, are two immense, flat-topped plateaus. They have Gaelic names, but most simply call them the MacLeod Tables. Not so long ago, King James V sailed around Scotland to pay a visit to the Western Isles, and our clan chief, Alasdair Crotach, wanted to impress him with a feast he would never forget." Lennox paused. "Our chief had boasted, during a visit to Holyrood Palace in Edinburgh, that he could offer a more impressive banquet hall on Skye. So, as the sun set, we led His Majesty and the royal party, by horseback, up to the top of the nearest plateau. There, a long table had been set. Instead of magnificent chandeliers, this setting offered a star-strewn sky, and the candles were replaced by clansmen standing all around the long table, holding flaming torches aloft. 'Twas a sight I will never forget."

"How splendid it must have been," sighed Nora. "Like a dream."

"Aye." It had been like a dream then, but now the memory was stained by the knowledge that he hadn't really belonged. Lennox opened his eyes. Although the little clearing was nearly dark, behind the clouds a luminous full moon shone. When he spoke again, his voice was husky. "The Isle of Skye is a mystical place."

"And the clan chief you mentioned, Alasdair Crotach—is he not your grandfather?"

He gave a harsh sigh. "Aye. He was."

"Was?"

Tears burned the back of Lennox's throat as he continued to look away. "'Tis not a subject I wish to discuss."

"Oh, I am sorry." Her hand touched his. "I've probed too far."

Slowly, he met her searching eyes and became aware of an emotional pull toward this lass. He felt she might even understand the conflict inside him. Before Lennox could even think about what he was saying, the words came out. "Ye should know, I'm no MacLeod. Not even a Highlander, I fear." His heart clenched, hard. "In truth, I don't know who the devil I really am."

Chapter Twelve

Nora blinked, confused. What could Lennox possibly mean? "Not a Highlander? I don't understand."

He raised one of his strong, elegant hands and rubbed his brow. "I forget how much pain this brings me until I must say the words aloud. Yet it is real."

"Whatever it is, you can say it to me," Nora said gently. Her arms went around his chest of their own accord, and Lennox leaned slightly against her as he spoke.

"This journey is actually a quest to discover who I really am. All my life, I have felt that I didn't quite belong among Clan MacLeod. I looked different, and my nature and interests were different. I thought that might be why my grandfather seemed to favor me less than my brother, Ciaran, but now I know the truth."

Nora listened in silence to the story about the day, only a few weeks ago, when Lennox had gone with Ciaran to Fiona's cottage. When he described the moment he'd accidentally knocked the silver casket from its shelf, dislodging the hidden panel on the back of the box, she held her breath.

"I have it with me."

In the shadows, Nora felt him reaching into the folds of his belted plaid. He brought out a leather pouch and opened it to reveal a small gold-framed oval portrait of a man. When Nora tilted it to catch more of the silvery moonlight, a shiver ran down her spine. The man looked exactly like Lennox. "Oh, my! It could be you but for his garb."

He gave a grim nod. "There was a lock of his hair as well that could have been cut from my head. The only difference, as ye can plainly see, is that this fellow is clearly no Highlander."

Nora's heart beat faster as she stared at the miniature. The striking green eyes looking back at her were identical to Lennox's. In fact, everything about him was identical to Lennox except his jeweled doublet, plumed cap, and the neat grooming of his hair and beard.

"What does this mean?" she asked.

In a hard, angry voice, Lennox said, "It means *this* fancy fellow is my da, not Magnus MacLeod. Since the day I found this, I've been tracking the pieces of this great secret. My mother ran away from Skye after a quarrel, nay—a *betrayal* by Da. Or, I should say, the man I believed to be my da for nine-and-twenty years. When I traveled to Falkland Palace, I learned from my Aunt Tess that Ma spent most of the time she was away at Duart Castle on the Isle of Mull. When she returned to Skye, I was already growing in her belly, but Da didn't know the truth until four years later, when he found a letter from her lover."

"Did he reveal the man's name to you?"

"Nay," Lennox replied harshly. "He swears he does not know it himself, that the letter was signed with only an initial: *R*."

Nora took it all in, more with her heart than her mind. "It must feel so confusing, to learn that the story of your family, of your life..."

"Is all a bloody *lie*," he finished. "I have never truly been part of Clan MacLeod, and my da and grandfather have known it all along, holding me at arm's length but never telling me the truth! It makes me sick when I remember the pride I once felt when I stood on the battlements of Dunvegan Castle, breathing in the air of the Minch, believing myself a Highlander through and through."

Nora wanted to say that his siblings were still blood relations, since they shared a mother, but this was not the time for such reassurances. Lennox was grieving a loss, and she could understand that well enough. It came to her that they were both adrift on the sea of life, unmoored from everything they had once depended upon. She burned with emotion, holding him tighter. His body was twice the size of hers, yet slowly she felt him yield. He turned toward her, returning her embrace, his heartbeat strong against the soft curves of her breasts.

It all happened so naturally. She reached up to touch the curve of Lennox's cheekbone then sank her fingers into his wild, golden hair. In the next instant, his mouth was on hers, hungry, insistent. Delicious. Gratefully, she opened to him, her tongue meeting his, her slim form straining against his hard-muscled body.

Nora lay back on the blanket and drew him to her, dimly aware that something painful was freeing itself inside her, banished by Lennox's mouth, hands, body. If she had been able to think, she would have remembered Sir Raymond Slater and the terrible night he had taken her innocence, and she would have been afraid. But this was Lennox, and fear was impossible. Everything about him blended strength with caring, power with kindness, and Nora knew in the deepest recesses of her soul that she was safe in his arms.

He framed her face with both hands and kissed her until a flame burned in her core, hotter by the moment. In the rising storm of their passion, clothing came away, and Nora burned to feel him touch her. Her nipples were taut, aching, and when his warm mouth closed over one of them, she gave an involuntary little cry.

Lennox touched her everywhere, and it felt so natural and right that soon she was returning his caresses. Nora loved the feeling of his fully aroused manhood against her belly, then pressing between her thighs in a way that made her open and arch upward, moaning. Lennox's fingers moved between their bodies, stroking her sensitized little bud, but Nora could not bear for him to linger. She was wet, aching, impatient. A primitive part of her wanted only him, inside her.

She reached down to touch the warm, thick length of him, and felt a new surge of arousal. For an instant, their gazes locked in the moonlight, then she raised her head to find his mouth as she brought him to her entrance. *This, this*, she thought, and then he was inside her, pushing upward. In that instant, it seemed Lennox could erase the past, her terrible mistake with Slater.

But then, he hesitated. Nora's heart seemed to stop as well, and she heard him murmur, "I do not want to hurt ye."

Of course. He thinks I am a virgin. She shook her head, eyes stinging. "I want this."

Lennox kissed her then, cradling her hips as he filled her completely, and the sensation was achingly satisfying. Nora tentatively lifted up to meet his thrusts, finding his rhythm, her soft moans mingling with the hoots of owls from the dark woods.

As they mated, the world seemed to spin away. All that remained was their mutual need and a white-hot bliss that needed no words.

Lennox held Nora in the moonlight, drawing the rough blanket more closely around them both. The scent of their mating was still in his nostrils, like an aphrodisiac. Just the thought of how it had been between them made him hard again, lusting for her. His eyes lingered on her sleeping face. The smudge of lashes on her cheek, her slightly parted lips, the faint crease in her brow…

What was she dreaming? Did she regret tonight?

He still didn't know why Nora had to flee the life she shared with her father at Stirling Castle. She'd left behind all her grand dreams of becoming the first female master weaver. What had she meant when she said William Brodie might be the one to threaten her in the future? Gently, Lennox brushed back her cloud of curls. He wanted to whisper, "What is your secret, lass? Ye can trust me with it."

But instead he closed his eyes. The journey to the Isle of Mull would not be an easy one, and he needed to sleep. The last thing he thought of before drifting off was the way Nora had gazed up at him just before he'd kissed her sweet mouth.

Minutes passed. Chaucer made a snuffling sound in his sleep. There was a soft rustling sound in the woods, followed by the quick cry of an animal that had become prey.

Nora cautiously opened her eyes. How long had she lain awake? All night, it seemed. Yet, even when she'd sensed that Lennox was awake, Nora had pretended to sleep. Thoughts raced in her mind. The familiar feeling of shame was back, but this time for the way she had behaved with Lennox. In the moment, it had all felt right, but now she saw the entire episode in a different light. Dear God, what must he think of her?

Her head hurt as if she had drunk too much wine, yet Nora knew that was not the cause of this sick feeling. How handsome his face was in repose! She wanted to nestle against his broad chest, to drink in the arousing scent of him, to touch his wondrous body again.

Yet she could not. It had been a terrible mistake. When Nora remembered the babe who grew deep inside her, she felt ill. Then a memory came: Grant telling her the story of his mother's friend, with child by a lover who disappeared. The friend found a respectable man and, once they had lain together, told him the babe was his.

Lennox and Nora had already exchanged vows. According to Highland tradition, they were wed. If she told him, at a later time, that she had conceived a child tonight, he would believe her. He would do the right thing, no matter what.

Never! Nora scolded herself, ashamed for even having so wicked a thought. She would tell him the truth. All of it, no matter how painful!

Tomorrow…

When Nora next opened her eyes, dawn was breaking. Warm, strong arms enfolded her, and she felt the hard curve of Lennox's cheekbone against her temple.

"Ah, she stirs," he murmured, a smile in his voice. "Ye made such a pretty sight, I didn't have the heart to disturb ye."

She felt her cheeks grow warm. "Is it late?"

"Nay, but Chaucer has gone off on his own to find some breakfast among the woodland grasses, and we have a long way to travel today. As much as I would like to stay right here with ye, we should rise."

Yet he gathered her closer still and she felt him sigh.

"Nora, I need to tell ye I fear I took advantage of ye last night. If ye have regrets, we will never speak of it again."

She wanted to weep. "I do not have regrets."

"I took your innocence, a precious gift. I will remain your husband if that is your wish."

Guilt rushed over her. To have him make such an offer out of obligation made her feel smaller than ever. *If he knew the truth…!* Reaching up, she touched the side of his jaw and managed to smile. "You are a good man, but what we shared last night was freely given on both sides, was it not? We are wed by chance, not choice, and I would not alter our arrangement."

She thought she saw relief in his face as he pushed up on one elbow. "Ye must be hungry. Shall we dress and see what there is for breakfast?

Watching as Lennox wrapped the length of tartan wool around his waist, fastening it with a belt as he rose to his feet, Nora resolved again to tell him everything.

Soon. Perhaps tomorrow she would find the right moment…

Chapter Thirteen

Contrary to Lennox's determined plans, he and Nora did not reach the Isle of Mull for several days. They were plagued by setbacks, including more drenching rains, impassable roads, and a lost horseshoe for Chaucer. The journey had been an ordeal Nora could never have imagined, for Scotland truly was a different world from anywhere she had lived before.

As they made camp at the end of the sixth exhausting day, Nora marveled aloud that England was far more civilized than Scotland.

"Believe it or not," she remarked under her breath, "in England it is not unusual to travel in a real coach, on real roads, suffering only minor discomfort before sleeping in a real bed in a real inn that serves—"

"Real food?" Lennox broke in, pausing in the midst of building a fire. His tone was dry. "Perhaps ye have noticed we have that here as well."

It came to Nora that she had doubtless offended him. The days filled with an unending succession of obstacles had taken a toll on both of them. "I think you must know what I mean," she replied evenly. "There is a difference between the sort of food we manage to scavenge in the woods or passing through a village and a hot venison pie or a roasted chicken, freshly cooked at an inn."

Lennox, whose even temper she had come to rely on, now gave her a sharp glance. "In case ye have forgotten the reason ye must endure this terrible ordeal, I would offer a reminder that it was your idea, not mine."

She felt like crying, but that was out of the question. Their entire situation was fraught with confusion, from the handfasting ceremony in front of her beloved father to the night they had mated under the stars. And most confusing of all was the fact that she carried the tiny baby of another man, a man she despised and had known for only one day.

Nora went to join Lennox, who crouched beside the kindling. "I beg your pardon," she said sincerely. "I must sound ungrateful, but nothing could be farther from the truth. I am tired and craving a bit of comfort, I suppose." Pausing, she swallowed. "Also, I had forgotten that, in spite of everything, you must still be loyal to Scotland."

There was turmoil in his green eyes. "In truth, I do not know where my loyalties lie any longer. I once would have sworn I was a Scot to the last drop of my blood, but now it's all a mystery." Turning away, Lennox muttered, "I'm going to find a rabbit or quail for us to eat. Tomorrow we'll reach Duart Castle on the Isle of Mull, where you'll doubtless find at least some of the comforts ye long for."

That night, Nora lay inches away from Lennox and listened to his deep, even breathing. She thought of the way it had been that first night in the woods, when he had held her, kissed her, touched her bare skin, caused her to feel sensations that were beyond anything she had ever imagined. Since then, Nora had doubtless done more to stay at arm's length than he had, for despite her resolution to tell him the truth, it seemed impossible. She felt ashamed for him to know about Slater and that she'd kept it from him. It came to her that perhaps he never needed to know. If their paths should diverge, they might part before he ever learned her true situation.

Lying there in the dark, Nora's heart ached. She could feel the warmth of his strong body, even though they weren't touching. A part of her longed desperately to be close to him, as they had been before. Perhaps if she touched his arm, he would not notice. Tentatively, she lay her fingers on the rough fabric of his tunic, feeling the iron-hard contour of his bicep, inhaling the masculine tang of his skin.

"Nora."

His whisper sent a thrill of panic through her. She began to remove her hand from his arm, but his fingers reached out to catch hers, stopping her. His hand was so warm, so strong.

"I'm sorry," she heard herself say.

"Let me hold ye, lass," came his soft reply. "'Twill do us both good."

Gratefully, Nora went into his strong arms. She could feel the power of his heartbeat against her cheek. When he put a hand up to smooth back her unruly curls, she ached for more. Memories returned of the night when Lennox's fingers and tongue had trailed fire over the most sensitive, secret places on her body, and just thinking of it spread heat to the part of her that longed for him most.

"Sleep," he whispered, as if reading her mind.

Soon, Nora heard his own breathing change, and she relaxed into his strength, closing her eyes.

The ancient MacLean stronghold of Duart Castle was built on a misty, emerald-green point of land extending into the waters of the Sound of Mull. As they sailed near in a small galley hired in the fishing village of Oban, Lennox heard Nora give a sigh of appreciation.

"It is magnificent," she pronounced. "When I was a child, Father spun tales for me at bedtime, of the Scots castles he visited while growing up, yet I could not have imagined this. It is so much more...*rugged* than what I knew in France and England."

Lennox wondered if she meant to launch into another unfavorable comparison between the Highlands and Europe, but he said nothing, concentrating instead on catching a wave to bring the boat onto a landing beach. After he'd swung down to push the galley completely out of the water, Lennox paused, his gaze drawn toward the massive bulk of Duart Castle.

He reckoned that he had been eighteen the last time he'd visited the Isle of Mull. Magnus gave him a small, fast galley to mark his birthday, and Ciaran suggested they test its sea-worthiness by sailing to Oban. Even then, Lennox reflected, he had felt an urge to wander away from the Isle of Skye.

"Do you know these people?" asked Nora, her eyes scanning the guards who lined the castle walls. "Will they welcome us?"

"I've been here before," he replied distantly. "The guards should not view the mere pair of us as a threat, and once we are inside, Hector Mór, the MacLean, will remember me. I hope."

With that, Lennox lifted Nora down from the galley and, carrying her satchel, they walked up the green slope toward Castle Duart. Damp winds swirled up from the island's moors, promising rain. As they drew closer, one of the guards waved, and Lennox raised his own hand in greeting. In the next moment, he saw that several other guards held drawn bows to their shoulders, arrows at the ready, and his heart skipped a beat.

"Hold your arrows," he shouted. "I am Lennox MacLeod, grandson of the MacLeod of Dunvegan."

So many thoughts and feelings were swirling inside Lennox as they neared the meters-thick castle walls that he nearly forgot about Nora. It seemed he must have been a different person during that long-ago visit with his brother, Ciaran, so much had changed in his world.

Even as the gates were opened by a half dozen of MacLean's fierce, burly guards, the heavens opened, and rain poured down.

"Halt," commanded a hulking, raven-haired man who appeared to be the Captain of the Guard, one hand on the hilt of his great claymore. "Ye will come no further!"

Lennox had started to reach toward his own weapon when he felt Nora grip his arm. She turned her wet face up to him, a flash of alarm in her eyes. It was the first time he'd ever seen her exhibit fear, and suddenly he realized that he might have put her in danger. There was nothing in her past to prepare her for this scene.

"Worry not," Lennox whispered to her with more assurance than he truly felt. Straightening he turned back to the guards. The others had formed a half-circle, flanking their leader, weapons at the ready.

Lennox arched a brow at the Captain of the Guard and inquired lightly, "Do ye imagine that this lass and I are a threat to this castle?"

The giant man had taken a step toward them, brows lowered, when a deep voice spoke from the arched doorway to the keep.

"Hugh, ye and your men must be at ease. I recognize the grandson of my old comrade, Alasdair Crotach." The older man who spoke was tall and dignified in his tunic and belted plaid, his long auburn hair partially covered by a tartan cap. Turning toward Lennox and Nora, he flashed a sudden smile. "I am Hector Mór, the MacLean. I remember your visit some years ago, young MacLeod." As more sheets of rain lashed them, Hector hastened to add, "Ye are welcome here, ye and your…" He paused, sweeping an appreciative look over Nora. "Ah…*lady*?"

Lennox felt a twinge of jealousy, and he instantly corrected, "Mistress Brodie is my *wife*." He sensed Nora's surprised glance, but kept his own eyes on Hector Mór.

"Ah then, is she indeed? Then ye and your lovely bride must come inside, young MacLeod, out of the weather!"

As they followed the older man back into the dark, forbidding keep, Lennox knew he should be grateful for this welcome, but suspicion tightened in his chest.

"I didn't realize we would be staying here," Nora whispered as she and Lennox were seated alone at the high table in the exceedingly damp and chilly great hall. Near her feet, a huge wolfhound gnawed at a smelly bone. "The housekeeper has taken my things to one of the bedchambers."

"I know I hoped we might speak to the MacLean and sail back to Oban by sunset, but 'twould be rude to refuse his invitation." Lennox, who had washed with real soap and combed his wild golden locks back from his face, gave her the briefest of glances. The MacLean was standing across the hall, near the doorway, speaking to a younger man, but he seemed to watch them with one eye. "Besides, it is storming outside," Lennox continued. "Chaucer will be just fine in the Oban stable, and we will have a hot meal and enjoy sleeping on clean, dry sheets." After taking a long drink from a goblet of wine, he added in a kinder tone, "Be grateful you brought your satchel, lass."

"I couldn't leave it at that stable. Everything that is precious to me is in it." She paused, willing her voice to be steady. "Every worldly thing, that is."

Lennox was watching her, and she knew he was trying to discern the secrets she held so closely. Not for the first time, Nora wished she had the freedom of a man and could have ridden away alone from Stirling, to make her own way in the world. But that was not an option for her, especially given her condition. It might not be obvious yet that she was with child, but certainly her belly would begin to swell soon enough.

"Are ye worried for your safety here?" He spoke in a low voice, all the while holding her captive with his intense green eyes. "I will not let ye come to any harm, Nora Brodie."

Before she could reply, Hector Mór strode to the table and took his seat across from them. A servant quickly appeared and poured ale into his cup while an old woman carried in a heavy, steaming pot and set it in the center of the boards.

Hector nodded to Lennox, but his attention was clearly on Nora, and soon enough he spoke to her. "Ye are not from the Highlands." It was a statement, not a question.

She nodded. "It is true, laird. I was born in Flanders. My father is a master tapestry weaver, and when I was ten, he brought me with him to the Tudor court in London. We lived there until this year, when King James V bade Father come to Stirling."

The MacLean's eyes widened in his weathered face. "And ye are educated?"

"My mother insisted upon it. She taught me to read and instilled a love of books and knowledge in me." Nora could feel Lennox's warm, strong body touching hers on the bench as he leaned closer, listening.

"Aye," Hector pronounced. "I could see it in your face and bearing. Ye are that rare beauty blessed also with a fine mind."

Nora bit back an urge to protest that beauty and intelligence were by no means mutually exclusive, but remembered that this was their host. Instead, she put on a smile. "You are kind to say so, laird."

Hector continued to watch her intently. "With so many gifts, what possessed ye to run off with young MacLeod?"

Before Nora could reply, Lennox interjected, "Have ye never heard of love?"

The older man paused in the midst of his first bite of mutton stew. "Aye, but *love* is fleeting, is it not? Ye will need something even deeper to make a lasting marriage."

"Speaking of marriage," Lennox parried, "Did I not meet your wife when I last visited Duart? Where is she today?"

His question hung in the air as more rain-soaked MacLean clansmen filed into the hall, taking their seats on the benches and helping themselves to the communal pot of stew.

"My wife, Mary," MacLean replied at length, "is in the ground."

"I'm sorry to hear that." Lennox put an arm around her waist before adding, "No doubt ye must miss her very much."

"Aye. This lass resembles my Mary," murmured Hector. "And how fares your own clan chief, young MacLeod? Alasdair Crotach must be a very great age by now."

"He is more than ninety years old," Lennox said tightly. "Irascible as ever."

"Did he send ye to Duart for a reason?" The older man used an oatcake to sop up some gravy then stuffed it into his mouth and chewed.

"In truth, I came for a reason of my own." He glanced around at the countless MacLean clansmen who were eating around them. "Perhaps we might discuss it when the meal is ended."

"None of these men have any interest in your affairs," Hector assured him. "And I cannot linger to converse after supper. There are preparations to be made for the return of my other guests, the Earl and Countess of Fairhaven, on the morrow. They were here at Duart recently with Ellen, the dowager countess, before sailing around Mull to the village of Torbermory."

"Have you known the earl and countess very long?" asked Nora.

"The earl's mother, Ellen MacLean, is my cousin, and I have known her all my life. Now that she is widowed, she longed to return to Mull to visit her kin. While she reunites with them, the new earl and his bride, Cicely, will return here." He paused to finish a second cup of wine. "I suggest you tell me now what you have come to say, young MacLeod."

Nora tried to eat, but she felt slightly nauseous and realized it must be because of the baby. She tried again to turn her thoughts away from the terrible problem she had, telling herself that somehow she would find a way forward, one step at a time.

Next to her, Lennox was making his case to Hector Mór, explaining the story of his mother's visit to Duart Castle nearly three decades earlier. Nora turned slightly to watch him. Even in the dim, smoky hall, she found him captivating. His tawny-golden hair and bronzed skin seemed to shimmer slightly, and his body was taut with emotion.

After explaining the circumstances of his mother's visit to Duart Castle, he asked, "Do ye have a memory of that visit?"

The MacLean scratched his head. "I couldn't have been more than a dozen years old. Too young to have an interest in this episode you recount," he said with a note of finality. "Mull is a favorite stopping point for travelers who are sailing to and from England, so we always had more visitors than I could count."

"I believe she was here most of the summer," Lennox pressed. "With her nurse, Isbeil, and my wee, black-haired brother, Ciaran, who would have been barely able to walk."

Hector stared into the distance. "Aye, I do have a faint memory of your ma and her bairn. She had raven hair? A rare beauty."

Nora could feel the tightly-leashed power in Lennox's body as he nodded, leaning forward. She expected him to continue the tale, explaining all of it to the other man, but instead he skipped over the painful parts. Bringing out the leather pouch from his belt, Lennox opened it and withdrew the painted miniature.

"Do ye know this man? He was here as well, I believe."

As the other clansmen continued to laugh, drink, and eat their stew, time seemed to stop in the center of the table as Hector Mór plucked the miniature from Lennox's golden-brown fingers.

He stared at it, squinting. "My eyesight is not the best any longer."

"This matter is more important than ye can imagine," urged Lennox. "Was he a friend of your da?"

"It could be. He has the look of a titled Englishman," mused Hector, turning the oval in search of better light. He sighed and shook his head. "I was but a boy. Noblemen and Highland chiefs gathered here often. We were a stopping place on every sea route, it seemed. After a time, they all look the same."

Tears pricked Nora's eyes as she felt Lennox's deep frustration. Where could he turn next if this long journey became yet another blind alley?

"There must be someone here who remembers," he said. "An older clansman? An aging servant?"

"Ye must stay the night." Hector rubbed his bearded jaw. "I

will sleep on it. Perhaps something will come to me. In any case, ye cannot return to Oban in this storm."

"We wouldn't want to impose on your hospitality," said Nora.

He laughed and shook his head at her. "Lass, ye are now in the Highlands. My Mary liked to say we have raised the practice of hospitality to an art form!"

Lennox caught her hand, squeezing it. "We are grateful for your generosity," he said.

"It is fortunate that ye two are wed, for there is but one chamber. The only other one fit for guests is already prepared for Robin and Cicely." There was a twinkle in his eye, as if he somehow guessed the truth of their arrangement.

"Aye," Lennox said firmly. "We are indeed wed."

Chapter Fourteen

When the time came for them to retire for the night, Hector Mór led the way up an exceptionally precarious circular staircase. His candle flame wavered eerily in the gloom, and once Nora lost her footing on a broken stone step. She cried out in surprise, but Lennox caught her and held her close until she regained her balance.

When they reached the top step and emerged into a stone corridor, Hector stopped in front of a heavy door. Pushing it open, he bent his head to enter, gesturing for them to follow. Candles were newly lit, and a peat fire burned low in the brazier, sending its welcome glow into the drafty bedchamber.

"If ye should need anything at all, just call for me." Pointing across the corridor, Hector added, "My own chamber is there, just steps away."

"You have been very kind," Nora told him.

"Aye," Lennox interjected. Stepping behind her, he patted her hip. "And now we must bid ye goodnight."

He felt a strong urge to demonstrate to the older man that the beautiful Nora belonged to him, but the reasons for this were a mystery to Lennox. He'd always had his pick of lasses, and though he was a kind and thoughtful lover, he'd been careful not to become entangled, usually departing on a journey when a moment of truth was at hand. Certainly none of them had kept his heart knotted up like Nora Brodie.

No sooner had the door closed behind their host than Nora turned to face Lennox. "What ails you?"

Although he wished he knew the answer to that question himself, he feigned surprise. “What do ye mean?”

“You are behaving like an overbearing…” Her voice trailed off, and she glanced away.

“Husband?” he supplied coolly. “I thought that the arrangement was one ye begged me to undertake.”

“But we both know it isn’t real.”

“Is it not? We were bound in a ceremony that seemed to satisfy even your own da.” They were standing so close together Lennox could smell meadow grass and the sea breeze in Nora’s hair. Her breasts were rising and falling as if she’d run up the steps, and he realized it was because of his effect on her.

“But it’s not like that!” Color rose in her cheeks, heightened by the firelight.

“Most would say that what we did under the stars a few nights ago seals this as a true marriage,” Lennox countered.

Nora did not take the bait. She stepped back, allowing the chilly air to waft between them. “Do not pretend to misunderstand me, sir. You act the devoted husband in front of our host, yet you know full well that we are not bound to one another in that way.”

For reasons he didn’t understand, her words pricked him. “Do not tell me ye didn’t see the gleam in Hector’s eyes! He would want ye for himself if I did not assert my claim.” Even as he spoke, Lennox realized how absurd he sounded.

“Your *claim*?” Nora echoed hotly, turning away to open the satchel Lennox had placed on a bench near the fire. “I see it all quite differently. It’s obvious that he is lonely, poor man, missing his dead wife. He doubtless longs for someone else to share his life in this godforsaken place.”

Lennox managed to draw a long breath, forcing his pulse to slow. “I only meant to protect ye, lass.”

Nora was taking slender, polished pieces of wood out of the satchel, setting them on the carved lid of the chest. “You have no understanding of the person I am.” She glanced back at him for a moment, the spill of her hair like molten copper, her expression proud and splendid. "Tonight, I do not need or want your *protection*. In fact, if I could have left Stirling alone, I would have. It is galling to me that I must depend upon a man for assistance during this difficult time."

Shocked, he could only stare at her. "That is not what ye said to me at Stirling Castle."

"Perhaps not, because I was desperate, but it is the way I truly feel. I have aspirations of my own, Lennox MacLeod, and the notion of romance only gets in the way of making them come true."

Of course, Lennox understood exactly what she meant about matters of the heart, for he felt the same. Why then did he feel a sting of rejection from Nora, a sting that recalled the black moments when he'd felt spurned by his own clan? As his heart squeezed, Lennox reminded himself that the true purpose of this quest was to discover where he truly belonged. Until that was revealed, was it not better to remain alone?

Silence calmed the air as Nora brought out two more carved, slender sticks, the tops wound with brightly colored threads. She arranged the pieces of wood on the carved chest, gradually relaxing.

Lennox was grateful for an opportunity to change the subject. "Now I know why your satchel was so heavy," he said wryly. "What do ye have there?"

She gave him a luminous smile. "They are a few of my bobbins, wound with silken threads I dyed myself. I use them at the loom." As she spoke, she reached inside the satchel for a thick piece of cloth, rolled up like a scroll. "Even though I cannot weave during our journey, I had to bring these things with me, or I wouldn't feel like…*myself*."

"I can see it brings ye happiness just to say it."

"You cannot imagine." Tears came to her eyes.

He could imagine, of course, because he felt that way about his own sketching tools. Most of them were in his saddlebag, in the Oban stable with Chaucer, but Lennox never went anywhere without a few of his charcoal pencils, just in case he might need them, as he had that day at Falkland Palace when he came upon Queen Mary holding her baby prince.

Nora unfurled the canvas to proudly display the small woven image of a gray rabbit sitting in front of a boxwood bush. "This is the very first tapestry I ever created," she said proudly. "When I was perhaps four years old, I begged Father to teach me to weave, and he did. He held me to a high standard yet praised and encouraged me every step of the way."

"No doubt ye miss him," Lennox said softly.

She nodded, eyes agleam. "Even though he was a gifted master weaver, working in the studio of the great Pieter van Aelst, Father found the time to make the pattern for this tapestry. The subject was my pet rabbit, Hugo. Do you see how the little rogue seems to flirt with us, one ear up and one ear down?" A smile lit her face. "I have always kept this with me. Not only because of the memories, but also because it clearly shows my progress, as my skills developed. Do you see? The weaving is much neater and tighter at the top than it is at the bottom, when I was first beginning."

Lennox knew an urge to put his arms around her. Compassion for others was an intrinsic part of him, but this was something deeper. He longed to hold her against him and kiss the soft tendrils that brushed her brow, yet he could sense her need for space. "It sounds as if ye found your calling at a very young age."

Smiling, Nora touched the rabbit's crooked ear. "It's as much a part of me as breathing."

"And your ma? How did she feel about the great gift that you and your da shared?" He watched her, remembering that her mother had stayed behind in Brussels when William Brodie and his ten-year-old daughter traveled to England.

"Mama could not understand. Or perhaps she *did* understand, and that's why she resisted so strongly." Nora's lovely smile turned sad. "When I first began to weave this little tapestry, Mama praised me every day. She was happy, until she began to realize that each stitch bound me closer to Father. As my passion for weaving grew, I went deeper into his world, where she could not follow."

Lennox felt a chill at her words. "And that is exactly what happened, it seems. Why didn't she travel to England with you and your da?"

"Her family and friends were all in Flanders. As Father became more and more absorbed in the world of tapestry weaving, Mama retreated to her own circle." Her eyes shone as she paused to sigh. "She is a strong woman, but I do not think she imagined she might lose us both."

"Do ye miss her?"

"I used to, but I had to remember that it was impossible for me to stay behind in Flanders, unable to weave. Father has always reminded me that it was my mother's choice not to come with us." Nora gave a great sigh and shook her head as if putting those thoughts from her mind. She picked up one of the bobbins, stroking the glossy wood. "It's calming for me to hold these things, but I won't feel complete until I have a loom and can truly weave again."

"When we left Stirling," Lennox murmured, feeling a twinge in his chest, "did ye have a notion of where ye might go to find that loom?" He still didn't know why she had begged him to take her away or what she meant to do in the future since she claimed not to want a marriage with him.

Nora looked up, her blue eyes filled with emotions he couldn't read. "London, perhaps? It's familiar to me, since we lived there before Father was invited to be master weaver at Stirling. King Henry VIII is intent on acquiring a collection of tapestries to equal those of the great rulers of Europe. If a permanent workroom could be established within the royal court, I believe my dream would be within reach."

It came to Lennox that fate seemed destined to separate them. In spite of everything, his chest felt tight. Raking a hand through his hair, he said, "I am very tired. Let us go to bed, lass. It is your chance to enjoy the comforts of the bed ye have been longing for."

Weak, gray light filtered through the bedchamber's single arrow-slit window. As Nora came slowly awake, she remembered that she and Lennox were sharing a real bed, in the shelter of a castle rather than a wet grove of trees.

If only things could be different. Lying there in her simple linen smock, a stirring memory returned of a moment during the night. She had been awake, turned on her side away from him, when she had felt him roll toward her and shape his strong hand to the curve of her hip. Heat and longing had blossomed under his touch, sending currents of need to every intimate part of her. Holding her breath in the darkness, Nora had remembered the intensely blissful sensation of his mouth on her nipple, and it came to her that perhaps he would make love to her again. She imagined him slipping his hand under her smock, touching her, and the very thought made her wet. If it could happen in the middle of the night, without a word spoken, perhaps they could pretend later nothing had happened…

But even as Nora had waited, Lennox had moved away from her. He was doubtless sleeping, dreaming perhaps of someone else.

"Lennox?" she whispered now. When he made no reply, she rolled over and found that she was alone. The only signs that he had been there were the rumpled covers and the crease in his pillow. Disappointment pricked her, but it was no surprise. Nora was growing accustomed to conflicting feelings when it came to Lennox MacLeod, and she knew he must think her slightly mad. One moment she was giving her body to him in the moonlight, and the next she was insisting on pursuing her dreams alone. Again, she thought of telling him the truth of her situation. She owed him that much, didn't she? And yet the thought of saying the words out loud terrified her.

With a sigh, Nora rose. Pouring water from a pottery jug into a basin, she washed as best she could. The morning air was chilly and damp, and she was eager to dry off and dress. The few garments in her satchel were travel-stained, but perhaps the castle housekeeper, Tilly, would let her do washing today.

After donning a simple long-sleeved gown of cornflower-blue wool, Nora stood looking outside as she tried with limited success to tame her mass of curls under a simple headdress. The view through the deep, narrow window was limited to a rocky green outcropping above the turbulent sea, yet she found it stunning. A wild, misty rain swirled once again, and the Sound of Mull was wave-tossed. Far away, Nora imagined she could see a flash of white sail. Thank heaven she and Lennox had not dared to cross from Oban in such perilous weather!

She was eager to go downstairs and discover what memories, if any, had come to Hector Mór during the night. Would he have an idea about the identity of the man in the miniature? Perhaps they soon would know where they would travel next. It had been easy enough to pretend calm last night, in the face of Lennox's questions about her own plans for the future, but the truth was that Nora had no idea what lay ahead for her…and her baby.

Chapter Fifteen

When Nora reached the foot of the stairs and emerged into the hall, she was met by a gust of cold wind and saw that the heavy doors were open to the courtyard. The big room had been scrubbed, fresh rushes were strewn on the stone floor, and Hector's aging wolfhound, Fergus, lay snoring near the fire. As she watched, servants, clad in the sort of fine livery she hadn't seen since leaving London, hurried in with bundles, satchels, and two small trunks.

Looking through the doorway, Nora glimpsed Hector Mór standing outside in the cobbled courtyard, wet with rain, surrounded by a mixture of rough Highlanders and more of the visiting servants clad in forest-green livery. The English couple Hector had been expecting must have arrived! What should she do? Go out to join them?

Before she could decide, a hand fit itself to the side of her waist, and she whirled around to find Lennox gazing down at her. He looked especially splendid, a blaze of gold in the dank, gray morning. "Hello, wife," he murmured with faint irony. "I believe the MacLean's noble guests have returned from Tobermory."

Remembering the moments when he had touched her in the middle of the night, Nora blushed. She was about to ask where he had been when a striking female appeared in the doorway.

"At last we have arrived!" exclaimed the young woman, drawing back the hood on her scarlet cloak. "Does it never stop raining in Scotland?"

The Countess of Fairhaven was not only beautiful, Nora observed, but also possessed a captivating aura that drew all eyes to her. In her wake trailed a tall, slender man with a long face. He was accompanied by a similarly tall, thin dog that Nora recognized as a greyhound.

Tilly and her housekeeping staff had quickly assembled, and now they curtseyed awkwardly.

"Welcome back, my lady!" exclaimed Tilly as she gestured for one of the girls to take the countess's sodden cloak. "Your chamber is ready. Would ye care for something hot to eat?"

"Thank you. How kind," the woman replied, smiling. "Nothing at this time. I'm going to change these garments for dry clothing and rest for a bit." Turning then, her gaze fell on Nora and Lennox. "It's quite difficult to believe the season is truly *summer*."

Before Nora could reply, Hector Mór rushed up to them, dripping with rain. No sooner had he made formal introductions than the countess smiled warmly and extended a hand to Nora.

"You must call me Cicely. How lovely to meet someone near my own age!" She turned her attention to Lennox, sable-brown eyes agleam with interest. "And you, sir, are the most attractive Highlander I have seen during our endless journey through the wilds of Scotland!"

The Earl of Fairhaven, Cicely's husband, appeared next to her, the look-alike greyhound at his side. "Fondling, do curb your tongue. You will give this fellow the wrong idea about your intentions," he scolded.

"Don't be absurd, Robin." Cicely merely laughed in his direction.

"Pay no attention to my lovely wife," said the earl. "My mother was born here in Tobermory, and we brought her north for a visit. In a fortnight's time, we shall fetch her and return to London."

"Not a moment too soon," Cicely parried, a slight edge to her teasing tone.

Nora watched her, fascinated. Petite and slender, Cicely was blessed with an expressive, heart-shaped face. Her dark eyes sparkled with wit, and no matter who was speaking, she remained the center of attention. Now, gesturing for her husband to follow, Cicely turned toward the staircase in a swirl of parrot-green skirts.

When the English visitors had disappeared from view, Lennox gave an ironic laugh. "That was *interesting*."

"The countess likes you, I think," murmured Nora.

Just then, Hector Mór, who had turned away to speak to Tilly, rejoined the conversation. "Ye must encourage a friendship with the Fairhavens. Her ladyship in particular may be helpful in your search for the man in the miniature. As a favorite of King Hal, she is invited to most functions of the royal court, and as ye might imagine, she listens to gossip. Furthermore, Cicely's brother is Andrew Weston, the new Duke of Aylesbury, one of the most sought-after men in England."

"Why is he so powerful?" asked Lennox.

The MacLean shrugged. "I have heard that he is not only splendid to behold but also a great artist in his own right. Henry VIII desires his friendship, but the duke comes round the court only when it suits him. He's more interested in his wife, a beautiful Frenchwoman, and their children." He paused, sharpening his gaze. "If His Grace deigns to help you, young MacLeod, ye may well find that person ye seek."

As soon as they were alone, Lennox took Nora's hand and led her out of the hall. She looked so beautiful, her burnished curls in contrast to the blue of her gown. Was it his imagination, or had the curves of her breasts and hips become even more alluring in recent days?

"I want to show ye something," he said conspiratorially.

"What is it?" Nora asked. For a moment she softened and

he had to resist the urge to press her against the wall of the passageway and cover her mouth with his.

"A surprise," he managed to reply. "Come with me."

"You are very mysterious!"

As they walked together out of the newer tower house and into a much older, timber-framed structure, Lennox was keenly aware of the charged atmosphere between them. What was the reason she was so determined to hold him at arm's length? A primitive male part of him was challenged to overcome her reservations, to hear her admit that she wanted—*needed*—him.

Yet, what then? He had no answer, for there were too many questions in his own life.

They had come to a low, splintered door in the wall, and Lennox stopped before it, savoring the moment. Nora looked up at him, brows raised in a question.

"How pleased you look with yourself!" she said with a soft laugh. "How could anything wonderful be on the other side of this broken door, at the end of a dark, damp passageway?"

"Close your eyes." Before she could react, he reached up to cover her eyes with one of his big hands. The contact between them brought with it a sudden shock of arousal, and he knew she felt it as much as he did. For an instant, Lennox imagined this as part of their love play, and he grew hard, aching for her.

"Lennox MacLeod," she warned, breathing against his palm.

He bit his lip, forcing himself to think of the surprise, and reached out with his free hand to lift the door latch.

"Look at this, lass."

Nora opened her eyes and gasped aloud. Tears filled her eyes. How could it be?

"A *loom*!" she heard herself exclaim. "How did you do it?"

The cramped room had only one high window, spanning the width of the far wall. A narrow beam of light streamed in, just enough to illuminate the old loom. It was nothing compared to those she'd stood before in the past, weaving with her father, but a visual appraisal confirmed it was a working low-warp loom.

At that moment, nothing could have thrilled her more.

"How—" Her throat was thick as she turned to Lennox, wanting to embrace him. "How in the world did you do this?"

His gentle, understanding smile went straight to her heart. "I only discovered it for ye. I couldn't sleep last night, and when I rose, I saw that Hector was also roaming about. As we talked, I mentioned ye were a weaver at the royal court, and he showed me this loom that belonged to his wife. It was her pride and joy, he said." Lennox paused, as if trying to decide whether to say more. "When I asked, he said ye might use it while we are here, but I confess I did not tell him this is your true passion. I feared he might try to convince ye to stay here with him and spend your days weaving tapestries for Duart Castle."

She saw that he was only half in jest. "I do not believe Hector Mór has designs on me, but even if he did, it's not possible for him to beguile me."

"It's only that…" He looked away, and she saw a muscle move in his jaw. "I know ye are meant for better things."

"I am," she agreed.

Their eyes met for a long, charged moment before Lennox swallowed. "Tell me, then: What do ye think of the loom? Will it do?"

Nora walked around it, lightly running her hands over the wooden frame, the rollers, the ratchet wheel, the half-filled bobbins, every part that she knew as well as her own body. It was much smaller than the magnificent looms she'd grown used to, but it would certainly do. She ached to create something new, right away.

"I could weave here," she said, "but I do not have a cartoon to use as a pattern."

"Do ye remember me saying I have been awake since the middle of the night?"

"I do." Their eyes met, and Nora remembered the interlude when he'd curved his hand over her hip and she had longed for him to lift her smock and continue touching her. Perhaps he had wanted it too—so much that he'd had to leave the bed.

Lennox went to a small chest that stood against one wall, opened it, and withdrew a large, loosely-rolled paper, probably twice the width of her childhood rabbit tapestry. "After Hector showed me the loom, I spent the next hours making this. I am not certain I did it right, but I remembered the few things your da taught me when I questioned him at Stirling."

Nora hurried to his side, bursting with excitement. Was it really possible he had made a cartoon for her? "Oh, please, show me!"

"I had only my charcoals," Lennox cautioned.

She put her hands on his, urging him to open the scroll. There was a sort of heat in the air between them and she thought she could hear the beating of his heart. "Please," she whispered. "I promise you I will love it."

Slowly, he unfurled the paper on the lid of the chest. "I didn't have the proper time to ponder a subject."

Nora gazed at his careful sketch, delighted. The bottom half of Lennox's cartoon was a multi-layered choppy sea. In the center was a Highland galley, like the one she and Lennox had sailed from Oban to the Isle of Mull. Both bow and stern curved up to slice through the wind, in the manner of a Viking ship, and a small sail rose up in the sky. There were two figures in the galley, and in the distance a great stone castle waited on a cliff.

Nora's heart swelled. "Oh, Lennox! It's wonderful. This is us, isn't it? And that castle is Duart!"

"Us?" Surprise crossed his handsome face for a moment, and his blond brows lifted. Lennox looked down at the galley he'd drawn, drew a thoughtful breath, and then gave her a smile that made her heart turn over. "Aye, lass. Of course it's us."

Nora felt consumed by emotions she couldn't name. How splendid he was! How thoughtful and caring and gifted, to have risen in the middle of the night and set to work on such an amazing gift. A gift to answer one of the deepest needs of her soul.

Was it also his way of communicating to her the deeper, wordless connection between them?

Before she could think or stop herself, Nora rose up on her toes and fairly threw her arms around his wide shoulders, pressing herself against him, urging his head down for her kiss. Lennox groaned as he took her mouth, and she felt as if she couldn't get close enough. He held her against him with one arm, while his other hand rose to cup the side of her jaw, angling her mouth so that he might taste even more of her. She pressed closer, kissing him back, aching with hunger.

"Christ, Nora," he rasped, lifting his head for an instant. "I—"

She waited, watching him, panting softly, dizzy.

Lennox squeezed his eyes closed and held her against his chest. She could hear his heart racing, feel him slowly shake his head. "Sometimes, when we are together, I feel a bit mad."

"I know," she whispered. "I feel it, too."

Chapter Sixteen

With an effort, Lennox forced down his ardor and put her from him. "Let me help you with the loom."

She swallowed, nodding. They spent the next hour testing the working parts of the loom as Nora chose the colors and threads she would use to weave the tapestry of the galley on the sea.

"I'm so pleased that Mary MacLean kept more than one blue bobbin. I will make each layer of the waves a different shade of blue," Nora enthused. "It will be beautiful."

"Do I remember correctly that ye will trace the pattern from the cartoon onto the threads? I have a charcoal pencil ye may use."

"Thank you."

Her smile made him want to take her in his arms again, but instead he reached out with one of his charcoals and their fingers brushed, striking sparks. "I am at your service, lass." He was smiling too yet as their gazes caught and held, another deep shiver of arousal ran down his spine and spread through his loins.

Soon, Nora was ready to begin working on her own. Lennox made an excuse about needing to speak to Hector, but in the doorway he couldn't resist turning back to watch her.

Her head of shining curls was bent over the loom as she gracefully arranged the vertical threads she called the *warp*. Every ounce of her was focused on the task at hand, and he felt a vibrant sense of creativity in the air. And something more… It was happiness, Lennox realized with a pang, and he had helped to cause it.

"This is us, isn't it?"

His mind returned again to the moment when she had spoken those words while pointing to his drawing. Each time he thought of it, a new, powerful emotion flowed through him like a river that had broken its banks.

The truth was, when Lennox had made the pattern that morning, he'd been thinking of his mural in Ciaran and Violette's Spirit Tower on Skye: a depiction of a galley sailing away from the MacLeod family home of Duntulm Castle, after it had been horribly conquered and stolen by warriors from a rival clan. Lennox, too, had sailed around the Western Isles since he was a wee bairn. The islands themselves were so rocky and wild, the best way to travel was always by sea.

But Nora, who had spent her life in more civilized lands, had no way of knowing or understanding that.

The strange new sensation swelled again in Lennox's chest as he watched her hold a bobbin of blue thread up to the light. If it pleased her to think the tapestry she was weaving depicted the two of them, sailing from Oban to Duart, he would gladly agree.

When Lennox emerged into the great hall, he found it empty except for Hector's elderly wolfhound, Fergus, who could barely rise from his place by the fire. Hector still gave the old dog an occasional bone, but otherwise he seemed to be largely ignored by the busy inhabitants of the castle.

"Hello, old fellow." Lennox went over to the great hearth and crouched down beside the wolfhound. "Do ye miss the hunt?"

Fergus slowly lifted his head and gazed at him with foggy eyes.

"It can't be easy to feel that ye no longer have value to your clan." Lennox stroked the dog's ears. Unbidden, the memory of Magnus's wolfhound, Dougal, came to him. Many times, it had been Lennox who remembered to feed the great beast, when Da was occupied with other matters.

Since leaving Skye, Lennox had done his best to put them all out of his mind, to remember the betrayals and secrets, but now the memories began to simmer inside him, bittersweet. Years spent waking up to a new day in Duntulm Castle, perched on a cliff high above the sea. How many sparkling mornings had he stood with Magnus and Ciaran in the courtyard, practicing with his claymore or learning to hawk? It was a stunningly beautiful and thrilling place to grow up, and in spite of Lennox's growing sense that he didn't belong, he'd loved his family and his clan.

His chest tightened at the cascade of memories and emotions. If only it were possible to pack the past away in a chest, lock it securely, and throw the key into the sea.

Fergus dropped his head onto Lennox's hard thigh and heaved a sigh. His breath smelled like dead rats, but the poor old hound needed to know someone still cared. Lennox gently stroked the pad of his thumb back and forth over the dog's brow, eliciting another sigh.

"You're a good lad," he murmured, and was rewarded with another deep sigh.

"Ah, I love a man who is kind to animals," a female voice proclaimed from the doorway.

Lennox looked up to see Cicely, Lady Fairhaven, standing there with her husband and their greyhound. Fergus seemed to understand the situation, for the hound shifted his head back to rest on his own two paws, allowing Lennox to rise.

The earl looked around the cavernous hall, sniffing hopefully. "We are ravenous. Is that venison I smell?"

"Aye. I think so." Lennox looked at the countess. "My lady—"

"Please, do call me Cicely." She gave him a charming smile.

"Cicely, can ye spare a few minutes of your time before the MacLean and his clansmen return? I would speak to ye about a matter of importance." When young Fairhaven shot him a glance, Lennox added, "Both of ye, of course."

"I would be pleased to help you," Cicely replied. "Do you seek advice? I'm exceptionally good at that."

She was already taking a chair near the hearth, where something savory bubbled in a hanging pot. Fergus barely stirred as the two men joined her.

"Where is your lovely wife?" Cicely inquired of Lennox, turning her face to bask in the fire's warmth.

After a moment, Lennox realized she was referring to Nora. "My bride is a weaver, and Hector Mór has kindly offered his wife's loom for Nora to use during our stay. She is very gifted." He heard the pride in his own voice. "I left her with the loom, choosing the best shades of blue to use for her tapestry."

Tilly and a few of the servants had begun to appear in the hall, laying the boards for the midday meal, and Lord Fairhaven watched them anxiously.

"Will there be venison?" he queried.

One of the girls gave him a cheerful nod. "Aye, sir!"

Realizing that his time was short, Lennox reached for the leather pouch at his belt and brought out the miniature. He hadn't told Hector the real reason he sought the man in the doublet, and he didn't plan to divulge anything so personal to these English nobles, either.

"I have a question." Lennox showed the miniature first to Lord Fairhaven then handed it to Cicely to study. "Do either of ye recognize this man?"

She scrutinized the painting, brows lifting, and his heart jumped with hope. "How long ago was this miniature made?"

"Nearly three decades ago."

"Robin and I had not been born then," came Cicely's reply. She shook her head. "How could I possibly recognize this man? Quite honestly, he resembles my own brother, Andrew, who was but a lad then." She studied the miniature again for a long moment, then gazed at Lennox over the top of the gold, oval frame. "Why exactly do you seek this gentleman?"

He managed an offhand shrug of one shoulder. "It is a family matter." Seeing that she would not be satisfied by this, he added, "The man may be a relative."

"Ah." Cicely cocked her head. "Are you truly serious about finding him?"

"Aye. It is the reason we have traveled to Duart Castle," Lennox replied, realizing that if these English aristocrats could help him, he should be more forthcoming. "I suppose it would be true to say I am on a quest."

She threw up her hands. "There is nothing for it, then. I feel certain my brother, the Duke of Aylesbury, can help you. You must come to London with us, and I shall arrange a meeting between you."

Even as Lennox considered this, his heartbeat accelerated. Was it possible that this new turn in the road might take him to his real father? "It would mean a long journey..."

"It would. Did you have other plans?" Cicely inquired sweetly.

The lass was shrewd. "Nay, although my horse waits for me in Oban." He paused, feeling a twinge at the memory of the expression on Chaucer's face when he'd left him behind with Tom, the stableboy. "I will find someone here who will return him to Stirling Castle, with a message for my family."

"It sounds as if you've made up your mind," Cicely said approvingly. "I feel certain your quest will bear fruit in London."

"London?" echoed a familiar voice. Lennox turned to see Nora walking toward them.

He rose to greet her, surprisingly cheered by her presence. "Come and sit down. Are ye hungry?"

"I am!" Her cheeks flushed becomingly. "Weaving is harder work than you know."

"We were just discussing the miniature your husband has shown us," Cicely said, watching her. "You know it, of course."

She won more of his regard by not giving anything away. "Of course."

"The two of you must come to London. We've decided," Cicely continued. "Haven't we, Robin?"

Their salivating greyhound was inching his way across the flags, clearly hoping to steal the dozing wolfhound's half-gnawed bone. Lennox couldn't suppress a grin when Fergus suddenly emitted a low warning growl.

"God's eyes, is that beast dangerous?" Fairhaven exclaimed.

"Robin, do pay attention to our conversation." Cicely gave him an impatient look. "Don't you agree that Lennox and Nora must come to London with us? I am hopeful that Andrew, who is so much older than we are, will recognize this fellow in the miniature. Since he is a painter himself, he may even know the artist."

As they all continued to talk, making plans, Lennox stole a glance at Nora's pensive profile. Was she thinking about her own future in London, the one she dreamed of creating as a master weaver? Something caused him to reach for her slim hand, clasping it in his own.

"Are ye pleased by this plan, wife?" he whispered, a hint of irony in his tone.

She lifted her chin and sent him an enigmatic smile. "It seems an answer to both our prayers."

Nora watched everyone else eat heartily while she poked around with her eating knife, feeling slightly sick. This time, however, she knew she couldn't blame her condition.

They were going to London. The identity of the man in the miniature would be revealed at last, and everything in their world was about to change. She felt it in her bones.

Yet wasn't this what she had wanted, to go to London and pursue her ambition to become the first female master weaver at the court of Henry VIII? And as she watched Lennox chat with Hector, Nora told herself that she must also wish for a wonderful outcome for Lennox. In London, he would discover the answers to all his questions, solutions to his problems. Quite possibly, he would find his rightful place in the world.

"What has put that crease between your brows?" Lennox asked with a bemused smile. "Is there a problem with our tapestry?"

Nora let herself look into his eyes, feeling a conflicting surge of emotions as she took in his use of the word *our*. She ought to be putting distance between this man and her vulnerable heart, but it felt impossible.

"The tapestry will take many hours to complete, even days, but it is begun," she murmured.

"I should have a private viewing, I think," he teased. "Later tonight."

His eyes touched her lips, and she felt an answering twinge between her legs.

"Now then, ye two lovebirds," scolded Hector with a grin. "Ye are surrounded by other guests—"

Just then, a loud pounding came at the double doors. "Help, help!" shouted a man's voice. "Ye must come. There's been a terrible shipwreck!"

The great hall became a scene of chaos as the messenger was admitted and Hector Mór heard his plea for strong men to aid in the search for survivors of the shipwreck.

"Some of us were hawking over on the west coast of the island, far from any croft or shepherd. The storm was rising and we sought shelter in a grove of trees when an awful cracking sound reached our ears. 'Twas the destruction of a great galleon, pushed by the wind into a narrow cleft in the rocks." The man paused, panting, overcome by emotion. "'Twas being crushed like a walnut. Men were screaming, but the cliffs were too high for any to reach safety. When we came to the edge and looked, we saw only the waves, sweeping them overboard!"

Hector Mór would hear no more of the man's story. He ordered whisky and a bowl of venison stew for the distraught messenger, while the rest of them hurriedly made preparations to leave on a rescue mission. It was no surprise to Nora when Lennox insisted on joining the MacLean warriors and clansmen, and even Lord Fairhaven gallantly proclaimed that he would go as well.

When Nora and Lennox were upstairs in the bedchamber, and he was assembling his possessions and weapons, he paused to look at her.

"Will ye worry for my safety, lass?"

His tone was light, and his teeth flashed in a smile, but when Nora came near, she thought she saw a sign of something deeper in his eyes. "Of course I will worry," she said sincerely.

Lennox wavered for only a moment before gathering her into his arms. "That means more than I'd like to admit," he whispered.

She could feel the power of him, warm and vital, as he bent to kiss her. Nora's own response surprised her, for tears sprang to her eyes as his mouth moved over hers, urging her lips to part so he could taste her. Her breasts tingled, her hips arched closer to him, and then he was lifting his head and setting her away from him.

"I must—" he began raggedly.

"I know," Nora interjected quickly, her cheeks warm. "You must go." She could hear the clatter of men, swords, and horses in the courtyard below. Aching to cling to Lennox, Nora instead stepped back, watching as he drew on doeskin gloves and a tartan wool cap. It felt so odd, knowing they were legally wed yet uncertain if she could show him she cared about his welfare in the way a true wife would.

He turned and left the room, and Nora hurried after him. A torch burned at the top of the twisting stone staircase. As he started down, she touched his shoulder, half-expecting that

Lennox would continue on. Yet, he turned to look back at her, and Nora stopped breathing.

"I beg you, have a care," she managed at last.

"Ye have my word, wife." He caught her hand and brought it to his lips, and that simple gesture made her heart ache with longing. "Fear not. No doubt I'll be back before ye notice my absence."

Chapter Seventeen

Days passed without word of the men.

Nora spent her days in the small workroom with Mary MacLean's loom, hoping the hours would pass more quickly if she lost herself in weaving. All her life, it had been her escape from cares and pain, helping her to forget when Father took her to England and it seemed she might never see her mother again. Distracting her from the temptations at the Tudor court, when young men had tried to pay her court. Offering a refuge when the world seemed fraught with uncertainty and even danger.

It should have been utter joy to bring Lennox's pattern to life, spending endless hours in the solitary pursuit of creative perfection. But her mind kept wandering to Lennox, imagining him in some sort of danger. Or perhaps the men had stopped to visit another castle, enjoying themselves. What if another lass had turned his head? After all, as he had reminded Nora on the day they left Stirling, their handfasting could easily be undone with a few words.

Perhaps that would be for the best, Nora thought, her heart twisting. She carried another man's baby, and soon it would be obvious to the world.

Each afternoon, Nora climbed the many steps to emerge onto the flat roof of the keep. Standing there inside the wall-walk, she could look over the low, crenellated wall and see miles in every direction. Her immediate view was out over the cliffs and the Sound of Mull, but soon she would turn to gaze across the misty green moors. The only sign of life she ever spied was a cow or hawk or rabbit.

Raindrops had begun to fall on the afternoon when Nora made her way back down the winding stone steps then back through the corridors to her workroom. To her surprise, she found Lady Fairhaven waiting beside the loom.

"Hello," said the countess, smiling. Even though the two of them were alone in Duart Castle, she wore an elegant gown of sapphire blue silk, the slashed sleeves revealing gold-embroidered puffs. "I hope you don't mind this interruption, but I am growing terribly lonely. I have read two entire books since the men left, and now I don't know what to do with myself."

Nora couldn't help smiling. She had shared a few meals with Cicely but otherwise assumed the noblewoman would be busy with her own pursuits. "I'm very pleased you are here, my lady! I confess that I am growing lonely, too."

"Have I not insisted that you call me Cicely?" The twinkle in her eyes belied her stern words. "Now, then, I am very curious to see your tapestry. How envious I am of people like you who have real creative ability. My brother is an exceptionally talented painter, but I am hopeless, even at the usual feminine pastimes like embroidery or playing the virginal." Cicely gave her an engaging smile.

Nora found herself opening up, showing the young countess how the loom worked, explaining about Lennox's cartoon, and then slowly divulging pieces of her life story.

"You and your father came from Flanders to live in London?" Cicely exclaimed. "Perhaps our paths crossed there."

"I doubt that, my lady. We were not part of your world." She shook her head. "For several years, Father oversaw the tapestry repair workshop that is part of His Majesty's Great Wardrobe. As you may know, the king moves among his castles and palaces every few days, it seems, and most of the royal tapestries go with him."

"I've never understood why the king is so restless,"

exclaimed Cicely. "It creates so much work for the rest of his household!"

"Indeed. And Father's real gifts were wasted. Eventually, he was granted the title of weaver, but most of the new tapestries are still being acquired from workshops in Flanders and France." Nora shrugged philosophically. "Eventually, the King of Scots made Father an offer he found irresistible. They are going to weave grand tapestries in a new workroom at Stirling Castle, and Father is the master weaver."

Cicely leaned closer to the loom, studying the way the colored weft threads had been woven into the grid of plain warp threads, then beaten down with the bobbin to create specific areas of color. "This is exquisite. No doubt your husband will be astonished when he returns and sees how you have brought his drawing so vividly to life." She straightened and met Nora's eyes. "What of you and *your* aspirations?"

"I want to become the first royal master weaver who is also a female," Nora replied without hesitation. "It has been my dream since I was a child."

Cicely clapped her beringed hands together. "Hear, hear!"

"My father, who knows my abilities better than anyone, has warned me it cannot be."

"But he is a *man*!" The countess's tone implied that this explained everything. She leaned closer. "When we are in London, I will help you. I know Jan Mostinck, who oversees the royal tapestries. He's very old, and no doubt he needs assistance."

Nora wanted to hug her new friend. "I know Master Mostinck but never imagined he might see me. It was one thing to work alongside my father, in his workroom, but quite another to imagine that those who are in power in the Great Wardrobe would welcome me, alone, a mere female, into the fold."

"You know well enough that, since the monasteries have been dissolved, the king has the funds to do as he pleases. It amuses him to acquire riches, especially precious tapestries."

"Yes, I do know that." Nora's heart was racing. For the first time since Lennox had gone away to help with the shipwreck, she felt able to focus on herself as an individual. "I would be very grateful for any help you can give me when we are in London, my—"

"Cicely! When we are together, you must call me Cicely. I will be delighted to assist you, Nora. Are we not friends now?"

Was it really possible? She wondered, feeling rather dazzled. "I would certainly like that… Cicely."

"Let us go and see what Tilly has for us to eat." She linked arms with Nora and led her to the doorway, inquiring casually, "How does your splendid Highlander husband feel about having a wife with grand ambitions?"

Nora tried to keep her tone light. "We will see when we reach London, I suppose!"

Two afternoons later, Nora looked up from her weaving to see a stream of golden light pouring through the long, narrow window. The sun was shining at last! Rising, she left her loom and lifted her deep violet skirts to hasten her progress up the winding stairs. The moment she emerged onto the rooftop, she turned toward the sea and saw a large birlinn sailing toward the castle, the colorful MacLean coat of arms billowing from the mast. Her heart leaped as she realized Lennox was coming back to her. The prospect of being in his arms again made her feel dizzy.

Laughing, Nora waved to the vessel with both hands. The two guards on the roof walk stared at her in bemusement, but she didn't care. "That's my husband out there," she explained, as giddy as if she had been drinking wine.

Turning, Nora hurried back down the steps and into the great hall, where she glanced around for Cicely. There was no sign of her, but Nora paused beside Fergus and crouched down to ruffle his fur. "Your master returns, as well as your friend

Lennox," she told him, wishing the old dog could rise and run at her side to greet the MacLean clansmen.

Out in the cobbled courtyard, the guards had already opened the outer gates, and Nora held her skirts aloft as she rushed down the hillside. A little voice in the back of her head fretted that she should not show Lennox how much she cared, yet it was impossible to stop.

The men were already disembarking by the time she reached the brow of the cliff, where a well-worn path led down to the landing beach. "Lennox!" she exclaimed, immediately spotting his golden head and broad shoulders above the others.

He shaded his eyes against the sun and grinned up at her, calling, "Patience, lass. I'll be there soon."

The husky promise in his voice made her stomach flutter.

Some of the servants and other wives were emerging from the castle and surrounding croft houses, chattering among themselves. Nora didn't want to socialize with them. She didn't want anything to get in the way of her reunion with Lennox, so to pass the time, she picked wildflowers and began to weave them into a wreath.

She chose red campion, purple thrift, and a few delicate bluebells, interspersing the vivid yellow of ladies' bedstraw among the blossoms. By the time the MacLeod clansmen started up the path, Nora had set the bright wildflower wreath atop her head and stood waiting, off to one side.

The men who marched past were grimy and sunburned, but when Lennox appeared, Nora thought he had never looked more splendid.

"Hello!" she called.

"Have ye come to greet me? I am honored," He cupped her cheek with his strong hand, and the simple motion caused pleasure to blossom in her very core.

"We have all been worried," she said. "What has kept all of you away for so long?"

Lennox caught her hand and led her behind a grove of larch trees. "It's been terrible. The ship, a Dutch brigantine, was crushed, first broken against the rocks during the storm, then further destroyed when it surged into a deep notch between the cliffs." A shadow crossed his face. "It took days to recover all the bodies, and even then I do not think we were completely successful. Finally, the MacLean himself fell ill. We were forced to take shelter at Torloisk, another MacLean castle nearby, until Hector recovered his health." He shook his head, and the sun struck sparks on his gilded hair. "'Twas not a place I would ask even Chaucer to sleep."

Nora wanted to tell him how worried she'd been, how filled with joy and relief she was to see him safely returned, but she suddenly felt shy. Would she seem like all the other besotted lasses he must have known? "It is so good to see all of you returned home," Nora said instead.

"Look at ye, wearing a crown," he teased lightly.

She put her hand up to the flowers, helpless to stop her face from growing warm. "I prefer these to jewels."

"Ah, Nora, ye have never been more beautiful." He traced the line of her cheekbone with his thumb. "Are ye blushing because ye care?"

He was gazing so tenderly into her eyes that she blurted out the truth. "I do."

"So do I, lass." Lennox lifted her up in his arms and covered her mouth with his. It was a kiss that ignited a flame of desire between them, yet it had an even deeper effect on Nora, as if he were speaking to her with his body. When at length Lennox raised his head, he murmured, "Let's go inside, shall we? I want to see what ye have done with the tapestry, and I am in sore need of a bath, if such a thing exists in that drafty old castle."

It almost felt as if they were truly a happily married couple as they walked arm-in-arm up the sloping green hillside to Duart Castle. Inside, they found Lord Fairhaven drinking a tankard of ale while talking with Cicely, and Hector Mór was already seated near the fire, propping his feet up on a stool.

"It seems I'm not a lad any longer," the clan chief

complained good naturedly, while Fergus limped over to join him. "Where is my whisky, Tilly?"

"You must be hungry," Nora said to Lennox.

"For food?" His smile held a wicked gleam, and her face grew warmer. "It is the least of my needs today."

The boards were being laid, and platters of cold meat, cheeses, and oatcakes were carried into the hall. Lennox snatched an oatcake and a wedge of cheese before guiding Nora into the corridor that led to her workroom.

"Every day I was away, ye and the tapestry were in my thoughts," he said. "Have ye had time to weave?"

She blinked. "In the midst of rescuing the crew of a ship that was dashed on the rocks, you were thinking about my tapestry?"

Lennox arched a brow, feigning surprise. "Is it not *our* tapestry? If memory serves, I've had a hand in its creation as well."

And so, as he ate his oatcake, they went into her workroom. The bobbins and shuttle lay where she had left them a short while ago, in front of the nearly-completed image of a Highland galley on a wave-tossed sea.

Lennox stared, awestruck. "How can it be that ye have done so much?"

"I have worked many hours each day, as long as I could in this feeble light. Sometimes, when I felt especially inspired, I brought in oil lamps to allow me to weave into the evening."

"It's exquisite. Ye are truly gifted."

He examined her creation with so much care, asking questions about every choice she had made, that Nora felt a warm glow spread through her body as they talked. This man saw and valued a deeply important part of her in a way no one else ever had, not even her father.

"I cannot ever express to you how much it means that you found this loom and created the pattern for"—she paused, her face warm again—"for our tapestry." She pointed to the small figures that, just this morning, she had woven inside the galley. "Do you see us?"

Lennox took a closer look, a smile lighting his handsome face. "Aye, lass. Ye have even added a touch of russet for your hair, I see."

"And for yours, I used the same color thread as the sun." Their eyes met, and her heart melted.

"Let us go to our chamber, shall we?" he suggested softly. "I want to show ye how much you've been missed."

Chapter Eighteen

Lennox poured one more jug of water over his head, savoring the feeling of being clean again. He stepped out of the knee-high tub and had just reached for a drying cloth when the door opened and Nora appeared, carrying a tray.

"Oh! I didn't mean to disturb you." She stared in shock then quickly averted her eyes, turning a delectable shade of pink. "I've brought you some more food. And cold ale."

"Disturb me? We are wed, are we not?" Lennox saw the tops of her breasts begin to flush, and her nipples puckered through the fabric of her bodice. He felt blood rush to his loins, but he didn't want to alarm the lass, so he covered himself with the towel. "Now that I've washed away those layers of grime, I feel like a new man. I don't even mind the scent of lavender from your soap."

"I think lavender is a fine scent for men as well as women." She set the tray on a chest. Still looking away, she asked, "Shall I get you a clean pair of hose?"

"Nay." The cloth was just big enough to wrap around his narrow hips, and he tucked one end inside to secure it. "That bed looks very inviting. Will ye join me?"

She glanced at the tray. "But…"

If it were anyone but Nora, he might have enjoyed a bit of cat and mouse, but this was not a time for that sort of love play. "It's not food I need now," Lennox said softly. He stretched out on the bed and held out a sun-darkened hand to her. "I have missed ye. Come and talk to me."

It seemed Nora's heartbeat was audible even to him as she obeyed. When she was lying beside him, all he wanted to do was to divest her of her gown, petticoat, and kirtle, but instead he pretended not to notice all the clothing that hid her from his sight. He rose up on an elbow and gazed down at her face, which was all the lovelier because of its character and intelligence.

"While I was away, missing ye, I had a lot of time to think." Lightly, he traced the curves of her face with one fingertip. Her eyes were huge, blue as sapphires, staring back at him.

"Think?" Nora echoed in a small croak.

By God, she was enchanting. A smile touched his mouth as he replied, "Aye. Thinking, even in my dreams, that perhaps there is a way to make this handfasting real. I know my future is filled with uncertainty. I have told myself that I should remain unencumbered by romantic attachments, at least until I know who I truly am and where I belong. Yet I have tender feelings for ye, Nora Brodie." He swallowed, wanting to say the word *love*, but unable to leap that chasm for the first time. "Do ye feel the same?"

Lennox paused, waiting, and the moments seemed to stretch into eternity. At last, she spoke, her voice thick.

"I do." She reached up to touch him, her slim hand soft against his hard, stubbled jaw, but he saw pain in her eyes. "I… I did not expect this."

Clearly, she was struggling inside. "What is it, lass?" He felt a powerful need to show her how right it could be between them. "That night we rode away from Stirling, when we lay together and I took your innocence… It was not what it should have been. We can have so much more together."

A long moment passed before he heard her soft whisper. "Yes. I do want that."

Every part of him burned for her, aching to taste her kisses, to be inside her, to say with his body what he could not put into words. Smoothing back her curls, Lennox bent to capture her mouth. She parted her lips and returned his kiss, her hands on the damp, bare breadth of his shoulders. He slowly trailed one hand up the curve of her waist, over her ribcage, and then used his fingertip to lightly circle her nipple over the fabric of her bodice. When her nipple tightened, he cupped her breast, feeling her response, determined to go slow and savor each caress, each taste, each throb of arousal. The night when they had lain together in the woods, a blind need had carried them away, but today would be different.

Lennox kissed his way from her mouth down her neck, burying his face in her meadow-scented cloud of curls. "All these clothes ye are wearing," he murmured, "are in the way."

Nora nodded, eyes closed. He found the laces of her gown, opening her bodice, drinking in the sight of her pink-tipped breasts, creamy in the soft afternoon light.

"Ye are so beautiful," he said hoarsely. "I mean to make this everything ye have ever dreamed of."

Bending, he kissed her again, exploring her mouth with his tongue, feeling her breathing change. And then he tasted salty tears.

Feeling as if cold water had been splashed on him, he lifted his head. "What's amiss?" he asked hoarsely. "What have I done?"

Now the tears spilled from her eyes, and she didn't trouble to dry them. "You have done nothing. It isn't you, Lennox, it's me. *I* am what's amiss."

"I do not understand." Suddenly, it seemed he was looking at a stranger, and yet perhaps this was simply what he had sensed for so long, the invisible barrier that existed between them. "What the devil are ye saying?"

Nora pushed herself up to a sitting position. "I have been keeping something from you." Now she was dry-eyed, determined. "I have been avoiding the truth, wishing it could be otherwise, but I should have told you long ago…that night we lay together in the woods."

It hurt her to see the pain and confusion on Lennox's splendid face, to feel his struggle to suppress the tide of his desire. But she could not keep the truth from him a moment longer, especially now that he had begun to speak of a future for them.

A *future!* The very word made Nora's stomach knot, for she alone felt the chasm of secrets yawning between them.

"I'm listening." Lennox pushed back against a pillow and watched her. "Whatever it is, ye can safely tell me."

Nora gazed at him, his tawny hair still damp and tousled, his serious, magnificent face darkened by the sun. When she looked at his mouth and thought of his sensual kisses, a shiver of wonder ran through her. How could she bring her troubles into the life of this good man? He had given her his protection, his friendship, and perhaps his heart.

"I wish all of it were different, that I could be the woman you imagine I am."

A shadow crossed his face, but he made no reply.

Unable to delay a moment longer, she took a deep breath, met Lennox's green eyes and summoned all her courage. "I was not a virgin when we lay together that night in the woods. I...had been with another man."

He paled then seemed to gather himself. "I was no innocent either, lass. I can understand if ye have cared for another."

She shook her head. "It was not like that." Pausing, Nora thought she might be sick. How hard it was to say these things aloud! "I lay with someone I did not love. I did not even want to do it, but—"

Lennox cut in. "Ye must tell me every bit of this tale," he said sternly. "I want to hear it."

"It happened at Stirling Castle. There was a man—"

"Which *man?*" he demanded.

"Why must you know that?" Her face heated. "He was simply a man of importance who visited the castle. One night, when Father sat at the high table with the king, I drank a goblet of wine in the company of this man." Remembering that Lennox had been at court that very night, she could not bring herself to identify Sir Raymond Slater. It would be humiliating if Lennox imagined Slater on top of her, inside her, putting his seed there to grow into a baby… "When I felt ill, he insisted on seeing me back to our rooms. There, I grew dizzy. Perhaps it was the wine. It could be that I imbibed more than I realized." Her voice broke.

"God's blood," Lennox ground out. "He took you when you were in that state?"

Nora clenched her trembling hands. "In truth, I am not entirely certain how it happened. I was lying on my bed, and he was there with me. Perhaps I encouraged him in some way? It seems I must have! Otherwise, it could not have happened."

"The snake who did this was Sir Raymond Slater," Lennox said abruptly. His eyes shone with fury, and a muscle pulsed in his jaw. Before Nora could speak, he continued, "I looked for you that night. I encountered Slater in the courtyard and asked if he had seen you. He said ye were unwell and required his escort to your room. The bastard!"

"I have never seen you like this," Nora murmured, dread coiling inside her.

"If only ye could have trusted me enough then to tell me!" Lennox's powerful body was taut with rage.

"That would have solved nothing. He left Stirling the very next morning."

"By God, I will kill him."

Nora stared at him in trepidation. "I have feared that, if I told you my sad story, it would bring pain to you as well." Her voice broke as a wave of hopelessness swept over her. It was impossible to change what had happened to her that night with Slater, even if she were not carrying his baby, and Lennox's rage made her world feel even shakier. "I cannot fairly accuse Sir Raymond of forcing himself on me. I was confused, and perhaps…"

"Perhaps *what?*"

She blinked. "Perhaps I unwittingly encouraged his… attentions."

"Are ye mad?" He reached out and gripped her soft upper arms, and she felt the fire inside him. "That devil raped you, Nora!"

Her eyes swam with bitter tears. "I cannot be certain what happened because I did not refuse him or fight against him. It was all a blur. I only know that I cannot undo it, and now I am changed. Soiled." Vivid, sickening memories returned of Slater pushing inside her, grunting. "I do not blame you for being angry, yet I had to tell you. I know a good man like you will not want me. I am tainted, but I can still make a future, with weaving the center of my life." Her voice broke. "I am grateful to have that remaining gift." Silently, she added, *A gift no man can steal.*

Lennox's grip relaxed, and now he gathered her against his broad chest, holding her in a way that only made her weep more. Had all these tears been stored inside all along? Even as Lennox held her, Nora waited for him to ask about a babe. He must know that would be the result, if Slater had planted his seed. She was struggling to find the words herself when Lennox lay her down again on the bed and gazed into her eyes.

"Lass, ye are not soiled, *not* tainted. Ye are as fine and pure as ever." His voice was raw. "That villain does not have the power to snuff out the light inside you, unless ye allow it."

"It is how I feel," she said honestly, fighting an urge to avert her eyes. "I made a terrible mistake and it stained me. I should have told you sooner, before you began to…care for me."

"It is too late." He shook his head, and she saw the corners of his eyes crinkle as his gaze warmed. "I already care."

Nora wondered if she were hearing things. "If you mean to be kind, I am grateful, but—"

His finger touched her lips, silencing her. "Nay. Of course ye deserve kindness rather than shame, yet much more as well. Ah, Nora, this does not change my feelings." The currents of emotion in his voice warmed the hidden recesses of her heart. He lifted her hand and kissed her fingertips then the tender base of her wrist. "The only stain is in your mind, lass. Together, we can wash it away."

A flurry of emotions began inside her, like the beating of a thousand tiny wings. Meeting Lennox's gaze, Nora could not bear to say one more hard thing.

"I want that," she whispered. "Very much."

"I know ye are strong and spirited, Nora Brodie, but today, in this bed, I would ask that ye surrender to me." The smoldering desire in his eyes made her heart leap. "Trust me."

"I will." She spoke the words like a vow. "But what shall I do?"

For an instant, his brow arched in invitation. "Your body will know."

Terrified and exhilarated all at once, Nora went into Lennox's arms. It was heaven, feeling the strength and tenderness of his embrace. The intoxicating scent of his skin, the texture of his hair, the hunger in his sea-green eyes, all combined to ignite a flame of arousal inside her. He kissed her with practiced lips, slowly drawing out each exquisite sensation, while his fingers found the laces on her gown.

"I want us to be naked together," he said in a ragged whisper.

Slowly, Lennox removed each piece of her clothing, his fingertips brushing her skin just enough to make her ache for more. When she lay under Lennox's gaze clad in only a silk smock, he levered himself on an elbow and lightly caressed from her knee upward, under the smock to graze Nora's sensitive inner thigh. Their eyes met, and she felt the heat in her face.

"Does that feel good?" he whispered.

She caught her bottom lip between her teeth, nodding. Warmth surged between her legs, building with each brush of his fingertips, and yet he avoided the place that ached most for his touch.

Please…

Instead, without moving his hand from her thigh, he kissed her, a deep, sweet kiss that only intensified Nora's ache. His mouth moved down the column of her neck, burning, until he reached her breasts, still covered by her smock. Her nipples puckered just thinking about his mouth, so close, and then she felt his tongue, hot and wet, through the whisper-thin silk. The erotic sensation was a shock.

"Ye are perfect, so beautiful," he murmured. He covered her nipple with his mouth and sucked it in, the silky barrier adding to the sharp currents of pleasure. At the same time, his hand lightly stroked inside her thigh, closer, closer.

Nora arched her neck, every nerve in her body alive. His fingertips brushed the curls between her legs and she moaned aloud, opening to him, lifting her hips to try to bring him in contact with the wet, congested bud that needed his touch so desperately.

"Ye were made for love," Lennox said softly. "Can ye feel it?"

She nearly sobbed when he finally touched her there, lightly pinching in a way that drove her mad. His fingertip moved in gentle circles, not quite giving her what she needed until her arousal became unbearably heightened. Nora had pleasured herself before, to the point of release, but these feelings went far beyond her imaginings.

Her eyes were closed in concentration when she felt him gently pushing her smock up and over her head. She barely had a chance to register her own nakedness, for Lennox was now kissing her hip, her abdomen, her inner thigh. Nora gasped aloud, daring to look. To her shock, she saw Lennox's unruly golden head, there, between her legs.

"Let go, lass," he murmured, sending her a faintly roguish smile.

It should have been shameful, but the sight of him there only intensified her arousal. When he replaced his fingertip with his mouth, she gave a low cry. He licked, swirled, flicked, and explored until the sensations grew wilder, insistent, nearly unbearable. Nora reached out for his hair, grasping what she could, trying to get closer to him. On the verge of insisting that he stop, she had to have more.

He was driving her completely mad. As Nora hovered at the

precipice, he pushed a finger deep inside her, tipping her over the edge. A glorious series of spasms shook her to her very core and left her disoriented. When the storm began to subside, she managed to focus on Lennox as he gathered her into his arms.

"I never imagined," she said, blushing.

He smiled into her eyes, tracing her cheekbone with the backs of his fingers. It was a tender gesture, and when he kissed her, Nora tasted herself. Suddenly she felt consumed with a need to touch him in return. Fleetingly, a shadowed memory of Slater darkened her thoughts, but everything about that night was so completely different from this light-filled interlude that it was easier to separate the two than she had ever dreamed.

Lennox was lying on top of her, skin to skin, and Nora could feel the strong beat of his heart against her breasts. Euphoric, she raised her hands to his face, framing it as he gazed down at her. Love welled up in her, rich and warm and sure, but before she could say the words, he was kissing her.

"This is all that matters," he said. "The two of us."

Their tongues met, fencing, as he moved back and forth inside her mouth, the rhythm reawakening her need. Nora traced the muscles of his shoulders with her fingertips then ran her hands down his tapering back. His body was like the statues she had seen in Europe, yet Lennox was thrillingly alive. His hard thigh nudged her legs apart and she was thrilled to comply, opening to him, moaning aloud when the hard, pulsing length of him settled against the hot center of her being. Instinctively, Nora rubbed against him, longing to topple into rapture again, but Lennox smiled against her mouth.

"Wait for me, lass..."

He was there, nudging at her slick entrance, and suddenly she wanted that more than anything. Lifting her hips, she invited him in, as their eyes met in a moment of raw intimacy. Lennox brought up a hand to push the damp curls from her brow, clearly in no hurry. He came into her an inch at a time. For an instant, she worried she would not be able to accommodate him.

Against her ear, his breath was warm. "Are ye all right?"

Nora nodded, drawing a deep breath just as he pushed all the way in, filling her. The sense of completion brought tears to her eyes. The coiled tension in Lennox's body was evident, yet she sensed he was taking his time for her sake. As he began to move inside her, drawing nearly all the way out before sliding back in, Nora wrapped her arms around his back and arched her hips in answer, again and again. Soon, she couldn't think at all, and as her passion mounted, Lennox's thrusts grew faster, harder. Each one took Nora closer to the fire she craved.

"Come with me," he urged. As he drove in one last time, groaning, Nora felt her world shatter again. Currents of exquisite pleasure radiated out from her core, and when the pulsing subsided, she was clinging tight to Lennox.

He eased onto his side and stayed inside Nora, holding her, gradually trying to sift through his feelings. His intention had been to not only make love to her but to carry her well past the notion that she was soiled in some way by what had happened with that devil Slater.

His sister, Fiona, who knew him so well, would accuse him of once again being tempted to rescue a damsel in distress. Other men might pursue victory on the battlefield, but Lennox had always seized the challenge of saving people.

Yet, he knew his feelings for this lass were real. Feelings that he hardly trusted himself to name. It was a complicated business, for this coupling was something far more serious than their stormy, wordless union in the woods.

Her mass of curls lay over his chest, deliciously fragrant. He ran his free hand down the creamy line of her back, over her hip, and cupped her lovely bottom.

"How do ye feel?" he asked.

She turned a glowing face up to him. "I feel as if I could fly away, like an angel."

Her words dispelled most of his doubts. "Aye, ye are an angel indeed. And now ye can fly away from the memory of that villain." He kissed her, savoring the sweetness of her mouth. "Together, we have burned away what he did to you. It's gone."

A shadow seemed to pass over her face before she whispered, "For now."

Lennox hated the thought of Sir Raymond Slater lurking in a hidden corner of Nora's soul. "*Now* is all that matters, love. This very moment." He felt himself begin to harden again inside her, and her answering, intimate response. "We'll find a way through whatever lies ahead."

Nora made no reply but kissed him instead. As the real world slipped away, Lennox told himself that was answer enough.

Hours later, Nora disengaged from Lennox's sleeping body and rose from the bed. She found her discarded smock in a pool on the floor and slipped it over her head. Her naked body was tender, almost bruised from so much lovemaking, yet she had never felt more like a woman.

Leaning into the deep stone sill below the narrow window, Nora glimpsed the full moon that silvered the nearby Sound of Mull. What time was it? Midnight at least, she supposed. Lennox slumbered, one brown arm thrown back over his head, but she could not find such peace.

It was a relief to have told him so much of the truth, to share the burden of her secret about Slater, to bring it out in the open where Lennox had done his best to destroy its power over her. Nora closed her eyes and pondered all they had said and the past hours she had spent in his arms, discovering the utter splendor of what could exist between a man and woman.

It meant so much that he had professed to care, to want to make their handfasting a true marriage, no matter what lay ahead for him in London. Yet Nora knew it was not so simple for Lennox. Who knew what lay waiting for him around the next corner?

Her hand went to her abdomen. She splayed her slim fingers, searching for a sign of the baby who was growing inside her, and tonight it seemed that the curve of her belly was a bit firmer. If she had told Lennox tonight about this baby, they never could have shared these stolen hours of passion and raw intimacy. Didn't they both deserve this interlude? Perhaps it would be all Nora would have to warm her heart in the years ahead.

Soon, I will tell him the truth.

A muffled groan of complaint came from the big bed. "Where have ye gone, lass?"

Turning, Nora pulled off the smock. Moments later, she was back in bed, molding herself to Lennox's lean, muscular body. He was warm, smiling sleepily as he rolled her over into the pillows and kissed her.

Nora let the waves of exquisite, deep happiness flow through her body and spirit. Opening her mouth to his, she reminded herself of his words: *This moment is all that matters…*

Tomorrow would come soon enough.

Chapter Nineteen

London, England
June 1541

Lennox found it impossible to stay seated as the Earl of Fairhaven's barge glided up the sun-spangled River Thames, surrounded by countless other vessels. It was as if he were in another world entirely, one that bore no resemblance to the Isle of Skye or even Edinburgh.

The legendary city of London that spread beyond the banks of the river was a jumbled maze of gabled rooftops, chimneys, and spires, filled with people of every description who moved about wherever he looked. Of course, there were no Highlanders among them and Lennox suddenly was conscious of his belted plaid, the sash fastened to his shoulder with a brooch. Some of these men wore soft plumed caps, quite unlike Lennox's tartan bonnet with its clan MacLeod badge.

Of course, he thought ruefully, envisioning the man in the miniature with the swan's feather in his velvet cap. *What did I expect?*

The voices that reached his ears, including the shouts of the watermen on Fairhaven's barge, did not sound like his Scots brogue, and certainly none of these Englishmen carried a giant claymore or wore a dirk at his belt.

"Are you looking forward to this adventure in London?"

asked Cicely. She had come to stand at his elbow without Lennox even noticing.

"I cannot truly say," he admitted. "If I can solve the riddle of the man in the painting, I will be glad to have come. Do I expect to enjoy myself in London?" He gave a wry shrug, surveying the outline of the bustling city. "It is very foreign to me. I feel…"

"Wary?" Cicely supplied.

"Aye." He paused, gesturing from his windblown locks to the folds of his belted plaid before adding, "And, as ye can see, I am a Scots thistle among these English roses."

"Ah, but a very handsome thistle, sir."

Lennox had no patience for her banter. Glancing away, he felt the tightening in his chest that had been coming more and more often of late. It was a sort of grief, he sensed, the prospect of trading his Highland identity to become a different person. Did he truly want this?

Swans glided over to the side of the barge, seeming to recognize Cicely. "They hope for a treat," she remarked. "I used to try to pet them when I was a child, but my brother forbade it, claiming to know someone who had a finger bitten off by a swan." She glanced back to the cushioned bench where Nora reclined next to Fairhaven, looking pale and dispirited. "Your lovely wife has not been herself for days. Do you fear for her health?"

It was true that Nora had suffered from what she called *mal de mer*, ever since they'd left the Isle of Mull. The seas were often rough, and Lennox had found himself on deck much of the time, working alongside the crew of Lord Fairhaven's sloop. And once they had neared London, he had been distracted by the realization that his whole life might be about to change.

Yet, looking back at Nora now, he felt an uncomfortable twinge of guilt. How could he be so focused by his own concerns that he had not kept a closer watch on her?

"Nora assures me that she has always been plagued by seasickness," Lennox said. He was about to go to her when Cicely put a hand on his arm.

"She has told me the same, and I know she also understands all that weighs on your mind. You are seeing this city for the first time. And you have come a very long way on an important quest for your...relative?" Cicely's voice trailed off expectantly.

"Ye will know more soon enough, when I speak to your brother," he replied.

He was relieved when she stepped back. "I think that meeting is at hand, but meanwhile, I will go to Nora and leave you to your thoughts."

Nora looked up as Cicely took a seat beside her, the yellow silk of her skirts billowing around her.

"Your splendid Highlander is very concerned about you," said Cicely.

She managed a weak smile. "I know that he is, but other matters must come first today for Lennox." Feeling the Englishwoman's watchful gaze, she added a small falsehood. "I am fine. No doubt my queasiness will be cured when we are back on dry land."

"Hmm. Do you think so?"

Nora was spared from thinking of a reply as Lord Fairhaven, who had been dozing on some nearby cushions, clambered to his feet. Shading his eyes to survey the shoreline, he exclaimed, "There it is. What a welcome sight!"

Cicely clapped her hands, beaming. "Andrew will be so surprised to see us."

They were drawing up before a water-gate that opened onto a series of wide stone steps. In the distance stood a grand home of rose-salmon brick, its diamond-paned windows agleam in the late-afternoon sunlight.

"Whose house is this?" asked Nora as the arched doors opened and an old man tottered out, followed by several other liveried servants. "Who is Andrew?"

"Have I not told you? Andrew is my brother, the Duke of Aylesbury."

Even as the waterman brought them alongside the steps, water lapping at the sides of the barge, Lennox turned in surprise to look at the Fairhavens. "Are we not going to your home?"

"Oh, no," said Lord Fairhaven with a shake of his head. He started forward, his greyhound obediently at his side. "Our home is not nearly so grand, and besides, it's the duke who will help you find the fellow in the miniature, whomever he might be."

Nora sat up straight, feeling the tension in Lennox's body even from a distance. "I didn't expect to be presented to a duke and duchess, let alone become a guest in their home," she protested. "Why didn't you tell us?"

"Because you doubtless would have refused," Cicely returned brightly. "And now you cannot."

When they had disembarked and climbed the shallow steps, Lennox felt his heart clench at the sight of the grand house and the servants coming toward them. By the saints, why had he ever embarked on this unlikely quest? For a moment, he envisioned the achingly familiar faces of Magnus, Alasdair Crotach, Ciaran, and Fiona. Had it been a mistake to spurn the fine life he'd been born to on the Isle of Skye in order to chase after the mysterious aristocrat his mother had loved?

Nora touched his arm, bringing him back to the moment. "You had to come," she murmured, her beautiful eyes rich with emotion. "We both know it."

The clear understanding Lennox felt from her was deeply reassuring. He straightened and took a deep breath. "Aye.

Thank God ye are here to set me straight, lass."

As more people emerged from the manor house, he perceived that he was about to meet the Duke and Duchess of Aylesbury. The duke, a handsome, fair-haired man with an air of wry charm, embraced Cicely. At his side stood a graceful, lovely woman, her cognac-hued hair partially obscured by a stylish French hood.

"What plans are you hatching now, child?" the duke was asking his sister in mock dismay.

"Will you call me child until we are both old and gray?" Cicely parried. Before he could reply, she rushed on. "Andrew, I've brought the most wonderful friends to stay here with us. You don't mind, do you? When you hear their story, you'll understand completely!"

"Allow me to greet our visitors," he said, and walked toward Lennox and Nora.

Cicely hurried in her brother's wake, clearly planning to take charge, but before she could speak, the duke extended his hand.

"Welcome to Weston House." His tone was affable, but he was staring at Lennox as if trying to place him from a previous meeting. "I am Andrew Weston, Duke of Aylesbury, but you must call me Sandhurst. I've only been a duke for a few months, but I've answered to Sandhurst all my life." Smiling, he brought his lady forward. "This is my wife, Micheline."

Lennox bowed to the noble couple, feeling more comfortable by the moment. "My name is Lennox MacLeod, of the Isle of Skye, and this is Nora Brodie, my—"

Before he could say the word *wife*, Nora spoke up. "I am Nora Brodie, and it is an honor to be with you both." She curtseyed to them. "You will not remember, Your Grace, but I met you a few years ago, when I was but a girl. My father oversaw the weaving of a new arras, a small hanging tapestry for your baby daughter's bedchamber. I accompanied the men who delivered it." She beamed at the duchess. "I have never forgotten the kindness you showed me that day."

Cicely interjected, "You already knew Andrew and Micheline, Nora? Why didn't you tell me?"

"Because the people I met were the Marquess and Marchioness of Sandhurst," Nora explained. "I didn't know of their...change in circumstances."

Smiling radiantly, the duchess spoke with a charming French accent, catching one of Nora's hands in both of hers. "Ah, *oui*! I do remember you, mademoiselle. You were an aspiring weaver, under the tutelage of your father, the master." She caught the sleeve of her husband's dove-gray doublet. "You remember Nora as well, don't you, Andrew?"

"I do." He gave his wife a bemused smile. "I suggest that we all go inside, where we can unravel this conversation at our leisure."

"Ye are very kind, Your Grace." Lennox felt a surge of hope as he smiled at them in turn.

"Not a bit," said Micheline. "And do call me Micheline. Titles only get in the way of friendships, we believe."

As they walked through the doorway, Sandhurst said dryly, "Later, after you've had a chance to rest and refresh yourselves, we'll regale you with the tale of our first meeting, when I traveled to France in the guise of a humble portrait painter."

The entry hall of Weston House was as warm and welcoming as their hosts, and Nora was pleased to see that nothing had changed since Lord Sandhurst became the Duke of Aylesbury. Throgmorton, the ancient steward, directed the green-liveried footmen to show the guests to separate chambers. Nora sensed that Lennox was about to protest that they were married, but she put a hand on his arm.

When they were out of earshot, halfway up the wide, oak-paneled staircase, she paused. "I beg you to leave it for now."

He stared at her as the servants continued on ahead of

them, carrying their meager belongings. "Why don't ye want to say that we are wed?"

Nora's heart hurt, wishing she could tell the world of their handfasting and share her husband's bed, but she steeled herself and held fast. "Wait until you know more. Trust me, please."

"Do ye believe anything I learn about my true father could change the way I feel about you?" he demanded in a hoarse whisper.

"No, of course not." Although his expression tore at her heart, she started up the stairs again, leaving him no choice but to join her. "So much is happening today, and you know I have not been feeling well. I will be glad to have a quiet respite to myself."

"We had so little time together during the voyage here." He looked stung. "I've missed ye, lass, and I am a stranger here in this city."

Nora could have wept. "I have missed you, too. But please, just for now, say nothing—" She broke off when one of the footmen appeared at the top of the stairs, clearly wondering what had happened to them. "There will be time enough later to say we are wed, but for now I long to go to my room and lie down for a bit. I have a feeling it will be an eventful evening."

Upstairs, the young footman whom Throgmorton had addressed at Bartholomew opened a heavy oak door and announced, "Your chamber, sir," to Lennox. The other servant ushered Lennox inside, and Nora followed Bartholomew down the corridor.

When he stopped before a door and opened it, Nora beheld a lovely chamber decorated in shades of rose and ivory. There were even dried rose petals among the fresh herbs on the floor, and the diamond-paned windows overlooked inviting gardens. She stared at the big bed with its carved posts, longing to crawl beneath the counterpane and stay there indefinitely.

"It's lovely. Thank you so much."

Bartholomew bowed. "One of the maidservants will soon arrive to attend you, madame."

When she was alone, Nora sank into a low chair near the windows. Tears of despair welled up in her. She felt nauseous much of the time these days and knew that her baby was making herself known. Slater's baby, though that did not change the love that swelled inside her for this tiny new life.

Could there still be a path forward for her with Lennox? That fragile hope had kept Nora going ever since the nights of bliss they shared at Duart Castle. Perhaps his father's identity would not be revealed here in London, or the man in the miniature would be lost without a trace. She could imagine Lennox making peace with that and returning to Scotland.

If they were left to make a life together on their own, Nora had hope he might accept another man's baby. Had he not made it clear he did not hold Nora responsible for what had happened with Slater?

But, before she could tell Lennox about the baby, she had to know what lay in store for him. Whenever she thought of the way the Duke of Aylesbury had gazed searchingly at Lennox, her heart felt heavy with foreboding.

A light tap came at the door, interrupting Nora's reverie, and before she could even speak, Cicely peeked in.

"Are you all right? Where is Lennox?" No sooner were the words out than Cicely seemed to assess Nora's mood and entered without an invitation. "Oh, I was right. Something is amiss! I can see it in your face. It's not just *mal de mer* after all, is it?"

Nora leaned back and turned her face against the cool oak-paneled wall. In her cloistered life spent mostly with her father, female friends had been few. Now she found herself yearning to open up to someone. "No. It is more."

Rushing over, Cicely knelt before her, her sable eyes penetrating. "Are you with child?"

This question caught Nora so completely by surprise, she couldn't think of a way to avoid the truth. "If I tell you, you must swear that you will not speak of it to another person."

Cicely dramatically made the sign of the cross. "I swear!"

"It's true. I am with child."

"But is that not a cause for joy? Why are you and Lennox keeping this news a secret?"

"In truth, it is a secret even Lennox does not know," Nora replied miserably.

Cicely blinked in confusion. "I still do not understand."

"I have not told Lennox…because he is not the baby's father."

Chapter Twenty

Nora had not meant to divulge so much, but now that the words were out, there was no going back. In fact, she felt a surge of relief, as if a great weight had been lifted.

Cicely was staring in shock. "What on earth can you mean?" she exclaimed.

The story emerged in fits and starts. "When I was at Stirling Castle, with my father, I was dedicated to my weaving, determined never to marry or even to be distracted by notions of romance."

"You are far too beautiful to live like a nun," her friend proclaimed. "What happened next?"

Nora took a painful breath. "An important Englishman came to court—"

"Indeed? What was his name?"

A sixth sense stopped her from revealing those details. After all, how well did she really know Cicely? "I would rather not reveal his identity. But everyone was very impressed with this man's reputation, and he was quite handsome. One night, he insisted on helping me to my rooms after I became ill in the banqueting hall." She closed her eyes for a moment, feeling Slater on top of her, pushing into her. "I'm not quite certain how it happened. I was suffering from vertigo, and then he was with me in my bed, and now I am going to have a baby."

"That is a shocking tale," Cicely pronounced. "Is it possible that he misunderstood somehow and thought you were willing?"

Nora shrugged in despair. "Perhaps. I felt so ill I can't remember anything clearly."

"But what about Lennox? How did you two come to be wed?"

She drew a painful sigh. "After that, I knew I couldn't stay with my father, especially once my condition became obvious. Lennox was leaving Stirling, setting off to look for the man in the painting, and he agreed to take me with him."

"How noble! He is like a hero from a fairy tale."

"Indeed." Nora felt worse by the moment.

"He didn't ask why you had to go?" Cicely pressed.

Guilt stabbed Nora as she realized how many times she had kept important truths from Lennox. "I begged him to trust me. I said only that I was in a desperate situation, which was quite true. It would have been impossible for me to stay there, working alongside my father, growing larger by the month."

"Perhaps Lennox was already falling in love with you."

"There was a spark between us from the first," she admitted. Remembering the night at Stirling Castle when she had gone to Lennox's bed, pleading for his help, Nora's face grew warm. Those kisses had ignited a flame in her that would not be extinguished. "My father discovered us as we were about to leave before dawn. He was furious, but Lennox insisted he loved me and intended to marry me. Father, in turn, demanded that we take handfasting vows there so that he might witness them." Nora sighed. "It almost felt real. And, as we traveled together and time passed…" She broke off, uncertain what to say next.

"You needn't say more. I can see it in your faces when you are together." Cicely rose and began to pace to and fro. "But *now* what do you mean to do?"

"Lennox is looking for the man in the painting," Nora replied. "He believes that he will not be whole until he finds him. I fear that, once he fulfills his quest, my condition might become an impediment in his new life. His dream must come first." She found it hard to speak the words. "I have deep aspirations of my own, as I have told you, so I understand."

Cicely slowly shook her head. "I don't know if you are a saint or a fool."

"Certainly not a saint," Nora replied with a touch of irony. "Now, my lady, I would have your word that you will not repeat anything I have told you. I don't want the duke and duchess to know that Lennox and I are wed, after a fashion, in case his future should take a dramatic turn."

"I promise, but you cannot simply wish away your wedded state," Cicely protested.

"It seems I can." Nora turned her face away, gazing out toward the gardens, and added softly, "When Lennox and I spoke the handfasting vows, I was stunned that he would take such a drastic step simply to set my father's mind at ease."

Her friend was watching her. "No doubt you were secretly thrilled to find yourself wed to such a splendid man."

"In all honesty, I suppose I was." Nora's smile was bittersweet. "But Lennox lost little time in disabusing me of such illusions. When I asked him why he would bind himself to me simply to ensure my escape from Stirling, he revealed that Scottish tradition decrees that handfasting can be easily undone with just a few words by either party." She paused. "That fact is never far from my mind."

When Lennox received a message inviting him to join the Duke of Aylesbury in the library, his heart quickened. Perhaps the moment of reckoning was truly at hand.

The servants had taken away all his travel-stained clothing, but there was one more clean plaid folded in his satchel. After washing and dressing, Lennox stood before the tall mirror and surveyed his appearance. In Scotland, he might win approving glances, but here in London he was a fish out of water. Sighing, he pinned the sash near the shoulder of his shirt and debated whether to add a jeweled dirk at his belt.

Nay, he thought with a faint arch of one brow, his host might fear Lennox meant him harm.

After scooping up the leather pouch with the miniature of an unknown nobleman, he went out into the corridor.

A door opened as he passed and Lady Cicely emerged, nearly bumping into him. "Oh!" she exclaimed. "How clumsy I am."

"Not at all." He tried to see past her, into the bedchamber. "Is Nora there?"

Cicely flushed, and he wondered what she thought about them having separate rooms. "I have just spoken to her. She is well but resting." Her dark-brown eyes softened. "I think that your lady will feel more at ease when your own future is resolved."

He suppressed an urge to simply go into the room and take Nora in his arms. "Your brother has asked me to join him in the library, so perhaps I will soon know more."

"I sincerely hope your conversation is fruitful," Cicely replied. In the next instant, she closed the door, ending his hopes of seeing or speaking to Nora. "Godspeed, my friend."

Expecting the library to be formal and austere, Lennox was surprised to enter and see three little girls holding out a ragged sock to an elderly spaniel.

"Do look, Percy, this is your favorite!" cried the oldest, a slim red-haired child of perhaps eight.

"Yes!" The littlest one, whose head was covered with golden curls, piped up, "Wouldn't you like to pull on it?"

The middle girl, a calmer beauty with a long auburn braid, held out both hands and looked from one sister to the other, clearly used to being the voice of reason. "Mama says Percy is becoming quite an elderly gentleman. We mustn't force him." She crouched down beside the liver-spotted dog and stroked his silky ears. "You need not frolic with us, dear boy, unless it suits you to do so."

Sandhurst was seated at his desk in front of a large window. Although an unopened ledger waited at his elbow, he was otherwise occupied, making sketches of the little girls and Percy the spaniel on a large sheet of paper.

"Ah, MacLeod, come in." Rising, he set down his charcoal pencil and looked to each of his daughters in descending order of age. "Susan, Tessa, Alison, will you not welcome Master MacLeod?"

The trio faced Lennox, and Percy obediently got into a sitting position beside them. The girls chorused, "Welcome to our home, sir."

"It is a pleasure to be here, my ladies," he said with a smile intended to charm. "How kind ye are."

The sisters stared at the sound of Lennox's Scots accent, before scanning his belted plaid, golden brooch, and tousled hair. Clearly uncertain whether she might be in danger, the smallest child hid partway behind her siblings.

"Pardon me," the auburn-braided girl said in a confident voice, "My name is Tessa. I am fairly bursting to know: Are you a *true* Highlander?"

Her words pinched at his heart. Lennox wanted to tell her that was the question that had brought him on a weekslong quest from Scotland to London, but instead he only nodded. "Aye, Lady Tessa. I've been a Highlander my entire life. I hope ye are not alarmed by my appearance."

It was Percy who responded first, coming forward to offer a gentle greeting. Lennox knelt and ran his big hand over the spaniel's head, causing Percy to close his eyes with pleasure. Little Alison came out from behind her sisters, beaming.

The duke came around the desk and Lennox straightened to clasp his outstretched hand. "This gentleman is our honored friend," Sandhurst assured the trio. "Now, then, my girls, will you kindly take Percy downstairs to the kitchen for his dinner? I must speak to our guest alone."

After bidding their father and Lennox goodbye, the trio rushed off, with Percy the spaniel following in their wake. The two men exchanged smiles as Sandhurst poured two goblets of garnet-red wine.

"Thank you for your kindness to my daughters," he said, lifting his glass in a silent toast.

"They are charming, sir. I must confess, I did not imagine I would find your ducal library filled with children and a dog."

"I beg you not to refer to this library as *ducal*." Sandhurst arched a brow. "I purchased Weston House long before I acquired my rather burdensome new title. As for the children, I love them fiercely. I want them to grow up surrounded by books," he said, gesturing toward the priceless volumes that filled the shelves. "Reading them, rather than admiring their leatherbound spines."

Lennox glanced back toward the sketches on Sandhurst's desk. "I see you are an artist."

"Ah, well, after a fashion." He shrugged self-deprecatingly. "I have always loved to paint and draw, much to the displeasure of my father, the last duke."

It suddenly made more sense that this Duke of Aylesbury would not be inclined to carry on the grand, haughty ways of his predecessor. "I, too, paint and draw," Lennox heard himself say.

"My sister tells me you are very talented. While you are here, perhaps we can sketch something together." The duke finished his wine and set the glass down on a side table. "First, however, I perceive there is something else you wish to discuss with me?"

For a moment, Lennox could scarcely breathe, let alone speak. "Aye," he managed at length, and reached for the leather pouch at his waist. As he drew out the miniature, the duke held up a hand.

"I must tell you, before you say another word, that when I first saw you at the water-gate, I thought you were someone else, magically made younger."

A wave of emotion washed over Lennox. *He knows!* His heart leaped with hope, yet another barrier might still wait ahead.

Holding his breath, he held out the small, oval portrait.

"Do you know this man? Is he the person you imagined I resemble?"

Sandhurst leaned forward, took it from him, and studied it. When he looked up, Lennox thought he saw a telltale gleam in his brown eyes. "It is. I knew him, looking just like this, many years ago. Before I tell you his name, will you explain your connection, and how you came to possess this miniature?"

As Lennox told the story of his parents and the quarrel that caused Eleanor MacLeod to flee from the Isle of Skye to Duart Castle, he was filled with mixed feelings. He longed to know the truth, yet a part of him sensed that a door was about to open that he would be powerless to close, no matter what lay on the other side.

"Before my mother died three years ago, she gave a jeweled casket to my sister Fiona. The box recently fell from a shelf, and we discovered a false bottom, with this miniature and a lock of golden hair hidden inside. Of course, it was as if I was seeing myself, garbed as an Englishman." Lennox paused, raking a hand through his hair. "I discovered that my brother Ciaran, who had gone with Ma to Duart Castle as a wee lad, knew the truth, that the man in this portrait was my true father. I then confronted Da, and he admitted he had known as well, after finding letters between Ma and this man."

"But they kept the truth from you," said Sandhurst.

"Aye. All my life. It seemed no one wanted to upset me, but I always sensed something was amiss." He met the duke's compassionate gaze. "And I never felt I completely belonged to clan MacLeod. I was raised to hunt and fight battles with rival clans, but in truth, I've always preferred to draw stags than to kill them."

Sandhurst nodded thoughtfully as he held up the miniature. "If you are indeed this man's son, it is no surprise that you felt uneasy as a Highlander."

"Are ye prepared now to divulge his name to me?" Lennox asked, unable to hold back another moment.

"I want very much to do so, but I hesitate to say too much until I have had a chance to speak to him myself. Once we can talk to him and learn whether he visited Duart Castle in the year of your birth, we will know much more." He paused. "And if all of this is true, he may wish to leave the past where it has been all these years. That would be his right."

"Ach." Lennox drew a deep breath and let it out as a sigh. The waiting was agony, but he had no choice. "I can see that ye are right, sir, and I am grateful for your help."

As if realizing that Lennox needed a few crumbs of information to sustain him, the duke said softly, "I will tell you this much: My friend is a fine man. We share a love of art. He is widowed and recently lost his only son to a sudden illness, so he has been grieving. And he is—" Sandhurst broke off. "No. I should say no more for now."

Lennox took in all that he had just heard, suddenly envisioning a real person in place of the painting. "I cannot thank you enough," he said, his voice hoarse with emotion.

"I will do my best to find my friend quickly." Sandhurst rested a reassuring hand on Lennox's shoulder. "I'll send word immediately to his London home. With luck, he will be in residence."

Chapter Twenty-one

That evening, the atmosphere at the supper table was warm and convivial. Because the sun did not set until very late on summer nights, the candles remained unlit, and light streamed through the tall leaded-glass windows.

Nora had endeavored to sit as far away from Lennox as possible. Their host made this easier, for he seemed to have taken Lennox under his wing, seating him to his left during the meal. The two men conversed quietly, and even from a distance, Nora sensed the shift inside Lennox. Had the Duke of Aylesbury given him information that settled his quest? She was anxious to know, but her inner voice warned that she must create a space between them until he knew more about his real father and the world he might be joining.

Susan, Tessa, and Alison joined the adults at the table, which delighted Nora. Cicely made introductions and, as they ate roasted lamb flavored with rosemary, she encouraged conversation between her nieces and Nora.

"Mistress Nora is a weaver of fine tapestries," she told them. "She may soon join the tapestry workshop of the king's own Great Wardrobe. Wouldn't that be thrilling?"

Soon Nora was chatting with the little girls, promising to show them the nearly complete tapestry she had brought from Duart Castle. When Micheline joined the conversation to say that she herself owned a small loom and would be happy to see it in use again, Nora's heart lifted. In the midst of so much uncertainty, the notion that she might soon be weaving again felt like she had been thrown a lifeline.

At the end of the meal, Nora copied the others, who used special spoons to sample green walnuts dipped in hot sugar syrup.

"It's called a sucket spoon," little Tess explained, when she saw Nora's curious expression.

Nora put the sweet walnut in her mouth and felt sick all over again. Hiding it in her napkin, Nora looked up to find Cicely gazing at her in concern.

"Are you all right?" her friend whispered.

"It's only more of the same," Nora replied softly, waiting for the wave of nausea to pass.

"Micheline claimed that she stopped feeling ill after three months. You must be nearly there if the baby was conceived close to Easter."

"Yes. I hope so."

As they rose from the table, Lord Fairhaven approached his wife, closely attended by their greyhound. "Shall we depart, my love?"

"Depart?" echoed Cicely.

"For our own *home*." His tone suggested he questioned her state of mind. "We have not been there for weeks."

"You are welcome to go, Robin, but I must remain here for now." She turned to smile at Nora. "Fortunately, I still have a bedchamber of my own here at Weston House. Andrew and Micheline were good enough to take me in after their wedding, when I was young and foolish, so that I would not be forced to live in Yorkshire with our dreadful father."

Lord Fairhaven took his wife's arm. "I must insist, my darling."

She removed his hand. "You are welcome to do so, sir, but I must decline."

Suddenly, Micheline was there beside them, exuding her own special Gallic charm. "*Mes chers*, how good it is to all be together! We have missed you during your sojourn in Scotland, and I know Andrew has been longing for a bit of time with

Cicely." She smiled into Lord Fairhaven's eyes and touched his arm. "Robin, will you not allow your bride to remain with us at least one more night? We will see her home ourselves, as soon as possible."

"Hmmph." He rolled his eyes. "I don't see how I can refuse."

"Ah, how wonderful you are," Micheline said, sounding quite sincere. "Allow us to walk you outside to the stables." She darted a tiny glance at Cicely, who obediently took her husband's arm as they left the dining room.

When the duke and the three little girls joined the others, Nora found herself alone in the shadowed corridor with Lennox. She thought he had never looked more handsome, his wild Highland looks in appealing contrast to the civilized Englishmen.

Lennox backed her up against the wall and put his arms around her waist. The nausea that had plagued her at supper was gone, replaced by a surge of desire. She wanted to tip her head back, part her lips, and welcome his burning kiss.

"Ah, lass, how I have missed ye," he said, his voice melting her bones.

He was kissing her sensitive ear, the fragile curve of her jaw, each tender spot on her neck. Nora wanted him so much she ached, but some higher part of her found the will to shake her head. "Lennox," she breathed. "We must not."

As he bent to kiss the first curves of her breasts, Nora yearned for more and made a soft, involuntary sound.

"Let us go to your rooms," urged Lennox. "We need to be alone."

He gently fit his hand to her swelling breast, and she felt a delicious cascade of arousal. Her mouth went dry. "If I agree, *this* cannot happen. Please, give me your word that we will only have conversation."

Lennox straightened as if he'd been slapped and stared down at her, his green eyes aswirl with confusion. "Is it something I've done that has turned ye against me?"

Nora led him to her chamber and, once inside, gestured toward the chairs near the windows. "Please, sit," she said.

Lennox shook his head, continuing to stand, illuminated by the rosy-gold beams of light that bathed the room. "Do ye imagine I can be moved here and there at your bidding, that ye can direct me as if our lives were a play?"

"I beg you to listen to me," Nora said, spreading her hands wide in supplication. "You must not think I don't want to be in your arms, to kiss you—"

"Then why won't ye do it? We are wed!" he shot back. "First ye tell me that we must not tell the duke and duchess that ye are my wife, insisting that ye must have a room alone. Now ye say conversation is all we can share. Did I fall short somehow that night at Duart Castle, when I did all in my power to show how precious ye are to me?"

Tears swelled in her heart. "Lennox, can you not see? It isn't as simple as you believe. I want you to complete your quest before we choose a way forward."

"My search is nearly ended." He told her then what he had learned about the man who could be his true father. "I do not yet know his name or circumstances, but Sandhurst says he is a good man." Nora heard the surge of hope in his voice. "His wife and only son have both died, so he lives with grief."

"Perhaps you will soon find that long-sought sense of belonging."

"I will confess something to ye alone." Lennox looked utterly vulnerable, the miniature in his extended hand. "I was worried that this Englishman might not be worth all I have endured to find him. After all, he lay with my mother, knowing she was a married woman! He could well have been without honor, a libertine like Slater."

Her heart seemed to stop when he said *Slater*. "Thank God you know that is not the case. Oh, Lennox, if he is the man you seek, this reunion could transform both your lives." She ached to put her arms around him, but that would be foolhardy. "Let us see what happens next before we talk about the future. I have dreams and needs of my very own, and if I could not weave, I would never be happy."

There was much more Nora could not say: that she was carrying the child of a man he despised, and that fact alone could prevent her from sharing his future. She loved him too much to risk hindering him in the wonderful destiny that waited just around the corner. Lennox might well refuse to accept those reasons, however, so her aspiration to become a master weaver seemed the best argument—at least for now.

Lennox stood now before the windows, looking out over the River Thames, bathed in the molten hues of twilight. A range of emotions passed over his face, and Nora knew him well enough to read most of them. Finally, Lennox fisted his hands and pressed them against his eyes.

"Why must ye make this so hard?" he asked, his voice raw. "If we love each other, can we not find our way through the rest?"

"Perhaps." It took all her will to resist him. "Let us talk again after you meet this man and learn more about him."

"I want ye to be there as well."

Her heart twisted. *He needs me.* "But how will we explain my presence?"

"I don't need to explain to anyone." Turning, his eyes burned through the space that separated them, scorching her heart. "Say ye will come."

Nora nodded. "Yes. I will come."

After a night of fitful sleep, Lennox awoke before dawn to find a message from the Duke of Aylesbury peeking under his door.

My friend will join us in the garden at nine o'clock this morning. Sandhurst.

Suddenly Lennox could not bear to stay indoors another moment. He dressed quickly and went outside, walking away from the Thames and into the heart of the city. The grand manor houses of the Strand gave way to twisting streets crowded with carts and horses, shouting vendors, and half-timbered shops, taverns, and chapels. And everywhere he looked, people stared back, clearly intrigued by his Highland garb. As he drew near the Fleet River, the stink of summer filled his nostrils, and Lennox found himself longing for the fresh, misty air of Skye.

By the time he found his way back to Weston House, it was nearly nine o'clock. The sky was hazy on this warm morning, and, in the distance, the River Thames was dotted with wherries and the white sails of tilt-boats. A tall, broad-shouldered figure waved at him from the knot garden that spread between Weston House and the water. Lennox had imagined he might go inside and wash up, but it seemed he'd run out of time.

Sandhurst, looking elegant yet relaxed in a buff doublet, walked forward to meet him. "I rather feared you'd changed your mind," he said with a trace of irony.

"Nay. My only intention was to explore London for a bit, not run away." Lennox didn't know how to explain that setting off on a solitary journey had always been his solution to life's thornier challenges. "I felt the need to clear my head."

"That's understandable." Sandhurst gestured toward a small table and chairs in a shady corner of the garden. "I thought we might sit outside, away from the bustle of the household."

"I very much want Nora to join us for this meeting," Lennox said. "Will you excuse me for a moment?" Without waiting for Sandhurst to reply, he went up the steps to the manor house. To his relief, Nora was standing in the hall, under a portrait of Cicely that dominated the far wall. Nora looked so lovely, slim and straight in her favorite simple gown of blue silk, her lustrous coppery locks set off by a French hood edged with pearls. When she looked at him, her eyes were tender.

"Ye are here," he said.

"I am."

"Thank God ye are better at following a schedule than I am," Lennox said, longing to take her in his arms. "I will confess that, after struggling to reach this day, I now dread it."

"All will be well." Nora reached up to touch his cheek. "I can feel it."

As they went back outside to the gardens, Lennox stopped at the sight of a fine barge gliding up to steps that led down to the Thames. "Ach," he muttered.

Sandhurst was waiting for them at the edge of the gardens. No doubt he was perplexed by Nora's presence but was too fine a gentleman to say so. "Good morning, Nora. It's nice to see you," he said kindly. "Excuse me, won't you? I will welcome our guest."

Lennox was grateful for Nora's calming presence at his side. Together they walked toward the table, where servants had laid out a bowl of cherries and a plate of cheeses, ham, and savory buns. He had never felt less like eating.

An older man was disembarking from the barge, accompanied by a stocky servant wearing livery of gold velvet. Lennox stared as Sandhurst went forward to greet his friend, and as soon as they started to walk up the lawn, he knew that the man was indeed his father.

"It's him."

"Yes." Nora was nodding soberly. "Without a doubt."

Chapter Twenty-two

The man who was walking toward them was so much like Lennox that Nora felt a shiver run down her spine. He held his head slightly cocked to one side as Lennox did when he was assessing a situation. He was the same height and moved like Lennox, if perhaps a bit more slowly. And the smile that spread over his aging face was exactly like Lennox's.

The main difference between them, besides age, was that this man wore the garb of a wealthy aristocrat. His doublet of dark blue velvet was slashed and set with gems. He wore a jerkin trimmed with silver braid, and a sapphire-studded pomander hung from a chain round his neck. His velvet cap sported a swan's feather, just like the man in the miniature made nearly three decades earlier.

Nora reached for Lennox's cold hand.

"He looks very kind," she whispered.

His only response was a slow nod.

Now, with a closer view of the man's face, Nora felt a wave of emotion. It was like seeing Lennox in the future, decades from now.

Sandhurst led his friend forward and sought to ease the tension. "This is an awkward moment, I suppose, but I trust you two very fine men will meet the challenge." He looked at Lennox. "I went to visit my friend late last evening, after discovering that he had not yet left London for the country. I have told him everything you shared with me."

Lennox straightened his shoulders, waiting for the page to be turned on his life.

"Hello, my boy," said the man, extending his hand. He wore rings set with precious gems. Nora noticed then that his fingers were like Lennox's: long and artistic yet masculine and strong. The older man studied Lennox, his sea-green eyes moving over his Highland garb then settling on his face as if he might find answers there.

As they shook hands, Sandhurst spoke. "Lennox MacLeod, it is my honor to present to you His Grace the Duke of Hastings."

Lennox went pale but did not flinch. "It is a pleasure to meet you, Your Grace," he said.

"But that sounds much too formal," the duke protested, a smile softening his handsome countenance. "I believe you are my son. Perhaps, after we have an opportunity to learn more about one another, you will do me the honor of addressing me as 'Father.'"

Nora's heart swelled as she watched Lennox, sensing the powerful emotions that must be rising up inside him. Thank God she had not divulged anything to him that might disrupt this moment. After waiting a lifetime, Lennox needed to be free to forge a relationship with his true father, without any outside obligations holding him back.

Lennox turned toward Nora. "Sir, I would have ye know Nora Brodie. This lass has helped me more than anyone else to stand here today." He looked hard at her, clearly wanting to say more.

Nora dipped a curtsy, relaxing under the duke's friendly regard. "Your Grace, Lennox made it possible for me to travel from Scotland to London. He has told me his story, so I know how much this day means to him."

"I suggest that we all be seated," Sandhurst said, pouring cups of weak ale for all of them from a silver pitcher.

Soon Lennox and the Duke of Hastings were leaning toward each other, deep in conversation. Nora cut herself a small wedge of cheese and watched them talk as if they had always known one another.

"You will never know what profound meaning this day holds for me," Hastings was saying. "How did you manage to find me?"

Lennox took out the miniature and handed it to him. "Ma left this behind, hidden in the false bottom of a jeweled casket, trusting I would eventually discover it."

"By God, she kept it." The duke's voice thickened as he stared at the small painting of a younger version of himself. "I will confess I never forgot your mother. Perhaps, if I had known she was with child, I would have been more courageous…and everything would have been different."

Nora could see the pain in Lennox's eyes and knew those words, *"Everything would have been different,"* held more weight than the duke could have imagined.

"Perhaps I risk causing offense by speaking plainly, sir," Lennox said. "But if ye knew she was unhappy with my da, and she loved you, why did ye let her return to Skye?"

Nora held her breath, waiting for the duke to turn frosty. She had spent enough time among nobility to know that they were used to being treated with respectful deference, and if one deviated from that code of conduct, a barrier of aristocratic reserve appeared.

Hastings glanced away for a moment before meeting Lennox's even stare. "I am not proud to admit this, but I was unhappy in my marriage to my duchess. I became fond of going away on journeys, and that year I escaped to the distant Isle of Mull to purchase sheep from Laird MacLean." He paused to sigh deeply. "I arrived at the forbidding Duart Castle to find another guest: your extraordinary mother, Eleanor, with her bold little son, Ciaran. I think we fell in love the moment we met."

Nora sensed the acceleration of Lennox's heartbeat as he

listened to his true father supply the missing pieces that connected their two lives.

"I wished with all my heart that I could change my circumstances...and those of your mother," the duke continued. "But we were both wed to others. We had children born of those marriages, and I carried the weight of my obligations as a duke." He paused, looking off as if he could see something the others could not. "So, you see, Eleanor and I stole those summer days, and nights, knowing we would have to make them last a lifetime. It was as if we had found another world, outside of time."

Lennox lifted a hand to rub his eyes, perhaps hoping that would help him to see more clearly. "Ye could be speaking of someone I never knew. When I was growing up on the Isle of Skye, my mother seemed content enough with her lot."

The duke shrugged, looking pained. "I surmise your parents worked through their differences, as I endeavored to do with my own wife. But I never forgot Eleanor. I sent her letters."

"Aye," Lennox said. "Da told me that's how he uncovered the truth when I was four. He found a letter from her lover, signed with an *R*."

The duke colored slightly. "My Christian name is Richard. Except for my close family, your mother was the only person who ever called me Richard."

"So, if ye signed an *R*, no one would suspect the writer could be the Duke of Hastings," said Lennox. Nora could guess how hard this must be for Lennox, yet she saw compassion in his gaze.

"There is so much more for us to talk about," said the duke, leaning forward. "My son, I hope you will agree to come with me to Greythorne Manor, my country estate in Surrey. I only ask for your time, long enough for us to become better acquainted...and discuss the future." He cleared his throat. "Perhaps you have heard that I lost my only child, Charles, just a few months ago. I've been lost in a sea of grief. As you may imagine, *your* unexpected appearance in my life feels akin to a gift from God."

Lennox nodded slowly. "Aye. I would like to go with ye to Surrey. But—" He looked toward Nora.

"Of course, Mistress Brodie is welcome to come with us," the duke hastened to say, every inch a gentleman as he sent Nora a polite smile. She could feel the man's questions in the air between them.

A shadow passed over her heart. "You are very kind, sir, and I deeply appreciate your invitation. However, I have business to attend to here in London. And in truth, I would not want to intrude on your time with your son."

From Weston House came the sound of Percy barking, followed by the happy voices of Susan, Tessa, and Alison. Nora looked over to see them emerging from the manor, hurrying out across the lawn. Seconds later, Micheline came into view behind the girls, utterly lovely in a jonquil-yellow gown.

Everyone began to rise, and Sandhurst went to join his family. Watching them move about on the clipped lawn with the River Thames as a backdrop, Nora reflected on the rarefied, often idyllic world of the English aristocracy. Was it possible that Lennox might find a place among these people, enjoying such pleasures on a regular basis? She imagined him traveling to Europe, studying painting with some of the gifted artists the Duke of Hastings would know. It was not a world Lennox would have chosen for himself, but perhaps he might find himself fitting in better than he could now imagine. And clearly, the duke had a great void in his life that only a son could fill.

The two men were standing close together, still conversing, clearly sculpted from the same block of marble despite the differences in their garb.

"How pensive you look," a feminine voice said near her shoulder.

Nora turned to find Cicely standing there, enchanting in a leaf-green gown and a fashionable French hood set with topaz. "I didn't see you."

"No doubt because your entire future is passing in front of your eyes," her friend said. "I'm so eager to know, now that

Lennox has discovered he is the son of a duke, do you intend to reveal your wedded state?"

Nora shook her head. "I can't say yet." Even if she had settled on an answer to Cicely's bold question, she wouldn't share it with anyone but Lennox.

Very soon, everyone will leave Weston House, Nora thought with a sigh.

During supper, she heard Micheline and Sandhurst telling their daughters to begin choosing the special belongings they wished to take to Gloucestershire, where they would spend the rest of the summer at the family's country estate. Susan, the oldest, was especially excited at the prospect of riding her favorite horse again.

Meanwhile, Lennox admitted that he would indeed be visiting the Duke of Hastings's manor house in Surrey. Over a dessert of plum tart sprinkled with sugar, the others peppered him with questions about his plans. Lennox had looked uncomfortable as he replied, casting frequent glances toward Nora.

It was Cicely, however, who delivered the news that most shook Nora's world. "I had a visit from Robin today. He insists I must return home tomorrow, or he will arrive here to take me by force." She pushed back her trencher and sighed. "Robin also brought some exceedingly sad news. Andrew, have you heard? Sir Raymond Slater's ship, *Hercules,* was lost in a storm off the coast of Spain. There were no survivors. How tragic, for such a man to die in the very prime of his life!"

Hearing these words, Nora felt shock ripple through her. Slater was lost. *Dead!* Trying to keep her expression calm, she leaned forward, eager to hear every word.

"Indeed?" Sandhurst was saying, brow arched. "I hardly think he'll be missed by anyone, except perhaps his trading patrons."

Cicely frowned. "Why do you say so? I always found Sir Raymond to be very charming, in a rather wicked way. In fact, before my Robin proposed marriage, Sir Raymond showed quite an interest in me, and I was tempted to reciprocate."

"Well, that would have never happened as long as you were living under my roof." Sandhurst's face darkened. "Sir Raymond Slater always struck me as unscrupulous, to put it politely."

Nora winced inwardly when Lennox spoke up. "I couldn't agree more. I detested him, almost on sight, when our paths crossed at Stirling Castle."

"By my troth," protested Cicely. "The poor man is dead! Will you not allow him to rest in peace?"

"Cicely is quite right," Micheline interjected in her soft French accent. "You men should save this conversation for another time. Shall we leave the table now? I know three young girls who must prepare for bed."

As the others rose, still talking, Nora hoped she could slip away. Sandhurst, however, appeared at her side before she had taken a dozen steps.

"I want you to know you are more than welcome to stay here for as long as you'd like," he said without preamble. "I've already spoken to Throgmorton and Mistress Goodwyn. They are here at all times, even when we are not, and they will be happy to serve you."

Nora's face felt warm. "You're very kind, sir."

"Nonsense. Micheline and I both want you to stay."

Pride stirred in her breast. "I do have plans to meet with the keeper of the Great Wardrobe," she professed, stretching the truth, "but until my situation is settled, I am grateful for your kindness."

"They will be very fortunate to have you," Sandhurst said, as his wife appeared, smiling by his side.

Micheline took his arm but leaned closer to Nora. "*Ma chère*," she said, smiling, "we must talk tomorrow. May I visit you in the morning?"

No sooner had Nora nodded agreement than little Alison

was spotted in the corridor, pulling Percy's feathered tail. Sandhurst called out to his youngest daughter, and Nora took that opportunity to bid her hosts goodnight.

Alone at last in her chamber, she went to the carved chest against the wall and took out her satchel. She had unpacked it and stored her clothing herself, not wanting the serving maid to know everything she had brought.

Now Nora opened the satchel, her mind racing with new possibilities. Inside, carefully rolled into cylinders, were her precious tapestries: the childhood weaving of the rabbit, the nearly finished creation made from Lennox's pattern, and another smaller tapestry, wedged between the other two. She closed her eyes for a moment and attempted to conjure up the magical power tapestry had always held over her very spirit. All Nora's life, when she had been weaving, she could leave the world behind and almost inhabit her creation.

Could she do it again, now that Lennox had planted himself inside her heart? One by one, she spread the tapestries out on her bed, gazing at each one in turn.

A soft tap came at the door. "Nora? Let me in."

Lennox's tone was firm, and she obeyed without question, seized by a need to be alone with him. *It may be the last time.* When she opened the door, he seemed to fill the space. It seemed he had bathed, for his wet hair was scraped back from his face and his linen shirt clung to damp patches of his torso. Nora stood back so that he might enter.

No sooner was the door closed than he took her in his arms. She felt helpless to resist the power and emotion of his embrace. Melting against him, inhaling his familiar scent, listening to his heartbeat, Nora wanted to say, *I love you*, but she knew that would only complicate matters tonight.

"I have some wine," she told him instead, stepping back. "Will you have a cup?"

"If ye will join me." He seemed to see inside her. As Nora poured the wine, he walked over to look at the tapestries she had spread on the deep-rose coverlet.

She brought the wine and came to stand beside him. After one drink, Lennox set the silver cup on a small table.

"I see ye have brought our tapestry from Duart Castle," he said, staring at the woven picture of the birlinn on the blue waves. "How gifted ye are, Nora."

If only she could tell him how much it meant that he'd made the drawing for her, and how close she had felt to him when she was weaving during the time he'd been away, helping with the shipwreck.

But instead, Nora avoided his gaze. "Why have you come here tonight? I know you must have a great deal to do, preparing to go with your…father."

"Ye know full well why I am here. I want ye to come with me."

"I am sorry, but it cannot be." Her heart ached with each word. "I think we both know that the time has come for us to part ways. We have grown close through all we've shared, but now your quest is ended, and you must go on to discover what your new life will hold."

"Aye, but *ye* must be at my side." Every muscle in his body was taut with emotion.

"No—" she began.

When Nora shook her head, Lennox grasped both her arms and lifted her easily off the floor. "Do ye imagine I can be fobbed off like someone ye barely know? God save me, lass, I have shown ye my very heart, yet ye will not even summon the courage to look me in the eye!"

"You are right, of course." She managed then to meet his anguished gaze. "Let us sit together and talk."

Nora brought their cups of wine to the two chairs near the window and sat down. Lennox, clearly unhappy with the space separating them, drew his chair around so that it was facing close to hers.

"Now, then," he said, "tell me, what has happened to change your feelings toward me? Have ye forgotten the vows we exchanged?"

Suddenly the room felt very warm. Pushing back her long mass of curls, Nora licked her dry lips. "Of course not, but perhaps you have forgotten what you told me moments after we rode away from Stirling Castle?" She watched his brows flick upward as if he suspected she was trying to trick him. "You said handfasting vows could be undone with just a few words, by either party, within a year. It seemed that our supposed vows were only spoken to placate my father."

One of the candle flames by the bed guttered out, deepening the shadows. "Do ye seek to confuse this matter by dredging up the nonsense I said so long ago? All of that was before we lay together in the woods, before we came to share our deepest feelings and secrets, before I made love to ye with not only my body but my very heart."

"Oh, Lennox, why must you make this so difficult?" Nora's voice broke on a sob.

"Because something is not right." He went down on one knee beside her chair. As if sensing her desire to hide her face, he captured both her hands in his. "I know ye are not the sort of lass who changes her mind with the wind. I bid ye, tell me the simple truth."

Her voice was barely audible. "The…truth?"

"Aye!" His eyes flashed. "Why have ye kept our wedded state a secret here in London, and why won't ye come with me to Surrey, as my wife?"

Never had Nora known anyone who had the courage to speak so directly, even though he risked being hurt by her answer. Her heart swelled anew with love for him.

"All right." Her voice shook, but she drew a deep breath. "I will tell you."

Chapter Twenty-three

Nora's lovely face was just inches away. He wanted to lift her off the chair, into his arms, but instead he waited, watching her, seeing the suffering in her eyes.

"I cannot go with you to Greythorne Manor because I am with child."

Lennox drew back slightly, stunned, but then her words sank in, and he wanted to shout with joy. "A babe! But that's wonderful!"

No answering smile came from Nora. Instead, she shook her head. "Do you remember the night I came to your bed and asked you to take me away from Stirling Castle? You knew I had a more desperate reason than I could share, and yet you were good enough not to press me." She paused, but he merely continued to watch her, waiting this time for a terrible blow. "The fact is I had to get away from Stirling because I already knew that I carried a child."

Silence filled the air, heavy as smoke, as the truth became real. "Slater's babe."

"Yes." Nora leaned forward and framed his face with both her hands. "I am so sorry. I wanted to tell you the truth the first time we lay together, but I suppose I was afraid and confused. At Duart Castle, when I revealed that I was not a virgin, I intended to tell you the rest, but—"

"Ye were too great a coward," he said flatly, feeling misled, betrayed, confused, angry.

Tears filled her eyes, as if he had strategically used his dirk to inflict a flesh wound. "Yes. I was. You were so good to me after hearing that I had lain with another man that I simply couldn't bear to shock you with one more hard thing. I knew how much uncertainty lay ahead, and I wanted to share that night with you." She turned her face away. "It was such a beautiful night. I'll keep the memory with me always."

Did she mean to bid him farewell, forever? Ignoring her last words, Lennox replied, "I see no sign that ye are with child. What if it's a mistake?"

"Women know," Nora said, flushing slightly.

"What the devil does that mean? This is too important for ye to speak in riddles. I have known my share of lasses, including my own sister, and I know more than ye might think."

She swallowed. "I have not had my monthly flow since that night with…him. The very sight of food makes me feel ill."

Her reference to Slater made him see red. "If that villain were not already dead, I would kill him with my bare hands. Slowly."

"Even that could not change the past." She shook her head again. "Besides, there is no point in this conversation. You must see that any thoughts you might have had about a future for us must end. You are going with your father to Surrey, and I will remain in London, weaving."

The anger he had felt just moments ago was gone now, replaced by a determination to change this outcome. "Nay, I do not see anything like that." Reaching up, he dared to pull her into his arms. "Ye may be with child, but the babe will need a father. Come with me, Nora. We'll tell the duke that we wed in Scotland, and no one need ever know the rest."

She made a token effort at struggling to free herself, then softened against him, clinging to his wide shoulders. "Lennox, can you not see? You have a new life ahead of you. I watched you today with the duke. I saw a bond that began to form the moment you first saw each other. If this is the life you are meant to have, the part of you that has been missing, you must go with him and explore it without anything to hinder you."

"Stop that. Ye could never hinder me." He heard the throb

in his own voice before he did the next, very natural thing and kissed her. His mouth slanted over hers, and she made a little sobbing sound as she opened to him, meeting his tongue. Arousal surged through him. His heart began to pound and his cock stiffened, aching for her in a way he'd never known was possible. There were no words for his feelings. He would simply have to show her.

Nora found herself kneeling with Lennox on the rush-strewn floor, her resistance burned away completely in the fire of their passion. His mouth was intoxicating. How she had missed him! His hands, so beautifully masculine, seemed to burn away her clothing, no longer gentle but confident, even commanding. When, for a moment, her mind engaged, and she started to draw back, Lennox clasped the back of her head and warned, "Nay. Ye are mine."

Oh, yes. She gazed into his gold-flecked green eyes. Perhaps they were meant to have this interlude to hold onto later, when they were separated. When he scooped her up in his arms and carried her to the bed, she made no protest. Instead, as he undressed her by the flickering light of one remaining candle, her fingers moved to unfasten the front of his tunic and then his belt. He was so gloriously made, sculpted yet warm and utterly human, and Nora wanted to touch him—every inch of him.

Only tonight, she reminded herself. Soon enough, they would have to deal with the real world, but surely they deserved to savor these moments of bliss.

Lennox straddled her hips, deftly unlacing her bodice then her kirtle, drawing them off, his expression frankly carnal as he rendered her naked. When her breasts were bared, he drew in his breath, and Nora wanted to cover herself. Her nipples had been tender in recent days, one more sign of her condition.

He cupped her right breast, squeezing gently, and she felt a lightning burst of sensation.

"Ah, how beautiful ye are," he said, his voice hoarse. He framed her slender torso with his splayed fingers and drew her up off the bed until his cheek lightly scraped her breast.

She smothered a gasp, wanting to beg him to touch her nipple. After an endless moment, his tongue, hot and wet, did just that, and an erotic response surged deep in her belly. She throbbed there, wet and warm, longing for just one thing. As he began to suck her nipple, slowly, like an artist wielding a paintbrush, she dropped her head back, her hair spilling over the coverlet. Lennox lowered himself slightly, leaning forward so that his erection brushed her nether lips, teasing, tantalizing, as he continued to suckle first one nipple and then the other. She opened her thighs wider. The storm was building inside her, cresting and retreating, driving her mad.

Suddenly impatient for control, Nora reached up for his shoulders and tried unsuccessfully to move him. "Let me, please, let me," she whispered urgently. Their eyes locked for an instant in the flickering light before he allowed her to push him back on the bed. She rolled on top of his powerful body, feeling exultant.

"What do ye mean to do with me, lass?" he rasped, arching a golden brow.

She replied by straddling him as he had done her, leaning forward over his hard-muscled chest to kiss him. Her hair fell around them like a curtain, and Lennox's hands roamed over her hips, her bottom, the small of her back, then back up to her sensitive breasts.

"Tell me what ye want, love," he invited, his gaze smoldering.

She thrust her breasts out toward him, cupping one herself so that the nipple brushed his lips. "I want more. Please, more."

He obeyed, sucking, licking, moving from one breast to the other until the waves of arousal broke higher and higher. She was nearly there. As if sensing this, Lennox reached around with both hands and cupped her bottom, his fingers straying between her legs, groaning when he felt how slick and ready she was. Nora sat down on the pulsing length of him, rubbing back and forth, finding her own rhythm.

"That's it, lass," he urged softly, just before the clouds opened, lightning struck, and pleasure cascaded out from her core like a hot summer storm.

For an instant, her vision dimmed. Damp with perspiration, she lay down over his body, her heart thundering. "Oh. Oh!" she panted.

"Now will ye let me have a turn?"

She heard the smile in his voice. "Not yet. Lie still."

"This is torture, lass."

Nora smiled into his eyes, loving the sense of play and trust between them. "Now you know how I feel, when you are on top and I am trapped, like a butterfly, as you have your way with me."

His voice held an undercurrent of sensual amusement. "Go on, then. I'll *wait*, and then ye will pay for this."

Love welled up in her. She kissed him lustily, and when she held his arms down, he pretended to be helpless. Moving lower, Nora caressed and kissed his shoulders, lightly running her fingertips over the muscled planes of his torso then leaning down to lick one of his flat nipples. He twitched in surprise and made a sound low in his throat.

"Ah, so you like that!" Delighted, she sucked at it, making it pucker.

"Ye should stop that," he warned.

Nora laughed. She turned her cheek against the crisp hair that lightly covered his chest, then kissed her way down the ridges of his belly, following the arrow of gilded hair that pointed the way to his sex. Reaching lower, she felt him, even hotter and harder than before, and wrapped her hand around him.

"That's *enough*, Nora." He sounded oddly breathless.

She smiled then dared to touch the tip of him with her tongue. For an instant, she feared he might come off the bed, but then he went utterly still, and even the rasp of his breathing ceased. He smelled of her, and that just made her feel more wanton, more connected to him. Using her tongue and her hands, she did her best to give him the same kind of wicked pleasure he had given her that night at Duart Castle. Lennox alternated between holding his breath and groaning, and once he reached down to hold her head, pushing himself into her mouth, which only increased the thrill of her arousal.

Then, suddenly, he caught her arms with both hands and brought her away from him, as if she weighed nothing at all. "Enough," he groaned. "One more second, and it would be over for me."

Effortlessly, he flipped her over into the pillows and stared down at her, his expression filled with wonder. "Ye are the most glorious woman in the world." He took her mouth in a deep kiss, fitting himself between her legs. It was as if they had been created to be together this way.

Nora desperately wanted to tell him how much she loved him, but knowing how this night would end, she held back.

"Later," he whispered in her ear, "ye shall be the butterfly again. But first…"

And then he was pushing into her, an inch at a time, and the feeling took her breath away. When he had fully sheathed himself inside her, they lay joined for several moments, their hearts beating in unison.

"I have dreamed of being with ye like this," he breathed.

Slowly, he began to move, the hard length of him withdrawing then filling her again, gradually finding a rhythm as Nora lifted her hips to meet him. It was like flying, soaring in his arms, higher and higher with each thrust. Her face was warm and damp, her heart pounding. Lennox held her tighter, muttering words of love just before he pushed all the way inside her one more time and released a primal groan.

Nora wrapped her arms around his back, dizzy with the sheer bliss of the moment. Eventually, he raised his head and met her eyes.

"Tell me ye love me."

"I do."

"Say it, lass."

"I love you."

"Ah. I knew it."

Nora felt his smile as he claimed her mouth in a sleepy kiss. He turned on his side then, cradling her near, and dozed off. She knew that Lennox assumed the future was resolved now. Bittersweet emotions tangled inside her as she rested her head in the crook of his shoulder. He smelled so good, and she felt safe from the world in his embrace.

Soon enough, he would hear what lay ahead…

The barest hint of plum was seeping over the sky as Lennox came awake. He reached for Nora, but she wasn't there. Sitting up, he wondered if it had all been a dream.

They had fallen asleep, limbs entwined, on top of the rose-patterned coverlet on her bed. In the dim light of early dawn, he recognized the three tapestries spread out along the other half of the bed, just as they had been when he came in last night.

"Nora." His voice was husky with sleep. "Where have ye gone?"

To his surprise, she emerged out of the shadows near the carved storage chest. Fully dressed in a simple gray gown, she was tying back her curls. As she drew closer, he saw that her beautiful eyes were sad.

"We must talk," she said.

He felt a chill. "We already talked last night. Everything is settled." The expression on her face made him reach out to catch her wrists. "We love each other. I will gladly be a father to the babe ye carry. No one need ever know—" He broke off at the sight of her shaking her head.

"But you will know." Her eyes shone as she tried to free herself from his grasp. "Lennox, loose me."

Immediately, he complied. "I must be having a nightmare. Did I harm you in some way when we lay together?"

"No, of course not." Her eyes roved over his naked body and she blushed, as if she had not kissed every inch of him mere hours before. "You should put something on." She handed him his linen shirt.

He pushed his arms into the loose sleeves and rose from the bed. "By God, if ye do not speak plainly to me, I shall go mad."

Nora started to pace then returned to face him. "Even if I were not with child, we could not be together. I could never go with you and the duke to Surrey or live with you as your wife in a grand manor house."

He had to stop himself from shouting. "Why the devil not?"

"I'm not that sort of woman."

Even though he sensed the truth in this, he couldn't resist arguing. "Micheline doesn't seem to find it a hardship to be a duchess!"

"We are not the same." She came closer then and took his hands. "I have given up everything, even my own mother, to be a weaver of tapestries. I have a deep passion for my art, my craft, and I have ambitions to fulfill. You know that very well! Did you imagine all of that would simply disappear because of our romantic notions?"

Lennox wanted to shake her. "Romantic *notions*?"

"Yes, of course it is more than that. But it cannot be. You have a destiny of your own that you *must* fulfill, and so do I." She reached up to softly touch his cheek. "I am asking you to release me."

A desperate sob rose in his throat. "But what do ye mean to do, all alone and with child in a city like London? It's impossible, Nora!"

Her face was pale but composed. "I have it all planned. I already have made arrangements to meet with the keeper of the Great Wardrobe, at Whitehall Palace, and I know I can find a position within the royal court."

Each word was like a blow. "But—the babe," he interrupted.

"I will present myself as a new widow. As a widow, I can make my way as an independent woman."

"That's why ye didn't want anyone in London to know we were wed." He found it hard to breathe.

"Yes. But until yesterday, I wasn't certain what the best course would be. When the duke arrived, and I saw you together, it all became clear."

"How will ye live?" Lennox demanded.

She led him to the other side of the bed, where the tapestries were spread out, and pointed to one he had never seen before. It was small but exquisitely made, depicting a maiden with a harp, sitting amid white and pink roses, with a castle in the distance. The colors were rich, the details were precise, and the weaving was impeccable. It was a work of art.

"Where did this come from?" Lennox asked, guessing the answer.

"It was hidden at the bottom of my satchel," she replied. "I wove the tapestry on a small loom about a year ago. It was meant to be a perfect sample of my work, to show the King of Scots when we would go to Stirling. Father always said I could sell it one day if need be. Many aristocrats purchase small tapestries like this one, called an *arras*, to hang in more intimate settings." She paused. "It is possible even King Henry or his queen might want it."

"And then you would have money to begin this independent life you desire." His voice sounded as hollow as he felt in that moment. "That's why ye brought it from Stirling."

"Yes. It would bring enough to have a fine loom and a house large enough for two. Soon enough, I will be weaving at the royal court." She smiled, as if anticipating that life. "I will find satisfaction, raising my child and pursuing my artistic ambitions."

"I see." He looked away, his heart twisted in a knot of despair and disbelief.

"Surely you must realize it is the right thing for you, too."

"Do not presume to tell me what is best for me." Lennox

turned his head and met her gaze, determined to try one more time. "Ye know very well that I have the highest regard for your gifts. I would never ask ye to choose."

"Then you understand why I cannot go with you," she said. "It would be impossible for me to be a master weaver in the world of the Duke of Hastings. And if I am your wife, I would have no power of my own."

Desperately he wondered why they could not find a way forward together, but clearly she had made up her mind. When he spoke again, there was a harder edge to his voice. "I would chart a different course for us, but it seems we are at cross purposes."

With that, he grabbed his plaid from the rush-strewn floor and hurriedly donned it. It seemed impossible to believe that they were truly parting. Fearing he might break down, Lennox started toward the door, but Nora followed and caught his arm.

"We should keep last night as a memory of how well we loved," she said, her composure crumbling. Her blue eyes swam with tears. "Our time was brief yet perfect, like a shooting star."

He wanted to turn and catch her up in his arms, to kiss her into submission, but he knew her too well. It would only prolong his suffering. "If it brings ye comfort to think that, do so, but remembering would only be a painful reminder of what I've lost." Opening the door, Lennox looked back one last time. "I love ye, Nora. Be happy."

Chapter Twenty-four

Nora stayed in her room until mid-morning, hesitant to emerge for fear she would encounter Lennox again before he left Weston House. She wasn't certain whether it would be more painful to see him one more time…or never again.

Numbly, she stood at the mullioned windows and watched the distant activity on the River Thames. When a knock came at her door, she felt a thrill. Certain it must be Lennox, she crossed the room and lifted the latch.

"Oh, my dear, look at you. You are so very pale," Cicely exclaimed, entering without an invitation. "Why have you not come downstairs this morning? Are you ill?"

Nora turned away from the doorway, unable to speak about what had happened. Her friend followed her.

"Sit down." Cicely put her in a chair then looked around the room, taking in the tapestries spread across one side of the bed, the rumpled coverlet on the other. And then her eyes fell on the two cups, still half full of wine. "This is about Lennox, isn't it? He was here!"

Nora felt an urge to be ill, but there was no food in her stomach. "He wanted me to come with him, as his wife." Weeping, she added, "He said he would raise this baby as his own."

"But that is wonderful!" Cicely rejoiced. "Why are you crying?" As she spoke, she poured some wine into another cup and lifted it to Nora's lips. "You are distraught. Drink a little of this."

Nora tried and felt somewhat revived. Sitting up, she sought to compose herself. "Once I saw him with the duke, who is clearly the father he's been seeking, I knew he must go with him. Alone."

"That sounds very noble." Cicely looked doubtful. "Did you truly mean it?"

"I love him. The duke is clearly a very fine man. Lennox has gone through his life feeling as if some important part of himself was missing. He must be free to discover it."

"And why couldn't you be by his side?"

She shook her head again. "It is Lennox's nature to want to help people in need; his own sister has told me so." Nora paused, remembering the day Fiona had teased Lennox about rescuing maidens in distress. "As you know, he only exchanged vows with me to placate my father during our escape from Stirling. His feelings for me now may be real, but I think he should have the chance to find out what's in store for him without me and my baby muddling the situation."

Cicely tilted her head as if in doubt. "Is that all?"

"Lennox despises the father of this baby. I don't see how he could truly raise it as his own, even if he was not involved now with the Duke of Hastings."

"I am *tormented* by curiosity." Cicely leaned forward. "Won't you please tell me who the father is?"

She swallowed, thinking that perhaps it didn't matter now that Slater was dead. "I think you know him. Sir Raymond Slater."

"Oh!" Cicely clapped her hands. "By my troth, you look as if you've bitten a lemon when you say his name. Sir Raymond was one of the most attractive, compelling men I ever knew, and surely you must have thought so too, in order to lie with him." Cicely wagged a finger, her ruby ring sparkling in the light that streamed through the windows. "I nearly married him, you know."

"Did he propose to you?" Nora asked in surprise.

"No. But if I had been a tiny bit more encouraging, I think he would have."

Although Nora didn't want to insult her friend's taste, she couldn't resist saying, "I think it is best that it never went that far."

Cicely sniffed. "There is a great deal you don't understand about men, you know, having spent your life locked up with a big, dull *loom*."

Nora's spirit stirred in protest. "I loved my life. I found it exceptionally fulfilling, and I didn't have to deal with heartbreak or scandal." It was thrilling to imagine being shut in a room with a fine loom, a glorious pattern, and plenty of vividly-dyed silk and wool thread. It would feel immensely comforting, like sleeping under thick, warm covers on a frigid night. But someone like Cicely could never understand that. "Besides, it doesn't matter now. Sir Raymond is lost at sea, Lennox has gone off to discover a new life as the son of a duke, and I am going to the court of King Henry VIII to pursue my dreams as a weaver."

"Who is going to look after the baby once he is born?"

"I will hire a nursemaid."

Cicely blinked. "You have thought of everything, it seems."

Pointing toward the bed, Nora told her about the exquisite tapestry that was spread out there, and how she meant to sell it to pay for a house and other essentials. "Of course, I will have to find a position with the Great Wardrobe, but you have said you can help with that."

Just then, a soft knock came at the door, and Nora immediately started to rise, as if she had glimpsed Lennox on the threshold.

"*Bonjour,* Nora." The door swung open, and Micheline appeared, carrying a tray as if she were a serving maid. "When you did not come downstairs today, I thought I might bring a bit of nourishment to you. Are you feeling unwell?"

Nora thought the duchess looked like an angel as she crossed the room. When she reached the chair, she glanced at Cicely. "Oh, I see you are here as well, Cicely. Help me with this, won't you?"

Moments later, the dishes from the tray had been set up on a small table. Micheline had brought enough for all three of them to share. There was warm, dense manchet bread with a golden-brown crust, served with a small pot of butter. Other small plates contained smoked fish, coddled eggs, and sliced plums.

"Goodness," said Nora, "I can never eat all of this."

"I noticed that you have been looking a bit under the weather," her hostess replied, "so I hoped at least one of these offerings might tempt you."

Cicely poured watered wine into enameled cups and passed one to Nora. "You should tell Micheline what is really happening," she said. "You can trust her, and she will be able to help, perhaps more than I can."

Nora's heart jumped. The old feeling of shame rose up in her, as it had for so long with Lennox. "Oh, I don't know..." She broke off, her face hot.

Cicely didn't hesitate. Turning to her sister-in-law, she said, "Nora is with child. It happened at Stirling Castle, when Sir Raymond Slater was visiting there. I know what you are thinking: Did he take advantage of her? Perhaps. She wasn't feeling well. But now we must help her. I have been thinking—"

Micheline interrupted her with a stern look. "Stop talking." As she turned to Nora, her expression softened. "*Chérie*, how do you know that you carry a baby?"

Before she had a chance to think, Nora was telling the kind Frenchwoman about the night when Sir Raymond Slater helped her to her room, and how she had lost her innocence to him. "I knew I was with child because he put his seed in me." The familiar feeling of disgrace came over her like a fever. "My monthly flow did not come. I felt too ill to eat. I grew very moody. Those are all signs, are they not?"

Micheline reached for Nora's cold hand. "You know, of course, that just because the seed is planted, it does not always grow?"

Nora considered this. "I suppose I did think, later that night, that I must conceive. I didn't realize it could be otherwise. I moved from Flanders with my father when I was ten years old and I haven't seen Mama since then." Saying this aloud, she felt a familiar pang. "No one ever explained these things to me."

"You were completely innocent," Micheline said. "In my own case, I was married before I ever knew Andrew, in France. My husband was killed in a joust. I soon discovered that Bernard had been repeatedly unfaithful during our marriage, and I questioned everything I ever believed about our love." She paused, a faint shadow of sadness crossing her face. "It was a terrible time, and I discovered that a shock can cause your monthly flow to cease. After my husband was killed, mine did not come for many weeks. Perhaps…?"

"I wish it could be true, but I am certain now of my condition." For a moment, Nora questioned whether she could speak of such personal matters but realized she could trust Micheline. And Cicely, for all her shortcomings, was determined to be her friend. "My breasts are very tender. The nipples are sensitive." She flushed, remembering last night with Lennox. "And my belly begins to feel changed. There is a firmness there."

"Oh. Well, then, it seems it must be true." Micheline sighed.

"Tell her about Lennox," urged Cicely.

Realizing that if she did not explain to Micheline about Lennox and the handfasting, Cicely would do it for her, Nora told her the rest of the story. However, she did not mention the nights of passion they had shared. Some things must remain private between her and Lennox. "He has helped me every step of the way, from leaving Stirling to coming to London. How fortunate I have been to have the help of such a good man. But now Lennox has found his true father, and it is time for me to make my own way forward."

"You two have tender feelings for one another though?" Micheline asked gently.

Nora felt her cheeks growing warm. "I am human," she replied, trying to keep her tone light. "What woman could resist him?"

"Indeed!" Cicely agreed. "That's very true." She leaned back in her chair and popped a slice of plum into her mouth, smiling dreamily.

"However, my condition prevents me from indulging in such romantic flights of fancy," Nora said. "I have more serious considerations. I mean to find a home here in London so that my child will grow up to be happy and secure."

Cicely spoke up again. "Nora has worked it all out quite brilliantly. She will present herself as a widow, thereby legitimizing her child and also making it possible for her to live independently, with some power."

"Widows have more rights than other women," Nora agreed. "I will simply have to make up a story about the death of my husband, in our country village. Who would question it?" Walking to the bed, she picked up the third tapestry and explained again, this time to Micheline, how she meant to sell it and start a new life with the proceeds. "It is my very best work," she added, putting it in the Frenchwoman's outstretched hands.

Micheline examined the piece, running her fingertips over the meticulously stitched figure of the maiden among richly colored roses. "But, my dear, it is exquisite!"

"I call it *Maiden with a Harp*. I concentrated every bit of my skill and love into this small tapestry. It was meant to convince someone important of my abilities."

"Do you mean to show it to Jan Mostinck, the Great Wardrobe's tapestry keeper?"

"Perhaps, although it has occurred to me that Queen Catherine herself, or one of her ladies, might desire to own it." Nora had thought of this after leaving Scotland. She could easily imagine the Scots Queen Mary, who cared deeply for beautiful things, purchasing such a tapestry.

Micheline lifted her brows. "Queen Catherine is too young

and frivolous to appreciate this work of art. Also, I suspect that she may be out of favor with King Henry."

"But is she not his *fifth* queen?" Nora wondered how the monarch could simply change his mind about his wives.

"Indeed," Cicely exclaimed. "He finds ways to dispose of the poor ladies if they begin to bore him or do not provide a male heir to the throne. But who would want to lie with him now, king or not? They say his fat legs are covered with oozing ulcers. He is grotesque!"

"Watch your tongue, or you'll be arrested for treason," Micheline's tone was light yet laced with caution. "Or perhaps His Majesty will find a way to dispose of Robin and claim *you* as the next queen!"

"I would have to drink poison before the wedding night," Cicely parried, laughing.

Micheline put a hand on Nora's shoulder. "My family is packing to leave London for the summer, but I will try to help you before we go. Andrew has said you are welcome to stay here, but I understand your need to be independent." She paused, looking thoughtful. "I may have an idea for a house that would suit you very well. What name will you take?"

Gratitude welled up in Nora. Although she felt strong and confident she could navigate the challenges ahead, underneath she was conscious of being alone and vulnerable. "You are so kind." She wanted to embrace the duchess but gave her a radiant smile instead. "I thought I might call myself Mistress Lovejoy. If I encounter anyone who knew me before, when I was weaving at court with my father, I will tell them I married in Scotland but am now a widow. What do you think?"

Cicely clapped in delight. "It's wonderful."

"I agree," said Micheline, clasping Nora's hands. "Welcome to London, Mistress Lovejoy!"

Chapter Twenty-five

The journey to Surrey was made in the Duke of Hastings's closed carriage, which had been recently imported from Belgium. Lennox had never seen anything like it, not even at the Scottish royal court. Of course, Lennox would have preferred to ride on horseback rather than shut up inside the dusty, jouncing coach, but he couldn't leave his father to travel alone.

Conversation was nearly impossible, given the noise of the wheels over the rocks and ruts of the roadway, yet it seemed the duke was content just to look at Lennox from the seat facing him.

"It was kind of Sandhurst to lend you a doublet. You look exceptionally fine in it," his father said when they came to a smoother, quieter stretch of road. "Heller, my tailor, will arrive at Greythorne Manor within the fortnight. I've described you to him and asked that he bring what he can—doublets, hose, and so on. Clothing that might fit you with a few alterations."

Lennox glanced down at the new spice-brown doublet he wore with his belted plaid. The relatively simple garment had been a first step, he decided, toward assimilating into this new world, though he couldn't yet imagine putting away his lengths of muted green tartan. *One step at a time*, Lennox thought, smiling at the duke. "Thank you."

Soon, the carriage rumbled up a long drive lined with beech trees. A fine manor house built of red brick, its rooftops decorated with ornate chimneys, came into view. It was laid out in four wings that enclosed a central courtyard, with a gatehouse facing the drive. His father was watching him, waiting for his reaction.

"Ye have a very impressive home indeed," Lennox said.

"Ah, it's gratifying to hear you say so, my son. I know it's very different from Scotland."

Unexpectedly, Lennox's heart tightened. This leafy estate, all red brick and sculpted gardens, was quite the opposite of wild, dramatic, stone-built Dunvegan, where one arrived by water and ascended through a sea-gate. He closed his eyes, seeing Magnus, Alasdair Crotach, Ciaran, Fi, and all the clansfolk he had known since birth. Yet he'd left Skye to seek out the truth, and now, here he was. Had the time come for him to stop thinking of himself as a MacLeod?

Lennox tried to draw a deep breath, but the knots remained inside him.

The coach moved past the gatehouse, where a barrel-chested, ginger-bearded man waved them through. In the open courtyard, a chubby boy rushed from the stables, smiling.

"Welcome home, Your Grace!" he called.

Lennox looked up to see the duke produce a large handkerchief, which he used to dab his eyes. "God's wounds," the older man exclaimed. "What's come over me?" As he spoke, he lifted a hand in greeting to the boy. "It's young Burley, Charles's groom. I suppose just the sight of him, coming out like that, reminds me of my son."

"How long ago did you lose him?" Lennox asked softly.

"Two days before Easter." His voice was choked.

"Just one season ago." Lennox wanted to lean forward and touch him. "I can well imagine the depth of your grief, sir. If I can help in any way…"

A liveried servant was opening the door to the coach. As the duke began to rise from the cushioned seat, he said, "You can, Lennox. I would ask you to address me as 'Father.'"

"Of course." It would be cruel to deny him such a simple request, yet the word seemed to stick in Lennox's throat. "Father."

For a moment, the older man paused, eyes closed. "When you say it," he murmured, "I can almost imagine it is my Charles speaking, your voice is so much like his."

The next few hours passed in a blur for Lennox. He was shown through the grand rooms of Greythorne Manor and encountered many servants, all impeccable in the duke's garnet livery. Except for Burley, the young groom who had greeted them outside, the servants were clearly trained to fade into the background. The duke treated them with an air of absentminded kindness, as if he didn't really see them.

"The original dwelling that stood here was in the Domesday Book, you know," his father said as they toured the house. Lennox reminded himself to find out what that meant. "King Henry gave it to my father, the last duke, but it's been up to me to do the rebuilding. My travels in Europe inspired me a great deal."

Lennox saw that there was no great hall, no common room where most of the guests would eat and sleep, while only the lord of the manor and possibly a few family members would have private chambers. It was all very different from Duntulm Castle, where Lennox had been raised, or Dunvegan Castle, the clan stronghold. The walls were hung with costly tapestries, though none could match Nora's artistry, Lennox thought. Much of the carved paneling was gilded, and the ceilings were elaborately decorated.

The duke paused to speak to a stone-faced steward named Wilton who led them up a wide staircase. Arched windows overlooked the stairs, spilling the pink hues of twilight through diamond-shaped panes.

As they ascended, Lennox realized that the duke was watching him from the corners of his eyes.

"Your home is magnificent," Lennox said, careful to be truthful without admitting that he didn't care for the style.

"I'm so pleased you approve. Are you not an artist?"

"Aye, I suppose ye could say that. I do like to draw and paint, when I have the necessary materials."

Hastings gestured toward the paintings ranged over the large wall beside the stairway. "I like to think that we have some very fine works of art here. Holbein himself painted these." He paused in front of two large portraits that hung side by side. One featured a timid-looking young woman, petite and rather plain, wearing an old-fashioned gable headdress. "That is my duchess, Jane, when she was a new bride." Even as he spoke, his gaze moved away to settle on the other portrait.

"Her Grace was very lovely," said Lennox before turning slightly to regard the painting of a young man. "And is this Charles, your son?"

The duke nodded mutely, tears filling his eyes.

"I am so sorry." Should he touch his father? Probably not, yet he could not resist laying a hand on his shoulder in comfort as they stood together. The young man looking back at them from the painting had an angular face and large, dark eyes that held a spark of humor. Lennox found himself returning his half-brother's wry smile. "Ye must be very glad to have this fine portrait. I can see how special he was."

"Can you indeed?" the duke asked hoarsely. "I still cannot quite believe he is gone."

Lennox patted his shoulder. "I am sorry," he repeated.

"You are a kind young man." Their eyes met for a moment. "I appreciate that. Now then, let us go up."

Wilton was waiting discreetly at the top of the stairs. He led the way down the corridor and opened a door. Lennox felt both men watching him now, and he guessed the fine, spacious room must have belonged to Charles. He went in, inhaling a faint but unmistakable scent of sandalwood. It felt as if the last occupant had departed only a short while ago.

For a long minute, Lennox stood silently, looking around the room. Clearly designed for a man, it was richly paneled and lined with tapestries depicting the drama of a boar hunt. The carved poster bed was covered in midnight-blue velvet, and precious leather-bound books lined shelves near the mullioned windows. One volume lay open on a polished desk, as if the room's occupant had just stepped out and would soon return to finish reading.

"You doubtless can perceive that this was Charles's room." The duke spoke from behind Lennox. After a brief pause, he added hopefully, "Do you mind?"

Lennox didn't know what to say or even how to feel. Briefly, he remembered the persistent sense of discomfort that haunted him while growing up in Clan MacLeod. It was a life that should have fit him like a glove yet never did, and the reason had teased and eluded him right up to that day at Fiona's cottage when he found the miniature.

Drawing a deep breath, Lennox tried to shake off the past. He considered Charles, who was his half-brother, and how this room honored him. In every way, Charles must have felt charmed and embraced by the world around him. Clearly, he'd been showered with every blessing, and the duke's aching heart was a testament to how much he had loved his son.

"Do I mind?" Lennox echoed softly. "No. How could I? It's a very handsome room, and I should be grateful to stay here, where your son lived."

"And now *you* are my son," his father declared. "Truly, a gift from God."

In the days that followed, Lennox told himself to be patient and wait to see what lay in store at Greythorne Manor. He often thought of Nora's words: "*If this is the life you are meant to have, the part of you that has been missing, you must go with him and explore it.*"

Lying in the carved bed at night, he ached for her. Memories of their past together ran through his mind. What was she doing? Did she miss him as much as he missed her? He knew now that he loved her, and so he wanted her to be happy, but at the same time he imagined that she would somehow send word to him and implore him to come back.

Although the duke was doing everything in his power to make Lennox feel welcome at Greythorne Manor, he still felt out of step. Would that change with time? The two of them dined together each evening at one end of a long table. There were no smelly, panting dogs lying on the floor, no uninvited guests from neighboring estates, no ribald jokes. At the duke's behest, the cook made an elaborate castle fashioned of sugar to welcome Lennox. The notion that someone had labored over this confection on his account was unsettling. He tried to imagine such a scene at Dunvegan, with his clansmen present. If one of the cooks, like Old David, had carried in a sugar castle, he would have been laughed out of the great hall.

The duke spent hours showing Lennox around the estate and invited him to ride Zeus, the impressive black gelding that had belonged to Charles. One day, when it rained, he beckoned Lennox to the library, where he taught him about their distinguished family history and showed him the numerous, valuable books on the shelves.

"You may take any of these to read," his father said, then paused. "Oh, I may have spoken too soon. Has someone taught you to read, son?"

Stung, Lennox straightened his shoulders. "Aye, of course I can read—and write, as well. My mother saw to that."

"I meant no offense, I assure you. I often forget that Eleanor was there with you until you were grown. She was very literate indeed."

"Ma was not the only learned person on the Isle of Skye, I can assure ye." Lennox softened his tone. "It's hardly a wilderness."

"Of course not. I have many friends who are Scots, and they are good people." With that, the duke turned back to the books, showing them to Lennox one by one and suggesting which volumes should be read first.

On Lennox's tenth day at Greythorne Manor, the duke made an announcement.

"Heller, my tailor, arrives within the hour," he said, looking especially pleased. "You will soon have a proper wardrobe, son. How splendid you will look!"

Lennox managed to smile, yet it felt as if he was in a hole that kept getting deeper.

When the tiny, balding tailor came into the courtyard on horseback, accompanied by two assistants riding pannier-laden steeds, Lennox was summoned to the duke's private apartments. His father stood off to one side but came forward to make introductions.

"It is an honor to meet you." Heller paused to rake Lennox with an imperious glance before exclaiming, "My good sir, I must inquire, what are you *wearing*?"

The duke spoke first. "I am certain I explained to you that my son has been living in Scotland. This sort of apparel is common in the Highlands."

Heller assumed a deferential posture, as if suddenly remembering how much income was at stake. "Ah, yes, Your Grace, so you did. I assure you I meant no *offense*." Turning to Lennox, he bowed. "Pray forgive me, my lord."

Lennox chafed at this term of address, but this was not the time to mention it to his father. Instead, he nodded to Heller. "I understand. Ye are not the first Englishman to stare at my plaid."

The little man parried, "That clothing *does* allow me to judge that you've a very fine pair of legs, my lord. You'll look splendid in these hose!"

With that, he snapped his fingers at the assistants, who began to display the hose, breeches, and doublets Heller had brought from London. The duke came forward to examine the pieces, inclining his head and nodding approval.

Soon, Lennox had been divested of his belted plaid and stood in the middle of the room wearing only a new pair of gray silk hose. Heller's assistants, who kept their eyes down as they scurried to and fro, brought a long shirt that was made of white silk. The shirt alone was finer than anything Lennox had ever worn.

"Trunk hose, I think," said Heller, and produced a pair in teal-blue velvet trimmed in gold that were rather like short breeches. Next came a matching blue-and-gold doublet with slashed sleeves and sapphire buttons.

Lennox wanted to protest that he felt ridiculous, like a cursed peacock, but the sight of his father's pleased smile made him swallow the words. Just then, one of the tailor's assistants appeared in front of him, holding out a soft velvet cap decorated with an assortment of gems and a swan's feather.

"Oh, I don't know," he said, suddenly yearning for his worn tartan bonnet with the clan MacLeod badge.

The duke came to stand at his side, turning him toward the mirror. "It's all a change, I know, but I can assure you you'll grow to appreciate these fine new clothes. Once we have you shorn, you'll be every inch a gentleman."

Lennox raised a hand to his wild golden hair. "Shorn?"

A moment later, Heller was putting something in his hand. "Don't forget this!" said the tailor.

Looking down, Lennox saw a yellow satin codpiece, its strings dangling between his fingers. *God save me,* he thought.

The next afternoon, Lennox was preparing to change into his riding clothes after dinner when he heard voices in the courtyard. Crossing to the arched window, he looked down to see the ginger-bearded guard speaking to a young man who held the reins of a horse. Two more of the duke's liveried men-at-arms emerged from another small building and seemed to be telling the dark-haired lad to go away. Lennox leaned forward, staring, as he realized that the newcomer wore a belted plaid and his chestnut horse looked familiar. His heart beat faster, swelling with something that felt very much like joy.

Was there a way to push the window open and shout to the boy? It didn't seem so, and Lennox could hardly pound on the delicately glazed panes of glass. Turning, he rushed from the room and ran down the stairs, nearly colliding with a serving maid who was carrying a box of candles.

"Sorry!" With a breathless laugh, he reached out for a moment to steady her then continued his descent.

Wilton stood near the entry, impassively watching the scene in the courtyard through a narrow window next to the door.

"Pardon me." Lennox reached for the latch on the big door.

"Sir, wait, please, you must allow me," Wilton protested.

Lennox was forced to ignore him. Emerging out into the warm afternoon, he saw that the men-at-arms had escorted the visitor away. The horse's tail was barely visible in the distance beyond the gatehouse.

"Stop!" shouted Lennox, sprinting toward them. The guard and men-at-arms turned to stare, clearly unused to hearing anyone in the duke's household behave in such a manner.

A moment later, the young man came back into view. As he entered the courtyard, a smile spread across his face, and Lennox saw that he had been right. It was Grant Carsewell, holding the reins of Lennox's own horse, Chaucer. The chestnut stallion brought his head up and down at the sight of Lennox.

"This youth is my friend," he told the guard, hearing his own voice catch with emotion. "I'll take charge of him."

One of the men-at-arms, a stocky man with a freckled face, spoke up. "We are tasked to keep His Grace safe when he is in residence. For all we know, this odd-looking, solitary fellow could have come here to do him harm."

"The lad's name is Grant Carsewell, and he's come from Scotland with my horse," Lennox said, thinking that they all must have thought he'd been odd-looking as well, before he'd traded his belted plaid for this new finery.

"We must confer with His Grace before a stranger can enter Greythorne Manor," asserted the stocky man.

"I will wait with my guest outside, then," said Lennox. Looking around, he saw Burley, the friendly young groom who had come into the courtyard on the day he arrived. Motioning for him to come forward, he introduced Burley to Grant. "And this is my horse, Chaucer." As he spoke, Lennox ran his hand over his horse's neck and felt him respond. "Will ye be kind enough to look after him for a bit?"

"I'd be honored, my lord!" cried the groom.

"I'm not a lord," Lennox replied dryly. "Just Lennox MacLeod." The act of saying his own name suddenly filled him with energy.

After Burley led Chaucer away to the stables, Lennox turned back to Grant. It seemed he had never been so glad to see a familiar face. Reaching out, he put an arm around the lad's shoulders. They were nearly the same height.

"Look at ye. So tall!"

Grant flushed. He was grimy and sunburned from the road, but a smile lit his face as he returned Lennox's grin. "It's not so long since we last met," he said. "Though Ma does say I am growing by the week."

"We'll go inside soon, where ye can have a cup of ale and some food, but first tell me how ye found me. And why did ye come all this distance?"

Grant's expression sobered. "When that MacLean from Mull fellow brought Chaucer back to Stirling Castle, I could barely contain myself. I read your message, and Stirling suddenly felt like the dullest place in the world!" He paused, grinning at Lennox. "Fiona bade me find out what fate had befallen ye. What a tale I will have to tell when I return to Scotland! How ye have changed!" He swept a hand through the air to indicate Lennox's silver-and-green doublet, soft hose, and breeches. "Ye are living the life of a prince, in this grand palace!"

He frowned, annoyed. "I can assure you I am no prince. I am still the same person you knew before."

"Ah, well, that's not the only reason I came. I was worried for Nora. She is one of the finest lasses I know, and I am honored to count her as a friend."

"Ye must know I would not let any harm come to her," Lennox protested.

"Perhaps not, but ye have left her behind in London all the same."

Lennox stared, his breath frozen in his chest. "Ye have seen her." He was aching to know more, yet half fearing what he might hear.

"Aye! How else could I know to come here? I sought out Lord and Lady Fairhaven, and her ladyship took me to Nora. She was in the midst of moving to a small house of her own."

"And did Nora send you here?" The possibility that she might have changed her mind and had sent Grant to fetch him lit a bright flame of hope in Lennox.

"She did send me, so I might bring Chaucer here." Lifting his brows, Grant gave a rueful smile. "She has never been more beautiful. Heartbroken, yet so determined."

The lad's words were like a dagger in the center of his chest. "She is truly making a new life, then?"

Grant nodded. "Already Nora has found a position at court, thanks to her friend, Lady Fairhaven. She's a lass of great resolve and I do not doubt she'll find her way forward."

"Alone."

"Aye, alone, though she'll have her babe, of course." Grant then brought out a small bundle he'd been carrying under his arm and opened it. "She sent ye something. She said she finished this on the Duchess of Aylesbury's loom, after ye left with your father."

Lennox took the rolled-up canvas that Grant proffered. Reluctantly, he unfurled it and beheld the tapestry they had conceived of together, combining his design with her weaving. There was the birlinn on the richly layered blue sea, with two small figures inside.

Tears burned his eyes, and for a moment he was back with Nora in the tiny room at Duart Castle, as she beheld his drawing for the first time: "*This is us, isn't it?*"

It might be, he realized, a gift that said farewell more eloquently than any words she could have written…

Chapter Twenty-six

"I'd forgotten how terrible the summers can be here in London," Nora remarked, glancing toward Master Jan Mostinck. He was in charge of all of King Henry VIII's royal tapestries, and she knew he had hoped to escape the city when the monarch began his Northern Progress at the end of June. Instead, a fever had held him back during the court's departure, and now it was too late. Trapped in London, he frequently showed his displeasure to those like Nora, who had stayed behind.

Mostinck walked over to stand behind Nora at her loom, where she was repairing a small, frayed tapestry that depicted the Royal Arms of Tudor England.

"It is one of the worst summers I have ever known. So hot! All of London stinks like the open sewers." He pointed a long, reddened finger at one of the heraldic lions. "Do you see the torn stitch here, on the beast's eye? I thought I could depend upon you, Widow Lovejoy, to do careful work!"

Nora wanted to tell him that this drudgery was an insult to her very real gifts. When she arrived with Cicely at the Great Wardrobe at Whitehall Palace in late June, Nora had been greeted respectfully by Mostinck and readily given a position among the men who labored in his workrooms. The Flemish tapisier remembered Nora's father, and when he saw the small, exquisite tapestry she had brought to illustrate her abilities, he had seemed genuinely impressed.

Encouraged about the future, Nora had settled into a small

house that the Duke and Duchess of Aylesbury had purchased for Throgmorton's now-deceased parents. Of course, it would take time to ascend to a high position among the Great Wardrobe's weavers, but once she convinced Master Mostinck of her talent and determination to work hard, surely Nora would reach her goals. Yet, as the weeks passed, London became stiflingly warm and Nora's size increased. Her lower back began to ache as she sat weaving for hours at Whitehall, and her longing for Lennox became a shadow over her heart. At least her swollen belly was still hidden under her gown. No one knew her secret yet, except those few of her own choosing.

"I regret that I didn't see that stitch," she told Master Mostinck in an even tone. Then, looking up from the loom, Nora summoned her courage and asked, "Sir, have you by chance heard whether the queen is interested in purchasing my tapestry?"

"Tapestry?" he repeated absently.

"Yes, the small one of a maiden with a harp and roses. I've been told it is an especially exquisite arras." Nora wanted to remind him that it had been his idea to take it and show it to Her Majesty himself, but she sensed that his temper was already stretched thin.

The Fleming stroked his short beard. "Ah, yes. I did show it to Her Majesty, but she didn't care for the lady's expression."

"I see." Nora's heart sank. She had been counting on the sale of the tapestry to fund her quest for independence, but clearly she would have to search for a new buyer. "In that case, I would ask that you return it to me."

He turned away, distracted. "I'll do that when I have a moment to look for the thing."

Nora rose and followed him. "I must request that you search for it now," she pressed. "It is my only possession of value."

They went to a large chest filled with small hangings, many of them waiting to be repaired. Master Mostinck rummaged inside before pulling out Nora's tapestry. "You are very assertive for a female! Did your good father, William Brodie, have no reservations about you coming to London alone?"

"I have told you, sir. In the short time after Father and I went to Stirling, I was married and then widowed. I had to consider my future. I have always wanted to become a master weaver for the royal court, but that wasn't possible in Scotland, where the tapestry collection is so much smaller." She took a breath. "I knew, as a widow, I could aspire to a higher position with the Great Wardrobe than I could in Scotland, with only my father to recommend me."

He stared at her over a pair of tarnished silver spectacles. "Hmm. You have bold dreams, Widow Lovejoy."

"I believe in myself." Nora spoke confidently, but she felt the throb in her voice. The days when she had enjoyed a single-minded purpose were behind her. So many things had happened to teach her that the world was not a place she could bend to her own will.

Her innocence had been stolen, and now she was carrying a child, conceived with that thief. She had parted from her father, who had been her anchor in the changing currents of life. But Nora's biggest lesson in powerlessness was Lennox MacLeod. Loving a man she could not have filled her with bittersweet longing, more powerful than any other emotion… except her hope that he was finding fulfillment in his new life.

"The heat is oppressive, and you are pale. Go home," said Master Mostinck, wiping his brow. "But leave your tapestry with me. I may yet find a buyer."

A summer storm was brewing as Nora navigated the crowded streets from Whitehall Palace to Cockspur Court. The sight of her modest, half-timbered house always gave her a surge of pride. She was making her own way in the city, honestly employed and determined to take care of her child once he or she was born.

Entering through the low front door, Nora was greeted by Mistress Joan Farthing, who had been sent by Sandhurst to look after the household.

"Ah, mistress, I am so glad you've come home ahead of the rain," the older woman said. Joan's countenance was pinched and angular, but her kind manner shone through. "If you will sit, I'll bring you a nice cup of weak ale."

"You're very kind. Thank you."

The dim parlor with its low ceiling would have been gloomy, but Nora had hung tapestries over the paneled walls. One was the hanging she had made as a child, the second was a hunting scene she found in a chest upstairs, and the third was a duplicate of the tapestry she'd sent with Grant, to Lennox. She had kept his cartoon, and Micheline had sent her own small loom to be set up in one of the Cockspur Court rooms. Since coming here to live on her own, Nora had spent long hours re-weaving the scene of her with Lennox on the Sound of Mull. The galley, with its Viking-style prow, bobbed on the blue waves, and when she looked closely, it almost seemed she could see the golden-haired figure smiling at her.

Looking at it now, Nora felt her throat thicken. It was strange: All her life she had relished the chance to work in solitude, but now she deeply missed human contact. Her father, who had been not only a parent but also a friend and mentor. Friends like Grant, Micheline, and Cicely. Even her mother, whom she had tried to block from her thoughts since leaving Flanders at age ten.

But most of all, she missed Lennox. She wanted to tell him about everything that she experienced and felt. She wanted to feel him draw her into his arms and rest her cheek on his warm, broad chest. Just to look once more into his sea-green eyes, glimpsing the flame of love in their depths, would be a gift beyond price.

Sighing, Nora blinked back tears and rested her hand on the place where her baby grew. Her belly felt hard through the layers of her petticoat and kirtle. Last night, lying in bed, she thought she could feel him move, like a feather brushing inside her. A wave of his tiny hand.

"We are together," she whispered.

Just as Joan Farthing came back in holding a silver cup, a knock sounded at the door. "Don't you move, mistress!" The older woman handed Nora the cup and went to the door. "Who's there?"

A muffled voice replied, "It is I, Lady Fairhaven!"

Nora's heart lifted. Rising, she hurried to greet her friend as Joan lifted the bar. There was Cicely, looking charming in robins-egg-blue silk. The sight of her animated face was almost like a dream.

"Can it truly be you? Do come in! I thought you and Lord Fairhaven had gone to Kent, to escape the summer heat." Nora reached out with both hands and they embraced. Glancing toward Joan, she added, "Will you please bring Lady Fairhaven a goblet of wine?"

Cicely came inside but immediately frowned. "It's *horrid* in here."

"I know. It's almost worse inside than it is out."

"You should stay at Andrew's house, on the river. At least it has wonderful views and lots of light, and there is a bit of breeze off the water."

Nora shook her head. "I prefer having a place I can make my own. I have a loom here. And it's a short walk to Whitehall, where I am employed in the Great Wardrobe."

"Oh, all right then." Cicely took a seat on a bench and accepted a goblet of wine from Mistress Farthing. "I suppose you should be able to decide for yourself."

"That's very generous of you," Nora replied, amused. "But why are you in London?"

"I had to return to town because…" Looking like a cat who has swallowed a canary, Cicely whispered, "I am *enceinte*. I think."

"But that's wonderful news!" Nora nearly exclaimed that their children could grow up as friends before remembering that Cicely was a member of the nobility, while Nora was merely a weaver of tapestries…whose baby would be, in truth, a bastard.

"I know," Cicely exclaimed. "Is it not thrilling? Robin insisted that we consult with his father's physician, so we came back to London for a few days." She paused, her cheeks coloring. "I know my Robin may be less heroic and handsome than other men we know, but he is just right for *me*. He lets me be myself, yet when the need arises, he can be quite forceful."

Nora wasn't certain how to reply to that. "That's lovely."

"But enough about me. How are *you* feeling?" Cicely pressed. "If you have awful stories to share about these past weeks, please do not tell me. I like to imagine that I'll become more beautiful with each passing day. Everyone will look at me and say how *serene* I am."

This made both of them laugh. Nora tried to assume an air of serenity herself, but it was difficult now that she was finally in the company of a caring friend who knew the truth about her baby's conception.

"I will confess that the past weeks have been a challenge."

Having swallowed the last of her wine, Cicely set down the goblet and bent close to Nora, clasping her hand. "Tell me, dear friend."

"It's not the baby." She touched the curve of her belly, irrationally grateful to be able to acknowledge the baby to someone. "He is my greatest comfort." Slowly then Nora allowed herself to speak about her loneliness, the unfulfilled dreams at the Great Wardrobe, and her mixed emotions about Lennox. "I think he must be happy in Surrey with his father. Our friend from Scotland, Grant Carsewell, came to Weston House with Lennox's horse. I encouraged him to take Chaucer to Lennox, and I confess I selfishly imagined Grant might return with news that Lennox missed me and wanted to return." She drew a painful breath. "Instead, weeks have passed, and there is no word from either of them. All must be well."

"You are not selfish," Cicely declared. "Not in the least! You could have kept him for yourself, but you wanted him to find his rightful place in the world, and it seems that has come to pass." She sighed. "And what of your exquisite tapestry, the one of the lady with the harp? Did the queen purchase it from you?"

Nora shook her head. "No. Thank God for the Duke and Duchess of Aylesbury's generosity, providing me with this house and Joan to look after me."

"And I take it Master Mostinck is not in any hurry to make you a master weaver?"

"No. Although he does appreciate my talents." Nora's eyes stung. "I must be patient. Perhaps I have only been dreaming after all, and now reality is here before me."

"Well, in any case, you should not be alone. I hate to say it, but it's a shame Sir Raymond Slater is dead. He could give you and your child a *very* fine life."

Nora hesitated to say anything too disparaging about the man Cicely had clearly found so compelling, so she glanced away. "That is neither here nor there, for he *is* dead, is he not? I must find my own way in the world. What sort of woman would I be if I gave up and looked around for a man whenever challenges appear before me?"

"You would be quite *normal*." Cicely rose and smoothed her pale blue skirts. "Let me give this situation some thought. Something should be done."

That sounded ominous to Nora. Following her friend to the door, she implored, "Please do not worry about me. I'm quite capable of making my way through the months ahead."

"But what about the baby? He needs a father."

"Nothing can be done about that." Nora watched her friend for a moment. What was in her mind? "Believe me, I will find a way. Dear Joan has already promised to look after the baby when I am away weaving, just as she would one of her own grandchildren."

Cicely rolled her eyes. "That's not good enough." Leaning

forward, she embraced Nora and kissed her cheek. "I will try to come again before we leave London. You are the bravest person I know!"

Outside on Cockspur Court, Cicely set off toward the comfortable home Robin owned a quarter mile away. One day she intended that they would live somewhere truly elegant along the Thames, but for now this cast-off family abode would have to suffice.

Her thoughts whirled as she wound her way through the crush. How could Nora possibly spend her days weaving while her child stayed in that gloomy house with Mistress Farthing? Was it folly to imagine that a suitable husband might appear, believing Nora to be a widow? But where could one be found?

"Watch out!" yelled a boy's voice.

Startled, Cicely saw that she was about to collide with a packhorse belonging to a young water carrier. The lad, who was going from house to house to sell water, spilled half his bucket. She stepped back, mumbling an apology, but he continued to scowl at her.

"Look where you're goin', mistress!" shouted the water carrier.

"See here, I certainly didn't mean—"

Before Cicely could utter another word, a hand gripped her elbow through the fine silk of her sleeve, and a shadow fell across her vision.

"Do *not* apologize to this varlet," a man's voice warned. Then, to the boy, her rescuer thundered, "How dare you speak to a noblewoman in that manner? Get away from us, this instant!"

Cicely's heart pounded in disbelief. She tried to focus. It couldn't be! Yet, looming above her, she saw the darkly handsome face of Sir Raymond Slater.

"Come into my coach," Sir Raymond commanded, leading Cicely to his nearby carriage and then lifting her off her feet. Her skirts were caught in the narrow doorway, holding her back, but he reached down and quickly freed her. "I will take you home."

She stared, still stunned, as he vaulted up into the vehicle and took the seat opposite hers. Resplendent in a crimson doublet trimmed with black and silver, his eyes sparkled as he stared at her.

"But," Cicely croaked, "you are dead!"

"Not at all." He flashed a wicked smile. "You should not listen to such vile rumors, pet. Did you really think a mere storm could kill *me*?"

"But where have you been? When did you return to London?"

"I stayed in Spain, with the wealthy merchant whose ship plucked me out of the sea." Slater looked bored. "I have only been in London for a day. I was just going to my house, but soon enough I will get out of this godforsaken cesspit and travel to the country."

Cicely put a hand to her brow, feeling overcome by shock and the oppressive heat inside the coach. It came to her that her meeting with Sir Raymond Slater had not happened by chance. It was clearly meant to be. "Raymond…"

"Yes, pet?" His voice was smooth, and his eyes wandered over her in a way that made her nipples tighten.

"There is something important I must discuss with you."

"Are you inviting me to come inside with you?" His dark brows flicked upward suggestively.

Cicely was tempted, but she reminded herself that when she married Robin she had made a sensible choice, leaving flirtations like this behind. "No, I can tell you here. Do you remember a lovely red-headed girl you met while in Scotland, at Stirling Castle? Her name was Nora Brodie."

"Ah, yes. The weaver's daughter. A bit too stiff for my taste." He paused. "How did you know of her?"

"We met when Robin and I went to Scotland, in the spring." They had begun to clatter along the cobbles, bound for her own abode, Cicely supposed, and in only a few minutes they would arrive there. Time was of the essence. Leaning forward, she tugged at the slashed sleeve of his doublet. "I have news about Nora that you must hear."

"You look pale, pet. Will you have one of my special sweetmeats?" He started to withdraw an emerald-studded case from a hidden pocket. "I brought them from the West Indies."

"No, no, I am fine. But kindly attend me. This is important." She began to tell him about Nora, relating the fact that she had found herself with child after the night she spent with Slater, and how she could not let her father know her predicament, could not stay at court.

"Are you suggesting the child is mine?" he asked coolly.

"Yes, of course it's yours. She was innocent before that night with you."

"I do recall that." A smile flickered over his mouth. "How did our little dove Nora come to leave Stirling?"

Cicely's stomach fluttered a tiny warning as he watched her, but now it seemed there was nothing to do but tell the truth. Besides, Sir Raymond had always enjoyed a bit of gossip. "A young Highlander who was leaving Scotland agreed to bring her with him. Lennox MacLeod. He came to England in search of his true father, and to everyone's surprise, it was revealed that Lennox is the son of Richard Gage, Duke of Hastings. Can you *imagine?*"

She saw him go white. "Indeed? How fortuitous for MacLeod, especially since Hastings's *legitimate* son died recently."

"I'm surprised that you know about that! Yes, fortuitous, for both Lennox and the duke. They've gone off to His Grace's estate in Surrey, to get to know each other."

Now Sir Raymond looked irritated. "It's so sweet my teeth hurt. Tell me again what the devil any of this has to do with me?"

"Why, Nora and her baby, of course. You should step in."

"What, exactly, did you have in mind?"

They were slowing down. Through the small window, Cicely saw her own front door come into view. "Why not court her? Nora is lovely, intelligent, and alone in the world, with your child growing inside her. Honestly, at your age, aren't you beginning to long for a quieter life?"

"Are you implying I'm in my dotage?" Although Sir Raymond sounded impatient, he rubbed his thumb and forefinger together thoughtfully.

"Do you feel it would be a sign of weakness to do the right thing?" Cicely dared to challenge. "I can assure you just the opposite is true."

"You're an interfering little chit." After a long moment, his expression softened and he smiled at her. "Perhaps you are right, pet. It might be rather amusing to change my ways. But you must promise me you won't tell Nora I have risen from the dead. I want it to be a splendid surprise…"

Chapter Twenty-seven

Lennox looked into the Venetian mirror and sighed at the sight of himself in a slashed blue doublet set with jewels, topped by a slate-gray jerkin trimmed in silver. "What do ye think?" he asked Grant.

The lad leaned against the table, where Lennox's papers and sketching tools were spread out. "Ye look like one of Henry VIII's fancy courtiers. Is that the impression ye were hoping to make?"

"What choice do I have? If I wore my Highland plaid instead, wouldn't the duke feel I was rude and ungrateful?"

"Aye, they would suppose ye are a heathen like me." Grant laughed. His voice was deeper now, and he was growing a fine pair of shoulders.

"These clothes are stiffer than Highland garb, but I suppose I'll become accustomed to them." Lennox bent his tightly clad arm and arched a brow. "All the same, plenty of Scots Lowlanders would envy me. And now I must leave you. There are guests for dinner, I am told."

"I saw them arriving. A finely-dressed older gentleman and an elegant, bonny lass." Grant raised his brows before adding, "If ye care for that type."

Lennox threw him a grin. "I am glad ye are here, lad, to save me from feeling completely lost."

"I can't stay forever, though. It's been weeks, after all. Ma and Bayard want me back at Stirling, and I confess I miss Scotland more than I thought I would."

Hearing these words, Lennox felt a familiar sharp pang. He

was saved from replying when a knock sounded at the door, followed by Wilton's austere voice. "His Grace requires your presence downstairs, sir."

"Aye," said Lennox. He reached for a blue-velvet cap with an ostrich feather. "I am coming now."

"How kind you were to invite Betsy and me this afternoon," Viscount St. John said as he speared a bite of roasted swan with his eating knife. His plump cheeks reddened, and his eyes grew wet. "I confess I have been concerned for you, Hastings, these past months. Such a tragedy you had to endure, losing Charles, and so soon after the loss of your dear Jane."

The duke blinked. "I am grateful, as always, for your abiding friendship, St. John."

Watching this exchange, Lennox sensed his father's discomfort with the viscount's emotional remarks. He had been told that the two men had been friends since boyhood, and it seemed that the viscount himself was grieving for Charles.

Lennox glanced toward Viscount St. John's daughter, Betsy. As Grant had observed, she was both elegant and lovely, fresh as a dewy pink rosebud on this warm August afternoon. Willowy, golden-haired Betsy was blessed with blue eyes and a demure smile that she turned his way every few minutes.

"Yes, it has been so difficult for all of us who cared for Charles," the viscount was saying. He inclined his head toward Betsy. "At times it seemed the world might end, and yet it did not. God has favored you with another son!"

To Lennox's surprise, Betsy murmured, "Favored us all."

The two fathers raised their glasses in a silent toast to her.

As the meal wound to a close, footmen appeared with another of the cook's sugar-paste creations. This time a gilded Cupid rose up from the platter, colored with spices and bright fruit juices. Lennox felt an odd twinge at the sight of it, pointing its bow toward him.

Betsy blushed and looked at Lennox under her lashes. "Your Grace, your cook is quite ingenious, for I have never found Cupid looking more appealing."

After the meal, Viscount St. John announced, "Hastings and I have business to discuss." Turning to Lennox, he said, "Would you be kind enough to take my lovely daughter outside for a stroll?"

The duke answered on Lennox's behalf. "My son would be honored. It's time these two attractive young people became better acquainted."

"Oh, look at the roses," exclaimed Betsy as they wandered through the knot gardens of boxwood and roses. "They are my favorite flower. Will you choose one for me, kind sir?"

Lennox found a white bloom that was just beginning to open. It had very few thorns and was easy enough to break off at its juncture with the branch. It was the sort of thing he had done countless times in the past, while charming the many lasses on Skye, but this time he could not feel lighthearted as he presented Betsy with the flower.

"I love it that you chose white for me," she said softly, gazing into his eyes. "It is apt, you know. I have kept myself pure for my husband."

Staring at the rose, Lennox thought back to the day on the Isle of Mull, when he'd returned from trying to save those seamen lost in a shipwreck. He had ached for Nora during that long absence, and even now he could clearly see her on the windswept bluff, waiting to greet him, a crown of bright wildflowers on her wild red-gold tresses. That night, he had made love to her with all his heart and soul, but there had been so much he didn't yet know. Secrets that were already building a wall between them.

"I had been saving myself for someone else," Betsy was saying.

Lennox came back to the present moment with a start, realizing what she meant. He looked at her. "Charles."

"How did you guess?" She came close enough to touch his arm with graceful fingers. "I loved him. He was a very fine person."

"I have no doubt of that."

"But Charles is gone, and all of my life is still ahead of me." She paused, her hand shaking slightly against the sleeve of his doublet. "My father tells me that His Grace has plans for you, in spite of the circumstances of your birth."

Although Lennox had no idea what plans she referred to, he could guess what Betsy had in mind for herself. He managed a smile.

"I can see in your eyes that you are a rare sort of man, but I should not say any more. I know all of this is new for you, and our ways must be different from those of Scotland." She stood on tiptoe and pressed a warm kiss to the edge of his jaw. "I just wanted you to know, I'm very glad you are now an Englishman, Lennox."

Later that afternoon, Lennox and the duke stood in the courtyard, watching as the coach bearing their guests passed by the gatehouse and turned down the long drive.

"I thought I'd go for a ride before the light goes," Lennox said, feeling a strong, familiar urge to get away. "Chaucer must be missing me."

"Chaucer?" the duke repeated distractedly. "Oh, you mean the horse that Scots lad brought."

"That's right. Chaucer and I had many fine adventures together before I came to England. Now that he is here, I don't want him to feel ignored." Lennox was grateful that his father seemed to have other things on his mind and hadn't objected to Lennox riding Chaucer instead of Zeus, the black steed once owned by Charles. Nor did the duke seem to care that Grant had been installed as Lennox's temporary valet.

To Lennox's surprise, his father said, "You show a great deal of consideration for the feelings of a horse." There was a slight edge to his chuckle. "Perhaps you might first grant *me* a bit of your time?"

"Of course." Lennox followed the older man as he walked back inside, up the stairs to his own large chamber. It seemed to Lennox that the air grew thinner with each passing step.

"Ah," said the duke, reclining in his favorite chair near the window. "That's better."

An unobtrusive footman poured wine into silver goblets and served the two men. A moment later, he slipped out of the room and silently closed the door.

Lennox took a chair near his father, feeling as if a weight was pressing on his chest. "Was there something ye wished to discuss with me?"

"I merely wanted to tell you how proud I was to introduce you as my son." The duke sipped his wine, a rueful smile touching his mouth. "I do not say that lightly. St. John is my oldest friend; he alone knows how I have suffered since Charles died." He paused. "It has been a dark time for all three of us, in fact."

Lennox could only wonder, with a faint sense of dread, where this was going. "I did glean something of that sort from Betsy."

"Ah, yes, you were alone together in the gardens." His green eyes were watchful. "Betsy is not only beautiful but also possessed of a fine character. I will confess, St. John and I remarked that you two would make striking children."

Lennox felt his entire body tense, yet the primal male in him could not help imagining, for an instant, what Betsy might look like naked in the candlelight, responding to his touch.

The duke broke into Lennox's momentary fantasy. "Have you been happy here this summer?"

"Aye." It was impossible to explain how conflicted his feelings were, but the one thing he did know was a sense of gratification that he could make his father smile again and offer him hope for the future. "At times, it still doesn't seem quite real."

"Ah, yes, I know exactly what you mean! St. John and I also marveled at the changing winds of fate. Mere weeks ago, I thought I had lost everything, and now it begins to seem God has granted me a reprieve, through you." His father leaned forward, holding his gaze. "As we survey the future, only one thing is lacking. Your legitimacy."

Lennox felt a muscle move in his jaw. "I don't think any less of myself for being born a bastard. In fact, I had nothing to do with it."

The duke seemed to barely hear him. "No, no, that's not what I mean." Rising, he paced across the floor which was swept daily and strewn with fresh rushes. "I am growing older. There are moments when my heart begins to gallop like a runaway horse, and I realize my life will end one day." Turning, he looked back, his eyes agleam with emotion. "I want to make you my son in every way, Lennox. I want you to be able to inherit my lands…and my title."

Lennox knew he should have seen it coming, but nonetheless he felt blindsided. "But don't ye already have a legitimate heir? A nephew?"

His father waved a dismissive hand. "Edwin? Oh, he is well enough, but you must understand, when I look at you, I see *myself*! There are moments when it takes my breath away. It is meant to be, that you are the heir to my legacy."

Legacy. It was not a word Lennox would have ever associated with himself. "It's impossible, though, isn't it?"

"No! That's what I am trying to tell you." The duke circled back to his chair, gripping its high, carved back. "King Henry VIII has grappled with this very issue. Without a living, legitimate heir, he turned to Henry FitzRoy, his son by Bessie Blount. His Majesty created the titles of Duke of Richmond and Somerset for the boy, and many felt he would find a way to make him the heir to the throne. It was outrageous, but our king is well known for breaking with precedent."

"Aye." Lennox nodded, searching his memory. "I have heard about Henry FitzRoy. Didn't he die a few years ago?"

"Yes, he was less than twenty years old, but his story remains. Why should I not remember it—and believe I might persuade the king to legitimize you, given his own history!" The duke's eyes grew moist as he continued, "I would beg him to allow you, my only living progeny, to inherit my title and lands. My dear son, nothing in the world could make me happier than to see you making a life here at Greythorne Manor. Perhaps I might even be able to hold a grandchild or two before I die."

The room seemed to tilt as Lennox struggled to find words. Hadn't he always been pushed to one side in Clan MacLeod, never even receiving a proper clan brooch from his grandfather, Alasdair Crotach? Now this good man desperately wanted to claim him before the world, even make him the next Duke of Hastings. As Lennox took it all in, the discomfort that had been plaguing him began to ebb. Could this be where he truly belonged after all?

"Ye have rendered me speechless, Father. I've longed my entire life to be accepted and cared for in this way."

The duke's eyes shone. "Care is too meager a word for my feelings. I want to do everything possible to make you happy here." His expression brightened. "What would you enjoy? I know you wish to create more art. Perhaps we might build a studio of your own, in the gardens, with a view of the fountain. Would you like that?"

Lennox felt rather like he had already overindulged at a sumptuous castle feast and was being offered even more fine wine, more rich food. Yet how could he explain that to his father? "It's very kind of you to think of it."

"Perhaps you might travel to Italy after your marriage, to see the magnificent art that exists there."

The duke didn't have to include Betsy by name; Lennox knew what he meant. She floated back into his thoughts, willing to be his after one afternoon's acquaintance. He could see why all of them believed this was a perfect plan. It was easy to envision himself living in this grand estate years from now, married to Betsy, their fair-haired children running about, the stable filled with horses. It would be an enchanted life remarkably similar to the one Andrew and Micheline enjoyed.

Nora appeared in his mind then, luminous, filled with passion, needs, and aspirations of her own. She loved him, yet he couldn't imagine her in this setting. Even if she were not carrying another man's child, Lennox knew she could never be happy here. She had said as much herself.

"I know it is a great deal to take in," said the duke, watching him. "I beg you only to think about it. I know you may have had other dreams…" He lifted his brows, as if indicating that he too remembered Nora.

Lennox felt tears prick his own eyes. "Aye, but some things can't be forced."

"I also hope you realize that marriage for people like us cannot be based on romantic notions of love, which fades with time. We have a duty to those around us and who come after us to marry for more solid reasons."

"Was that how it was with my mother? A romantic notion that had to be put aside?"

The duke was silent for a long moment before he gently replied, "I fear it is true."

Chapter Twenty-eight

Nora pushed open the window and breathed deeply of the wild red roses that climbed up the back of her little house in Cockspur Court. August, with its stifling heat, was on the wane. Nora paused to savor the feeling of well-being that swept over her. At last, it seemed her life might be coming together.

That very week, Master Mostinck had announced that he might have a buyer for Nora's *Maiden with a Harp* tapestry. To Nora's astonishment, Mostinck later reported that the wealthy merchant man purchased it on the spot, so entranced by the hanging that he'd insisted on paying even more than the asking price. Her small, handmade tapestry purse, filled with gold sovereigns and angels, was now hidden in a cabinet. It was enough for Nora and her baby to live on for a long time, perhaps even enough to buy a house of their own.

She now turned back to the loom, loaned to her by Micheline, that nearly filled this snug room. She looked forward to this time to plan a small tapestry for her baby. Nora had even made the cartoon herself, knowing that she must practice the skill of sketching her own patterns if she truly aspired to be a master weaver.

Yet the effort had made her miss Lennox more than ever. There were no words to describe the ecstasy of a true artistic collaboration like theirs. Nora kept his original cartoon close by her loom. Each time she unfurled it and remembered when Lennox had first shown it to her at Duart Castle, she felt anew that sense of bliss. Completion.

And the pain of loss.

She prayed Lennox was finding happiness with the Duke of Hastings. It wasn't hard to imagine him, splendid and strong, in the garb of an English nobleman, perhaps riding through the woods with a group of new friends. She hoped he felt the sense of belonging that he'd been searching for all his life.

Nora supposed she would always ache for him, but each day she felt stronger, more certain that she would find fulfillment for herself and her baby.

Her loom always brought her joy. Now she wondered which shades of tan and golden thread would be best for the rather friendly-looking lion in this tapestry. Nora was poring over her collection of wool, silk, and metallic threads when a knock sounded dimly at the entrance. It continued for a bit before she remembered that Joan Farthing had gone to care for her ailing aunt and wouldn't return until tomorrow, at the earliest.

As Nora rose, the baby kicked. Because of the style of her gown, she could still hide her condition from others, but very soon that wouldn't be possible. Gently, she patted her belly and murmured affectionately. "Don't worry, little one, I have not forgotten you."

Joan's big gray cat, Samuel, was napping on a stool near the hearth, seemingly unbothered by the knocking. It came to Nora that the person at the door might well be Joan, returning for something she had forgotten.

"I'm coming," called Nora. With one motion, she lifted the bar from the door and pulled up on the latch. A tall male figure filled the portal, cast into shadow by the light behind him.

"Ah," said the caller in a deep, chillingly familiar voice. "What a relief to find you at home, Nora."

Quickly, he came forward into the small parlor and reached back to close the door. As Nora focused on the man's face, her heart froze.

"I must be seeing things," she said. "You… You are—"

"Dead? Not a bit. Such a nasty rumor," Sir Raymond Slater replied, smiling. "But you look frightened, pet. There's absolutely no need. Did you really imagine a storm at sea could kill a man like me?"

Nora took a deep breath, trying not to let anything he said distract her. "How did you know I was here?" Heart pounding, she reminded herself that he could not possibly know about the baby. "Why have you come?"

As Slater swept a hand around the small, neat parlor, Samuel narrowed his eyes and rushed from the room. "Won't you invite me to sit down?" Slater took a chair. "That's better. Might I trouble you for some refreshment? Ale will do if you cannot offer me wine."

She wanted to refuse but realized that could be dangerous. Instead, she brought him a cup of ale and took a seat near the cabinet where her coin-filled tapestry purse was hidden. "Will you now answer my questions?"

"May I say, first, that you are even lovelier today than when we last were together in Scotland?" He inclined his head slightly to indicate what he meant by *together*. "You have a certain glow, pet."

Nora felt sick. *He knows*! She told herself that he must not see her panic. "How kind of you to say so." She looked at him, waiting.

"I have spoken to your friend, Lady Fairhaven," he said. "She has confided all your secrets. For your own good, of course."

Of course. Forcing a smile, Nora murmured, "That does sound like Cicely."

As Slater continued to speak, he sounded almost sincere. "I have taken some time to think about this situation, and now that I am here, seeing you, my feelings are…" He swallowed. "Quite tender. Do you remember how it was between us that night? How sweet you were, giving yourself to me?"

She wanted to protest that she did not remember any such thing, but his manner was disconcerting. There was so much about that night that was a blur in her memory. Was it possible that Sir Raymond remembered it all differently?

"We both may have drunk a bit too much wine," he conceded, leaning forward, holding her gaze. "I realized, once it was clear that you were innocent, that perhaps we should have stopped sooner. But in that moment, when you were responding to my kiss, I lost my head."

"I suggest we both put it behind us, then," Nora managed to say, her mouth dry. "Let us pretend it never happened."

"But that is impossible, is it not? Cicely tells me you are with child. What sort of man would I be to turn my back on you at a time like this?"

Her face felt hot. "What are you suggesting?"

"I will confess something to you alone, pet. Perhaps I was more shaken by my brush with death than I have cared to admit. Perhaps I have had cause to examine my life, and I find it…wanting." His voice seemed to thicken. "Perhaps all that has happened between us is a sign from God."

Rising, he came closer and dropped to one knee before her. Nora fought an urge to recoil from him. She searched his face for a sign of deception, but he appeared to be completely in earnest.

"I want an heir," he was saying. "I have wealth and a position at court, and we have already determined that we deal well together, if you take my meaning." He smiled now, his short, pointed beard lending him a jaunty air. "Come and live with me so that we might make a home for this baby."

At a loss for words, Nora replied, "This was the last thing I expected you to say today."

Jeweled rings glinted on the hand he stretched out to capture hers. "Have I told you how beautiful you are?"

"Yes, you did," Nora replied quickly. "Just a few minutes ago."

"Don't you miss the touch of a man?" As his dark eyes fell on her bodice, his nostrils flared slightly. "There is so much I want to teach you, pet."

Nora firmly withdrew her hand. "I must ask you not to press yourself on me, sir." Breathing evenly, she forced herself to remain calm. "I appreciate the offer you have made." What it had been exactly, she wasn't certain, for he had never mentioned marriage. "However, I already have settled on a way forward with my life. I am quite capable of raising my baby without your assistance."

"Raising a child on your own? That's ridiculous!"

Nora lifted her chin. "I assure you it's not. I'm doing quite well, fending for myself and selling my work to those who appreciate my gifts."

Slater narrowed his eyes, clearly incensed. "Are you *refusing* me?"

"I am."

The Englishman bolted to his feet. "You will regret this." Looking around the room, his eyes fell on the tapestry Nora had replicated of her with Lennox in the galley. Stalking closer, he pointed at the fair-haired figure and sneered. "It's *him* you dream of, isn't it? That Highland bastard who dares to lord over his betters! No doubt he's a fine fellow now, swaggering about in his doublet and hose, beside his doting father, the Duke of Hastings. Surely you don't imagine he will ever make *you* his duchess?"

In the next instant, Sir Raymond Slater stormed out the front door, slamming it in his wake. Nora's heart was pounding as she rushed over to replace the bar.

With all her heart, she prayed he would never come back.

"Where is your fine claymore?" asked Grant as he walked with Lennox toward Greythorne Manor. "Have ye thrown it in the sea?"

"I've done no such thing," Lennox protested. For good measure, he reached over to lightly cuff the lad's arm. "I couldn't bring it here in the coach, though. I had to leave it behind at Weston House." He paused, feeling the accusing heat of Grant's stare. "It still belongs to me. It always will."

"Oh, aye. I suppose so." His young friend looked doubtful.

The two of them were returning from a few hours at the archery butts, a fine practice field built near the stables. Even the duke had joined them for a few rounds, impressing Lennox with his skill, yet now it seemed his father's every glance carried extra weight. It had been a relief when he went off to meet with his steward.

"I know what ye are thinking," Lennox continued. "Ye wonder if I could truly find happiness here, in this world." He took a deep breath. "Without Nora."

"Amen," Grant intoned soberly.

"Nora herself urged me to give this a fair chance." He stopped at the edge of the knot garden, where gardeners were clipping the boxwood hedges. "And now that I've been here for weeks, my doubts grow. But I do not see how I could turn my back on the duke. He is, after all, my true father."

"Is he?"

Lennox met the boy's level gaze. "Ye know he is. Can ye not see it clearly, every time we are together?"

"I see that you two look just the same, and he is a fine man, but there is more to being a father than that. Magnus MacLeod was by your side from birth."

"I suspect Fiona told ye to say these things."

"I may have heard them from her mouth," Grant conceded, smiling. "I have spent a lot of time with her, after all. Fi is like an aunt to me, and Bayard is like a father. Your sister-in-law, Violette, has been there to guide me when my own ma was too selfish to be bothered." He paused. "True family is more than blood."

Emotion rose up in Lennox, stinging his eyes. "The duke has suffered so much loss. My appearance in his life has brought him hope and happiness. He wants to petition the king to make me his rightful heir. How can I turn away from him now?"

"'Tis surely a dilemma," the lad agreed. "But I thought ye set out on this quest to find your own destiny, Lennox. What do *ye* want?"

Grant's words were like a dirk in Lennox's heart. When he spoke, his voice was choked. "God save me, I want to make a life with the woman I love. Nora." Leaning against a tree, he raked a sun-darkened hand through his hair. "I do not want to interfere if she is happy in her new life, as you have said she is. Yet, before I make a decision about this life with the duke, I must know if there is a chance for Nora and me. Will ye go to her, Grant? Ask if she will see me."

His young friend seemed to suppress a smile. "What about her babe? Could you love her when she is heavy with another man's child?"

Lennox gave an impatient nod of his golden head. "I already do."

Chapter Twenty-nine

On the first day of September, Nora was surveying a newly restored tapestry when Master Mostinck approached her.

"I have been impressed by your work," he said without preamble.

She lifted her chin so that she was perhaps an inch taller than the stout Fleming. "Thank you, sir. I am pleased to know it."

"I want you to oversee a group of weavers who are about to begin work on a new tapestry, the one we are calling *The King's Joust*. It will be a test for you, Mistress Lovejoy. Even though you are a woman, I think you may be up to the challenge."

Her heart sped up. She had seen the large cartoon for the new tapestry when it arrived in sections from France. Nora had wondered if Mostinck would choose her to be one of the weavers, but this news was beyond her hopes—though not, of course, beyond her dreams.

"I would be honored to accept such a position, sir," she said, smiling. Soon enough, he would know that she was with child, but by then the new tapestry project would be well underway. She would prove to him that she could do the work, no matter what.

"Good, good!" Mostinck nodded several times. "Tomorrow we will meet with the weavers."

When he had gone, Nora sat at her loom and tried to absorb the news. Slowly, her future was unfolding as she had envisioned. The baby would complicate matters, but if Nora kept her focus clearly on what was in front of her, she knew she could successfully navigate each challenge.

"Mistress Lovely?" A boy's voice broke into her reverie.

"Lovejoy," Nora corrected as she looked up. There stood a liveried page, gazing at her as if she were an angel.

"From my mistress, Lady Fairhaven," he said, holding out a sealed message, and Nora realized the page was wearing Lord Fairhaven's livery. "I'm to wait for your reply."

The brief note informed Nora that Cicely had returned from the country and was staying at Weston House. Could Nora meet her there today to address a matter of some urgency?

"You may tell your mistress that I will come as soon as my work here is finished," Nora told the boy.

"Her ladyship instructed me to escort you myself," he said earnestly.

"How nice. What's your name, young sir?"

"Ted." He beamed back at her.

An hour later, Nora was allowing Ted to lead the way through the crowded streets of London. When they came to a flower seller, Nora stopped to purchase a posy of pale blue love-in-a-mist blossoms for Cicely. As they drew near Weston House, she realized how much she had missed her friend.

It was a fine day, and Nora felt her spirits rise. The bright sails of tilt-boats dotted the Thames like colorful flowers, and children were running over the garden pathways. It came to her that Andrew & Micheline must have come home as well.

As Ted brought Nora around to the gardens, Cicely rose from the bench where she had been sitting and rushed forward, skirts lifted.

"My dear friend!" she cried. "How are you feeling? Do join me." Glancing toward the page, Cicely added, "Ted, will you let Her Grace know that our other guest has arrived?"

They sat together at the same table where Lennox had first met the Duke of Hastings. Remembering the splendid night and the heartbreaking morning that followed, Nora closed her eyes for a moment. That night in Lennox's arms, giving every bit of herself to him, might have to last her for the rest of her life.

"I have been simply longing to speak to you," Cicely said abruptly. She looked charming as always, in a fashionable gown of pink and silver. "I would have asked you sooner, but I have been beset by the most terrible siege of something very similar to *mal de mer*."

"Seasickness?" Nora puzzled over this and smiled. "Oh, yes, now I understand. The baby. I suffered from that as well."

"Don't you find it is sometimes quite unbearable to be a woman?" Without waiting for an answer, Cicely continued, "I have a confession to make. The last time I left your house, I encountered someone."

"I know, it was Sir Raymond Slater. I do wish you had not spoken to him about me." Nora gave her a chastening look. "He came to visit me just a few days ago. He offered, I believe, to make a home with me for the baby."

Cicely gasped. "Sir Raymond proposed marriage to you?"

"Oh, no, I don't think he intended that at all." She smiled ruefully. "Something much less proper. I declined."

"Thank God you were able to send him away! I meant well, telling him where you lived and that you were increasing with his child, but after Robin and I returned to Kent, I had second thoughts. There was something faintly sinister about him, even when he was offering me a fancy sweetmeat. I wanted to trust him, yet doubt crept in."

Something shifted in the depths of Nora's memory. "A sweetmeat?"

"Yes. He keeps them in a jeweled case. It was all innocent enough, no doubt, but I didn't care for the way he watched me, like a cat stalking its prey." She shook her head, as if to dispel the memory. "I began to see him in a different light, but by then it was too late. I had already encouraged him to involve himself in your affairs. Can you ever forgive me?"

"I know you were only trying to help, and everything

worked out fine, so let us put it behind us." Nora's heart softened at the sight of her friend's repentant expression. "It is fortunate that Lennox has removed himself from my life, for if he'd been there when Sir Raymond appeared, I hate to think what might have happened. Lennox despises him."

Cicely looked nervous. "How did you manage to turn Sir Raymond away?"

"I simply told him, quite firmly, that I prefer to manage on my own." Nora smiled at her friend. "And it is true."

"But he is the father of your baby," mused Cicely, "and he could make your life very comfortable."

"I beg you, put any lingering notions you may harbor about Sir Raymond out of your mind. I do not need his help! Everything is coming together after all. I've sold the tapestry, so I have means, and now Master Mostinck has assigned me to oversee a large tapestry project. It's a step forward toward achieving my goal."

"I am very happy for you, but…" Cicely's voice dropped to a whisper. "Do you never tire of being alone? You are a woman, after all."

"Are you asking me if I miss Lennox?" An abrupt wave of longing swept over Nora, and her voice broke. "Of course I do, but—"

She was interrupted by Cicely, who had half-risen and was waving toward the manor house. "Here we are! Do come and join us."

Nora turned her head and saw Micheline gracefully making her way down one of the pathways, clad in a fresh-looking gown of apricot silk. Walking beside her was a familiar-looking young man with a head of unruly dark hair. Nora's heart leaped with joy.

"It's Grant!" she breathed. As their eyes met, a broad grin spread over his face and she rose, hurrying forward to embrace him.

"By my troth," Cicely exclaimed. "I believe we managed to surprise Nora after all!"

Warm greetings were exchanged all around. Micheline inquired about Nora's news before sharing stories about their weeks in Gloucestershire, where the family passed the summer riding and breeding horses.

"We are fortunate the girls love horses as much as we do," she said, smiling. "We can all be outdoors together. Andrew had a special saddle made for his horse, Hampstead, after our babies began to come, so now it is little Alison's turn to ride up high with her papa."

"Oh, it sounds wonderful," Nora said with feeling. Their life was like a fairytale, she thought.

"We did have a fine time," Micheline agreed. "Our dear friend, Sir Jeremy Culpepper and his new wife recently paid us a visit." She glanced at Cicely. "He has grown more stout than ever. I could sense his wife wanting to give his hand a little slap when he continued to reach for the sweets."

They laughed together until Grant cleared his throat. Suddenly Micheline was getting to her feet. "Cicely, won't you help me gather the children for supper?"

"What? Oh, yes, I suppose I should go with you." Cicely suddenly smiled as if she knew a good secret. "You and Grant have a nice chat. I'll be back soon."

When Nora and Grant were alone, she reached out to clasp his hand. "I can hardly believe you are here. I think you must be growing taller every week."

He beamed at her. "Ye are a welcome sight."

Nora wore a French hood lined with pearls and now she raised a hand, sensing that some of her long curls had come loose. "I came from weaving at Whitehall Palace. I know I must look very untidy compared to the ladies you've seen at Greythorne Manor."

"Your cheeks are pink, your eyes sparkle, and your hair gleams like polished copper in the sun. That's real beauty as far as I'm concerned."

"How did you know I needed to hear a few words of flattery?" Nora felt his hand tighten on hers. She remembered the day at Stirling Castle when they had been together in the lion's den courtyard, and she had trusted him enough to confide that she was with child. Grant had declared that he would wed her himself if he could. "What a good and true friend you are to me, Grant. Tell me now what brings you here." Her heart was in her throat. "I hope Lennox is well?"

He shrugged. "Not sick or injured, if that's what ye are asking, but he is not himself."

What could that mean? Nora's thoughts skittered toward hope then backed away. Certainly, she would not wish for Lennox to be unhappy in his new life.

"What is it then?" she managed to ask.

"I will be plain. Do ye still have feelings for him?"

Emotion rushed through Nora in a wave so powerful she felt ill. Looking into Grant's big gray eyes, she replied, "I will always love Lennox, yet I know it is impossible." Her hands went instinctively to her thickening middle. "I could never live in his world, with the duke."

"Because of your weaving," Grant supplied.

She nodded. "It is as much a part of me as breathing, and Lennox well understands that. I might want to *try* to be different, but I would not thrive among the aristocracy."

"Yet ye love him."

She fought an urge to weep. "Yes. Of course."

Grant leaned closer, tightly holding her hand. "He bade me to ask if ye would see him. He didn't want to just appear if it would be painful, but if ye will agree…"

"It is surely folly!" Nora drew a shaky breath, smiling as elation rose up in her. "But, yes, I will see him. Gladly."

Chapter Thirty

After she returned from Weston House, Nora was so excited she could scarcely sleep that night. She dreamed of Lennox coming to her, then she lay awake on her rope-strung mattress and relived every memory they had shared.

The next day, Nora kept busy meeting with the weavers who would work under her supervision on *The King's Joust* tapestry. Four of them were men, who eyed her uncertainly, but the three female weavers appeared delighted to be led by Nora. One was a former nun who had come to the court after the dissolution of the monasteries. Another, Peg Horner, gave Nora a winning smile and proclaimed that she had known William Brodie during his time as one of the royal tapisiers. Peg declared that if Mistress Lovejoy was Brodie's daughter, that was a fine endorsement.

Returning home late that afternoon, Nora felt a mixture of satisfaction for a day well spent and hope for the evening ahead. Was it possible that Lennox might be on his way to London, even now? Perhaps not, for Grant had confided that there were plans afoot to match Lennox with a young noblewoman who was a favorite of the Duke of Hastings. Although Grant insisted that Lennox felt uneasy about this match, he could not assure Nora that Lennox would refuse.

Perhaps he was with that other woman now. He might have changed his mind and wouldn't come to London at all. Or perhaps he was coming to tell her himself that he had settled into his new life and he planned to wed another. Would he ask her to release him from their handfasting vows? It wasn't necessary, of course. No one in England would pay any attention to the simple ceremony that had bound them together, almost by accident.

She sighed, wishing she had never let herself think about Lennox and the beautiful lady who might be on his arm at that moment, miles away at Greythorne Manor.

Inside the little house on Cockspur Court, Nora found Joan Farthing holding her basket and petting Samuel, the cat. "Hello, mistress," said Joan, a smile softening the lines of her pointed face. "I was just telling Samuel here that I'm off to the fish seller to see if they've gotten more fresh oysters. If you don't mind, I will stop to visit my sister on my way back."

"Of course I don't mind. Enjoy your time with your sister."

"Oh, mistress, I nearly forgot." Joan opened the parlor cabinet and took out a folded message. "This came for you a short time ago."

When Nora was alone, she stood beside a small mullioned window and looked at the letter. *Mistress Nora Brodie, Cockspur Court* was written in an ornate hand. Perhaps it was from Lennox, for who else knew her true name? Her heart began to pound. Breaking the seal, she unfolded the paper and read,

My beloved, I will soon be kissing your sweet lips.

Listen for my knock at your door.

Your own, Lennox.

Heat flooded her cheeks. She stared at the paper, trying to imagine him writing those words with a swan's quill. Every part of her seemed to come alive with joy, anticipation, and arousal. Was it truly possible that soon they would be together in this very room?

After setting out a flagon of wine, goblets, and a dish of cheese, nuts, and figs, Nora rushed up the narrow steps to her bedroom. Off came the plain woolen dress she had worn to Whitehall Palace that day. Quickly, she washed at her basin and donned the cornflower-blue gown Lennox had liked best. It fit more snugly than in the past, and her breasts strained above the laces of her bodice. Should she tug the neckline of her chemise higher, for modesty's sake? Nora looked in the mirror and shared a secret smile with her own reflection. Realizing that there was no need to hide any part of herself from Lennox, she felt like a woman again, for the first time in many weeks.

She was brushing her long curls when a knock sounded downstairs. For a moment, her heart stopped. *Listen for my knock*, he had written. Her feet scarcely touched the steps as she descended to the parlor, fumbled with the bar, raised it, and threw open the door.

When Sir Raymond Slater stepped into the room, Nora felt raw fear. Samuel the cat hissed and hid behind the chair.

"What are you doing here?" Nora asked. Sensing that she could be in real danger, she kept her tone even.

Slater pulled the door shut and replaced the heavy bar. Over his doublet, he wore a wide-shouldered, fur-trimmed jerkin that made him appear even more formidable. "I thought perhaps, by now, you might be ready to listen to reason, pet."

"I have not changed my mind," Nora said firmly.

"No? Perhaps this will help to persuade you. Does the title *Maiden with a Harp* mean anything to you?" He came closer, flashing a sinister smile. "Did you imagine that someone really wanted to *purchase* that little tapestry you made, enabling you to support yourself without a man?"

Nora felt the blood drain from her face. "Are you implying that it was not a merchant but *you* who purchased it from Master Mostinck?"

"Oh, I'm not *implying* it. I'm telling you! You needed to be taught a lesson. If we cannot reach an agreement today, I shall be forced to take back all those beautiful sovereigns and angels you need so much."

Feeling sick, Nora glanced toward the door. If only Lennox would appear!

The Englishman seemed to read her mind. "Ah, of course, you are expecting someone, aren't you? Let me guess…'*Soon I will be kissing your sweet lips*'."

She stared at him in horror. "Y-you wrote that note? And signed Lennox's name?"

"My ruse succeeded very well, I see, for you have made yourself look especially lovely, pet. And look at the refreshments you have prepared, expecting to enjoy them with MacLeod. Oh, wait, he now aspires to be an English nobleman, does he not?" Slater's tone was mocking. "Soon he may have a title. Did you really expect MacLeod to turn his back on life with the Duke of Hastings and come back to you, especially knowing you carry *my* child?"

Nora pushed through a tide of rage and forced herself to think. She might feel a powerful urge to pick up the flagon of wine and smash it across his head, but if that failed, Slater could retaliate in a way that would put her baby in danger. No, instead she must use her wits to overpower him.

Striving to sound conciliatory, Nora said, "I suppose I must recognize that there is truth in all that you are saying."

He came closer, watching her. "You are sensible as well as beautiful."

"I cannot escape the fact that you have sired my baby, Sir Raymond. I may wish at times that it were not so, but it is."

"Very wise, pet." He poured wine into both goblets and helped himself to a wedge of cheese. "Shall we agree to be *friends*?"

Nora nodded slowly. "I can finally see that we must work together, for the sake of our child."

Slater hovered closer. As usual, he wore a jeweled pomander on a chain around his neck, its musky scent filling the air. Reaching for her hand, he guided it to his gold-striped codpiece and forced her to touch him. "We can do much *more* than work together."

It took every ounce of Nora's control to refrain from giving him a shove. Instead, she lowered her lashes and moved her hand away from his body. "You are so virile. I can't help remembering how shy I felt the last time we were together and how your delicious sweetmeat helped me to relax. Do you by chance have more of them?"

"What a good idea." He lifted both brows and reached inside his jerkin for the emerald-studded case. "For you, pet, anything."

Nora accepted the sweetmeat he proffered and gazed at it longingly. "Let me sip my wine first, for I am thirsty."

Slater nodded, but he was looking across the parlor to the cabinet, where Nora's tapestry purse peeked out from the open door. "What do I see there?"

"That purse contains all the money I have in the world," she said in a defeated tone. "Not only my meager savings, but also the payment for the *Maiden and the Harp*. I had been so proud to earn it honestly, but I now realize those funds came from you, sir."

Striding to the cabinet, Slater withdrew the purse and opened it. As he counted the coins, Nora took one of the figs, furtively poked a hole in it, and pushed the sweetmeat inside.

"Indeed, there is even more than what I gave for your unremarkable tapestry," Slater announced, slipping the purse inside his jerkin pocket. "But don't worry, you won't need any money of your own. You'll be in my care." He returned to her side. "Now then, where were we?"

"I have just eaten my sweetmeat. Will you have a fig?" She held out the plump fruit. "They are exceptionally good."

He took the fig and ate it in one bite. "God's teeth, I've never tasted anything so delicious. Now for some wine. Let us drink together, pet, and then you will take me to your bedchamber so that we may *seal* our new arrangement."

Nora's heart was beating like a drum. What if the sweetmeat did not have the same effect on a big man like him as it had on her at Stirling Castle? As she raised her goblet to answer his toast, her hand trembled. Slater frowned and gripped her wrist.

"What's this?" He stared at her suspiciously, searching her face, and she felt herself flush. "I hope you don't imagine you can *deceive* me!"

Nora knew she should attempt to return his stare with wide, innocent eyes, but hatred welled up in her, burning her heart.

"Why don't you simply tell me the truth?" she asked, defiant.

He slammed down his goblet and grasped both her arms, his thumbs digging into the soft flesh above her elbows. "Which truth do you mean? I've already enlightened you about your ridiculous dreams of a future with Lennox MacLeod. And I helped you realize that your fantasies of being a master weaver are laughable!"

Nora thought she heard his voice begin to slur. Did she dare to hope that the sweetmeat was having an effect? "I am referring to that night at Stirling Castle," she said. "What truly happened between us?"

He laughed a bit too loudly. "You can blame the sweetmeat you ate then, which will soon be affecting you again."

"The sweetmeat?" Nora feigned surprise. "Why, what have you put in it?"

"I use a variety of herbs, including Linden flower, which causes sedation, especially when taken with wine," Slater said proudly. "There are also other exotic substances, given to me during voyages to distant islands. I think I have the mixture just right, don't you?"

"Does it excite you to render a female like me defenseless?" She wanted to kill him, but first she had to hear why he committed these terrible acts.

"Of *course*. Especially when my victim is an innocent maiden like you. Can you imagine how arousing it was to deflower so proud a beauty?" Slater tried to bring his crotch in contact with her hip, pressing against her. "Some ladies become utterly senseless and have no memory at all afterward. I can do all sorts of wicked things to them." He drew a ragged breath. "Others, like you, are more resistant, yet you were unable to move or struggle against me. Later, I'm quite certain your memories were muddled. Yes?"

Nora tasted tears at the back of her throat. "But why would you choose to violate me? I had done you no harm."

"Because Lennox MacLeod wanted you." Leaning closer to her ear, Slater muttered, "I saw how he stared at you in the banquet hall that night. He would have liked to have you himself, so it amused me to take you instead. I despise men like him, who behave as if their righteous code of honor puts them above the rest of us. The sort who's too virtuous to stick his cock in a common kitchen maid, given the chance."

Listening to Slater rant, Nora realized that all his instincts were twisted. Everything that had happened that night at Stirling Castle now came clearly into focus for the first time. "You are a monster."

"Yet my babe grows in your belly." Drawing back, he leered at her, his lids heavy. "You have no choice but to join your fate to mine."

Over Slater's shoulder, Nora glimpsed a movement on the steps leading to the upper story. Her heart leaped. Surely she must be seeing an apparition, for midway down the stairs stood Lennox. How could he have gotten inside? The door was barred! He wore his belted plaid, the sash fixed to one broad shoulder. His unruly golden hair was crowned by a tartan bonnet bearing the Clan MacLeod badge.

Yes, it was Lennox, still a Highlander, and he had come back to her! Nora wanted to cry out to him, but somehow she managed to remain unmoving in Slater's grasp, waiting to decide what she should do next.

She watched as Lennox pressed a silencing forefinger to his mouth, then sent her a heart-melting grin. In one brown hand he gripped the hilt of his claymore, and she saw that a dirk was thrust into his belt. Shadows played over the hard muscles of his legs as he soundlessly descended the remaining steps.

Just then, Slater lifted his head and peered at her with glazed eyes. "What are you looking at?"

Remembering how strangely dizzy she had felt after eating the sweetmeat at Stirling Castle, Nora pointed toward the corner behind them. "Over there. Is that a rat I see?"

Slater drew back and attempted to peer in the direction of the corner. No sooner did he turn his head and look down than he began to topple over. Wildly, he reached out for Nora, as if she might keep him upright, but only succeeded in pulling her down with him.

"Do you think to trick me?" Slater demanded as they toppled together to the rush-strewn floor.

Nora found herself imprisoned under his body. His breath smelled of wine and the tainted fig, and when she tried to move and couldn't, she began to panic a little. Was it possible to dislodge him by bringing her knee up, hard, to the place where it would hurt him most?

She was saved from trying by the sound of a beloved, familiar voice. "Slater! Did I not warn ye, at Stirling Castle, that I would see your head on a pike if our paths should cross again?"

Lennox towered above them, the sharpened point of his claymore pressed into the middle of Sir Raymond Slater's back.

Slater suddenly broke out in a sickening sweat. "MacLeod! How—"

"Get up," ordered Lennox.

"Don't kill me, I beg you." Slater's words were garbled.

Leaning down, Lennox grabbed Slater's arm and easily pulled him over, freeing Nora to roll away. Lennox quickly lifted her to her feet, and she buried her face in the tartan sash covering his chest. He smelled wonderful. As familiar as her own breath.

"Are ye hurt?" Lennox asked. He kept one arm firmly around her while he continued to hold the claymore inches from Slater's throat. "What's happened here?"

"He ate one of the poison sweetmeats," Nora said in a rush. "Just like the one he gave me that night at Stirling Castle, when he took my innocence. It is rendering him insensible, I think." She clung to Lennox in disbelief. "Can you be real? How did you get in here?"

He laughed. "I have my ways. Grant and I were arriving when we saw Slater through the window and realized what must be happening. I decided it would be better to enter through the upstairs window. 'Twas easy enough for a Highlander like me, trained from the time I was a bairn to scale cliffs and castle walls."

Slater gave a low moan, and Nora whirled to look at him. He was lying on his back on the floor, arms at his sides, eyes nearly shut. Was he watching them, waiting for a chance to leap up and turn Lennox's claymore against them? As if reading her thoughts, Lennox shook his head.

"He isn't getting up, but I'll take no chances." He looked down at her with the sea-green eyes she'd dreamed about every night since their parting in June. "Nora, can ye go to the door and lift the bar? Grant is waiting outside."

She did as he bade, and moments later Grant was rushing into the parlor, brandishing his own dirk.

"Mistress Farthing, the housekeeper, returned from her errands a few minutes ago. I asked her to summon Lord Fairhaven and the authorities," Grant exclaimed as he bound Slater's wrists together. "They should be here at any moment!"

Love swelled inside Nora as she watched Lennox and Grant stand together over their captive, boldly united in their Clan MacLeod plaids. Neither was a MacLeod by birth, but really, what did that matter? It was all so much deeper than that.

She walked over to look down at Sir Raymond Slater, who was now as incapacitated as she had been that night at Stirling Castle. Nora felt satisfaction in seeing him open his mouth as if to speak yet be unable to make a sound. She remembered that terrible feeling all too well, when she had wanted to cry out in protest against what he was doing to her.

"He's not worth another moment of your pain, lass," Lennox said in a low voice. "We can begin now to put it all behind us and look to the future."

The feeling of his strong arm around her meant more to Nora than she could have imagined. *Us*, Lennox had said. She let herself smile. At that moment, Samuel the cat emerged from hiding and walked soundlessly over to the prostrate Sir Raymond Slater, sniffing his face with a moist nose. For an instant, their captive seemed to focus, and an expression of horror crossed his face.

Nora couldn't help smiling. "He is doubtless afraid of cats," she observed. "Joan told me that some of our neighbors think cats like Samuel are possessed by the devil."

Samuel purred loudly then flicked his whiskers over Slater's mouth. When Nora looked up to share her amusement with Lennox, she could see that his thoughts were far away.

"Is something wrong?" she asked.

He drew a short breath. "We know this man is a criminal, and the authorities should arrest him, but what crime can he be charged with tonight? There must not be a possibility that they will release him."

Even as he spoke, the front door opened, and Joan Farthing appeared, with Lord Fairhaven at her side. Following them was a burly fellow carrying a lantern, a bell, and a pike slung over one shoulder. Nora recognized him as Barnaby, the night watchman who patrolled the area surrounding Cockspur Court. Barnaby held out his lantern, scanning the small room, and scowled.

"What's all this?" he shouted, indicating Sir Raymond Slater.

Slater, who seemed to be reviving, mumbled, "Help! I am a…nobleman!"

Barnaby glared at Robin and the others. "Is that true?"

"Sir Raymond Slater may indeed be a knight," Lennox allowed, "but he's also a thief—and worse. When the king learns of his crimes, even he will agree the man must be punished."

"What crimes, then?"

Nora intervened. Stepping close to Slater, she reached into his jerkin pocket and drew out her tapestry purse. "I made this purse myself. You can see my mark on it." She crossed to the watchman and pointed to her small N, woven into one corner. "All my savings are contained inside this purse, and Sir Raymond Slater stole it. Not only that, he attempted to force himself on me, much against my will."

Barnaby looked around at Robin. "Lord Fairhaven, do you support the accusations of Widow Lovejoy?"

All of Nora's friends joined to stand beside her. "Every one of us does," Robin asserted.

"Then this is a matter for the courts," declared Barnaby. "I'll summon the authorities to take Sir Raymond to Newgate, where he will await trial."

"What will happen then?" Nora asked.

Barnaby shrugged. "Stealing is often punishable by death. As a nobleman, Sir Raymond might mercifully be beheaded rather than hanged." The watchman glanced toward the prisoner before adding, "Many thieves' heads are displayed on pikes along London Bridge."

Amidst the general commotion in the room, Lennox drew Nora off to one side. "We have wasted enough time with that villain. I want to be alone with ye, love. Come away with me to Weston House."

"Oh, yes, please." His nearness kindled a flame inside Nora, casting out all the dark moments of that day. "When can we leave?"

"Now." He brought her hand to his mouth and kissed it, his eyes full of promise. "Is that soon enough?"

Chapter Thirty-one

In the dead of night, Weston House was still. Only Lennox was awake.

When he and Nora had fallen into bed, they hadn't bothered to close the draperies, and now moonbeams streamed through the mullioned windows overlooking the River Thames.

The light silvered her naked body as she lay in his arms. His nose grazed the back of her neck, still damp from their lovemaking. Was she sleeping at last? His own emotions consumed him.

His gaze swept over her, lingering on the increased swell of her belly. When he thought about the babe growing inside her, Lennox was filled with wonder and a tangle of more conflicted emotions. He loved her, and loved her babe, yet his heart instinctively fisted whenever he remembered that the villainous Sir Raymond Slater was the father. When Lennox and Nora were able to make babes of their own, would he love this one any less?

As he considered this, Lennox recalled something he had said to the Duke of Hastings, his own birth father:

"I don't think any less of myself for being born a bastard. In fact, I had nothing to do with it."

It came to him that this babe inside Nora was as innocent as he himself had been. He thought of Magnus, the man he had called Da all his life, who had carried him on his shoulders when he was a bairn and taught him how to sail a galley. Da, who had talked to him about the right way to be with a lass, no matter what other lads might suggest. Da, who learned along the way that he hadn't fathered Lennox after all yet had continued to do his best to love him anyway.

Tears burned his eyes and he drew a painful breath.

"What is it?" whispered Nora. She turned halfway in his embrace, looking up at him with luminous blue eyes.

"'Tis nothing. Ye need sleep, lass."

"There will be other nights to sleep." She smiled, and it seemed to Lennox that God had never created a more inviting mouth than hers.

When he thought of how they had loved that night, arousal coursed through him again and he felt himself stiffen, hot and urgent, against the curve of her bottom. "Aye, we'll have a lifetime of other nights to sleep," he agreed softly. "So let me show ye again how much I've missed ye."

She had turned toward him, enough so that her breasts were close enough for him to bend his head and kiss. Already that night, he had lingered for long minutes over her nipples, savoring them, making them harden under his questing tongue. Now, Lennox cupped one of her full breasts in his free hand and gave a low groan. In that moment, it seemed that he had slept alone for years rather than months. He made his fingertips like feathers, grazing her nipple and the underside of her breast, then slowly moved over her belly, down to the wet, aching core of her desire.

He could feel her breathing change, her thighs open ever so slightly. As he angled her toward him, Nora put a hand on his chest.

"Wait. Please, I want to talk."

Their eyes met in the moonlight. "Soon," he coaxed, nudging her close enough to feel his urgent need at the apex of her thighs. "But first…"

"Lennox!" Nora caught his dark hand and brought it to her heart. "Must I cover myself? We have loved already tonight, and now we must talk."

He gave a sigh but smiled as she held his hand to keep it

from wandering. "I suppose ye wonder what happened while I was away."

"I do. You have seen the house where I now live, you met Joan Farthing, you know I was weaving at Whitehall Palace. And you can see that I am hardly in a state to embark on any new romance."

Lennox lifted both brows. "Are ye suggesting that's what I was doing?"

"Tell me about life with the duke. You went with him because you thought you might find the place you finally felt you belonged, the world you were born to. Have you truly decided against that?"

"I missed ye so much," he said, aching to kiss her again. He wanted to press every inch of his naked body to hers, to be inside her, to stay like that, in this bed for days. But Nora's gaze demanded an answer. "I missed ye, but there's more to it, of course."

"I assumed as much. I beg you to be honest." She was still watching him. "You were unhappy there?"

"Aye." He started to nod, then shook his head. "Nay. There is no plain answer. Father did everything he could to make me feel comfortable. He hoped I would slip into a new role, as the son of a duke."

"You were to have a title?"

"That was the duke's intention. He meant to petition the king. His legitimate son, Charles, died not long ago, and he yearned that I might be heir to his title."

"I can only imagine what it was like for him, to find a son who so closely resembled him and then to hope that you would be with him forever." She paused. "Did you come back because you knew I could not live in that rarefied world, even if I were not carrying this child?"

"In part, but it was more complicated. My father meant well, but the longer I was there, the more I realized I did not fit in his world. The more plans he made for me, the more uneasy I felt."

"What sort of plans?"

Lennox really didn't want to talk about it, especially now, but her eyes told him he must. "It was assumed I would wear the clothing of an Englishman, made for me by the duke's pretentious tailor. He wanted me to ride Charles's horse, to sleep in his room, to sit in his chair at the table. Before I left, my father even made plans to acquire a nearby monastery that was abandoned during the dissolution. He thought we could renovate it, and that would be my estate."

"And who would live there with you?" she asked softly.

"I can see that ye suspect I was with someone else during these past months." As he spoke, Lennox wondered at the spark of indignation he felt. Perhaps it was because he had indulged in a fantasy or two of a future with Betsy, including fleeting images of her in his bed. But that did not mean he had been unfaithful to Nora! Just the opposite, for those thoughts of Betsy had given him no pleasure, only a sense of loss for the woman he truly loved. "I will say that Father had a plan for that as well, but I could not do it. None of it felt right, no matter how sorry I felt for Father's empty life or how rewarding it was to make him smile again. In the end, it wouldn't have been fair to either of us."

"You have told him how you feel?"

"Aye. I was plain with him." Lennox felt anew the pain of disappointing the duke, whose hopes had been so poignantly high. "He assures me he understands. I know we will see each other again. I care for him."

Nora's eyes shone. "Do you know, now, where you belong?"

"Aye." He traced the delicate line of her jaw with his fingers. "I belong right here, love, with ye in my arms. My identity doesn't rest on the name of my father, whether it's MacLeod or Hastings. I can take a bit from both of them and make a new family."

"You are a splendid man, Lennox MacLeod." Eyes shining, Nora moved closer so that they could embrace. "But…what of my baby?" She rested a protective hand on the curve of her belly.

"With all my heart, I will be a father to this babe. I've learned well enough that what matters is not who plants the seed, but who loves and nurtures the child. I love ye, Nora Brodie, and I want us to make a life together."

Tears spilled from Nora's eyes. She pressed her face to his chest, and he held her so tightly he could feel their heartbeats mingle.

"I believe you," she murmured at last. "And I love you, too."

"I want to take you back to the Isle of Skye, to meet the people of my clan." Lennox thought of the last time he'd seen Magnus, when he had told Lennox he couldn't change the past, only try to do better going forward. Love for Da welled up in him, bittersweet with the promise for healing. "I want to find my place among them at last. How they will love ye, lass."

"Oh, I want that, too." Nora lifted her face, gazing at him soberly. "But… I have accepted an assignment with the Great Wardrobe, overseeing a group of weavers who are making a new tapestry. It is an honor to have been selected by Master Mostinck for this project."

Their eyes met in the moonlit shadows. Even as Lennox considered asking her to put it aside, to return with him to Scotland where they could begin a new life, he remembered every word she had ever spoken to him about her passion for tapestry-making and her dream to one day become a master weaver.

"I am deeply proud of ye, lass," he said, his voice husky with love. "Perhaps we might live together in your little house in Cockspur Court, until your project at Whitehall Palace is finished."

"You would do that for me?"

"Anything ye desire, lass. I can sketch and paint again. And perhaps we can create new art together during those weeks."

"Oh, I would love that! You'll never know how often I've remembered our time at Duart Castle, working on the tapestry you designed." She was beaming at him in wonder. "I've been endeavoring to make something new, for the baby. I still have so much to learn about sketching a pattern. Will you help me?"

"Aye, of course. What subject have ye chosen?"

"A lion." She laughed softly. "With a friendly face, of course."

Lennox closed his eyes, holding Nora tightly, remembering his ma's habit of calling him her *golden lion.* How happy she would be to see this new path for his life.

"Clearly, we have many plans to discuss, but it is late." As he spoke, he turned Nora back into the pillows, his mouth hovering just above hers. "I propose we stop talking for the rest of this night. Starting now."

Nora wrapped her arms around his wide shoulders, parting her thighs so that they fit together in a way that was keenly, exquisitely arousing.

"Mmm," came her reply, muffled but happy. As his mouth captured hers, an intoxicating heat began to build between them.

It was, Lennox realized, only the beginning of a lifetime of kisses.

Chapter Thirty-two

Isle of Skye, Scotland
May 1542

Nora followed Lennox up the narrow, twisting stone steps that took them high into the tower his grandfather, Alasdair Crotach, had added to Dunvegan Castle decades ago.

"I want ye to see the world from up here," he explained when they reached the top step. "'Tis a magnificent view."

In the days since they had come to Skye, Nora had gained a new understanding of her husband. It was one thing to hear tales of this western isle where he had been raised but quite another to be there herself. The Isle of Skye was tinged with magic, legends, and accounts of faeries that everyone seemed to accept as truth. The gloriously windswept land boasted virtually no roads or other signs of civilization, yet the people Nora had met all seemed to be part of one big family.

Lennox caught her hand, drawing her forward to an arrow-slit window. "Look!" His voice was hushed with wonder.

She did as he bade, leaning against him to gaze out over the rooftops and parapets of Dunvegan Castle. The clan MacLeod stronghold crowned a rocky pedestal surrounded by Loch Dunvegan and was only accessible by water. On the far bank of the loch, Nora recognized Ciaran and Violette's tower house, where they lived with their year-old baby, bold little Niall. Looking westward, Nora drew in her breath at the sight of the azure loch gradually widening until it reached the wilder waters of the Minch.

"I can only imagine how stirring it must have been to grow up in such a place," she murmured.

"Aye. Because my grandfather was also our clan chief, this was where we came to visit him and so many of our people. But I was raised at Duntulm Castle, on the tip of Skye's Trotternish peninsula." His voice caught for a moment. "I know I have told ye how we lost Duntulm to the evil MacDonalds, but I confess that it hurts even more now that I have come back to Skye." Pausing, he wrapped his arms around her. "For too long, I didn't want to feel the deep bond I have with the Highlands, but it is all different now that I have my own family with me. Thank God I could be here today, with my clan, as Grandfather makes my uncle William our new chief and then sails away to that monastery on the Isle of Harris."

"I'm so glad we were able to come and that I could meet Alasdair Crotach before he retires to the Isle of Harris." Even as she spoke, Nora wondered where they might settle and make their own home. Would Lennox want to remain on the Isle of Skye? Uncertainty squeezed at her heart. Perhaps, with time, she too might feel more connected to this wild, beautiful place.

"I know tiny Brienne won't remember what happens today," Lennox said, "but it will be part of her all the same."

She knew he was right. Every person and event that touched them was woven into the fabric of their souls…even a force for evil, like Sir Raymond Slater. Nora would never be able to banish him from her memory, but at least he could never bother them again. Before she and Lennox had left London, Slater finally went to trial. Sandhurst, who had known King Henry for years, spoke to the monarch, and in the end Slater had been beheaded, just as Barnaby foretold.

Slowly, day by day, Nora was teaching herself not to think of him. She reminded herself that justice had been served in the end, and that she'd grown stronger through the entire ordeal.

Now, Nora went into Lennox's arms and they shared a slow

kiss that soon caught fire. "People are gathering outside to witness your grandfather's leavetaking," she murmured when they paused for breath. "And Violette has her hands full, watching both Brienne and Niall. I suggest we go down to join them."

He kissed her again before raising his head with an air of regret. "Have I mentioned that ye are looking especially bonny, wife?"

"Thank you, but I'd say that you are the bonny one today, husband." Beaming, Nora thought how true that was. She swept her gaze over his tall, splendid form, from his windblown, tawny-gold hair to his powerful torso to the length of MacLeod tartan wrapped and belted round his hard waist. "Let me straighten your sash." Reaching up, she fussed with the long end of his plaid so it was draped perfectly over one shoulder.

As they descended the treacherously narrow steps, the aromas of food and cooking smoke drifted up to them from the hall, lingering after the final feast shared by Alasdair Crotach with his clan.

"Ah, the scent of haggis. Would ye care for another bite?" Lennox teased. "Old David always makes more than enough."

Nora laughed, wrinkling her nose. "Please, no. I did my best to swallow it at the table, when everyone was watching me, but the only thing I want right now is to hold our daughter."

They found the baby with her aunts, Violette and Fiona, and cousins Niall and Lucien. Three-year-old Lucien de St. Briac was sitting astride the dozing bulk of Raoul, his family's great French hound. "Listen," he commanded his small cousins. "I will tell ye a story! It is about the blue men of the Minch."

Nora's heart leaped, as it always did, at the sight of Brienne. Blessed with deep blue eyes like Nora's own and a head of red-gold curls, Brienne Brodie MacLeod was nearly six months old. She sat now on a small woven rug, wobbling slightly, and when she saw her parents, she giggled and toppled over.

Lennox scooped her up effortlessly. "Ah, my wee lass, have ye hurt yourself?"

The baby cooed as she pressed a damp hand to his cheek. Nora's heart swelled anew with a love more powerful than she could have ever imagined. Perhaps it was even sweeter to watch them together because Lennox loved Brienne just as if she were his own child. Once, soon after the baby's birth, Nora had ventured this observation and he had given her a hard stare.

"What are ye talking about? This babe *is* my own child."

Still, Nora was glad their daughter resembled her rather than Sir Raymond Slater. If she had been born with Slater's black hair and dark eyes, perhaps it wouldn't have mattered, but Nora was grateful not to have to find out.

Just then, Magnus MacLeod strode into the castle hall, filling the space with his energy. "Ah, there ye are!" he boomed, fixing his weathered gaze on Lennox and Nora. "Come and join the others in the gun court. The time has come to bid farewell to our clan chief."

"Walk with me, lad," Magnus said to Lennox as they began to leave the hall.

Lennox glanced at Nora, who smiled and held out her arms for Brienne. As she joined Violette and the others, he kept pace with his da. The air outside was cool and refreshingly damp from the morning's rain, and cobbles were slick under their boots.

"I've something to say." Magnus's voice was gruff. "To ye alone. I need to tell ye again how deeply I regret the mistakes that were made when ye were young. The secrets we kept…"

Looking over at Da, Lennox felt a tide of emotion. In that moment, surrounded by walls of their clan stronghold, he was more certain than ever of his identity. "I know, Da." He patted Magnus's thick shoulder, thinking of his own Brienne. Would he one day reveal that he was not her natural father? It was a question Lennox could not yet answer. "No doubt you meant to do what was best for me."

"Aye! How can it be that ye have gained that understanding?"

Lennox searched for the right words. "When I was away, I discovered that the destiny I searched for had been inside me all the while, and I came to appreciate the love ye gave me all through my life."

"Ah, lad." Pausing, Magnus cleared his throat, watching him. "I suppose that *man* must've disappointed ye in some way?"

"Nay." Lennox squinted out at Loch Dunvegan, where a handful of galleys and birlinns bobbed near the sea-gate. "I could see how he and I are connected too. But Skye is my true home, with our clan, even if it's not MacLeod blood in my veins. I suppose I had to undertake that quest before I could fully understand."

"Can ye forgive me, then? I've suffered every day since ye came here with that cursed portrait, demanding the truth." Magnus's bloodshot eyes grew wet.

"Oh, aye. Of course I forgive ye." Lennox felt his heart open. "Ye will always be my da."

They embraced then, Da squeezing with all his might. What Lennox didn't say aloud was that he'd discovered there were no easy answers. No heroes or villains, just a lot folk who were flawed yet tried to love him all the same. The truth was all of that mattered less now that he was forging a path of his own, with Nora and the family they were creating together.

Ciaran's shout reached them from the gun court. "Da, Lennox, come on, then!"

The others were gathered below, near the stone-lined tunnel of steps that led down to the sea-gate. There, supported on either side by his legitimate sons, William and Tormod, stood Alasdair Crotach, the great MacLeod himself. Bent and frail, his flowing white hair covered by a tartan bonnet, he had ruled over their clan for seven decades.

"'Tis hard to believe he is truly going," muttered Magnus.

Lennox nodded. For years, the old man had dreamed of sailing away to the Isle of Harris to live out his remaining days at the monastery there, but he had been unwilling to relinquish his leadership of the clan…until today.

Now, as dozens of clan members gathered in the gun court, Alasdair Crotach formally proclaimed that, henceforth, his eldest legitimate son, William, would be the ninth chief of clan MacLeod. With that, the old chief put his own massive claymore in William's hands.

Lennox was about to move back in the crowd to stand with Nora and Brienne when his grandfather suddenly raised his voice.

"Lennox MacLeod! Come here, lad. There is one more act I would perform as chief."

All eyes were on Lennox as he walked forward to stand in front of the old man. Wounded many years ago by a battle axe, Alasdair Crotach had lived most of his adult life with a hunched back. His legend was about more than his injury, however, because the grievously wounded MacLeod had found the strength to wield his own dirk. After killing his attacker, young Alasdair had cut off his head as a trophy.

Now, looking down at his frail grandfather, Lennox felt a tide of affection for the old warrior. "How may I serve ye, Grandfather?" he asked.

"I am pleased to see ye back among your own people," Alasdair Crotach rasped. "There is something I have been keeping for ye, waiting for this day."

With that, the old man opened his hand to reveal a gleaming clan brooch. Crowned by a gold bull's head, it featured the MacLeod clan motto: *Hold Fast.*

Lennox's heart began to pound. His eyes stung. For so long, he had believed his grandfather withheld this honor because Lennox didn't meet Alasdair Crotach's standards for a fierce clan warrior. Later, upon learning the secret of his parentage, Lennox had assumed it was his illegitimacy that prevented him from receiving this sign that he was a true MacLeod.

Yet now, Alasdair Crotach was reaching up to pin the MacLeod clan brooch to Lennox's sash. At last. For a moment their eyes met in silent understanding.

"That bull's head looks very fine on ye, lad." A smile flickered at the corners of his grandfather's thin, dry mouth. "Ye have always been a MacLeod. But, as I said before ye went away, 'twas a discovery ye had to make for yourself."

"Aye." Lennox's voice was hoarse. "I'll wear this brooch all my days, Grandfather. I am grateful to be a MacLeod."

Lennox turned away then and went to stand with Ciaran, Fiona, and their families. They stood together, watching as William, Tormod, and Da guided Alasdair Crotach to the sea-gate and then half-carried him down the winding path to the birlinn that would bear the ancient clan chief away from the Isle of Skye. Gray clouds scudded over the sun and a misty rain blew in from the Minch.

"Remember the day Ma died, when we still lived at Duntulm Castle?" Ciaran asked, looking from Fiona to Lennox. "We three have come a long way since we joined at her bedside to bid her farewell."

As Fi leaned against him, sighing, Lennox saw that she was wearing the serpent brooch Ma had given to her on the day she died. It had been stored inside the same case where Lennox had later discovered the miniature of the Duke of Hastings.

"Ye were a rogue through and through, Ciaran MacLeod," Lennox replied to his brother. Laughing, he added, "Praise the saints for sending this magnificent woman who tolerates your shortcomings."

Violette wrapped an arm around Ciaran, who held a sleeping Niall in his strong arms. "Let's go inside," she said with a smile. "This is a conversation best served with wine."

The birlinn holding Alasdair Crotach and his sons pushed out into the loch, followed by other assorted galleys filled with his servants and an array of possessions. When it had been rowed out of sight, passing behind a wooded bend in the coastline, Lennox and Nora followed the others back to the castle. Brienne cuddled close in her mother's arms.

As they walked, Christophe St. Briac fell into step beside Lennox. "I have been waiting for an opportunity to speak to you," the Frenchman said. He sent Nora a smile and added, "Both of you."

The hall quickly grew crowded with MacLeod clansfolk, hounds, and children, so Lennox found a corner where they could sit together on a bench and talk. He was filled with affection for St. Briac, who had brought Fiona home to Skye to see her grandfather one more time before his departure.

"You are looking quite splendid in that clan brooch," St. Briac remarked, leaning back against the stone wall. "Yet I cannot help wondering what this means for your future. Do you and Nora intend to make a life here on Skye? Will you now become a warrior against the MacDonalds?" He glanced toward Nora, devils dancing in his blue eyes. "Perhaps our fair Nora wishes merely to weave here in the castle, surrounded by her new relatives? No doubt Old David can teach her to make haggis."

It came to Lennox that although Skye would always be his home, he couldn't imagine living there with Nora. One look at her told him she felt the same. Turning back to Christophe, he said, "Do ye truly have a message to deliver, or are ye merely toying with us?"

Christophe laughed. "I do have a message. Everyone at Stirling Castle misses you both." He turned to Nora. "Your papa has not been the same since you went away. He yearns to meet his new granddaughter."

"What sort of villain do ye take me for?" protested Lennox. "We intend to return to Stirling for a visit. Soon."

"And then what?" The Frenchman pushed lightly at his chest. "I suggest that you come back to stay. In fact, I have a proposal to make to you."

Nora tightened her grip on Lennox's hand, and suddenly it became clear that this was what she wanted.

"Tell us, please," she said. "I confess to missing Father more than I have been able to admit, even to myself."

"Nora, your papa needs you. I think he regrets not elevating you sooner to the position that you deserved." St. Briac arched a brow at Lennox. "And I have an important offer for you,

MacLeod. Perhaps you remember the portrait medallions we had begun making for the outer hall at Stirling Castle? Each is the head of a different person who plays a role in the king's life. I want you to oversee the design and painting of the remaining medallions. Bayard and Grant have worked closely on the carving, so you would be collaborating with them."

"Oh, what an inspired idea!" exclaimed Nora. Her voice caused Brienne to stir, looking around. Lennox held out a finger to her. She grasped it with both pudgy hands and gnawed on it with her gums.

Christophe stood, looking pleased with himself. "You two must talk in peace. I look forward to your decision."

Lennox felt a stirring in his soul, as if the future were opening before him like the yellow gorse flowers along Loch Dunvegan. He met Nora's eyes. "Tell me, love, how do ye feel about St. Briac's proposal?"

Her face lit up. "Oh, Lennox, I think you would be a brilliant choice for that position. You'll be creating art again! And how happy you would be to work with Bayard and Grant every day." She paused. "I haven't known how to say it, in case you felt differently, but I should love to be back at Stirling Castle. I don't think I realized how comfortable I was there, working with Father, until I went away."

"Then that is where we must live." Lennox felt a frisson of anticipation, already imagining how he might transform the great wooden medallions into unique works of art. Nora came into his arms, her eyes agleam with emotion, and baby Brienne snuggled between them as they embraced.

"We will create a home of our own in Stirling," Nora said.

"Aye." Embracing his wife and daughter, Lennox leaned back against the wall and drew a deep breath of happiness. His quest had brought him back to the place where he had started, yet everything had changed. "Together, we'll make the life of our dreams."

Epilogue

Stirling Castle, Scotland
December 1542

Nora served the midday meal of cod, boiled carrots, and oatcakes with honey. No matter how busy she and Lennox were at the castle, they made a point each day of meeting in their apartments to eat together, share stories about their work, and play with Brienne.

"Your food is hot," Nora reminded him, smiling. "It's fish again, but that's the best I can do during Advent."

From the wash basin, he sent her a grin that melted her heart. "Aye, love. Brienne and I will be there as soon as she dries my face."

It was Lennox's habit, upon returning from work on the great Stirling medallions, to pour fresh water into a basin and clean away the wood dust and paint drops that clung to him. Brienne loved to watch this ritual, laughing when he splashed his face with water, shook his head, and sent droplets flying her way.

Now Lennox carried Brienne to the table, tossing her up in the air to make her squeal in delight. Nora laughed too, awash with joy.

Before they sat down together on the bench, he drew Nora near and kissed her in a way that told her how much he loved and wanted her. "I missed ye today."

From her chair, Brienne reached out to tug at his plaid. "Me, Da."

"Oh, aye, wee one, I missed ye, too."

Nora poured ale for him and put a small cup of fish stew in front of their daughter. As they all began to eat, she told him about the latest developments in the great *Prodigal Son* tapestry project she was leading for her father. "Will you come later, to see it? I want you to look at the cartoon for the third panel. I'm not certain if it is quite right. With Father away in Edinburgh, you are the only person I trust to save me from making a mistake."

He reached out to touch the side of her face with his strong, elegant fingers. "Of course I will come, but I do not think ye truly need saving."

"I will feel better once you look at it." Nora watched his face as she spoke. "In fact, after the medallions are finished, I wish you could work with me, making the cartoons for our tapestries. I find myself dreaming every day of how wonderful it would be to have you as my partner." What Nora didn't say was that she had noticed her father's eyesight failing, his hands growing gnarled after years of working at the loom, and his attention wandering. Already, she had been sharing the duties of master weaver with her father. The day might not be far away when he would step aside completely.

Lennox cocked his head at her. "Ye do not doubt your own abilities, I hope."

"No! But I do love working side by side with you." Leaning closer, she kissed him.

"Why do ye suppose your father went to Edinburgh in the middle of winter?" Lennox mused "He's been away a full fortnight. Do ye think he has found romance there?"

"Father? I doubt it," she scoffed. "Although I can't remember him ever going off on a journey alone like this. He was quite secretive when I asked him about it."

Lennox pushed his empty plate away. Taking an apple from the bowl in the middle of the table, he remarked, "Speaking of mysterious fathers, I received a letter today from the Duke of Hastings."

Nora stared. "Indeed! I am surprised a message could get through from England to Scotland since the terrible battle at Solway Moss."

Just days had passed since they learned of the shocking English victory over King James V and his Scottish troops. The tenuous relationship between James and his uncle, King Henry VIII, had ruptured in late 1541 with the death of Margaret Tudor. Mother to James and sister to Henry, Margaret had been a link that kept the peace between the two countries, but Henry's patience snapped completely when the young Scots king refused to break from the Catholic church. The ensuing attack by King Henry's army at Solway Moss resulted in the capture of more than a thousand Scots, including many prominent figures. Now, according to the latest messages brought to Stirling Castle, James V was in seclusion at Falkland Palace, while the queen awaited the birth of their child at Linlithgow.

"It is true that normal relations have ceased between the two countries," Lennox agreed. He took a folded letter from the pouch at his waist and showed it to her. "The duke must have employed a special courier."

"What does he say?" Nora wiped a smear of broth from Brienne's dimpled cheek then set the baby on the floor so she could totter along the bench, holding on. Her proud father predicted that she would be walking by Christmas.

"He wishes us well, of course, and is glad to know I am being challenged creatively here at Stirling." A wry smile touched Lennox's mouth. "Oh, and I almost forgot. My father has taken a new bride."

Nora gasped. "Are you very surprised?"

He shook his head. "Not really. The duke is determined to have an heir, and since I would not cooperate, he must have taken matters into his own hands. Already my new step-mother is with child."

"Do you know this woman?"

"A little. She is a great beauty, the daughter of Father's close friend, Viscount St. John."

His tone was a bit too casual for Nora's liking. "I see. Could it be the same woman the duke wanted you to wed?"

"Ye are a perceptive lass." He smiled into her eyes. "I could not have done it, of course. Father told me once that noblemen like him cannot marry because of 'romantic notions that fade with time.' I suppose that was the moment when I realized I could never belong to that world. I had to come back to London, to discover if you would still have me."

Nora longed to go into his arms, but part of her attention was on Brienne, who was always at risk of taking a tumble. As if reading her mind, Lennox reached out and scooped their daughter onto his lap, holding both mother and child close to his heart.

Just then, there was a knock at the door. Before either of them could respond, it flew open to reveal William Brodie. His face was flushed with cold, and snowflakes clung to his heavy cloak and grizzled beard.

"Nora! I have returned." He paused, his voice choked. "I am not alone."

"Oh, I am so glad to see you, Father, to know you are safe." As she rose, a tingling sensation came over her. The scent of lavender faintly touched her nostrils, her memory. Even before William Brodie reached back to bring a woman into view, Nora knew she was about to meet her mother again.

Ada Enloe Brodie had grown older since their parting a dozen years ago, and yet her deep blue eyes, tentative smile, and the delicate hands she extended were all the same.

"Mama." As Nora rose and crossed the room, time fell away.

"My darling." Ada began to weep softly as they embraced. Her cheek was cold and damp against Nora's, and she patted her back, as if to comfort her. "I am so sorry."

"But I was the one who left you." It hurt to say the words aloud, to let herself feel it all again after so many years of making herself numb to the separation from her mother.

"Nay, child. Ye were but a wee lass!" declared William

Brodie. "Blame *me.* I forced you to choose between us." He looked from Nora to little Brienne, who watched with interest from her father's lap. "Watching ye with your own babe during these past months, I finally faced my crime."

"Always so dramatic!" Ada shook her head at him and wiped a tear from her eyes. Looking at Nora she explained, "William wrote to me, and fortunately I was still living in the same house in Brussels. When he invited me to sail to Scotland, I could not refuse. In fact, I have waited ten long years for this day."

For a moment, Nora could not speak. They had been parted when she was beginning a delicate adolescence. Her mother's absence had been a wound in her heart, but perhaps it was possible for them to weave a new, stronger bond now that Nora was a mother herself.

"Is this only a visit?" Nora dared to ask, looking between her parents. "Or will you stay in Scotland, Mama?"

"We shall see," Ada replied, glancing toward William. To Nora's surprise, her father reddened. "I hope to remain here, with my family."

As they spoke, Lennox rose and carried Brienne across the room, pausing before Nora and her parents.

Nora reached out to draw him closer still. "Mama, I want you to meet Lennox MacLeod, my splendid husband. And *this* is Brienne Brodie MacLeod..."

Lennox smiled as he finished her sentence. "...our bonny daughter."

Thick, wet snowflakes made a lacy curtain beyond the castle windows as Lennox and Grant carried the newest medallion into the tapestry workroom. He had expected the large space to be a hive of activity, as usual, with William Brodie back in charge, sternly ordering his weavers about while Nora guided the project more quietly.

Instead, William was sitting in the corner, seemingly oblivious to the tapestry that was taking shape on the great loom. He bounced Brienne on one knee while Ada beamed at them from a nearby stool. From time to time, she said something in a low voice and William replied.

"Ye may go," Lennox said to Grant. "There's a lass who was looking for ye in the outer hall. Barbara?"

"Oh aye!" Grant's eyes opened wide. "I'd better discover what she might need."

As the lad turned and rushed away, Lennox shifted the medallion in his arms and looked for Nora.

"I'm here," she called, peeking around one corner of the loom.

They met each other halfway. Lennox inclined his head toward her parents and said dryly, "What's that all about then? Your da seems besotted."

She glanced heavenward. "Yes, quite. But I must confess I'm very happy to see them together like this."

"Ye don't mind if he forgets about his work?"

"No. In a way, it's easier," she said in a confidential tone. "I don't have to defer to him or correct the mistakes he sometimes makes."

"Then ye are already master weaver, by default." He set the medallion down on her worktable. "What do ye think of this head I'm about to paint? It's James V."

"Oh, yes, it's a perfect likeness!" She studied the carved likeness Lennox had designed of the Scots king, nodding. Bayard had done the carving, expertly depicting his sad eyes, short beard, and hands clasped in an attitude of majesty. "How pleased he will be to see it."

"I hope so." Lennox felt deep sympathy for the despondent king. "I thought to make his clothing crimson and gold, the Stewart colors."

"Those are perfect choices. It will be magnificent," she said, nodding.

Their eyes met, and he yearned to take her in his arms. Nora grew more lovely by the day, Lennox thought, her burnished curls shining, her face aglow, her body appealingly lush since she had become a mother. In a low voice, he suggested, "Perhaps we should go somewhere and talk. Don't ye have a new question about the tapestry pattern to put to me?"

"I might..." Nora leaned closer, tipping her head back as she smiled.

"Do ye, now?" Lennox laughed softly. "I can think of something I'd like to put to ye as well."

"You are very wicked, sir." She pretended to look shocked. "One of the many reasons I enjoy having Mama here is that she loves to take care of Brienne, thus allowing us more time alone."

Lennox imagined having Nora in their bed, undistracted by the chance that Brienne might hear them. Perhaps there would even be enough time to divest her of her gown and kirtle so they might make love properly. Nora was looking at him as if she would like that very much.

"Let's be away, lass." Arching a brow, he reached for her hand. "Quickly, before ye change your mind."

Before they could turn to leave, Lennox heard footsteps, and a tall female figure appeared in the doorway.

"Lennox MacLeod, there you are at last! I've searched this entire castle." His Aunt Tess stood before them, richly garbed in emerald green and a gem-studded gable hood.

"What a fine surprise." Lennox tried to summon the proper enthusiasm as he embraced his aunt. Turning back to Nora, he introduced the two women.

"I am very pleased to meet you at last, my lady. Please, do come and sit down," said Nora, gesturing toward a nearby bench.

Tess looked her over approvingly. "Fiona has written to me all about your adventures with my nephew." She sent Lennox a reproachful glance. "I expected a visit from *you*, telling me everything that you learned about Eleanor, but no doubt you have been too busy. Thank goodness for your sister."

"Ah, men," Nora rejoined. "Aren't they all the same?"

Tess nodded approval. "Indeed."

Lennox held up both hands in mock defense. "Surely ye have not come to Stirling simply to scold me for being a man!" Sensing that his aunt was avoiding a more serious subject, he continued, "I would not have expected ye to journey here from Linlithgow now, when Her Majesty is about to deliver a child." Even as he spoke, he felt a strange chill of foreboding. "I hope nothing is amiss."

"Indeed, I do come on a sad errand." Suddenly Tess looked as if she might weep. "I have just spoken to Fiona and Christophe. I bring two pieces of news that are shaking all of Scotland." At that, Nora brought her a cup of wine, and Tess took a long drink. Her tone then became deeply serious. "On the sixth day of December, our queen was delivered of a healthy babe. A girl, called Mary."

"How wonderful!" Nora said with feeling.

"Aye." Tess's strong face grew pinched. "Although, after the tragic loss of the two princes, we had deeply hoped for a boy. I know it was a great blow to the king, who was already laid low by the loss at Solway Moss."

Her words brought back the memory of the day at Falkland Palace, when Lennox had sketched the queen with her new baby prince. Not long after, both of her little sons had fallen ill and died. He prayed that this infant princess would be healthy.

Yet, watching his aunt, Lennox felt a shadow of foreboding. "What is the second piece of news?"

"His Majesty, King James V, sank into a fever and died, just days after the birth of his daughter. The tiny babe is now Mary, Queen of Scots."

"By the saints," Lennox muttered as he tried to make sense of what Tess had told them. "What will happen now?"

"His Majesty lies in state in the chapel at Falkland Palace before being removed to Holyrood Abbey in Edinburgh." Her voice quavered. "He was only twenty-eight years of age, you know."

Lennox thought back to the chess matches he had shared with the monarch at Falkland Palace, while waiting for his chance to speak to Aunt Tess. James could be imprudent, selfish, even cruel to anyone he believed to be disloyal, like his old friend Hamilton of Finnart, yet he was also charming and dedicated to artistic pursuit. His youth had scarred him, Lennox reflected.

"I wonder if the little queen will be able to stay with her mother or instead be in the care of regents, as James was," Lennox mused. If he were separated from Brienne, it would tear his heart out. The infant Mary had been born into a world of privileged nobility, one Lennox had glimpsed when he was with the Duke of Hastings. Yet it could be a cold, dangerous existence. Her father, the king, was dead, and if they took her from her mother, there was no telling what heartache and peril might lie in store for tiny Mary, the new Queen of Scots.

"We pray they will not be separated," Tess replied, and he saw in her eyes that she shared his concern.

"Indeed, it would be tragic," Nora nodded gravely, then rose to her feet. "I hesitate to interrupt this sober conversation, but I see that my parents are approaching."

William and Ada had clearly grown curious about their visitor. When Nora guided them near, Lennox stood to make introductions. Tess was gracious to both William and Ada, but the sight of Brienne transformed her expression.

Little Brienne leaned out of William's arms, straining toward Lennox, and he felt a familiar surge of love as he lifted her into his strong embrace. "This is our daughter," he said proudly. "Brienne Brodie MacLeod."

"Indeed she *is* your daughter!" Tess smiled broadly, looking from Lennox to Nora. "I would know my wee niece anywhere. What a welcome reminder that life goes on, even in the midst of tragedy."

Lennox felt a bit guilty, letting her think they were related to Brienne by blood, but for now, it was the only way. *Besides*, he thought, *it matters not.*

"Brienne, will you sit with your auntie?" Tess spread her skirts to indicate the place on her lap for the baby.

Lennox carried Brienne over to the bench and took a seat beside his aunt. The others joined them. He expected the babe to be a bit shy with someone new, but to his surprise, she clambered over and sat on Tess's lap as if they were old friends.

"She looks just like Eleanor when she was a wee babe, right down to the shape of her face, the tilt of her nose, and the dimples in her cheeks," Tess marveled. "It is truly a miracle!"

Stunned, Lennox let her words sink in. He looked past his aunt to meet Nora's startled gaze. Was it possible that she had not been with child at all after that night with Slater and that Brienne had been conceived when they were together that night in the woods? His mind raced with the possibilities.

"And look," Tess was continuing, "this wee beauty will soon have green eyes, just like her da."

"They are blue, like Nora's," Lennox corrected.

"Oh, no. The eyes of a babe often begin as blue but change with time. See for yourselves!"

Both Lennox and Nora leaned forward to look more closely at their smiling daughter. It was true, there was now a discernible green tint to Brienne's blue eyes. When had this happened? Had they simply been so convinced that Lennox could not have fathered the babe that they never noticed the gradual change in her eye color?

Nora stood up. "I just remembered something I must tend to." Her voice shook slightly as she looked from Tess to William and Ada. "If you three would not mind entertaining Brienne, I will steal Lennox away to assist me."

William waved a hand at her. "Go on, lass. This babe will be safe with us. And we can become better acquainted with her ladyship."

Taking Lennox's hand, Nora led him quickly out of the workroom, down the passageway, up a twisting stone staircase, and into their own apartments. When the door was shut, she turned to face him.

"I think it may be true!" she exclaimed, pressing her hands to her flushed cheeks.

"Can it?" His heart was pounding. "Ye were so certain that you were already with child when we left Stirling!"

Nora came into his arms and clung to him. "In my innocence, there was much I didn't understand. I thought, because he had put his seed in me and my monthly flow did not begin, it must be so. But when I was in London, Micheline told me things that now make so much sense."

As she spoke, Lennox picked her up and carried her to a long cushioned stool near the window. Snowflakes continued to drift from the pale gray sky, while embers glowed in the nearby hearth.

He drew off Nora's French hood and smoothed back her curls. "Tell me," he whispered.

"She said every seed that is planted does not grow." Tears filled Nora's eyes. "And a trauma might cause a monthly flow to cease. But because I was already clearly with child when we talked, I thought no more of it." Nora gazed into his eyes. "Oh, Lennox, I believe your aunt is right. Brienne is *your* child, born of our love."

Slowly, he nodded, filled with a new sense of peace. "It never mattered to me. Ye know that. She was mine, in my heart, all along."

"Perhaps it weighed more on me, deep inside, more than I could admit even to myself. Now I can begin to completely blot that evil man from my memory. Will you help me?" She caressed Lennox's rough cheek, smiling, and his heart filled with love.

"I suggest we begin together." He kissed her slowly, tasting her sweet mouth. "This very moment."

~ *The End* ~

Author's Note

After spending time with Lennox MacLeod in my other Scottish books, it was a joy to finally be able to write his story for you. I hope you enjoyed it!

It was a treat to revisit the Isle of Skye in this newest book, and also to take you to Stirling Castle. During both my visits to Stirling, in 2017 and 2019, I became increasingly fascinated by the history of tapestry making that is on display at the castle. I was so pleased to be able to introduce you to Nora Brodie, my heroine who aspires to be a master weaver.

Also at Stirling Castle, there is a wonderful exhibit of the Stirling Heads—the wooden medallions of famous people that decorate one of the ceilings. I have a post about both the tapestries and the "heads" on my Pinterest board.

Last time I was in Scotland, we spent a few days in Oban on the west coast, and we took the ferry to Duart Castle on the Isle of Mull. It was pouring rain, but I fell in love with the castle and its history all the same. I'll include some images on my Pinterest board.

It was so much fun to return to Tudor London and reunite with Andrew, Micheline, and Cicely from OF ONE HEART in this book! If you haven't read Andrew and Micheline's love story, please page ahead to read an excerpt and download your copy today.

I'll be returning to 19th century Cornwall in the coming year, to revisit the marriage of Justin & Mouette St. Briac from HIS MAKE-BELIEVE BRIDE. I'm excited to cause some trouble for Justin—and see how their son, Anthony, is doing as he enters manhood. Stay tuned!

Thank you again for reading my books and spreading the word to your friends. I appreciate you more than you can imagine.

Your grateful author,
Cynthia Wright

Meet Cynthia Wright

Cynthia Wright is the *New York Times* and *USA Today* bestselling author best known for her *Rakes & Rebels* series, 13 intertwining historical romances starring the irresistible Raveneau and Beauvisage families. Her other acclaimed series are *Crowns & Kilts* and *Rogues Go West*. Romantic Times Magazine hails Cynthia's novels as "Romance the way it was meant to be."

Cynthia's latest releases are RETURN OF THE LOST BRIDE, Book 4 in her *Crowns & Kilts* series, set in 16th century Scotland, and HER HUSBAND, THE RAKE, a *Raveneau Family* novella and QUEST OF THE HIGHLANDER (Lennox & Nora).

Cynthia lives in northern California. She enjoys riding a tandem bike and taking road trips in an airstream trailer with her Colombian-born husband, Alvaro and their corgi, Watson. She is also devoted to her two adorable grandsons who live nearby.

You are invited to visit Cynthia's website (where you can sign up for her newsletter and peruse the Books Page):
http://cynthiawrightauthor.com/

You can "Like" Cynthia's Facebook Author page here:
https://www.facebook.com/cynthiawrightauthor

View her "Behind the Books" boards on Pinterest:
http://pinterest.com/cynthiawright77/

Novels by Cynthia Wright

Crowns & Kilts

THE ST. BRIAC FAMILY
YOU AND NO OTHER
OF ONE HEART
ABDUCTED AT THE ALTAR
RETURN OF THE LOST BRIDE
QUEST OF THE HIGHLANDER

Rakes & Rebels

THE RAVENEAU FAMILY
SILVER STORM
HER HUSBAND, THE RAKE
SMUGGLER'S MOON
THE SECRET OF LOVE
SURRENDER THE STARS
HIS MAKE-BELIEVE BRIDE
HIS RECKLESS BARGAIN
TEMPEST

THE BEAUVISAGE FAMILY
STOLEN BY A PIRATE
RESCUED BY A ROGUE
TOUCH THE SUN
SPRING FIRES
HER DANGEROUS VISCOUNT

Rogues Go West

BRIGHTER THAN GOLD
IN A RENEGADE'S EMBRACE
THE DUKE AND THE COWGIRL

Boxed Sets

RAKES & REBELS: THE RAVENEAU FAMILY 1
(Silver Storm, Her Husband, The Rake)

RAKES & REBELS: THE RAVENEAU FAMILY 2
(Smuggler's Moon, The Secret of Love, Surrender the Stars)

RAKES & REBELS: THE RAVENEAU FAMILY 3
(His Make-Believe Bride, His Reckless Bargain, Tempest)

RAKES & REBELS: THE BEAUVISAGE FAMILY 1
Stolen by a Pirate, Rescued by a Rogue)

RAKES & REBELS: THE BEAUVISAGE FAMILY 2
(Touch the Sun, Spring Fires, Her Dangerous Viscount)

ROGUES GO WEST
(Brighter than Gold, In a Renegade's Embrace, The Duke and the Cowgirl)

View all of Cynthia Wright's unforgettable novels here:
http://cynthiawrightauthor.com/books.html

Made in the USA
Monee, IL
25 February 2021

61340819R00184